Praise for Ni

"*Night Theater* is astonishing—stark and luminous, nimble and tensile, powerful and propulsive in the moment, but also full of lingering wonder." —LEAH HAGER COHEN, author of *Strangers and Cousins*

"Yes, *Night Theater* is an exquisite fable about what we need and what we want, and a beautiful meditation on what it means to be alive. But it reads like an urgent thriller, full of characters pumping with blood and guts, twisting and turning and twisting again. This novel actually kept me up all night and then some, clutching my mortality, listening to my heartbeat, drawing that line between the living and the dead until it blurred." —AJA GABEL, author of *The Ensemble*

"Magic realism is a difficult genre to pull off but Paralkar has managed to do so with aplomb." —RACHNA CHHABRIA, *Deccan Chronicle*

"A book that delivers one hundred per cent in terms of thrill, drama, atmosphere and eeriness." —IVINDER GILL, *Financial Express*

"Equal parts speculative fiction, medical drama and a philosophical treatise on death . . . Perceptive and absurdly humorous in ways I hadn't expected. By the time I reached its smashing final line, I was hoping Paralkar would resurrect the dead for a sequel." —KARTHIK SHANKAR, *The Hindu*

"A beautifully fearsome meta-fiction on death, the dead and the living." —JINOY JOSE P, *BusinessLine*

Praise for *The Afflictions*

"Disease is made into something new and strange through the eyes of writer-scientist Vikram Paralkar . . . Paralkar shares with Borges a collector's delight in details."
—BRENDA WANG, *The Believer*

"The beauty of *The Afflictions* comes from the fact that it is an unabashedly entertaining narrative that revels in weirdness and impossibility while also packing a much more profound layer in which Paralkar explores the frailty, failures, and absurdity of human nature . . . Vikram Paralkar is a talented author with a knack for the fantastic. He knows medicine, but it's his understanding of the relationship between diseases and the human mind and spirit that make *The Afflictions* a great read."
—GABINO IGLESIAS, *Atticus Review*

"Paralkar's tragicomic imagination, sly sendup of pseudo-Latinate medical prose and fine sense of irony make for an arresting read . . . A haunting take on the ills of flesh and soul."
—*Kirkus Reviews*

"Marks the birth of a fiction writer who must be followed closely." —SELVA FLORENCE MANZUR, *Uno*

"The whole book has a deeply Borgesian air." —MERCEDES HALFON, *Página/12*

"Beautifully narrated, with Pythagorean prose . . . Borgesian in style. The sentences are polished till they gleam . . . *The Afflictions* is not only the delicious fruit (hilarious at times) of an overflowing imagination, but is also filled with erudition. Paralkar trades in philosophy, history, anthropology and theology, among other disciplines . . . This is a book to devour with relish." —GUILLERMO BELCORE, *La Prensa*

NIGHT THEATER

NIGHT THEATER

A NOVEL

VIKRAM PARALKAR

CATAPULT
NEW YORK

Copyright © 2020 by Vikram Paralkar

First published in India in 2017 as *The Wounds of the Dead* by
Fourth Estate, an imprint of HarperCollins Publishers
First published in Great Britain in 2019 as *Night Theatre* by
Serpent's Tail, an imprint of Profile Books Ltd
First published in the United States in 2020 by Catapult (catapult.co)

ISBN: 978-1-948226-54-7

Cover design by Nicole Caputo
Book design by Wah-Ming Chang

Catapult titles are distributed to the trade by Publishers Group West
Phone: 866-400-5351

Library of Congress Control Number: 2019941064

Printed in the United States of America
1 3 5 7 9 10 8 6 4 2

NIGHT THEATER

ONE

THE DAY THE DEAD visited the surgeon, the air in his clinic was laced with formaldehyde. His pharmacist had poured some into a beaker in the operating room and given it a night to scour every corner. Once the door was opened, the acrid fumes spilled into the corridor and death leached out of the walls. This was the usual death, the mundane kind—that of insects and vermin.

The previous afternoon, a farmer had slit open the forearm of another with a sickle. They rushed up the hillock and crowded into the clinic, five farmers with a red trail behind them, holding the wound shut with a grimy rag.

The surgeon peeled off the cloth and saw the laceration from elbow to wrist.

"How did this happen?"

The injured man snarled through gritted teeth. "This dog did it."

Beside him, the accused hung his head. "I was cutting the

grain, Doctor Saheb. I didn't see him bending down to pick up the bundle. Please stitch him up. I'll pay."

The surgeon pressed the rag back onto the wound. "It may not be so easy." His pharmacist was standing by his side, ready with gloves on her hands. He passed the farmer's forearm over to her and let her lead the man to the operating room. The surgeon followed, stepping over the drops of blood in the man's wake. The other farmers stayed in the corridor. One of them pulled out a pouch of tobacco from his pocket.

"Don't spit on my walls," warned the surgeon, and he closed the door.

The pharmacist laid a drape over the stone slab of the operating table, and the surgeon asked the farmer to sit on a stool and stretch his arm across the cloth. He snapped on a pair of gloves and lifted the rag again. Blood oozed into the gash. The farmer puffed as the surgeon pulled the arm out straight along the length of the table.

The cut was long and irregular but shallow, confined to the skin for most of its length. The sickle had dug a little deeper in one place, but at least it hadn't nicked the artery. The sun was still up. There was enough light. The surgeon painted the skin brown with iodine and poured some into the wound itself, and with a piece of cotton soaked in alcohol, he traced the margin of the torn skin. The alcohol, as always, spread like oil on a lake, leaking into the cut. The farmer, who'd been biting his lip at the iodine, now threw his head back and started cursing someone's mother and sister.

"Enough," the surgeon said. "If you want me to do my work, you'll have to be quiet."

"Saheb, the liquid burns."

"Yes, I know. But it's necessary. And I'll tell you right now that I have very little numbing medicine—just two vials. I'll inject some of it here, but I won't be able to numb your whole arm. If you're shouting so much now, god knows what you'll do when it's time for the stitches."

"I'll be quiet, Saheb."

"And don't move your arm. Otherwise you can go to some other clinic and find another doctor to sew you up."

The surgeon injected lidocaine into the edges of the wound and prepared his needle and suture while the numbing took effect. When he began stitching, the farmer bit down into his turban and whimpered, though without another word. And so it went.

Something scurried across the corner of the surgeon's vision. It was a cockroach at the base of the far wall, rustling its wings, curling and waving its antennae as though claiming the clinic for itself. The surgeon wanted to bellow at someone, but the pharmacist had stepped out to hand medicine to an old woman with a porous spine who visited the clinic every week with her unending complaints, and the farmer just sat there with his eyes clenched and his bloody arm extended before him. There was no one at whom the surgeon could holler: Why is there a filthy cockroach in my operating room? Am I supposed to play the exterminator around here as well? Mortar the cracks in the tiles? Pack the walls with poison?

The numbness in his fingers made the surgeon realize how hard he was gripping his forceps. He tried not to pour his anger into the needle and suture, but the more the cockroach scampered, the louder the farmer puffed into his turban. Then, after a stab that the surgeon himself thought regrettably brutal, the farmer gasped and raised his wet eyes. The surgeon slammed down his instruments and marched to the wall. The roach darted away. The surgeon stamped, but twice, thrice it dodged him. Then he suspended his leg in the air, waited until the cockroach stopped running around, and, when the moment was right, ground it under his heel. The rest of the suturing, he completed without interruption.

Just when he'd started to wonder if the pharmacist had fallen down a well, she returned to help him bandage the forearm. He wrote out a prescription for a tetanus shot and a course of antibiotics. The farmers outside the room had all left, except for one, who snapped up from his haunches as soon as the surgeon walked out into the corridor.

"You're the culprit, aren't you?"

"I'm sorry. I swear on my mother I didn't cut him on purpose. I didn't see—"

"Go buy these things from the city pharmacy. There should be a train leaving in fifteen minutes."

"As you say, Doctor Saheb." The man bowed and ran off.

The surgeon called the pharmacist, who'd left the operating room after bandaging the man's arm. "Sterilize my instruments and fumigate the room."

"Tonight?"

"Yes, tonight."

"But, Saheb, there'll be children here tomorrow. For the polio drops."

"Children? What do they have to do with this? There's a

dead cockroach in there, and god knows how many live ones hiding in the walls. A cockroach in my operating room. What a disgrace. Only in *this* bloody clinic."

The pharmacist winced as the door slammed in her face. Perhaps Saheb's back was troubling him again. She peeled away a fleck of rust from the edge of a metal tray and gathered the used instruments and the drape from the operating room on it. Saheb had clearly spent some energy in flattening the cockroach, and it took her some time to scrub its remains off the floor. A line of ants had already started to form, so she swept and mopped the rest of the room as well.

Then she taped shut every gap she could find in the windows, all the cracks in the frames, the spaces around their blunt, rounded corners. From the cabinet under the sink, she pulled out a large beaker and set it in the middle of the room. She poured the formalin halfway up to the black line—the clinic would be unbearable the next day if she filled it all the way. After confirming that she hadn't dropped anything in the room, especially not her mangalsutra, she added a few tablespoons of permanganate to the beaker. The mixture started bubbling, and she hurried out with the roll of tape and sealed the door behind her.

"What about the vaccines?" the surgeon called from his consultation room. "Have they been delivered?"

"No, not yet, Saheb. They were going to come today."

"Then what are we supposed to do for the polio drive? Spray the children with rose water? Worthless, all of them. Some lazy official must have spent the day eating mutton at his aunt's place instead of delivering the cases. If he isn't here by tomorrow morning, I swear I'll file complaints in the head office every week till they fire him."

He emerged, the newspaper rolled in his hand like a policeman's club. "I'm going. If patients come for me and they aren't dying, tell them to return tomorrow."

"Yes, Saheb."

A full bladder pulled the surgeon from sleep, and the rattle of the ceiling fan kept him from returning to it. The fan wasn't loud, but it had a maddening rhythm, a monotonous, creaking pulse. He thought about prisoners who'd reportedly lost their sanity after enduring such things—dripping water and the like. Who knew if those tales were even true? At this hour, they sounded plausible.

It was almost exactly three years since he'd come to this place. Three years in these rooms, in the tiny quarters adjoining the clinic. The windows were just as they'd been when he arrived, actually a little worse now, their squares of mosquito netting perforated by the constant pecking of sparrows. And what protection had the netting provided him against that bout of dengue anyway? The illness had come and gone, but it had left a fatigue that still lingered all these months on. He sometimes wondered if the disease hadn't affected his brain as well. When he first moved here, he'd resolved never to let his mind stagnate, no matter how bad things got. He'd brought his library with him, three tall bookcases to surround his bed, his bulwarks against this unlettered village.

When was the last time he'd taken a book from the shelves? The tomes were just chunks of yellow paper now, collections of purposeless sentences trailing each other from cover to cover for no good reason.

These menial chores—draining abscesses, treating coughs and diarrhea, extracting rotten teeth, and now, another great feat, squashing cockroaches. All for what? To live in this hovel?

He could walk across the room and turn the creaking fan off, but the effort didn't seem worth it. Sleep wouldn't come either way. He cradled the back of his head in his fingers and watched the blades chase each other in gray circles.

At dawn, the pharmacist strapped on a surgical mask and stepped into the eye-watering cloud of formaldehyde engulfing the clinic. She threw open every window, even set out small bowls of ammonia in each of the four rooms, but the fumes wouldn't dissipate. She tried to switch on a fan.

The run back home left her too breathless to get her words out.

"Wake up, wake up. The clinic lights aren't working. The fridge is warming up. Doctor Saheb will be so angry."

Her husband looked barely conscious as she dragged him up the hillock, but the noxious fog at the top blew the sleep right out of him. She didn't want to torture him like this, but who else in the village knew the clinic's wiring?

"The fuses," he said. "Third time this month."

She let him grumble. With his red eyes, his uncombed hair, and the handkerchief tied across his nose and mouth, he could have been mistaken for a bandit. He pushed a ladder up against the door of the operating room and climbed to the electrical box. When he opened it, even she, from where she stood, could see black mustaches on either side of the fuse beds—remnants of repeated burnings.

"Give me the screwdriver. And that wire."

She dug in the box. "Can't you do something to stop it burning again?"

"I'll talk to Saheb about this machine, a 'surhjagard,' they call it, I think. I've never seen one. It's expensive. And I'll have to change a lot of wiring to make it all go through one line."

"Don't talk about it today, then. It's going to be a bad day, I know it."

He unscrewed the wrong connection at first, then tightened it again, then coughed until she was afraid he would fall off the ladder. Every few minutes he leaned down, and she wiped his eyes with the same cloth with which she was wiping her own. Finally, he twisted the last copper wires together, and when he pressed the fuses into place and turned the switch, the lights, the fans, the refrigerator, all began to hum and creak.

As he was putting the ladder away, Saheb walked up the steps. "What happened? Why are you crying?"

"Not crying, Saheb. Just the fumigation."

These fumes never seemed to bother Saheb. Maybe it was part of his training all those years ago. That, and the cutting open of corpses, the pharmacist had heard. Doctors were brave people. She would die if she ever had to watch something like that.

Saheb went to his chair. "Have the vaccines arrived?"

"No, not yet." She tried to retie the straps on her mask, but it was too large for her face.

"What are those rascals doing? Did anyone call to explain the delay?"

"I tried, but no one picked up the phone."

"Fine. If that's the way it's going to be, I don't care. It's not my vaccine drive anyway. What do I have to lose?"

Over the next hours, the mothers started arriving. They squatted on the grass at a distance, covered their faces and fanned their children. If it hadn't been for the fumes, they would have crowded into the corridor and piled on the benches in twos and threes. Perhaps it was a blessing they weren't doing that now. Not even a week had passed since the pharmacist's husband had hammered the planks back together.

For the past few days, the tiny television in the village square had been broadcasting the same public service announcement on the Marathi channel—round-faced mothers in saris and burkhas smiling and holding hands while a deep, kind voice said, "Give your babies a gift. Protect their futures. Just two pink drops." Then a child's sweet face—one that always made the pharmacist's eyes fill—would appear. She knew what would come next: the shrunken leg, the crutch in the armpit, the sunset. "Make sure you come," she'd said to every woman she'd met. "Early in the morning. Tell everyone."

Now it seemed that ten villages' worth of mothers had taken her advice. And the vaccines seemed more likely to rain from the sky than be delivered.

She closed the pharmacy window and started rearranging shelves that didn't really need her attention. When the day crept past noon, she avoided the eyes of the complaining crowd as she carried lunch and ice water to the surgeon.

He placed a tablet on his tongue and gulped it down. "Look, if the man doesn't show up in another half an hour, send the women away. If they start yelling, tell them to march to the district office and set up a hunger strike there. Just tell them not to bother me. I don't brew vaccines in my kitchen. Understood?"

"Yes, Saheb."

"And tell them all to be quiet. My head is going to explode. Let me at least have a peaceful meal."

"Yes, Saheb."

The surgeon was polishing the last morsels off his plate when the pharmacist's husband knocked.

"He's here."

The surgeon looked out the window. A corpulent shape in a faded blue safari jacket was puffing up the hillock. The man had an exuberant mustache and square glasses, and was carrying six large polystyrene boxes. The sea of squatting women parted to let him pass.

The surgeon washed his hands and stepped into the corridor, every ounce of his flesh already pickled with contempt. The visitor laid down his load.

"Here are the vaccines."

"You were supposed to bring these yesterday."

"I was delayed."

"That's it? You were delayed? And what about us? Are we beggars, waiting for you to throw us alms?"

The official looked at the women who had hurried into the corridor after him, and who were now tugging at the corners of their saris, veiling their faces against his eyes.

"It's no business of yours why I'm late. I'm here now, am I not?"

"Not a shred of responsibility. Is this what you're paid to do? Every other day is a vacation for you people. Who gives a damn about the doctor? For all you care, he can get holy water from the Ganga and drip it down his villagers' throats."

"Don't raise your voice, Saheb. I'm not some peon."

"You think I'm scared of you?"

"I've been placed in charge of this village, this clinic. I'm your supervisor. You don't want to get into trouble with me."

"Really? What kind of trouble?"

The official rubbed his mustache and then inspected his fingers as if afraid he'd find them stained with dye. "I didn't want to bring this up here, in front of all these people, but there have been irregularities reported in this clinic. Questions about how your money is spent."

The surgeon packed as much derision as he could into his laugh. "You mean the money that doesn't even *reach* us? The money that turns to smoke the moment you and your comrades touch it?"

"Saheb, look, you have vaccines to give out. Why are you wasting time with this kind of talk?"

"Don't teach me how to do my work. I would have been dispensing them since eight if you hadn't been so lazy. But now that you've brought up irregularities, let's talk about irregularities. Just wait. I'll make sure you learn every financial detail about this clinic."

He gripped the official's arm, digging his thumb and fingers deep into the man's biceps. The man's eyes widened. The surgeon strode into the consultation room, dragging the official in with him, and then released him with enough force to make him fall into a chair. The glass door of the wall cabinet gave a piercing rasp as the surgeon slid it aside, and he yanked out his tattered moss-green ledger and slammed it on the desk.

"Here's my account book. Pay particular attention to this section, page fifty-two onward, where I've listed the amounts I've had to spend from my own pocket to keep this place from turning into an archaeological ruin. *That's* an irregularity worth noting, isn't it?"

The official sat as if every part of him, down to his fingers, were welded to the chair.

"I've been working here without a nurse. I've asked the head office to budget me one, to issue advertisements in the district newspaper, but no, my application's been pending in your office for months. I need a new autoclave machine—the old pressure drum we have could blow up in our faces any minute. I need an EKG machine, a suction unit for the operating room . . . No one can run a clinic like this. A morgue perhaps, not a clinic. Every month I have to spend my own salary to keep this place together. I buy antibiotics and sutures. And kerosene for the generator. I know how much money is assigned to this clinic in the government budget, but you middlemen eat it up, you fat pigs. Sit here, sit with this ledger.

Conduct your investigation. Prepare a detailed report for your superiors. I'll wait."

The look on the official's jowly face was the most satisfying thing the surgeon had seen in months. As if he were thawing himself out of a block of ice, the man started tapping his fingers and making grinding sounds with his teeth. A woman in the crowd behind him giggled. The official scowled, pulled a small booklet out of his pocket, and compared some scribblings in it to the numbers in the ledger. A few times he made as if to write something, but his pen never actually touched paper. Finally, the formaldehyde seemed to get the best of him, and he pressed a handkerchief to his nose.

"I'll need to look around the clinic."

"Look all you want. It's just four rooms, so take as long as you need. Do you require a magnifying glass?"

The official turned and went into the corridor. The women moved aside as they might have for a serpent.

The surgeon snorted. This one was a novice. The experts among his kind knew how to play their hands with more skill. They knew how to sniff out the naïvely dishonest; erode confidence with pointed observations, ominous frowns, knowing *hmms* and *tsks*; apply the slow, escalated pressure that they'd all learned from their bastard supervisors, who'd learned it from the endless hierarchy of bastard supervisors above them. Once the prey was cowed enough to reveal some slight indiscretion, some minor misuse of government funds for personal gain, the bastard's work was done. He could then put his feet up and recite his lines: "Never mind, never mind, everyone makes mistakes. A single mistake doesn't make you a bad person.

Of course the government is very strict about its rules. It has a responsibility to the public. But I would never wish your reputation to be soiled. Perhaps we can reach an arrangement. Seal everything within these four walls."

The seas would boil before he'd tolerate such nonsense in his clinic.

While the surgeon was unpacking boxes and arranging vaccines in the refrigerator, someone pointed at the window. He looked up to see the official worming his way out through the crowd. The surgeon cupped his hands around his mouth and shouted, "Next time forget the vaccines. Just bring us some water from the Ganga."

The safari jacket receded at a faster pace.

If only the day could have ended there. But now there were these women. The hillock was crawling with their offspring.

The pharmacist's husband stood in the corridor like a traffic guard, organizing the crowd into queues, directing them either to the surgeon or the pharmacist.

The surgeon squeezed two pink drops onto an infant's tongue. It coughed and burst into a wail, the vaccine bubbling on its lips in pink spittle, and its mother gathered it up on her shoulder and patted it.

"Done. Next."

"Thank you, Doctor Saheb. Your blessings on my daughter."

"Come on, come on. Next. What am I, a priest? There are other people waiting."

The young mother, barely more than a girl herself, was replaced by another who could well have been her twin, for all he knew. This one had a three-year-old in a shabby brown tunic. He was rubbing his eyes and mewling.

"My eyes hurt."

"I know, I know." She was trying to hold him steady. "Just take this medicine and we'll go."

"But it's burning. My eyes are burning."

"Saheb is waiting, my child." She tried to pry the little mouth open, but the boy squirmed, twisted his head this way and that.

The surgeon clenched his jaw. Who did they think they were? They could take the vaccine or get out, it was nothing to him either way. What did they know of his qualifications? Of his skills? He was glad the fumes were burning their eyes, the eyes of their brats too, so they could know that he was a surgeon and not some village quack. He hoped their eyes would burn all the more with that knowledge.

He said little else as the chain of mothers and children trickled through the clinic. The afternoon passed, and the assembly on the hillock thinned.

After the last of them had left, and the formaldehyde had wrung out all the tears it could and drifted away, the surgeon sank into his chair. The sun was a bag of blood sliced open by the horizon, smearing the squat brick houses. The parched ground stretched before him, covered with a rash of dry yellow weed.

Every speck of this village seemed created to crush the life out of him. He felt an intense hatred for it all—the dust that lay heavy on the earth, the bone-white trees clawing with ludicrous ambition at the sky, even the mongrels that limped from door to door for scraps of meat. If it could all vanish, the world would only be enriched.

He faced the window and ran his fingers through his hair—what little was left of it—as the sun extinguished itself on the huts in the distance and darkness dripped like pitch over the dreary village. "No more." He yawned. "No more." From this day on, not a paisa of his own money would be spent on this place. Whatever savings he had, he would gather them and leave. Two months at the most while he arranged for a house somewhere. Anywhere. The official could take this bloody clinic and turn it into a tomb.

TWO

THE SURGEON, HIS HEAD buried in a ledger, was adding a long string of numbers when someone said, "Doctor Saheb."

The nib of his pen halted, and he watched an inky halo blossom around it and spread through the cheap paper. The calculations in his mind evaporated. He looked up.

There were visitors in his doorway. He hadn't heard them step into the clinic.

"The polio drive is over. The vaccines are all finished. Nothing left."

With his pen, the surgeon pointed at the boy, an oval-faced child with untidy hair sticking out behind his ears. "How old is your son?"

"Eight," replied the man.

"Then he doesn't need this vaccine. It's only for children five years and younger."

"We aren't here for the vaccine, Doctor Saheb."

Fingerprints smudged the surgeon's bifocals, and he had

to pick them off his nose and wipe them clean to take a better look. He couldn't remember having seen these people before. The man was slim, his face oval like his son's, but stubbled. The woman standing behind the boy was perhaps a little younger than the man. Probably the wife. Her odhni was wrapped so strangely around her neck and chin that he couldn't see a mangalsutra.

"What is it, then?" the surgeon asked, returning to his ledger. First the encounter with the official, then his confinement in this room, monotonously forcing drops into bawling children—it had ground him down to his marrow. And then there was his misplaced perfectionism, his inability to fill the vaccine ledger with meaningless scribbles and be done with it. The ledgers would be filed away in some government archive and never opened again, but still he needed the serial numbers on the invoices to match the boxes, the boxes to match the aliquots, the aliquots to tally with groups of children. And he was almost done. Fifteen minutes without interruption—that was all he needed.

What the hell was the pharmacist doing, anyway? Last he knew, she was in the storeroom, folding cardboard boxes to line the medicine cabinets. Instead of doing her origami, that girl should have stopped these three at the front steps. "It's late," she should have said. 'The clinic is closed. Come back tomorrow."

But she was nowhere in sight. He would have to deal with them himself.

"Are you deaf? What do you want?"

The visitors flinched. "We need your help," the man said. "This will seem like a strange request."

"Strange request? What nonsense is this? Just state your business or get going."

Now, finally, the pharmacist rushed in, panicked. "What are you doing here? You can't disturb Saheb like this. Wait outside, wait outside." She began to usher them out.

But when the boy moved aside, the surgeon noticed the bulge under the woman's loose clothing. He raised his hand.

"Is your wife in labor? Did her water break?"

"No. She's almost at term, as you can see, but that's not why we're here. Or at least, not just that."

The man paused, rubbed his mouth with the back of his palm. His eyelids parted farther, and he stammered out his next words.

"We—we're seriously injured. All three of us. And we need surgeries. Tonight."

The visitor clearly wasn't a bumpkin. He was educated—his choice of words left no doubt about that. But surgeries? Had the surgeon heard him right? What could the man possibly—

"Show me," said the surgeon.

Like merchants displaying their wares, the boy rolled up his vest and the man unbuttoned his shirt and lifted his right arm over his head. In the man's side was a slit, its edges white and still, like lips paused in speech. It was enough to fool one into thinking that the ribs had been penetrated. The boy's abdomen was bloated. Two cuts in the upper left, under the rib cage, formed a cross whose corners curled outward.

And then the woman finished peeling away the many loops of odhni wrapped around her neck. It couldn't be. He had to be mistaken. The wound in her neck—surely it was a trick of the light? Could those be the ends of her muscles? And was that—no, it was impossible—the *larynx*?

But there was no blood gushing out, not even from that neck. What kind of hoax was this? Who were these charlatans?

Out of the corner of his eye, the surgeon saw a jerking motion. It was the pharmacist. The surgeon had forgotten that she was still in the room. She looked rigid, as though in the grip of a seizure. The man with the cut in his side sprang to her and grabbed both her wrists with one hand. Stepping behind her, he clapped his other hand over her mouth. She was thin, but seemed to match him in strength as they struggled. He grimaced as he twisted her forearms and muscled her to him, her back against his chest, her torso immobilized by the pressure of his arm folded across her, locking her twitching hands against his shoulder.

The air seemed to clot, grow viscous. The surgeon pushed through it, tried to reach the pharmacist. He felt his books fly off the desk as his hand struck them. The woman with the monstrous neck blocked his path, clasped his wrist, pressed a finger to her lips.

"Please, Doctor Saheb, please," the man said. "I won't hurt her, won't hurt you. We are good people. We just need your help."

"What—" the surgeon began, but could find no suitable words to add. So he just stood and watched—watched the man signal the boy; watched the boy run to the window, close and latch it, bolt the door; watched the woman go to the pharmacist and reach out to cup her cheek, all the while speaking rapidly, calling her "sister," begging her not to scream.

This was no hoax. The pharmacist, twisting in her captor's grip, arched her body back like a bow at the woman's advance, making the man stumble a step back to maintain his hold on her. The girl's eyelids had opened as far as they could go, and her eyes were fixed on the woman's obscene neck. The surgeon felt his own muscles knot and pull at the point where the nerves threaded out from his skull. He pressed his hand on the cold glass plate of the desk behind him.

The man with the cut in his ribs opened his mouth, but if he said something, the surgeon could not hear it. The woman fell quiet and, probably realizing the effect her injuries were having, raised her odhni and let it drape back around her neck, removing her wound from view.

The surgeon's eyes darted around the room. Could he use his pen as a weapon, was it sharp enough, solid enough? It lay on the floor, its nib snapped off. A spray of ink stretched across the tiles. What else? He had scissors in his drawer somewhere, he was sure, but he'd have to dig for them.

He gripped the table's edge tighter, leaned against it. "What is this? What's going on?"

The visitors stood like effigies. The woman and the boy turned to the man, who was opening and closing his mouth like a fish thrown to land. The girl he held captive had stopped her struggle and now just hung against him, breathing heavily with her eyes squeezed shut. He, too, closed his eyes and heaved, as though gathering his breath for some feat.

"I'm a teacher, Doctor Saheb. This is my family. We've never harmed anyone. We just want to live our lives in peace."

THREE

"WE'D GONE TO A fair near our village," said the man who called himself a teacher. "It was sunset by the time we left it. The street was dark. The bulbs in the lampposts had burned out. I didn't think much of it then, didn't turn back. God knows how much I've repented that."

The pharmacist started squirming again in the man's grip. His words spilled out faster.

"Four men were hiding there. They jumped out, took our money and jewelry. And then they stabbed us, Doctor Saheb, stabbed us and left us on the roadside. Like sacks of garbage. They just left us there and disappeared."

The visitors were pale. There was a sickly tone to their skin, that was true. But how—

"When did this happen?" the surgeon asked.

"This evening."

"But, but there was no fair here. I didn't hear of any—"

"It didn't happen here, Saheb. We're from another district."

"But that doesn't make any sense. How did you get here? The sun just set, not even an hour ago. And how did you stop your bleeding?"

"We didn't."

The surgeon felt his toes curl in his shoes, press hard against the leather. "But then how did you survive?"

"We didn't."

This was unacceptable. One could string letters together to say anything, anything at all, no matter how outrageous. The surgeon wished his thoughts would connect, one to the next, turn the man's words into something that made sense.

He took a step toward the family. The teacher's wife, as if she'd read his mind, lowered the odhni and tilted her neck away, letting her wound gape. The sight was suffocating, and the surgeon staggered back and collapsed into a chair as his legs gave under him. How was one to shake off such a hallucination? Perhaps he ought to bash his head against something—the desk, the wall . . . fracture his skull if need be. Would that do it?

The silence felt like an awful pressure on his eardrums. His eyes kept flitting to the drawer, the one that supposedly had scissors in it. At one point, he heard a sob, and it took him some time to realize it was the pharmacist. She was hanging limp in the teacher's hold.

The surgeon sat up in his chair. "Let her go."

"I—I can't, Doctor Saheb. She'll wake up the villagers. I can't let that happen."

"She'll be quiet. Let her go."

The teacher turned to his wife with an anxious look, then

pinched shut his eyes and loosened his grip. The girl tore away from him and flung herself into the farthest corner of the room. There she whimpered, high and soft, but did not scream.

The surgeon leaned forward, pressed his thumbs hard into his eyelids. Webs and vortices danced in the darkness.

"We need you, Doctor Saheb. There's no one else."

"What are you saying? What are you—"

"Without your help we will remain dead."

"The dead do not walk," said the surgeon, his head reeling with vertigo. "The dead do not speak. The dead have no choice but to remain dead. You are lying to me."

"I understand what you're feeling, Saheb, believe me. If I were in your place, I would have found this as impossible as you do. When I was alive, I never believed stories of ghosts and possessions and haunted houses—the tales that old men told their grandchildren to scare them. All nonsense, I knew. I always taught my students to reject superstition. You have no reason to trust my words, Doctor Saheb, I understand that. But trust our wounds. Examine them, and then tell me. Who could stay alive with injuries like ours?"

The surgeon released the pressure on his eyes. The vortices spun away and vanished, but the family remained, shrouded by a haze as though their bodies were fraying at the edges, unraveling. He couldn't will them out of existence. Every blink of his eyes brought the family more into focus, made them more solid.

"Look, are you a thief of some kind? Just say so if you are.

I have money in my safe. Take it and go. You don't need to do this elaborate—"

"Please, Doctor Saheb, please listen. At dawn, we will live again."

It couldn't be. It just couldn't. "Why have you come to me? Go find a priest, a sorcerer. Leave me alone."

"We need you to fix our wounds. At sunrise, our bodies will fill with blood again, and we'll no longer be walking corpses."

"How? Why? How is that possible?"

"The answer is long and complicated, Saheb, and I don't understand everything myself. I can only tell you now that an angel took mercy on us. I'll explain everything else later. We have so little time. I know nothing about surgeries, but I'm sure that injuries as severe as ours will take you all night to stitch up."

The surgeon's chest felt cold, tight. "Are you mad? You want me to operate on you here? In *this* clinic? I don't even have instruments to set a fracture, let alone repair torn blood vessels and whatever internal injuries you have. Whatever this is, this insanity, it can't be done here. You must go to the city. Go."

"But, Doctor Saheb—"

"There's a train that leaves every hour. It will take you there."

"Saheb—"

"Maybe the train isn't a good idea. You can drive there. Here, take my car. I don't care, you don't even have to bring it back. Can you drive? No? Okay, then, I'll drive you. I'll drop you off at a proper hospital. You can explain everything to the doctors there, get them to treat you."

He went to the pharmacist. She was pressed to the wall, as though trying to percolate to the other side.

"Come." He helped her up, began to steer her to the door.

"Wait," said the teacher. He looked desperate. "We can't go to the city. Whatever you can do here, in this clinic, is all we're allowed. If we even step beyond the boundary of this village, the angel will snatch our lives back."

"What? But that doesn't make any sense. Why would angels care about village boundaries?"

"I swear to you, Saheb, it's the truth. It was his most important condition."

"But that's just ridiculous. You must have heard him wrong. Look, I'll just drop this girl off with her husband and get my car ready. Let's not waste time."

He was almost at the door, reaching for the bolt, when the teacher spoke, so softly that even a breeze might have swept his voice away. "If we were to drive with you, Saheb, our bodies would stop moving at the boundary, and you would be left with three corpses to keep you company for the rest of your journey."

The surgeon jerked to a stop. Something settled in his skull, dense as lead, a sudden condensation of all the grotesquerie of this evening. He could already imagine the family on his operating table, lying there as he worked on their bloodless flesh, corpses laid upon stone slabs in preparation for autopsies—his mind rebelled against that word, but what other name could one give to surgeries on the dead? This night contained nothing but absurdities.

"Have mercy on us," the teacher was saying. "If our wounds

aren't closed, we'll die another death, as bloody and horrible as the first. If you can't do anything for me, at least help my wife and son. Give life to them, to my unborn child, I beg you. I have nothing on me, no money, but I'll do anything you ask. Just don't turn us away."

The man threw himself at the surgeon's feet. The doctor stood like an imbecile, unable even to recoil from the dead fingers clutching his shoes, able only to repeat, "No, no, don't do that, don't do that."

FOUR

"WAIT HERE, IN THIS room. I need some time," said the surgeon to the dead as he helped the pharmacist out into the corridor. She hung from him like a dead weight, her face so gray that he thought she would faint at any moment.

He closed the door behind him and set her down on a bench, propped against the wall. After raising her lids with a thumb against her eyebrows to confirm that there was life still there, he sank beside her.

To be freed, even for a moment, from the dead and the dreadful hope in their eyes was an intense relief. The breeze wafting in through the entrance of the clinic was warm, and outside the shuttered room, no longer faced with bloodless wounds, he could once again breathe. Far below, oil lamps flickered in the windows of the village at the bottom of the hill. Behind those windows, the villagers were probably washing dishes, tossing leftovers out for the crows, dousing embers, unrolling mattresses. As though this night were no different from any other. As though it were obvious that the sun would rise again.

The girl was whimpering. The surgeon knew that something was required of him, consoling words perhaps, but all he could do was grip his kneecaps. It was the only way he could still the shaking of his hands. There would be no one to console him—it was best he accepted that first.

"This is just . . . just so impossible," he said. "I don't know what to think."

The girl swallowed, then coughed, choking on her tears. "They're ghosts, Saheb." She could barely get the words out past her chattering teeth.

Something rustled outside the entrance, and even though the surgeon could tell it was only a rat in the grass, the muscles in his arms and shoulders tightened. The pharmacist didn't even notice. The effort of speaking seemed too much for her.

"A ghost climbed into my sister's body, Saheb. We had to tie her to a bed. She kept turning, one side to the other, kicked at everyone. Said things, Saheb, that no one could understand. Her eyes, they were rolled up; her body became hot, like burning coal—so hot that no one could touch her. And her mouth was full of foam, as if she'd eaten soap."

The girl had never mentioned her sister before. Would he have remembered if she had?

"My father, he called a tantrik. Told him to do whatever magic he could to save her. The tantrik had to beat her with a broom to drive the ghost out—that's how tightly it held her, like a crab. On the third day, it left her body and went into a coconut. The tantrik broke it open and blood spilled out. So much blood, I thought I would die. My sister woke up, but she didn't recognize any of us."

"How long ago was this?"

"Six years. No, more. Eight. She lived, but what kind of life is this? The ghost made her mind weak. She can't even feed herself. My mother still has to change her clothes every day. No one will marry her."

The surgeon had witnessed spectacles such as this before—charlatans with hair that had seen neither comb nor water in god knew how long, wearing bone necklaces around their necks, jumping and chanting to the goddess Kali and spraying so much red water around that the room looked washed with blood. The trickery was always so transparent, but the gullible believed what they wanted to believe. A few days of antibiotics would have done the poor girl more good than a lifetime of holy water and chants.

But it was hard to dismiss ghosts so glibly now, with three of them waiting on the other side of the wall.

"We have to run away, Saheb. We have to leave the village before something bad happens."

The clock in front of them had only one hand. No, there were two, overlapping between eight and nine. A small green lizard was pasted to the wall next to the clock, as still as its hands.

"If the man had wanted to strangle you," said the surgeon, "he would've just done it. He already had his hand around your mouth. There was nothing to stop him."

With a click, one hand of the clock stepped out from behind

the other. The lizard slithered off to the wall's edge. If even a word of what the dead had said was true, they couldn't just sit here and keep talking like this.

"Their wounds need to be repaired. I don't know how I'm going to do it, but they need to be repaired."

From the look on the pharmacist's face, he might have been speaking a foreign tongue.

"Look, either we help them, or they die. Die again, that is—however you want to think about it. It's not a question of whether any of this makes sense. It's a question of . . . of whether we're going to just kick them out of the clinic or not. And if not, we have to do something."

Her eyes had already begun to widen. It was clear she knew what he would say next. So he said it.

"I'll need your help for this."

"Me? No, Doctor Saheb, no," she almost screamed.

"Quiet. We have to be quiet."

She dropped her voice, which only made her sound more hoarse. "What are you saying, Saheb? I can't stay here. I can't. This is not right. These things shouldn't happen, it's not right, it's not right."

He leaned against the wall. Whatever he was feeling now— the fear and fatigue—the night would only magnify it. Perhaps her instinct was the right one. Perhaps he should just leap into his car and drive away in any direction, abandon the village and everything in it. In the morning, the villagers would find three cadavers in the clinic. Or the visitors, recognizing the idiocy of their plan, would decide to walk to the boundary of the village and fall there. Either was infinitely preferable to his involvement in this dreadful matter, the raising, no, the mending of the dead.

"You've always done everything I've asked," he said. "If you want to leave, I won't stop you. Maybe if things were any different, I would have left as well. But the woman is pregnant. Her son is just eight. We have to do something."

At first it seemed as if she hadn't heard him, but then her face turned to the ground and her chest began to shake. The way her braid hung between her bony shoulders made her look more like a child than ever. He thought of placing a hand on her head, but couldn't bring himself to do so, not even at a time like this. "It will be fine" was all he managed to say, his hands still on his knees. "It will be fine."

But he couldn't ask her not to weep. As the lights in the village winked out one by one, he tried to push away his own disquiet while he waited, but it was like trying to sweep a fog aside with his fingers. Whatever this was, this inescapable madness, he would have to get through it. He would pretend that the visitors had been wheeled in on gurneys, with lolling heads and frothing mouths, victims of some mysterious accident. He would just do his job, and let the pieces fall as they would.

The girl finally wiped her face. Taking that as a sign, he stood up.

"Your husband must be wondering where you are. I'll need his help as well. Let me explain everything. And we have to be careful. If the villagers hear about this, they'll bring down the sky."

FIVE

THE LIGHTS IN THE operating room flickered on. The faintest trace of formaldehyde still hung in the air. Glazed tiles with bluish veins covered the walls to a height of four feet. Many were chipped and broken. Despite the pharmacist's regular scrubbing, grime had settled into the grout, and the paint on the wall above, once a shiny white, was now blistered with green geographies of mold.

A loop of sturdy metal hung from the plastered ceiling. The large tungsten reflector lamp that was intended to hang from it had never been delivered, vanishing, like so many things, into the bureaucratic ether. The room was lit instead by a fluorescent tube mounted high on one of the walls, and by two tall Anglepoise lamps that the surgeon himself had purchased. Together they cast a modest illumination, suitable for minor procedures such as the suturing of shallow cuts or the extraction of glass shards, but certainly not for any real surgery. Only a lunatic would suggest doing anything here in the middle of the night.

These last few years, the surgeon had wondered if he had the right to operate at all any more. With a well-lit surgical field, he might still have trusted his skills. But in this room, where lamps cast shadows, concealing more than they exposed, every nerve or blood vessel or loop of bowel could hide in a dark corner and conspire to brush against his scalpel's edge. It was impossible to operate safely here. Inflamed appendices, gall bladders, bowel obstructions—he sent them all to the city hospitals. What did he have to offer anyway? No nurse, no blood bank, no light. If a patient had to die, she would die from her disease, not from his surgery.

A glass cabinet on the wall housed his instruments—relics of his past. It was the pharmacist's job to keep them sterilized and bundled in thick green cloth. Their shine was rarely marred by use. The surgeon would just unwrap the green wombs and sort through his collection, arrange his tools by size and type, hold them up to the light one by one as though approving them for surgery, until he could no longer ignore the absurdity of this farce.

"These need to be autoclaved," he would say, and drop them back on the tray.

"Yes, Saheb."

The instruments were sterilized far more often than they were used, but the pharmacist never complained. She would just wrap them back in the squares of cloth, pack them into fenestrated metal boxes, set them in the autoclave drum, and wait while the machine steamed and whistled. Then she would extract the contents with sterile gloves and stack them back in the glass cabinet until the surgeon felt the need to inspect them again. Because of this pointless routine, all the instruments in the cabinet were always ready for surgery. And they were ready now.

Still, it was just a humble set of implements—basic tools for mundane surgeries, nothing very specialized. The dead seemed to think him a magician, with mystical devices and superhuman powers. How many disappointments was he destined to inflict on them?

And what agonies? The surgeon had worried about this since the beginning. Would they feel pain? He had no equipment for anesthesia—no propofol, no thiopental. And even if he did, how could the drugs work on the dead without a bloodstream? He might have to crack their chests open without the basic luxury of lowering them into slumber. Did they understand that?

To these concerns, the teacher said, "Our wounds don't hurt. We don't even feel them. It's part of our state. We won't feel any pain for the rest of this night."

"And what about tomorrow morning?"

"We'll have life and blood at dawn, Saheb, so I assume we'll also have pain. When that happens, we will endure it. We'll endure whatever we have to."

The surgeon knocked on the door of the pharmacist's house. The pharmacist stood at his side, wringing her hands as though trying to scrub them clean of some unseen stain.

Her husband opened the door. "What is it, Saheb? You here? At this time? Is there a problem?"

"Yes, a problem. You could call it that."

"Go get Saheb a glass of water," the man said to his wife, but his eyes didn't leave the surgeon.

"No need for water." The surgeon waved his hand. "This will seem like a strange request." It struck him, after he'd spoken, that these were the same words with which the dead had begun explaining their predicament.

"Saheb?"

"Walk up the hill with me."

The clinic sat on the hillock like a lantern. They walked in silence past the houses and huts of the village, and then, once they had started climbing, the surgeon spoke in slow, careful words, some of which he had to dig out of a vocabulary he'd never dreamed he'd use. The windows of the clinic seemed to grow brighter with every step. The moon had not risen, and it was as though the foot of the hillock were the rim of the world, with only nothingness beyond it. When they reached the top, the surgeon found himself short of breath, as if he'd hiked a great distance, and he stopped speaking.

A few yards from the entrance, the pharmacist's husband squatted on his heels and slapped his hands to his cheeks. A string of fearful questions poured out of his mouth. What good could possibly come of this? The only reason ghosts ever came back was to harass the living. What if they wanted to possess them all? Haunt them and drive them mad? Maybe even kill them?

The surgeon, exhausted by his own incomprehension, offered answers that barely convinced even himself. What right had he to the allegiances of these two? It humiliated him to be placed in this position, but how else would he get through the night? The pharmacist just knelt at her husband's side and avoided the surgeon's eyes.

The man would run, and he would take her with him, the surgeon felt sure. It was futile to hope for anything different. And why indeed should the man not do as he wished? If corpses could walk, what remained to guide any other action?

A silhouette moved in the clinic's light. The teacher's son was leaning against the entrance. With the bulb at his back, his outline threw a long shadow across the bright strip that stretched from the clinic door, out over the grass. Behind everything was the sky—an inky spread with pinpricks of white. When the surgeon's eyes met his, the boy inched back into the corridor, and his face fell in the bulb's light. He looked guilty, as if he knew he didn't belong there, in this place and this world. The boy's parents appeared behind him. "What are you doing here? Saheb told us to wait inside," said the teacher. He cast a nervous glance at the pharmacist's husband, then at the surgeon, and began to lead his son away, but the surgeon gestured for them to stay.

The pharmacist clutched her husband's arm. "There they are, there they are."

"Yes, there they are," said the surgeon. "The dead. They're here to regain their own lives, not to steal yours."

The pharmacist's husband slumped back. He rubbed his eyes, stared, rubbed them again, trying perhaps, as the surgeon had tried not that long ago, to scrub away the hallucination.

The surgeon himself, observing the dead for the first time from outside his clinic, was struck by how like the living they looked, standing there surrounded by bulbs and benches and discolored paint, as though the corridor were the place where all the entities of this world and the next could blend together seamlessly. Nothing more than a doorframe separated the dead from the living now, and who could say in that moment who stood on which side?

The pharmacist rose, helped her husband up. The surgeon looked away, tried not to eavesdrop as they murmured to each other. Nothing he could say would accomplish more than the sight of the dead themselves.

"If you think this has to be done," said the pharmacist's husband, his lips a dull white, "we trust you."

"If you want to leave, go now."

"You have done more for us, for the villagers, than anyone else, Saheb. We are in your debt."

"If you want to go, I understand," repeated the surgeon, perversely hoping they would take the opportunity to fly. "Really, I understand."

"We can't leave you here. We'll do whatever you tell us. The rest is in God's hands."

The surgeon nodded. It was the most he could manage by way of gratitude. His face felt permanently carved in a grave expression of foreboding. He turned and made for the clinic.

The teacher came up to him at the steps. "I was wondering, Saheb, if you think it's wise to involve more people in this. The fewer who know, the better, don't you think?"

"There won't be any more," said the surgeon. "And without these two to help me, you might as well prepare for your second death."

Responsible now for both the living and the dead, he dragged himself up into the corridor. The teacher appeared to have more to say, but the surgeon was in no mood to hear it.

SIX

"KEEP WATCH HERE," THE surgeon said to the pharmacist's husband. "If you see anything, call out for me and hide the others."

"Yes, Saheb."

"I might have more work for you later, but first I need to find out what these surgeries will involve."

"As you say."

"Do you think, Saheb," the teacher asked, "that someone might be suspicious if the clinic lights stay on all night?"

"I sometimes sit here through the night if I can't sleep. The villagers are used to it. But yes, it's possible the light might attract someone. We'll just have to risk that. So, who's first?"

The teacher patted his son's shoulders. "Operate on him, Saheb, then my wife. Treat me only after you're done with both."

His wife looked away. From her demeanor, it was clear that this matter had already been decided, that the two had argued over it while the surgeon was away.

The surgeon led the boy to the operating room. The child had appeared quite calm through the evening, but now he hesitated, pulled back at the door. The tiled room seemed to frighten even him, he who had traveled distances that the surgeon couldn't even begin to imagine.

"Go in, my baby," his mother said. "It will be done soon. So soon, you won't even realize it."

The teacher clasped his son's hand. "I'll be with you. Don't worry."

The stone slab was covered with a single thin drape, and the surgeon had the boy strip and climb onto it. Over his thin, supine body, his abdomen now rose like a dome, as if he too bore another life within him. His wound still seemed like an elaborate disguise, and the surgeon was tempted to peel back the fake skin and reveal the real one underneath. He hoped that the teacher was right—that the dead couldn't feel any pain. With gloved fingers, he examined the wound and the skin around it, squeezed the sides and pinched the skin, gently at first, and then quite hard between his nails. As promised, the boy felt nothing.

The surgeon adjusted the Anglepoise lamps to illuminate the boy's abdomen as best he could, and with the help of the pharmacist he cleaned the skin and wound with iodine. He then masked and scrubbed and gowned as was customary, swabbed the wound with alcohol, made it sterile, draped it. He took every precaution he would have taken with any other patient. The bodies of the dead might well be immune to infection now, but that would change at dawn. He also took care to arrange the drapes so that the boy wouldn't be able to see his own bowels. Surely there were sights that all humans, alive or dead, were better off not seeing.

With his scalpel in hand, he paused to plan his first incision, and now couldn't help wondering if the dead were just soulless contraptions. Divine puppets, perhaps. Was this a fiendish test, meant to force him to pluck at his core and emerge with god alone knew what? An outrageous test, if so, by a deity who would stoop this low to wring belief from his subjects. What if he were to turn to the stars and cry out, "I was wrong, I was wrong"? Would the visitors vanish and the three worlds open before him?

He lengthened the wound with his blade, and found himself both fascinated and repulsed by the quality of the boy's flesh. It resembled nothing so much as the flesh of a corpse—not yet mottled or putrid, but dead enough that the blood had coagulated in the vessels and no longer oozed out as he sliced through the skin. It reminded him of his work in the office of the city coroner. Of course, those corpses never climbed up on tables themselves.

The teacher was seated on a low stool next to his son. He whispered and cooed to the boy, ran his fingers through his hair. The boy's eyes were half closed, his hands by his side under the drapes. They remained that way until the surgeon said, "Maybe this is a good time for you to explain what's going on. Explain how you got here."

The teacher's eyes, when he raised them, first fell on his son's abdomen, which was in the process of being opened. He immediately jerked them away.

"Are you sure, Saheb?"

"Don't you think I have the right to ask?" replied the surgeon.

"Yes, of course. I didn't mean that. But maybe—maybe you might not want to know."

"And why would that be?"

"Only the dead know about the afterlife. It's not something the living are supposed to learn."

"That may be, but all kinds of things are happening tonight that aren't supposed to happen. Besides, if I'm supposed to treat you, I need to understand exactly how the three of you ended up here."

The teacher looked at his son's face for a few moments, then at the floor.

"The moment we died, all the pain stopped. Then, for who knows how long, we couldn't move. There was no light, no sound, nothing. Slowly, we began to see and hear again. Our senses returned, but not the pain . . . thank god, not the pain. We were on this—this plain. It went on and on in all directions. There was no end to it. This was the afterlife, Doctor Saheb, where we all go when we die.

"There were dead people there from every part of the world, all mixed together. They spoke so many different languages, but it was strange, we could understand all of them, and they could understand us. Many had died from old age, others from sickness or epidemics. Some, like us, had been murdered. Our deaths were unjust. Everyone must die some day, yes, but not like this. One person killing another, there's nothing worse than that.

"We met so many people, and each had his own story.

Really interesting stories too, from times and places I'd never even heard about. I tried to look for kings or famous people from history but, as you can imagine, most of the dead there were as ordinary as us."

While the teacher was speaking, the surgeon had deepened the incision in the boy's abdomen through the thin layer of subcutaneous fat. Within the peritoneum, he could see glistening clots in copious volumes. If an injury to a major blood vessel had caused this bleeding, it would be disastrous, impossible to mend here. The question couldn't be answered through the limited aperture of the wound. He would need to make a larger incision, inspect the contents of the entire abdomen through a long vertical cut.

"Weren't you attacked this evening, after sunset? And yet you were on this plain. How much time did you spend there?"

"In the afterlife, there's no way to keep time, Saheb. There's no sun that rises, no days, no weeks. That's not to say it's dark, not at all, but there's just this . . . this light that glows. It never becomes any dimmer or brighter. And there's no need for sleep either. When we got there, the shock of everything was so great that we tried to hold on to the one thing that was as natural to our lives as breathing. We tried, we forced ourselves. We would close our eyes, lie down, try to imagine that it was night—even imagine we were dreaming, to see if that would help. In life one sleeps and then dreams—I thought in death maybe it would work the other way around. But that didn't help either. Once you're dead, you don't need any rest, and so we've been awake ever since.

"It's very difficult to describe the way time works there.

Here on earth we're always reminded of it—ticking clocks, summer and monsoon, even little things like food on a stove. If you take it off the fire too soon, it's raw, too late and it's burnt—that's a measure of time too. And even if you lock yourself in a room, turn off all the lights, sit in complete silence, you can still hear your heartbeat. There's nothing like that there. Someone mentioned to me in the afterlife that the only point when any living being experiences this kind of time—this absence of time, rather—is inside the womb. But who can claim to have memories of that?

"In any case, to answer your question, Doctor Saheb, after what might have been a week or two, I was completely disoriented. And the opportunity to return here came later, much later. After all that wandering, time is again the most important thing for us tonight. I have to remind myself that it's ticking, that things are different now. Or the same again, depending on how you look at it."

The surgeon turned to the pharmacist for a pair of forceps. Her masked face was turned away from the surgical field. But she was listening, he could see.

"Then we met a celestial being, you could call him an angel, and we told him about the crime done to us. Not just the crime of being stabbed, Saheb, but the crime of being killed. Not everyone who is stabbed dies. Humans decide whom to stab, but someone up there decides who will live and who won't. It shouldn't have happened. We had never harmed anyone. My son deserved to live and grow and have a family that would care for him when he was old. The angel asked us what we wanted him to do.

"'Send us back,' we said. 'Let us live again.'

"'There are laws even we can't break,' the angel told us. 'The valley between life and death can only be crossed from one side. Once you're here, it doesn't matter how it happened, how unjust the circumstances. It's done.'

"'But then what about rebirth?' we asked. 'Our priests insisted it happens. Were they lying?'

"'There is rebirth, yes,' the angel replied, 'but not the kind they talk about in your land, where you can be reborn as an insect or a lion, something different each time. You can only be reborn as a human, through a woman's womb. People are chosen for it based on their virtues, based on how they lived their lives. Have faith. You will have the opportunity, but it won't happen right away.'"

The surgeon's new incision laid the boy open from the tip of his breastbone to his navel. The surgeon cut through the skin and fat, and then through the fibrous strip running down the midline of the abdomen between the muscles on either side. Once the peritoneum was cut, the solidified blood spread before him like a russet sea. He reached in and started scooping out the clots. This part was more bewildering than anything else so far—the fact that the boy could lie there awake while his bloodstream piled up on a tray next to him. The pile grew larger as the peritoneum emptied out, and the contents of the abdomen became visible.

There was a large cut in the edge of the spleen. It just lay there now, dry and pink and feigning innocence, but one only had to imagine how a puncture that size might have bled in life. It took a good amount of time, but the surgeon scooped out every clump of blood that had collected under the liver, in the omentum, and in the folds around the intestines. He then carefully searched for other injuries.

When he was done, he placed his instruments on a tray and took a breath.

"Is something wrong, Saheb?"

"Nothing, nothing's wrong. It's just that I've discovered what killed your son.'

The man flinched at this, and the surgeon regretted his choice of words.

"What was it?"

"The knife cut into his spleen."

"Did it hit anything else?"

"Doesn't seem like it."

"Does that mean that if—if it had missed the spleen, he might have survived?"

"Yes. Perhaps. Yes."

The teacher turned away, his lips twisting, his face slowly contorting. He blinked, appeared almost to be in pain himself. Then, shielding his eyes from the surgeon and pharmacist, he buried his face in his son's hair. He cried for the first time that night, at this unexpected moment, as if some barrel of emotion he'd been balancing had just been overturned.

The surgeon coughed—two short, blunt coughs—to master any emotion that threatened to spill from himself at the man's display of anguish. It was a technique he'd perfected early in his training. Perhaps too well, for it'd been far too long since he'd felt any emotion worth mastering. Health itself appeared so bleak a state that sickness and death wrung little pity from him any more. Sometimes, when a patient's final breaths seemed no more than the last turns of a wheel, leaving behind an object to be removed, charred, turned to ash, and stirred into a riverbed, his indifference terrified even him.

"In a sense, we're lucky it's the spleen," he said, hoping to clear the gloom. "If the knife had cut the liver or the intestines, or, god forbid, a big artery, we'd have had no chance at all."

The teacher raised his head. Not a muscle moved on his face as he listened.

"It won't help if I just stitch the spleen shut. It will bleed again. But I can remove the whole thing—he can live without it. I can't promise you we won't discover new problems in the morning, but this might be all that's needed."

The man clasped his hands together so hard that his knuckles looked like rows of rounded bones. "You're our savior, Doctor Saheb, you're a saint. There's nothing I could possibly do in a thousand years to repay your mercy. Please save my son, Saheb. Please do whatever you think is best."

He rained kisses on his son's cheeks and forehead. "Saheb is going to fix you. He's going to make you better." The boy, infected with his father's enthusiasm, started to prop himself up on an elbow. "Shhh," the teacher said, caressing the boy's brow, trying to calm his son though clearly unable to contain himself. "Don't move, don't move. Lie down."

The surgeon let himself be lifted by an unfamiliar, buoyant sensation. The one thing that could have confounded this surgery—the tyranny of a relentless bloodstream—he wouldn't have to face tonight. During the early years of his training, he'd once had to extract the spleen of a young man who was struck by a bus. The spleen, ruptured like an egg, had lain at the bottom of a red pool that constantly refilled itself no matter how much blood he suctioned out. By contrast, this was almost absurdly easy.

"Go on," he said.

"Yes. Where was I? Yes. The angel. We asked him to just send us back to our old lives, but he refused. So we begged him to let us be reborn, but he told us it wasn't our turn yet, and disappeared. But we called him again."

"How do you call an angel?"

"You have to think of him, imagine his face, ask for his help, and he appears."

"Just like that?"

"Not exactly—sometimes it works, sometimes it doesn't. I'm sure angels have their own preferences, whose calls they will answer, whose they won't. For whatever reason, our angel appeared more often to us than any of the other angels did to any of the dead."

"Why?"

"I really don't know, Saheb. I honestly don't think there was anything special about us, but this angel was definitely different from all the others. In fact, he always had more questions for us than we had for him. He asked us about our families, our childhoods, our wedding, the birth of our son. He was interested in the customs of the living—our festivals and foods, the way we traded money for objects. Even small things—the way we kept our houses, painted our walls, grew potted plants in the yard. He had watched these things from the afterlife, but he didn't always understand what he was seeing."

"Didn't understand? What do you mean? Wouldn't angels be all-knowing?"

"Well, those are two different things, Saheb: knowing and understanding. I'll give you a simple example. The angel knew that the living like to fly kites, but never understood why it was such a popular thing, why it should deserve a special day of celebration, why people would drop everything and climb on rooftops for it. There are no kites in the afterlife. There's no wind there, not even really a sky . . . there's just that plain. I tried to explain to him the joy when something that's nothing more than a square of paper stretched across two sticks catches the breeze and goes up, up . . . so high that sometimes you can't even see it against the sun, so high even birds won't get near it. I tried to explain it a few different ways, but none of them made any sense to the angel.

"And so I told him that it felt like toying with death. It was like tying your life to a thread, sending it out to a place over which you had no power, working all day to keep it from being lost, and then, in the evening, if you were lucky, pulling it back unharmed, admiring its colors again, and storing it in a safe place for another time. That's when the angel understood. That was his language, Doctor Saheb, the language of life and death."

The teacher's story was like a bizarre fable—something a priest might deliver in a religious ceremony. But there were no flowers here, no lamps or burning incense to make the unreality more palatable. The surgeon felt a constant tightness at the base of his throat. He had to loosen it occasionally by swallowing the spittle in his mouth.

"What do these angels look like?"

"They look human, just like everyone else. No shining eyes, no aura of light. They don't ride on any animals, they don't fly, they walk on their own two feet. Our angel was about my height, shorter than you. He looked a little overweight, but I think their bodies are just disguises they wear in front of us."

"So what happened next?"

"It became a regular thing. I would call for the angel, and he would appear. I would ask that we be sent back, and he would smile and decline my request. And then he would ask his own questions. I have to admit that even though the likelihood of returning to life seemed to diminish with each of his visits, I still kept calling for him, just to see what new question he would bring me. I've always wanted to help people see things in different ways. That's why I became a teacher. When students couldn't understand something that seemed obvious to me, I took it as a challenge to figure out what the basic misunderstanding was, and use that to explain things better. I don't want to suggest that the angel was my student, of course not. I wouldn't even dare call him a friend. But I valued the time I spent with him, answering his questions.

"And then, during one of his visits, when I wasn't expecting anything at all, he said that there was something he could do for us. Something that was within his power."

By now the surgeon had freed the spleen of the scaffolding that had held it up against the diaphragm and the other organs. He checked its surfaces and prepared to tie off the vessels that would, in life, have fed it blood. The teacher had paused, so the surgeon looked up at him, signaled that he was still listening.

The teacher glanced at the pharmacist. "The very first thing the angel said to me was that all of this had to remain secret. I can tell you, Saheb, you have every right to know. But I beg you, none of this can leave the clinic. We were ordered to keep it to the smallest number of people possible. Forget the rest of the world, even the rest of the village cannot know of this."

The surgeon nodded. He turned to the girl, who nodded as well, though with some hesitation.

"The angel told me that there are limits to what any single one of them can do. Each has a few specific powers. They can perform what we would consider miracles, yes, but only with the skills of four or five put together.

"He offered to send us back, but he didn't have the ability to fix our wounds. He couldn't manipulate human flesh, he said. We would have to return just the way we were. That was enough to dash all my hopes. What were we to do then? Bleed to death again? Empty our lives into the mud? The angel said he could help us in one way—he could keep us from coming alive for some time. He could keep us like this—bloodless, the way we appear to you now—but for no more than one earthly night. That was all. While everyone was asleep, we would have to get our wounds fixed. Blood would start flowing through us at dawn.

"Now, Saheb, you can imagine what I thought when he said this. The offer sounded hopeless enough already, but the restrictions didn't end there. He reminded us again and again that what he was offering was completely forbidden. Apparently, angels can be punished too. By even talking about helping us, he was putting himself at risk. He told us that his power extended only to a small village—this village. He couldn't allow knowledge of this plan to ever spread outside it. No other angel could ever be allowed to see us. We could never cross the boundary. If we tried, our bodies would drop like corpses right there, and we would be pulled back to the afterlife. It also meant that we could never visit our old town; never see our families. We wanted life, didn't we? Well, now we could get it, with all of these conditions binding our hands and feet.

"But I should bite my tongue before I say another ungrateful word. Please understand, I'm not blaming the angel. He was offering us the very best option he had. But still, to be sent here after sunset, with just a night before we died again . . . it seemed so pointless. Until he told us that within this village lived a very skilled surgeon."

The surgeon felt his hands go slack. "The angel mentioned me? Your angel specifically mentioned me?"

So his paranoia wasn't entirely unjustified, was it? There was a prickle in his hair, a wash of fresh sweat, new rivulets tickling their way down the sides of his neck and face. He pretended to stretch his shoulders, turned his neck this way and that, and looked up at the ceiling so that this sudden wave sweeping over him wouldn't be so obvious.

The plaster of the ceiling was plain gray, featureless except for the metal loop embedded in it. From this angle, and with the shadows cast by the lamps around it, the loop looked like an eye, a single sinister aperture set at the center of a gray face. He allowed himself to indulge this theatrical cliché. Why not? Why not see eyes everywhere? Even in the bulbs, hot and unblinking? Examining, documenting. Perhaps this really was a test, not of his belief but of his surgical skills. What was the examiner looking for? Would a certificate descend from the clouds to declare him competent? Competent at what?

"Yes, Saheb. That's why he made this offer in the first place. If it weren't for you, he would never even have mentioned it. He told us to consider everything very carefully. We could refuse if we wished, but he would never offer us this choice again. So we accepted."

It was now time to individually tie off and cut the vessels that streamed, bloodless, from the boy's spleen. The surgeon needed to be meticulous. He couldn't allow the absence of blood to lull him into complacency. A single untied vessel, and that would be the end—an open tap through which the boy's life would gush out in the morning. The phalanxes of questions within him would have to wait.

The surgeon ligated the vessels, freed the spleen, and then scooped out the fleshy organ and placed it on a tray. The boy craned his neck forward while this was happening, but his father patted him back, covered his eyes. The surgeon inspected the liver, the stomach, the intestines, the vessels again. Once he was as certain as he could possibly be that the murderer's blade had missed them all, he picked a long, thin strip of corrugated rubber from his tray. He threaded it in through the stab wound, and positioned the inner end within the peritoneal bed where the spleen had been. The other end he kept free against the skin on the outside. It would catch and drain any blood that might leak through the vessels and pool in the abdomen in the morning, he explained.

Then he sutured back the layers of flesh, one after the other.

Once the skin was closed and dressed, he tried to make the scene less grisly by covering the spleen and the pile of clots with a drape. The boy had said nothing during the surgery, but now he looked impatient, eager to be done.

"Careful, don't sit up too quickly. The stitches are delicate. You don't feel them now, but you could pull them out if you run around too much. And don't touch the bandages. They need to remain clean."

The boy listened with just half his attention, but his father nodded at everything.

The surgeon began to list to the girl the instruments he wanted sterilized right away, but stopped when he actually looked at her. She hadn't spoken during the surgery, and the parts of her face visible between the green stripes of her mask and cap were as bleached as the moon.

SEVEN

Out in the corridor, the teacher's wife clutched her son and covered him with kisses. For the first time that night, their despair seemed to have lifted. The surgeon looked away, wondering if, in his optimism, he had promised too much. Their expectations would be even greater now. And the boy might succumb to any number of complications in the morning.

Supporting the pharmacist, the surgeon stepped into the night. Gravel crunched under his feet.

The girl's husband ran up to them and put his arm around her, saying, "It's all right, it's all right." He caressed her hair, pressed her into his neck. She leaned against him, pale and stiff.

He cast a fearful glance at the dead. "Did they do anything to her?"

The surgeon compressed his lips and winced, afraid that the family had overheard this needless slander. "Just sit her down somewhere. She's not used to this. Nothing more."

The man led his wife to a flat rock a few yards away. She sat there with her arms wrapped around her ribs.

During her time in the clinic, the pharmacist had assisted in childbirths and minor procedures, learned how to change dressings, clean ulcers, administer injections. But she'd never taken part in a surgery in which the depths of the bowels were plumbed and the organs carved out. With his mind so crowded with otherworldly matters, the surgeon had overlooked this simple fact. Perhaps it was best he kept her out of the operating room from this point on.

Apart from the whispering of the dead in the corridor, the silence was almost deliberate—as if the crickets had been bribed and the dogs strangled. The village at the base of the hillock was perfectly still, its houses like polyps erupting from the soil. The rising moon had dusted them all with white talc. They appeared to have receded in the hours after sunset, abandoning the clinic to its unnatural deeds.

The surgeon returned to his consultation room. From a drawer in his desk, he picked out a syringe, a needle, and two thumb-size glass vials with rubber corks. From a jar of anticoagulant salt on a shelf, he tapped a few crystals into each vial. In another drawer, he found small paper labels. He wrote a couple of words on two and pasted them around the sides of the vials. With his left sleeve rolled up all the way to his shoulder, he tied a tourniquet around his biceps, pulling the end of the loop with his teeth until blue veins bulged on his forearm. Then he guided the needle into one of them, drew the plunger back with a thumbnail, and pulled out half a syringe of blood. This he divided between the vials, tilting and turning them until the crystals dissolved. Some empty polystyrene boxes had been left over from the vaccination drive. He filled one of them with ice cubes from the refrigerator.

He then began drafting his list. He would have only one opportunity. This wasn't the time to rush, to forget something important. He wrote and erased, crossed things out, calculated, estimated. Would eight of this item be better than four? Would twenty of those suffice? Maybe the larger ones instead of the smaller? There were limits to what he could ask for, of course. He had to be realistic.

When he was satisfied—or rather, when he was done—he waved to the pharmacist's husband. The man was with his wife. It took the surgeon a couple of attempts to catch his eye.

If indeed this entire fantastic premise was true, and the sun would melt the clotted blood in the vessels of these visitors, the challenges of this night would pale before those that the dawn would bring. Since all medical care would have to take place within the walls of this clinic, the pharmacist's husband would need to travel to the city for supplies. He would have to fetch intravenous lines, tubing, catheters, sutures, needles, syringes, gauze, bandages, antibiotics, tetanus shots, lidocaine, opiates, sedatives. The clinic would have to be stocked as never before. There were some bags of saline in the pharmacy, and while those would likely not be enough, it was unreasonable to expect the man to bring back more than a few liters. If those ran out too, they would have to make do with boiled, salted tap water and accept the risks.

But perhaps the most important of these requirements was blood. Who could predict which stitches would hold and which would give way, and what streams would flow unstemmed?

The surgeon placed the blood-filled vials in a small box and handed them to the man. "List me as the patient at the blood bank. Get four bags. Bring more if they'll allow you. Make sure they cross-match it well. It needs to match my blood type exactly. O-negative. Look, I've written it right here. If you get the correct match, it should be safe to transfuse into anyone."

From his safe, he picked out a small bundle held together by a rubber band, and counted the notes before handing them over.

"This should be enough for everything, I hope."

The man's eyes kept flitting to the window.

"Perhaps I should first ask you," the surgeon said, "if you would be willing to let her stay here while you're gone."

The man shifted his weight from one foot to the other without answering.

"They won't harm her." The surgeon hoped his tone was reassuring. "That much I can say."

The man fidgeted and scratched his ear, turned the list over a few times. Then he nodded with the resignation of one unaccustomed to challenging instructions. "I should leave now, if I'm to get back before morning."

He went to the back room and picked out a bedsheet from the cupboard. Then he slipped out quietly through the corridor, careful to keep as great a distance as possible between himself and the dead, to the point that the surgeon saw him almost jump into a wall when the teacher tried to thank him. There was an old pile of bamboo rods outside the clinic. The man picked a thin one, waved it around to make sure it was sturdy, and fashioned a makeshift sling with the bedsheet. He then walked his bicycle to the pharmacist, spoke to her briefly, and pedaled off. The surgeon watched him through the bars of his window. The railway station was a few miles away. Even if the stars all lined up, it would be at least two hours by train to the city.

The surgeon walked to the rock. The pharmacist hadn't moved from her spot since her husband had brought her there.

"You look tired. It's very late."

She sat looking out into the darkness. The surgeon flicked a mosquito from his neck.

"You won't have to be in the operating room with me anymore. I can see that it's too much for you."

The rattle of the bicycle had completely faded by now.

"But it would be good if I could still have your help. I've already used half of the instruments and drapes, and there are two more surgeries left. While I operate on the woman, could you wash and autoclave the used items? You don't have to stay awake all night—in fact, I don't want you to. You could turn the drum on and then take a nap in the back room. I'll wake you when I'm done."

She said nothing. The surgeon sat beside her on the rock, his joints making their usual clicking sounds.

"Maybe I should do a fourth surgery tonight. After I'm done with the dead, I should just replace my knees with oiled hinges."

There was a feeble smile at this.

He was asking too much of her, he knew. It wasn't fair to expect her to brush aside all her fear and disorientation for his sake, just because he'd taken upon himself this delusion of reviving the dead. It would be better if she went home.

But before he could suggest it, she asked, "Could this be a mistake, Saheb?"

"Mistake?"

"The man says that the angel doesn't want him to leave this village. Isn't that something to worry about?"

"Yes, it is. It's very worrying. Even if your husband returns with every single item on that list, it still won't be anywhere near to what's necessary for something like this. But what can we do? We work with what we have."

"Forgive me, Saheb, but that wasn't what I meant. I was talking about . . . about this being a secret. That's what I'm worried about."

"What do you mean?"

"They're breaking the law. The dead man didn't say it that way, but he knows what he's doing. He knows it's not allowed, coming back like this, like corpses. And now he wants *us* to break the law too. What if some evil spirit sent them here against God's wishes? What if it's a sin to help them? I'm afraid, Saheb. I am nobody to question you, but what will happen to us? Won't we be punished with them?"

The surgeon looked up at the sky. It seemed charred, as if some great and distant immolation had finally been completed. When he was the girl's age, already filled with doubt about everything he'd ever been told, he'd wondered how astrologers assembled all those creatures from the stars—rams and fishes and scorpions. All he ever saw were silent threats—the way the dots of light hung there, deceptively stable from one night to the next, preparing to dash themselves to the earth at the slightest provocation.

"Ask any priest and he will tell you exactly what God wants you to do. What prayer, what fasts, what lockets and threads to wear. And then ask another, maybe an imam or father this time, and see what answer you get. There are many people who pretend to know God's wishes. But God Himself never says a word."

"But then, Saheb, how do we know what to do? How do we know we're not doing something wrong tonight?"

"We cannot know," said the surgeon, surprised at the bitterness in his own voice. "We cannot know. That's the most difficult thing about this, and not just tonight. We hope that before we die we'll find some final truth, a magic bulb to switch on and make all the wrong paths disappear. Until then, all we can do is walk through thorns and try not to trip."

"Then why not leave it to fate, Saheb? Whatever will happen, let it happen. Why try to change it?"

There was an ache in his calf. He was tempted to remain seated on the rock and indulge it; rest while he ruminated on the questions the girl kept tossing at him. But she was too young. Maybe she thought her doubts original, and maybe someday he would have time enough to explain to her just how ancient they were, and how unanswerable.

But now it was almost eleven. He raised himself with his palms anchored on his thighs, straightening his knees first and then his spine. He was an old man now. His reluctant bones had to be prodded into motion.

They were at the very edge of a circle that the clinic lights had carved from the darkness. Beyond it, a cloud blotted out the moon. A few selfish fireflies idled in the grass, doing nothing to illuminate the shape moving up the hillock. It wasn't an animal, that was all the surgeon could tell. And it wasn't on a bicycle.

He pressed a finger to his lips. "Shhh . . ."

The pharmacist raised her head, confused, and then she too saw. For a moment she sat there, as frozen as he. Then she said, "I'll hide them," and headed to the clinic.

EIGHT

No, it was too absurd. That he could even think it was evidence enough of his slipping mind. Why would an angel appear in this way? He could materialize from the air, spy on them through walls. He wouldn't trudge up with this slow, ominous walk.

But then why was he himself clinging to his little limbus of light? If it was some villager—and who else could it possibly be?—surely it'd be better to stop him as far from the clinic as possible. And if it were indeed the angel, what shield would the dim light provide? Yet the surgeon found himself unable to step forward. It wasn't fear, he insisted. And what if it were? The hour was late, after all. Why not remain where he had a sliver of an advantage against some madman with a knife?

Hushed words were uttered behind him. A door closed, soft and slow as the creak of a tree. The angle from which the visitor was approaching wouldn't allow him to see directly into the clinic. For that at least, the surgeon was thankful.

"Doctor Saheb."

The voice was slurred, and the surgeon instantly recognized it. A mortal, and the basest of them all. His blood rose into his temples.

"What are you doing here? This late?"

The man was closer now, his rosaceous nose entering the light before the rest of him did. He was taking one step at a time, as if confirming that the first knee wouldn't betray him before he trusted the next with his weight.

"My leg, Doctor Saheb."

"What happened to your leg?"

"Blood, so much blood."

The man's dhotar was folded to the middle of his thighs, and his shins were coated with mud. He had the breeze at his back, and even at this distance, the surgeon could smell the stench. Alcohol and vomit, and everything else about him.

"What blood? I don't see anything?"

"Look, Saheb."

"Stand right there. Don't come any closer."

The surgeon twisted his neck back. The corridor was empty. The girl had managed to conceal them in time. The man walked past him, made for the clinic. The surgeon considered reaching out and grabbing him, but the very thought of touching the drunkard made his nerves curl.

"Go home. It's late, I don't have time for you now."

The man started wailing at a grating pitch. "Doctor Saheb, the blood, do something. I'm dying."

"Quiet. What nonsense is this? It's just a little scratch. Go home."

"I won't go back. Why should I return to her? She threw me out, at this time, this late, Doctor Saheb. What kind of wife—"

On any other night, all the surgeon would have had to do was cup his mouth and yell in the direction of the village, and a few strong farmers would come and muscle the man away. But now the dog was already at the clinic entrance.

"What do you want? Money? Here, take this and go."

The man studied the two notes the surgeon had pulled from his wallet, grasped at them. His hand missed a few times, and then he let a wave of martyrdom wash over him.

"Don't want it, Doctor Saheb. What'll I do with money? Money is for educated people like you. Not for us. We'll stay this way, live and die in the ditch."

The man was actually bleeding, the surgeon could now see. There was a cut on his calf.

"Sit right here, on the grass. I'll bandage you up. Do you promise you'll leave after that?"

"Yes, Saheb, I'll go, I swear on my mother's ashes, my father's ashes. They're both dead. I swear on them, I'll go." With these words, the man lurched into the corridor.

The surgeon scrambled ahead, squeezed past the drunkard. The doors to the pharmacy, the back room, and the operating room were all closed—hopefully bolted from the inside so that if the man fell into them, they wouldn't fly open. Only the door of the consultation room was ajar. The surgeon confirmed with a quick look that no one was hiding there.

The man collapsed on a bench. The surgeon had to bite back the urge to kick him out, physically toss him on the gravel. Who cared if he broke a bone or two? How could the dead, with their corpse-like bodies, smell less revolting than this living creature?

Under the lights, the gash in the man's calf was more visible. The surgeon considered just bandaging it and sending the man away, but that wouldn't work. The bandage would soak through, and then he'd be back.

"You'll need a few stitches. Don't move. Do you understand?"

"Yes, Saheb." There were red cobwebs around the man's irises.

All the supplies were in the operating room. The surgeon walked up to the door and pushed the handle, but it was latched from the inside.

"I'll check here," he said in a raised voice, as if to no one in particular, and tapped his knuckle softly on the doorframe.

The latch on the inside clicked. He looked back at the bench. The man was still there, his leg stretched in front of him, the rest of his body bent sideways like a sack of grain. He didn't seem to have noticed. The surgeon stepped in and latched the door shut behind him.

The pharmacist was there, sweat beading her brow along the line of her hair. "Where are they?" he mouthed, and she pointed toward the back room.

The lamps were all switched off, and only the ghost of the moon seeped in through the thick, frosted windows. In the near dark, he put on a pair of gloves and picked out a needle and thread, some cotton and gauze and tape, a bottle of iodine, a small tray. He also picked up his very last vial of lidocaine. Not out of compassion, it had to be said. He just couldn't afford to have a screaming man in his clinic now. The trays around the operating table were as he'd left them—the instruments, the spleen, the clots, all there under a blood-drenched drape. Drained of color by the moon, the drape glistened in silvers and grays. It was terrible to leave the pharmacist in the dark in a room like this, but what else could he do?

She didn't need to be told. She flattened herself against the wall as he opened the door.

The drunkard had wandered from his bench. He was at the door of the back room, trying to rattle it open.

"What are you doing? I told you to sit there, didn't I?" He grabbed the man's shoulder, pushed him down the corridor, forced him back where he was.

The man was blabbering. "I was trying to find you, Saheb. Didn't know where you went."

The surgeon knelt down and placed his tray on the floor. He'd forgotten the forceps. With his gloved fingers, he bundled a piece of cotton, soaked it with iodine, and swabbed the wound. He then drew the lidocaine into the syringe.

"This may burn a little." He guided the needle into the edge of the wound.

"Oh, God," the man cried out when he was pierced. "Save me, it hurts so much, I'm dying, I'm dying."

The surgeon ground his jaw. He'd seldom felt such rage. The man yelled as the surgeon stuck the needle in at one angle and then another, into the right edge of the wound and then the left, emptying the lidocaine into the wound. Then the surgeon raised his face to the drunkard and roared, "Shut up or I'll smash your teeth in."

The man cowered under him, muttered something incoherent. A black crust coated his gums—the foul residue of tobacco he'd been chewing on for god knew how long. The surgeon felt the urge to retch.

But the lidocaine worked. The man didn't even notice when the suturing started. It was a pity there was no drug to paralyze his tongue.

"She's a whore. She lets anyone enter her. Nothing but a whore. I should charge the neighbors—fifty rupees to look, another fifty to touch between her thighs, another fifty to spread them and—"

"Don't you have any shame, talking about your wife this way? You could search for ten lifetimes and never find someone like her. You beat her every night, and still she stays with you, I have no idea why. Any other woman would have returned to her parents by now."

"Her parents are dead too. All gone. Ashes, Doctor Saheb, it's what everyone becomes in the end. No difference between a man and the wood they use to burn him. And I'm telling you, I never touched a bottle before my marriage. Ask anyone, ask the sarpanch if you want. All of this, it was only after she—she came to my house, the *witch*. *She* did this to me, turned me into this."

The surgeon tried to block him out.

"Don't want this life, nothing of it. Better to be dead than to live like this."

"Stop talking and let me do my work."

"I'm telling you, Saheb, I have a bottle of rat poison. After I go back tonight, I'm going to drink it, drink the whole bottle. Don't want this life."

The man had done this thrice already, his theatrical attempts at suicide. He'd swallowed some DDT the last time, then walked to the village square to beat his chest and announce it to one and all. They'd brought him to the clinic with his beard white with powder, more DDT outside his mouth than inside it. But the surgeon did what he had to do. He put a tube down the man's nose, washed out the contents of his stomach, pumped it full of charcoal powder to absorb any remaining poison. The man then vomited all over the clinic, and the smell took forever to wash out of the mattresses. The same farce now, on this of all possible nights. This imbecile threatening to take his pathetic life while the dead waited in the next room for a resurrection. And it was half past eleven already.

"If you want to kill yourself, why are you here at all? Why do you want me to stitch up this scratch? Just go home and drink your poison. And lock yourself in your room so that no one brings you here half-alive again. I hope that when they find you, your bones are as cold as ice, and you're gone, once and for all."

These words penetrated even the drunkard's thick, intoxicated skull. His eyes opened wide and he slumped back, finally silent.

The surgeon finished stitching the wound and knotted the ends of the sutures together. Not a drop of blood squeezed through them. He rolled a bandage around the calf and shin and taped it in place.

"Up." He lifted the man without taking off his gloves, steered him out.

The drunkard pushed up against the wall, tried to slither out of his grip. "I know who you're hiding."

Had the man seen? "What are you talking about?"

"What will the villagers think, Saheb? It's not right."

"Just say what you have to say or get out."

"Does it suit you, someone of your position? With that girl? I saw her run in and hide. Look at your age, look at hers. And she's married, too."

The surgeon felt fury burn his throat. "Go. And if you ever come back, I swear I'll smash every single bone in your body."

The drunkard showed real fear now. Perhaps the alcohol was wearing off. He almost lost his footing on the two short steps and limped his way down the hillock, turning back once or twice but not stopping. The surgeon stood at the clinic entrance, arms crossed, as though he were the keeper of some forbidden cave.

"He's gone. You can come out now."

The dead emerged in a huddle from the back room. The boy clutched at his mother, shrinking behind her when the surgeon looked at him. The surgeon couldn't help his irritation at this. What did they expect him to do, keep up some charade of benevolence all night? There were limits. He wasn't a saffron-clad monk. If they couldn't put up with the way he did things, they were free to leave.

Yes, he remembered now, he'd been talking to the pharmacist when the bastard interrupted them. She hadn't appeared from the operating room.

He pushed the door open. She was clearing away the trays.

She'd already gathered the soiled drapes, and was emptying some of the remains into a plastic bag.

"You should go home and sleep," he said with a dismissive wave.

"No, Saheb. You working through the night alone? What will my husband say when he returns? I'll sterilize the instruments."

NINE

WHATEVER TRIUMPH THE SURGEON had let himself feel after mending the boy's injury was completely dulled now, partly by his lingering ire over the drunkard, more at the prospect of facing the woman's wounds. He felt a deep resentment against all creation for putting him in this position. Why had the neck been designed this way in the first place? All those vessels, so close to the skin. Countless necks had been slit since man sharpened his first stone, but each new one came into existence as flimsy as the last.

The woman's odhni hid her injuries, and the three appeared deceptively whole, a family like any other. Apart from the pallor of their skin, there was no hint of their trials and migrations, or of the strangeness of their bodies. When he said, "Come," the woman patted down her hair and adjusted her clothes. Even in death, it seemed, the habits of life were not entirely lost.

"The two of you should stay here," he said to the teacher and his son.

The woman tried to pull her fingers from her son's grip, but the boy kept grabbing at them, higher and higher, tugging at her hand, her wrist, her forearm, first one side, then the other. The teacher tried to restrain him, and the boy resisted, but neither made a sound. Father and son grappled in pantomime until they were locked, larger fists imprisoning smaller ones as though doubled in prayer.

The pharmacist wasn't done clearing the operating room, so the surgeon walked to the entrance and surveyed the hillock for loiterers. Nothing he could do would jeopardize the woman's life beyond what was already fated, he told himself. It was tempting to adopt the pharmacist's way of thinking about the world and everything in it. Whatever would happen would happen, she'd said . . . or something similar, some aphorism of endless absolving circularity.

Without turning, he said to the dead: "This will take at least a few hours. You'll have to be patient." He cast one last look outside. There was no sign of the drunkard, or the pharmacist's husband, or anyone else.

In the operating room, he now became aware of another astonishing aspect of the visitors' physiology, if that word could even be applied to the bodily mechanisms of the dead. Before the first surgery, he'd listened to the boy's chest with his stethoscope, more out of custom than with any specific intention, for what changes would he have made to his plan had his findings been abnormal? And abnormal they certainly were. The boy had no heartbeat, which, given that there was no blood to flow, wasn't particularly unexpected. It would've been more startling if the familiar *lub dub, lub dub* had reached his ears. But the boy breathed, and his chest rose and fell. The stethoscope confirmed the steady tide blowing through the maze of his airways. Now, what need could there be for respiration when there was no blood to be oxygenated? No obvious answer presented itself, and since the boy's injuries involved only his abdomen, the surgeon abandoned that line of questioning and proceeded with the surgery.

But in the case of the woman, due to the nature and location of her injuries, he was forced to give the mechanics of her breathing greater attention. Her larynx was cut in such a way that there was a good chance her vocal cords had been damaged. And the cut had definitely produced an air leak, a direct connection between the inside and outside of her throat. How could she possibly speak with such an injury?

This led him to an extraordinary discovery—a phenomenon every bit as bizarre as her silent heart. Her voice appeared to form not in her larynx but in the back of her mouth, somewhere in the space behind her tonsils—from empty air as best he could tell. How that could possibly be, he hadn't a clue. Her speech was unconnected to her lungs and her voice box, and though her words were coordinated with her breathing, they didn't seem to depend on it in any way. He found that she could, with little effort, overcome the innate habits of her body and speak without interruption throughout both inhalation and exhalation. And, astonishingly, even with her breath held.

The anatomy of the dead was incomprehensible. Some of their bodily systems worked, others didn't, but it was all just enough to allow them to impersonate the living. If his old EKG machine hadn't been roasted by a power surge, he would've taken tracings from their chests. What scrawls might the box have produced? Waves and peaks? Flat, monotonous lines? Or something else? Patterns, letters, perhaps; messages in some ancient, unbreakable code. Equations containing the deepest enigmas of death. He would keep the tracings running endlessly, paper every wall with EKG strips. Years, perhaps decades later, when his mind had become weak and every memory doubtful, he could return to read the chronicle of these hours plastered from floor to ceiling. Perhaps then he would see everything more clearly.

The disconnect between the woman's voice and her larynx resolved a purely practical concern. He'd expected that the surgery would leave her unable to speak. He'd been in half a mind to tell her that—to have her say to her husband and son whatever she needed to say while she still could. But this fear no longer appeared warranted. No matter what he did, she would still be able to speak. At least until dawn.

But this insight could not blunt the savagery he was seeing. The surgeon gritted his teeth, pressed his lips together, forced his face to remain expressionless as he examined her. The tips of her earlobes were torn; the sides of her arms scraped raw, skin peeled away along the bony parts of her wrists. The bandits had been thorough in their plunder, ripped out her earrings, torn off her bangles. But the wound in her neck . . . The hand that did this had not sought only money. There was craving here, a hunger for whatever arousal was to be gained by sinking a blade into flesh. This was no theft complicated by unintended murder.

Before this night, he'd found it easy to fill medical silences with chiding banter and rebuke, but none of that could help him now. No words of consolation, nothing he could dredge up, held any truth or meaning. All speech was blasphemy before these wounds. And then there was her massive abdomen, looming at the edge of his vision. He couldn't speak of that either. Surely it was never far from her mind, but what purpose would it serve to bring it up, to remind her that the life of another creature hung in the balance of her own?

Decades ago, when he was working at the coroner's office, he'd been assigned the autopsy of a young woman who'd hanged herself after learning that her husband had frequented a brothel during her pregnancy. She would have been at term in a few weeks, and in her suicide note, she wrote of her intention to free herself of this unjust life and take her child with her. And that she did, for on the slab, her thin corpse was distended with what lay still within her. As part of regular autopsy protocol, he was required to extract the inhabitant of her womb, a cold and unmoving fetus that had never known the world outside her and now never would.

Later that day, unexpected visitors had knocked on his office door.

"Doctor Saheb."

Raising his eyes from his papers, he, a young man then, saw two aged, myopic faces.

"The girl on whom you performed an autopsy to-day . . . we're her parents."

"The morgue is to the left. A man there will have you sign

some paperwork, and then you can take her for your rites. It shouldn't take much time."

It was a perfunctory response, his attempt to make the meaninglessness of death bearable through protocol. If only mourners could just occupy themselves with the mechanics of planning a funeral. Second door to the left. Sign here, here, and here, that form too. And don't forget to write the address of the crematorium.

But this elderly couple couldn't be dismissed so easily. They stood there, waiting for something else.

He peeled his glasses off his head and laid them on the desk. It was a trite gesture, but it helped him offer his trite sympathies. "It's so terrible this happened. So terrible you have to bear this. My condolences."

"Did she really take her own life?" the mother asked.

His throat felt dry. He now noticed two shabby, discolored bags on the floor behind them. They'd just traveled here from some distant village. Probably on the first bus they could board, jostled for hours by strangers who had no idea how their world had just been smashed. There was a good chance this morgue, and maybe his office, was their first destination from the railway station. Perhaps all they knew of her death was the little they'd been told over a bad telephone connection.

"Did she really take her own life?" she asked again.

What answer was he supposed to give? The simplest and truest?

"Yes, she did."

From beyond the swinging door came a distant guffaw.

The attendants in the common room were sharing some lunchtime joke.

"But why?" the mother cried. "Why didn't she just come to us? Did she think we wouldn't take her back?"

All he could do was fidget with the pen in his hand.

And then she asked, "Was it a boy or a girl?"

Her words fell on his ears but did not sink in.

"Was it a boy or a girl?" she asked once more.

"A boy or a girl?" he repeated. Then the meaning of her question dawned on him. "Why are you asking me that? Why do you want to know?"

The woman put her palms together. "Forgive me, Doctor Saheb. We know you're busy. We won't take any more of your time. Please tell us if it was a boy or a girl, and we'll go."

"It was a boy," he said, faltering, and then corrected himself. "It would have been a boy."

At this, the old woman clasped her bony fists to her mouth and sobbed, as though with his words he had made flesh before her the tiny hands and toes and lips of her unseen grandchild. And not just that, but also the swollen face of her daughter and the furrow of that noose imprinted in her neck. He closed his eyes and turned away. The swinging door creaked as it swung again, and even after it stopped, he could still hear the sobs as the old man led his wife away.

In the coroner's office, he steeled his heart against his work, dissociated from the subjects that lay uncomplaining on his slab. After all, what hope would he have of keeping his sanity if he took it upon himself to probe into the life of every corpse? He only needed to think of them as clocks that had stopped, and of himself as the watchmaker assigned to list the springs and coils that had failed. No obligation to repair anything. He did this for two years, but then it became too oppressive, and he wanted something more. The empty ambition of youth, as he thought of it now. Look what it had brought him.

"I'll have to shave your hair," he said to the teacher's wife.

She looked startled. "All of it?"

"Just the back of your neck and a little way up. Is that all right?"

"Yes, Saheb, I didn't mean to question you. Whatever you need to do."

"Put on this gown."

He thought of stepping out of the room so that she could change in private, but it would require him to reshuffle the cart and trays he had arranged in the cramped space behind him. So he just cleared his throat and turned to the wall. Behind his back, the dead woman undressed from the waist up and slipped on the tattered green surgical gown.

"I'm ready."

Using a fresh razor, he shaved her nape and the back of her head. Fine strands fell on her shoulders. The hair of the dead, no more or less dead than the hair of the living. He brushed it into a tray. The rest of her hair he helped bundle into a surgical cap. He positioned her, neck arched backward, head elevated with wooden blocks, contorted into a pose that would allow him full advantage of the meager light. The position would have been unbearable to anyone capable of feeling pain, but he found that she could hold it without complaint, as if she were a mannequin. After cleaning her wounds with iodine and alcohol, he draped her so that only her neck and its injuries were exposed. Only when he'd laid a drape across her face, covering her eyes, did his shoulders relax a fraction. He didn't want her looking at him while he worked. He could not bear her unreasonable hope.

Her neck had suffered at least two deep strokes and a few shallower ones. The skin was shredded and hung in strips, and the tissues beneath were sliced at jagged angles. Some muscles had been partially cut as well, even the one that was supposed to be necessary for her to turn her head. That she could support and move it naturally despite this was as remarkable as her ability to speak.

Part of the larynx lay open before him in a macabre display of cartilage. Now, with her neck bent back, air puffed through the opening with every breath. Blood vessels with dull red clots within them poked out of the ravaged mess. The most prominent vessel—the carotid artery—was also the one that had suffered the most ominous damage, for the two deepest knife strokes had cut into it at different angles, detaching a flap from one of its sides. This had carved a window into the vessel, through which her blood had probably spurted out with such speed that her suffering had likely been the shortest of the three. But the flap had somehow stayed in place, attached by a strip of tissue so narrow that he was surprised it hadn't fallen off in the few hours since she'd appeared in his clinic. If it had, there would have been a gaping hole in the vessel, and nothing here would have allowed him to close that.

He wasn't trained to deal with injuries like these, to the neck, to the larynx. Even recalling some of the fascial planes, the names of the smaller muscles, the positions of the nerves, was beyond him now. There was a volume of anatomy in his cupboard somewhere, three decades old at least, its binding tattered. He wished he'd thought to skim through it earlier, but it was too late for that now, and he wasn't sure it would have helped. He would have to feign a mastery he did not possess, and braid together the frayed threads of her life as best he could.

He unwrapped the suture casing and grasped with his forceps his thinnest needle and suture. With it he pierced the lower half of the carotid stub. The needle made too large a hole in the gossamer structure, and the suture looked thick and unwieldy, a jute rope hooped through silk. He passed the needle through the corresponding point in the upper half of the vessel and tried to bring the two edges together, but one of the ends had retracted between the muscles of the neck, and his thread tugged at the vessel's edge, threatening to tear it. Only the first stitch, and already there were premonitions of defeat. In slow, painstaking loops, his needle crept one stitch at a time around the curve of the vessel.

The night wore on, his back stiffening as he stooped over his work. Finally, with difficulty, he stood upright again. Over an hour had likely passed since the surgery began, and the woman hadn't made a sound, hadn't moved, hadn't so much as inflated her chest. Surely she was just holding her breath to help him, but perhaps it wasn't a bad idea to confirm that she was still there, still alive. Though *alive* wasn't the right word, of course. There was no vocabulary for this kind of thing.

"Is everything fine?" he asked.

There was a movement under the covers, lips brushing against drapes, neck muscles twitching as she moved her jaw to speak. Was that even necessary, though? Maybe the dead could speak like ventriloquists if they wished, with mouths slack and tongues still.

"Yes, Saheb."

"Any pain? Any discomfort? Do you need to change your position?"

"No, Saheb, don't worry about me."

It was remarkable how one could get accustomed even to such things. The surgeon no longer felt the deep, acrid bite of moments like these. He could speak calmly to a woman whose neck lay open before him, forceps sticking out between her cartilage and muscles. A glaze of unreality had settled over everything, as though his vision had permanently warped.

He looked up at the wall to his right, but it was bare. He'd forgotten to hang the clock up again after he changed its battery. And he'd removed his wristwatch and left it on his desk in the other room. Unless he either broke his sterile field and ventured out of the room, or called out to the pharmacist, who was probably sleeping as he'd instructed her to, he had no way of knowing what time it was. He closed his eyes for a moment, trying to add up every stitch he'd placed and multiply that number by the time each one had taken, and at once devious sleep hooked its anchors on his eyelids. He opened them in panic and stamped hard on one foot with the other, making his toe pulse with pain. It was still night. He had to stay awake.

Pushing all other thoughts away, he again took stock of the surgical field. All this time spent, and so little accomplished.

He'd sutured the upper edge of the carotid flap to the margin from which it had been torn, and just begun working on the other. The flap bristled with sutures. Clumsier than the precise work he'd once been capable of, his stitching had pulled and constricted the artery into an angular shape, as though an unskilled plumber had forced together a series of crooked and ill-fitting pipes. And the hole in the vessel still gaped. Any attempt to close it would only twist it further.

The fluorescent light emitted a low electric buzz that he hadn't noticed before. Outside the window, a lone crow cawed—a cry of insomnia and longing, if indeed the fauna of this earth were subject to the same torments as mankind. He looked up at the metal loop in the ceiling and shifted his neck this way and that, but it no longer seemed like an eye. It just returned to him the bland look of an inanimate object. The ceiling had no sight, nor did anything beyond it. The dead had been flung at his feet and abandoned.

What was he going to say to them? How would he tell them that she wouldn't survive?

The sweat was making his brow itch, and he dabbed at it with his sleeve, careful not to let his glove touch anything that might not be sterile. He abandoned the suturing of the carotid artery for now. He would tackle the trachea instead.

"This part of your throat, the part through which air flows to your lungs, it's damaged. If I leave it this way, you'll have trouble breathing in the morning. So I'll have to make another hole right here, lower in your neck. To help the air flow."

The surgeon explained the plan with as much optimism as he could summon up, and the woman nodded under the drapes. Whether she understood a word, he had no way of knowing. She would have nodded at anything he said.

He rolled his gloved fingers over the skin that covered the cartilaginous bumps under her larynx, and decided on an appropriate spot at the midline of the neck, just a little above the point where the collarbones met the sternum. It would have to be a little lower than was customary, yes. The murderer hadn't thought of surgical convenience when he slashed with his blade. The surgeon sliced the skin cleanly and teased away the thin, bloodless layers of tissue with his knife and forceps, pushing aside the muscles that ran like straps along either side of the trachea. Her thyroid was a little larger than he'd expected, and its bridge gripped and covered the front of the trachea. He cut through it. Now he could feel the tracheal rings, and he made a neat cut through them as well. Even though he had no need to fear that she would die on him, his heart still pounded at this step from force of ancient habit. He didn't have a tracheostomy tube, but he'd managed to dig out an endotracheal tube from some old supplies. He inserted one end into the trachea and closed the skin around it. The other end protruded from the neck, and he harnessed it to the skin with loop after loop of suture. The sutures slipped against the smooth plastic, and some fell loose even as he placed them. The tube wasn't designed to be tied like this. He secured it as best he could.

Then he turned to the larynx and began to sew the torn sections of cartilage back together. It was slow, painstaking work, and there was really no way to hurry. There were other arteries and veins too. Diligently he addressed them, trying to pretend that the most crucial problems had been resolved, and now he was just finessing the details. But the carotid would determine whether she lived or died, there was no doubt about that. He felt like a laborer pressing a thousand pellets of clay into hairline cracks in a breached dam, as if all that toil would somehow compensate for the enormous rift in the center. Holding sleep at bay with every blink, he focused on the blood vessels, one by one, reconnecting some, tying the superfluous ones into blind stumps.

Finally there was nothing left to do but put the last sutures in the flap of the carotid. As he tightened the last knot, he couldn't help but cringe. But he could either do this or just leave it open, and there was no possible world in which the second choice was the better of the two. The result was terribly unsatisfactory. The vessel looked deformed. There was none of the craftsmanship of which he'd once thought himself capable. He imagined the vessel pulsing with blood, and then imagined it immediately tearing or clotting.

He stitched the torn ends of the muscles together and closed the tissue planes. There was no clean incision along which to close the skin, so he sewed it back along the lines of its rupture, along the blueprint that the murderer had forced upon him. The jagged rows of stitches looked like railway tracks placed by a deranged engineer, crossing each other at strange angles. If the carotid were to leak, the mesh of skin and nylon would never endure the strain of the expanding pocket of blood.

Perhaps he could save her husband, so that the boy wouldn't end up all alone.

And then, just for a moment, he allowed himself a thought

that was unacceptable for him: perhaps it might be better if he sabotaged the surgeries, made sure that they all died, all three of them. At least in the afterlife they would remain together. Dawn would come, and it would all be over. The dead would return to where they belonged, and the living would mourn and, in time, forget them. And he would sleep, let his eyelids fall and sleep, let all darken, let the world grow quiet. It would be so easy, nothing much, a couple of cuts, a few slit blood vessels. So many people died every day, what difference would it make if there were a few more? He would be doing them a favor anyway, sparing them so much agony. In the long run, they would be thankful, and they really had no business on this side anyway. This was the side of the living. The dead ought to have known better, ought to have stayed where they were so that the living could continue with their days and nights, with their work and their sleep. Perhaps he could turn them out into the dark, force them across the village boundary, by trickery if need be, so that they could drop there. What a silent, painless end it would be. If only everyone could be so fortunate, blessed with the option to just walk into an invisible wall and disrobe from their skins, walk into the embrace of death, which would welcome the dead, so that the living could go on to live, and rest, and sleep.

It was dreadful, what he was capable of thinking, what he might even be capable of *doing*, just to appease the demons of his exhaustion.

The surgery was done. He undraped the teacher's wife and raised her from her reclining position, supporting the back of her head so that the sutures wouldn't pull. He then wrapped and taped bandages around the neck, around the endotracheal tube, until the neck appeared almost twice its natural thickness. The tube protruded from the front like a proboscis, bobbing under her chin with every movement. He screwed an inflatable bag to the tube's outer end and forced air through it, confirming with his stethoscope that both lungs filled with each puff.

"The less you move your neck, the better. I've stitched the tube in place, so it shouldn't fall out. But be careful. Your ability to breathe will depend on it."

Then the surgeon busied himself gathering and wiping his instruments so that he wouldn't have to answer her eyes. She sat still, so still, and for so long, while he cleared his trays, that his silence began to feel more and more unacceptable. Since he couldn't bring himself to offer her a prognosis, he just said, "Come, I've finished. I did what I could."

Her face appeared taut. "I'm not afraid of death, Doctor Saheb. Just save my son and my unborn child."

The walls of the operating room, gray and yellow in the murky light, seemed to close in on the surgeon. He willed the claustrophobia away, wished for it to be replaced with light and air and breath, but he had as little power over this as over anything else. So he just helped the woman down from the table.

TEN

THE PHARMACIST WASHED THE drapes and instruments from the boy's surgery and packed them in a drum that she lowered into the pressure autoclave. After tightening the screws around the edge of the lid, she pressed down a switch on the wall, and a small red light glowed. The temperature gauge was broken, its hand stuck at the fifty-degree mark, so she wet the tip of her finger with her tongue and touched the drum a few times to make sure it was heating as it should. When it began to hiss and steam, she wiped her finger on her dress.

There wasn't much else to do at the moment. Saheb had told her to get some rest while he operated on the boy's mother. She went into the back room and pulled the door shut. After a moment's thought, she slid the latch into place, but slowly, so that the dead wouldn't hear her.

The room held two beds, each a simple frame with a webbing of rusted iron strips holding up an old mattress. The bedsheets were threadbare. She searched the cupboard for better ones, but they were all the same. She picked one that seemed cleaner than the others and spread it out on a mattress. From the pile of blankets in the cupboard, she chose the one at the very bottom. It was quite coarse, and smelled of mothballs, but she, who had washed every conceivable human secretion off these blankets, knew it to be the cleanest.

She lay down on the mattress. The frame creaked so loudly in the still room that she was worried that the iron strips were coming apart under her. With her eyes shut tight, she began to take slow, long breaths to make herself fall asleep. When she found herself lying awake as time drifted by, she blamed the moonlight and the breeze. Rising on one elbow, she closed and shuttered the window and buried her head under the blanket.

Her body felt sore. She tossed on the bed, tried this position and that, but every lump in the mattress seemed to prod her. The pinwheels in her mind showed no sign of slowing down. The more tightly she closed her eyes, the more it seemed that sleep was being squeezed out of them, and the blanket's sickly sweet mothball odor didn't help. She surrendered, threw the blanket off, and stared at the wall at the foot of the bed.

The calendar hanging there had a picture of the goddess Durga printed above the days of the month. When the pharmacist first started working in the clinic, she'd thought of asking her husband to put up a little shelf on that wall, on which she planned to arrange little statuettes of Ganpati and baby Krishna, a picture of Vithoba, maybe one of Sai Baba. But after witnessing Saheb's tantrums at the mention of anything religious, she dropped that plan. The lack of gods in the clinic troubled her, though. In a place that people visited for fear of death, there needed to be *some* source of hope. Then one day it struck her, while strolling through the district market. A calendar with a different god for every month. Twelve gods at the price of one. And Saheb couldn't object to that, could he?

She shuffled to the foot of the mattress and examined the picture, her face inches from the paper. Even in the darkness, she could appreciate Durga's ten hands with their weapons, her large eyes, the lion on which she was seated. The tip of Durga's spear was in the belly of a demon writhing at her feet, his blood splashing on the lion's paws. A violent picture, but the face of the goddess was serene, as if she were barely aware of her victim. Perhaps that's what it was like to be a god—to perform bloody deeds and remain completely untroubled by them.

The calendar was hanging a little crooked on its nail. The pharmacist straightened it and looked around. There was a single spot of light in the room, coming through a hole in the door where there'd once been a doorknob. She'd never been in a position to observe the door from this angle before, with the room darkened and the corridor lit. She left her bed and crept up to the door, placed her eye against the circle, careful not to let the dead see her.

The boy was on the bench, leaning against his father's shoulder. There was a scar on his knee, a little below the point where his short pants ended. It was an old, healed cut, unlike the wounds the three had brought for Saheb to fix. His father was rocking him, humming a lullaby, singing a word once in a while. Why the lullaby, since they couldn't sleep? Was that something the dead did on that plain of theirs—rocked each other and hummed, unable to sleep, unable to stop wanting to sleep?

She stood, looked once again at the calendar, joined her palms in front of her mouth and muttered a few lines of prayer, and then undid the latch and nudged the door open. The man fell silent. The boy raised his head from his father's shoulder and sat straight, as if anxious not to be thought of as a child. She glanced at them out of the corner of her eye, but jerked her head away when she saw them looking back. In all the hours they'd been here, she hadn't been able to bring herself to say a word to them. When the drunkard had appeared, she'd relied on a few frantic gestures to herd them into the back room.

She slipped into the pharmacy, feeling her way in the dark, careful not to dislodge the empty boxes she'd piled so foolishly high on every shelf. One pile almost fell over, and she steadied it, her heart pounding. She inched along the room, feeling the ground with her toe, and stopped when it hit the base of the stone platform at the end. Her eyes had again adjusted to the dark by now, and she lifted the stove that sat atop the platform and gave the tank a quick shake. There was enough kerosene in it. She opened the small bottle of alcohol tucked against the wall. The alcohol spilled as she poured it, but she steadied her trembling hand enough to get a teaspoonful into the spirit cup under the burner. The first match broke in her grip, the next two refused to spark, but with the fourth she managed to light the alcohol. The small flame heated the burner in the center of the blackened brass rings, and she pumped the drum to get the kerosene flowing.

Once the kerosene in the burner was hot enough, it ignited, and blue jets rose from the stove.

The burner made a soft sound, and she sat there a moment, looking at the little roaring ring of fire. In the dark, it seemed to hang in midair. And it seemed impossible that something so beautiful and blue could also be so hot. It looked like something she could just scoop up and steal away in her pocket.

She felt under the kitchen platform for the covered bowl she'd left there in the afternoon. It still had some okra in it. She scooped half out into a small copper cup and placed it on the flame. The rest she left for Saheb, in case he should want any. She'd also had the good sense to make extra chapatis for lunch that day. She unwrapped two and felt around for some butter to brush onto them, but couldn't remember where she'd kept the can. She didn't want to switch on the light. That would only draw the attention of the dead.

So she put the chapatis, dry as they were, on a plate along with the bhendi, and folded her legs under her on the ground. She held the plate where the thin ribbon of light from the corridor fell across it. Her grandfather used to tell her to chew every morsel thirty-two times, once for each tooth. Only old people ever had time for habits like these, but now seemed as good a time as any to give it a try. With each bite, the okra grew more slimy and flavorless. It was missing something, salt perhaps, or ginger, though it had tasted fine that afternoon. But she was hungry, and she wiped the plate clean with the last piece of chapati and rinsed it under a quiet stream in the sink.

There was no reason to expect another attempt at sleep to

be more fruitful than the last. So she went into the corridor. The eyes of father and son followed her as she sat on the bench opposite them, her hands pinched between her knees. Above the dead, insects were buzzing against the fluorescent light.

"I—I would have made you something. Some tea at least, and biscuits for the boy. But Saheb said, in your condition, you don't—"

"We don't eat," said the teacher. "We don't need food. But thank you. We'll eat again once we're alive, won't we?" He patted his son's shoulder.

"If you need something, just call me. I'll be in—"

"Sorry about—about earlier this evening."

"About what?"

"When I had to hold you like that. I didn't want to hurt you. I was just afraid you would scream."

"I did scream. Inside my own mouth."

The man smiled meekly. "I hope you aren't afraid of us any longer."

She tightened her fingers against one another. "No, I'm not afraid."

She didn't really have much else to say, and it wasn't clear the teacher did either. She rose.

"Did you study in the city?"

"Me?"

"Your pharmacy training? Was it at the university?"

"I'm not . . . not really a pharmacist. I only did seventh standard in school. No training or anything. It's just—there's nobody else here, and Saheb needs someone to look after the place. So my husband and I, we help him take care of it. Saheb registered me as a pharmacist so I could get a salary from the head office."

"Really? I wouldn't have known. The way you were assisting him during the surgery, it seemed that you knew every instrument, Saheb didn't have to ask twice. How long have you been working for him?"

She sat back on the bench, her ears warm. "Two and a half years. Since my marriage, when I came to this village. Saheb was looking for someone who could read and write. I don't know English, but Saheb taught me the names of the medicines and instruments. He writes them out, and I practice them every morning. Right after my prayers."

"And how long has Saheb been here?"

"Six months before me."

"That's all? Who was here before him?"

"No one. Actually, there was a doctor, but the villagers say he was as good as absent. He visited once every two weeks, wrote something in the account books, and left. The government didn't care, so this went on for many years. And then that doctor disappeared, god knows what happened to him, and Saheb started here. He began to sit in the clinic all day, even when there were no patients. The villagers didn't know what to think at first. They were afraid he was going to steal their organs and sell them to rich people. Why else would a city doctor come to a village like this? Saheb paid my husband to fix the pipes and the wiring, and then, when I came here after my wedding, he gave me work as well. It looked like an empty godown, this place, the rooms were full of cobwebs. It's so nice now, look." She pointed at the ceiling so that he could see with his own eyes how clean she kept the corners.

A sharp whistle made her jump, almost fall off the bench. But it was just the autoclave machine. The teacher started at the sound too, as did the boy, but the boy recovered first, and he giggled and poked his father's arm, teasing him for being as scared as a mouse. The pharmacist found herself glancing at their legs.

The teacher wiggled his toes in his slippers. "No, our feet don't point the other way."

She brought her hand to her mouth in embarrassment. "I was just, my mother told me, many years ago—"

"Yes, yes, I know. Ghosts are supposed to leave footprints that point in the wrong direction. Or they're afraid of mirrors, because they don't have a reflection. As if life and death were so simple: just turn one little thing upside down, and the living become dead. All those ghost stories are just that—stories."

"You can laugh, but they can't *all* be false. I've seen a ghost with my own eyes, I'm telling you. Outside my parents' village, there's a broken-down house. The roof has fallen in, the walls are covered with vines. The man who used to live there, he cheated many women, one after the other—married them with false names and then killed them on the wedding night, can you imagine? He kept doing this—ten times, they say—until the police finally took him off and hanged him. But his wives remained in that house, even after their bodies were burnt and gone. Their souls still roam, looking for some innocent person to haunt, to take revenge for what that demon did to them. I saw one, I swear, once when I was walking back at night a few years ago. I heard a scream that was so loud my ears kept ringing for days afterward. There was a woman in a red sari. Her face was white . . . whiter than milk, and swollen like a balloon. She was floating in the air, above the roof, and she jumped at me. I ran so fast, I didn't even realize when a piece of glass cut my foot—that's how scared I was. My mother always says there are things in this world that no one can explain."

She stopped, wondering if she should've told such a gruesome story in front of a child. But the boy didn't seem to mind. He was scratching something into the wood of the bench with a rusted nail he'd found somewhere. Maybe he'd seen worse things himself. She felt it strange that she should be trying to convince the dead of the existence of ghosts, but when she'd finished speaking, the teacher just nodded, his face serious. It seemed that he agreed with her mother. There were things in this world—and, who knew, maybe even the next—that no one could explain.

"I'm sorry you have to be part of all this," the teacher said. "To have to deal with us showing up in this state."

"No, no, I didn't mean it that way. You're not that kind of ghost, I know. And don't worry about me. One night without sleep isn't that bad. Sometimes if we have really sick patients, I stay awake to take care of them."

A feather blew in through the entrance to the clinic, and the teacher's eyes followed it as it floated all the way to the closed doors of the operating room. His gaze stayed there.

"Everything will work out, with God's mercy," the pharmacist said.

"I hope so. It's all in Doctor Saheb's hands now."

"There's nothing Saheb can't fix. So many people come here, so sick, with their legs and stomach so swollen they can't even stand. And then Saheb does his work and in a few days, the men walk out on their own feet. There's nothing he can't cure."

The man gave a sad smile. "Has he ever cured death? Brought a corpse to life?"

"Have faith. You're half-alive already. Let Saheb worry about the other half."

The teacher was looking down at his palm, as if reading its lines. The pharmacist took the opportunity to change the subject.

"Did you find out who you were in your past lives?"

When the teacher didn't answer, she said, "Our family astrologer used to tell us that when we're born, our souls lose their memories. So we live every life as if it were our first. But all of us, we've had many lives before. Hundreds. When we die, we remember all of them. Is that true?"

"Well, I'm—I'm not sure. It might be, but we didn't, at least I didn't, remember any old lives."

"Oh? Maybe it takes time for those memories to come back."

"That's possible. Who knows?"

"Our astrologer told me I was a devoted wife in my past life. My husband had an illness in that life that made him bedridden from birth. I served him day and night, washed him and cleaned his sores right up to the end. I don't remember any of this, of course, but the astrologer saw this in the chart he drew up for me. He said that because of my service to my husband, and because I kept away from all sin, from now on I would enjoy the fruits of my good deeds. He told me all this before my engagement, before I had even seen my husband's face, just after the astrologer had checked our horoscopes and told my father that we were destined for each other, lifetime after lifetime. I had forgotten all about it, but I remembered it just now, when we were hiding from that drunkard. What I'm trying to tell you is, I understand tonight why our astrologer took me aside and told me this, though I hadn't even asked him. He must have seen in my chart that a time would come when I would be very scared, that I would want to run away, but it would be a test from God to see if I would serve others in this life just as I did in the last one. The astrologer just wanted me to know that because of my good deeds, nothing would be able to harm me. So I've decided not to be scared. I will help you come back to life, I'll do whatever I can to help Saheb with his work. I know now that I don't need to be afraid of anything, for myself or for my husband."

All of a sudden, the teacher's lips were trembling and his face looked as though it would crack. The pharmacist wasn't sure what she'd said that could have brought about this change. He started to say something, but then a latch sounded, and the door of the operating room opened. She jumped to her feet, as did the teacher and his son. The man kept his face turned to her, with a look she couldn't read. It was a strange reaction from him, but it lasted just a moment, because then they all ran down the corridor. The surgeon walked out of the operating room, leading the dead woman. Both appeared stiff, as if cut out of cardboard. The pharmacist had to stop herself from gasping at the sight of the neck swollen with bandages.

The teacher touched his wife's arm. "How are you feeling?"

"Fine." The woman's face had no expression on it, none at all.

"Are you sure? Was the surgery painful?"

"No. No pain."

"Careful," the surgeon said. "The inner end of that tube is in her windpipe. We'll need it in the morning to ensure that she can breathe."

The pharmacist wondered if that wouldn't hurt. If a small crumb in the windpipe could make a grown man fall to his knees and choke, wouldn't this plastic thing be much worse? And Saheb wasn't saying anything about how the operation went. Nothing about whether the woman would live. They'd been in the operating room for three hours, and the only things he said now were about the bandages and the tube.

The teacher kept asking his wife, "Does the tube hurt?" to which she kept saying, her eyes turned away, "No, it doesn't." The boy pulled at his mother's fingers, but she avoided his face as well. Though the pharmacist was afraid of what it might be like to touch the dead, she reached out to the boy. She felt his shoulder, skin and bone and soft flesh, there under the shirt, no different than if she'd touched a living child. She kept her fingers there for a few moments, tentatively feeling with their tips, trying to build up the courage to actually rest her entire palm to comfort him, but the boy turned to her with an expression of such anger and annoyance, and shrugged her off so violently, he might as well have slapped her across the face. In an instant, the words she'd just spoken with the dead seemed more remote than the sight of that ghost floating over the house all those years ago. When the surgeon told her to clear out the instruments and replace them with new ones, she was glad to have an excuse to leave the corridor.

She put on a pair of gloves and entered the operating room with a sterilization drum, preparing herself for god alone knew what. The boy's belly had contained so much blood, there'd been a mountain of it at the end of his surgery. It was as if a butcher had sacrificed chickens and goats there and thrown their innards all over the place.

But this time, the drapes were clean. The scalpels and forceps and trays were barely flecked with red. She'd always assumed that the amount of blood spilled said something about how the surgery had gone. But maybe that rule too, like everything else, no longer held with the dead.

She collected the instruments and drapes, washed them in the sink, placed them in layers inside the drum. She peered at the dead through a gap between the doors of the operating room, and then tiptoed to the autoclave machine. The drum inside had now cooled enough for her to reach in and jiggle it loose. As she replaced it with the new one, the surgeon came from the consultation room, carrying a narrow-mouthed glass jar with a rubber lid, half filled with water. She'd seen the jar in the cupboard, she'd dusted around it before, but there was something different about it now. Yes, Saheb had made two holes in the lid, and stuck plastic tubes through them.

He took the sterilized drum from her, pushed the door of the operating room open with his foot, and waited there with his back to everyone else. "It's my turn now," the teacher said to his wife and son, and the door closed behind the two men.

Only mother and son were left on the bench under the fluorescent light. The pharmacist stayed at the end of the corridor. The bulb in the ceiling above her had burned out. She felt like a ghost herself, hidden in the shadows, spying on the dead.

The boy's eyes were on his mother's neck, on the tube sticking out at the front.

"Doctor Saheb said this is to help you breathe. Is that true?"

"That's what he says, so it must be true."

"Why did he put this tube in you and not me?"

"Because my neck is hurt. The air we breathe passes through the throat, right here."

"Will Baba need a tube too?"

"I don't know. We'll find out soon, after his surgery is done."

"Does this mean that without the tube you wouldn't be able to breathe?"

"Saheb's just being careful."

"And is it fixed now?"

"I'm sure it is."

The boy didn't seem satisfied with her answers. He folded his arms and sat back with a sullen pout.

The pharmacist remained flattened against the wall, her shoulders aching from the effort of concealment. The autoclave machine whispered beside her instead of making its usual whistling sound. Was the seal not tight enough? She moistened her finger on her tongue and pressed it to the lid.

The heat was like an electric shock. She bit down on the scream that tried to burst through her throat. Tears squeezed from her eyes as she pressed her fist shut to numb the finger.

The boy was saying something. She ignored the burn. They still hadn't noticed her.

He had snuggled close to his mother. "Aai, I want to taste food again."

"Yes." The woman's voice broke. "I want to cook for you. When we're all well and healed, I will cook you the best food I've ever cooked."

"Will you cook me mutton?"

"Yes, my baby, I will. I'll cook it just as you like it—spicy, and with plenty of coconut."

"And will you make me solkadhi?"

"Yes, I'll make you solkadhi, as sour as you want it to be."

"And we'll have mango pulp?"

"Yes, fresh mangoes. You can drink the pulp till your stomach is full, so full that you'll fall asleep at your plate and I'll have to wash your hands and mouth and carry you to bed."

The woman folded her arms around her son and looked out through the doorway of the clinic. She seemed to be pleading with someone, with God perhaps, or the stars.

Her son rested his head on her pregnant belly. "After we come back to life, what if we die again?"

"Why are you asking that, my baby?" She combed away a twig stuck in his hair with her finger.

"What if someone attacks us, and this happens again?"

"It won't happen, I promise. Those were bad people, but they're far away now."

"But aren't there any bad people in this village? What if they don't want us here?"

"Don't say that, my child. Most people aren't like that. Most people are kind, they want to help others, even strangers."

"But not all. How do we find out who the bad people are?"

"God will keep us safe. He'll protect us."

"And will the angel protect us?"

"Yes, I'm—I'm sure he will. Baba has great faith in him."

The woman sat that way for a while, looking down at the side of her son's face, and then her eyes moved to the village beyond the hillock.

"That looks like a school," she said. "That's where you'll study, and that's where Baba will work, too."

"Will we ever go back to our house?"

"We can never leave this village, no matter what happens, you know that. Maybe when you're older you'll understand this better, but for now you have to trust your father and me. You can never cross the boundary of this village, not even for a second. Not even if there's a pile of gold and diamonds on the other side."

"But where will we live?"

"Saheb is generous. He'll help us. I'm sure the villagers will help too. It won't be easy—we won't have any money, and we'll have to live on what others give us. But you're a big boy now. I know you won't be stubborn if you don't get everything you want. Someday we'll have our own house. Right here, at the foot of this hill."

The boy pointed at something. "Is that a temple?" The pharmacist could see it from where she stood, and yes, a pennant fluttered above it in the moonlight. The boy had a good eye.

"Maybe. It looks like one," said his mother. "We'll go there to pray every morning. Those white flowers you like, we'll make garlands out of them. I wonder what kind of statues they have. I hope they're made of stone, I like those better than the metal—"

The boy stood up and held his face against his mother's, pressed his forehead and nose to hers, his left cheek to her right. "I'll take care of you, Aai. I know you're really hurt, but I'll take care of you."

His mother cupped his cheeks in her hands. "I know you will, my baby, I know you will." She pulled him to her breast.

The pharmacist, as she watched this from the end of the corridor, couldn't help but feel that there was something strange about the woman's face, something unnatural, though she wasn't quite sure what it was. Then a drop rolled down her own cheek, and she realized. The woman's eyes were as dry as paper. They remained dry while she rocked her son back and forth, though her chest shook with sobs. So the pharmacist let her own eyes spill, drop by drop, what the woman strained to spill but could not, for flowing tears, like flowing blood, were denied to the dead.

ELEVEN

EVEN WHEN THEY WERE in the operating room and the door was closed, the teacher did not ask, "Will she live?" and so the surgeon did not answer, "I don't think she will." The man just took off his shirt and raised himself onto the operating table, and the surgeon put his stethoscope to his ears.

On the right side of the chest—the side of the stabbing—the surgeon couldn't hear any air filling the lung. When he tapped in the spaces between the ribs, the cavity rang dull under his fingers, as if he were tapping on stone.

"You bled into your chest. How long was the blade?"

The teacher held his thumb and forefinger about six inches apart. The surgeon looked at the wound, and the teacher brought his outstretched fingers close to his chest in response. With the thumb placed against the gash, his forefinger curved all the way along the rib to the breastbone. A knife that size, driven to the hilt, could have hit anything. The surgeon scratched his stubble, kneaded a knot in his jaw with his thumb.

He had the teacher lie on his side, facing away, his right arm folded up over his head. He picked up the razor he'd left on the shelf. Strands of hair still clung to it, long, fine hair from the back of the woman's head. He unscrewed and washed the razor, snapped on a new blade. With it, he carefully shaved the man's armpit and part of the right side of his chest, clearing a broad margin around the wound. Then he scrubbed the chest with iodine and covered the upper and lower areas with drapes, leaving only a strip of skin exposed at the level of the injury.

"Hold your breath."

The chest under the drapes stopped moving. The surgeon put his scalpel to the skin and extended the wound in both directions—toward the breastbone alone the line of the rib, and backward, first under the shoulder blade and then curving upward along the spine. The teacher's arm was raised, and his skin was stretched. The edges of the new incision parted as soon as the scalpel passed through them.

"There was a palmist at the village fair," said the teacher. His chest did not move. He too could speak without having to breathe.

"Um?"

"Sorry. I can keep quiet if you'd prefer—"

"No, go ahead. What were you saying?"

"At the fair, on the day this happened, we had our palms read."

"Really? You believe in that kind of thing?"

"Not me, Saheb, no. But my wife used to. Who knows, maybe she still does, even after everything."

"And what did the palmist tell you?"

"That all three of us had perfect lifelines, stretching all the way to our wrists. Not a single break."

"You should ask for your money back."

"He was sitting on a mat, Saheb, under a tattered umbrella for shade. He had these dusty signboards around him, with drawings of palms and lines and numbers."

"And you took pity on him?"

"His clothes were torn. He looked old and tired . . . probably hadn't eaten much that day. People were walking by without even noticing him. It was just a few rupees, and he spoke to my son as lovingly as he would've to his own grandchild."

"Well, it's all a question of the right setting," said the surgeon. "Sit an old man on a mat, and no one looks his way. Put him in a clinic, and even angels refer patients to him."

He had finished cutting through the fat under the man's skin. He pulled aside the fleshy muscle that ran across the surface of the rib cage and cut through others, careful not to injure the nerves in the region. He then sliced through the muscles that held together the ribs flanking the wound, right down to the pleura on the inside of the ribs. He used to have a rib retractor, but the pharmacist had dropped and broken it over a year ago, and he hadn't felt the need to purchase another. So he just pulled the ribs apart with his hands, as though he were prying open the bony lips of a cavernous maw. The interior of the chest was as he'd expected.

"It's full of blood."

"Can it be fixed?"

"Don't know that yet."

If the heart had been punctured, or one of the arteries

around it, this was the end. There was absolutely nothing here that would allow him to repair that. But there was just too much blood. Liters of it, from what he could estimate, obscuring everything.

The teacher's face was turned away from the surgeon, half covered by the edge of the drape. It was clear the man wasn't feeling any pain, but the surgeon now wondered if he had any sensation at all, any awareness of what part of him the scalpel was cutting at a given moment. Maybe one could pluck out every organ, disjoint the bones, reduce the man to just a head, then trim even that down—the cheeks, the lips, the tongue. Would words still issue from a bare skull?

"These villagers are lucky, Saheb."

"Are they?"

"How many villages have someone like you, someone with your skill? There's so much money to be made in cities, but still, here you are, serving the poor."

The surgeon had begun to clean out the interior of the chest, and found that it wasn't easy holding the ribs apart and digging out clots at the same time without a retractor or an assistant. Removing one of the ribs to make some space wasn't a bad thought, but it would probably be more trouble than it was worth. It was a mercy the man was thin. No roll of fat around his chest to force apart every time.

"There are very few people like you, Saheb, who willingly sacrifice their comforts for others. Everyone's just concerned with their own lives, interested in adding to their wealth. All greed and selfishness."

The teacher paused, considered his own words.

"But what right do I have to judge anyone else? I want life, don't I? Life on earth, even after my death. The one thing that no one's really supposed to have. Maybe that's real greed, worse than wanting money or fame."

The surgeon smiled. "Philosophy is for the elderly. You're much too young for thoughts like these. Leave them to people my age."

"But don't they say that philosophy is for those who struggle with death? If that's true, who could be more qualified than me?"

The cuffs and sleeves of the surgeon's gown were a deep red by now. The sides of the incision closed over his forearm each time he reached in, and a wet, sucking sound accompanied every handful of clots he pulled out. They came in clumps and threads—dark, shiny, teasing their way free through his gloves. Try as he did, he couldn't keep some of them from slipping to the floor. He would have to remember to clean them off later, or the whole clinic would be smeared.

"My son's feet ached," the teacher said. "He wanted to take a rickshaw home from the fair, and I teased him, 'You're a big boy, you should be able to walk, it isn't that far.'"

"Don't say that. It wasn't your fault. You shouldn't blame yourself."

"If only I'd listened to him, Saheb, if only I'd taken a minute to stop and think. It was getting dark. My wife shouldn't have been walking in her state anyway. But I wasn't thinking. I just wasn't thinking."

It was clear where this conversation was headed. The surgeon thought of enforcing silence on the teacher, under the pretence of medical requirement if need be. But the time when he could have done so came and went, and the man just kept speaking. The surgeon pulled his hand out from between the ribs and placed his bloody glove on the cloth covering the teacher's shoulder. He knew full well that the man would feel this gesture as little as he did the cuts and tugs on his insides.

"They twisted my arms behind my back, Saheb. Held me as if I were nothing more than a child. They started pulling off our valuables. 'Take everything,' I begged them. 'Take her mangalsutra, her bangles. Take my ring, my watch. My wallet has a week's pay. Take it. We won't fight, won't make a sound.' And still the knives, Saheb. Why?

"I could see their teeth. They were smiling. And then this pain . . . I'd never felt pain like this. Every single breath, it felt as if someone were tearing out my ribs. My wife's clothes were covered with blood. My son was on the ground, he was holding his stomach, 'Baba, I'm hurt, I'm hurt.' The men had already run away. Imagine me, Saheb, trying to breathe, trying to stop her bleeding. It kept flowing through my fingers, hot as boiling water. Imagine, Saheb, her face all red, her eyes rolled back, and my child . . . *our* child, our baby, ready to be born . . . we even had names for it, one if it was a boy, another if a girl, dying inside her, and I could do nothing. I couldn't even kneel there and cry. My son was screaming behind me, so I left her. She was gone. There was nothing I could do, so I left her.

"His shirt was wet. I grabbed his arms, dragged him— my boy, whom I used to swing over my back but whom I couldn't even lift off the ground now. Who knows how long we went like this . . . it was so dark, the street was swaying from side to side, it was as if I were walking on a rope. So I fell. What lies I whispered in his ears then. 'Don't be afraid, help is coming, I'm here with you.' Yes, I was there with him, Saheb, as nothing but a witness. My boy stopped breathing in my arms, and I could do nothing. May this never happen to any father, Saheb, may no one ever have to feel what I felt. I tried to scream, but there was no air left in my lungs. And who was there to listen? I felt only hate, nothing but hate. And my greatest hatred wasn't even for the bandits. It was for that palmist at the fair. That poor old man, he had done nothing to hurt us, but as the pressure in my chest became unbearable, and the next breath became impossible to take, I could only think of his promises, about our lifelines and how long they were supposed to be. And then I died."

The man spoke in a smothered voice, as if he were strangling himself with restraint. The surgeon could only see the side of his face, not even that, really, just his ear and the back of his cheek. The rest was either covered by the drape or in shadow. There was no consolation fit for such an unburdening, and so a silence fell between them. Something as raw and horrific as this, the surgeon couldn't bring himself to scrape at it with words.

"We've suffered so much, Saheb. I feel so terrible about all the trouble we're putting you through, putting the girl and her husband through, but please understand, we've suffered so much."

The surgeon loosened his grip on the shoulder and searched again between the ribs. The clots the man's chest surrendered were as gruesome as his words, but at least the surgeon knew what to do with them. He scooped them over to a tray, shook them off his fingers.

Then he said, "I'm not here to serve the poor."

The teacher turned ever so slightly toward him. His eyelashes caught the light from the Anglepoise lamp.

"I've been here, in this village, for almost three years, and every single day I've thought of just packing up and leaving. It would be dishonest of me to let you think otherwise."

The teacher's face remained where it was, his eyes turned in the surgeon's direction without actually looking at him.

"I used to practice in a large private hospital in the city. We had conveniences there—luxuries compared to this place—that I would barely even notice. New instruments, imported machines, trained nurses. I just assumed I would have all of those resources until I retired—all I had to do was snap my fingers.

"And then one day one of my patients became unstable after surgery. I did everything I could, but he kept worsening, and the patient's family demanded that he be shifted elsewhere. The hospital they wanted was at the other end of the city. Late that night, an ambulance managed to get him there alive.

"I called early the next morning to find out how things had gone. The staff at that hospital told me that the patient was in the operating room, undergoing a second, emergency surgery. I asked them who was operating, and they told me the surgeon's name.

"It was a man who'd worked in the same hospital as me. Actually he'd been my subordinate—this was a decade earlier. He was a terrible surgeon—lazy and impatient, bothered only about getting through his quota of cases for the shift and going home. Neglecting so many details that he would routinely put patients' lives in danger. I had to fix so many of the problems he caused that finally I had him fired. It had been ten years since I'd even thought of him. And now here he was, operating on my patient.

"When the surgery was finally done, they connected me to him. I could hear it over the phone—his triumph—from his very first word, from the way he greeted me. He asked about the old hospital, about how things were, how the other doctors and matrons and ward boys were doing, pretending he had no idea why I'd called. He had been operating since dawn, but there wasn't a trace of tiredness in his voice.

"I let this go on for some time and then asked about the patient. As if tossing off a minor detail, he said, 'Oh, he's going to die.' And then he told me he'd identified a surgical error when he opened the man up. I had cut something I shouldn't have cut, he said, tied a vessel I shouldn't have tied.

"I racked my brain, tried to remember every minute of the surgery, every suture and knot, but I just couldn't believe I'd done as he claimed. I kept questioning his findings, hoping to clarify some detail that would prove him wrong. I asked to speak to one of the surgeons who'd assisted him, to see if that person had the same opinion of the case. That's when his voice changed.

"'I don't have time,' he said, 'for fools who can't accept their own mistakes.'

"It was reasonable that he would want revenge, I understand that now. I was a fool, yes, and like a fool I tried to reason with him. We'd worked together. He knew me, he knew how careful I was. I was just requesting him to consider this a special case.

"'A special case?' he said. 'Really? Well, if that's so, let's see how special you're willing to make it. I'm open to changing my report. Assuming you're willing to reach an arrangement. Five lakh rupees. I don't need to tell you there won't be a receipt.'

"I'd been lucky until then, I have to say. I'd managed to get very far in life without being forced into a corner like this. If it took six extra months to get a telephone line installed, that was fine, I could deal with it. If a hundred other people paid under the table to move things along faster, best of luck to them. But I'd never dreamed that this would happen . . . that I'd be blackmailed for a mistake I couldn't even remember making.

"I yelled into the phone, cursed him and his kind—termites hollowing out every institution. But every word I spoke just gave him more power over me. He was only trying to help me, he said. It'd be easy. All I had to do was take a briefcase to my bank and then bring it to him. 'Don't try to complicate simple things,' he said. 'And don't try to negotiate me down, I'm not some jewelry salesman.'

"'You're nothing *but* a jewelry salesman,' I shouted, 'trying to hawk some diamond you've dug out of a corpse. Buying a new Mercedes, are you? How many bribes is that going to take? I hope your mother isn't alive to see this. If she'd known what kind of snake you'd turn out to be, she wouldn't have let your father fuck her in the first place.'

"The man disconnected. I kept calling, but he wouldn't

answer, and in the evening, I learned from a nurse that the patient had died—"

The surgeon felt a wetness on his forearm. He yanked his arm out of the teacher's chest, tugged at the knot at his waist, tore off his gown. A red band circled his wrist above the level of the glove. He turned the tap in the sink on full, but only a sluggish stream came out. Under it, he scrubbed a bar of soap into a pink froth. The water's ropy pressure was excruciatingly gentle. He had to hold his skin against the tap to coax the foam down into the drain.

Blood, it was just blood. The little that had soaked through his sleeve. It was harmless. It wasn't acid, it wouldn't corrode his flesh. Nor were the dead branding him as one of their own with some demonic ink. The surgeon gripped the porcelain rim with his dripping hands to hold the world steady. The water reached from the mouth of the tap to the floor of the sink in a thin, silent column. Every so often, it would lose its inner harmony, and a gurgle from the spout would scatter the glassy stream.

The surgeon let the thudding in his chest fade. Then he shut the tap, gowned and gloved again, returned to the table. The teacher's face was blank. Without comment, the surgeon dipped into the man's open chest again, with greater care for his scrubs this time. The teacher did not react to that, either. It was clear he was waiting for the story to resume.

The surgeon sighed. "I've often thought about that conversation. Maybe, at the bottom of all this, his findings were real, and I was too conceited to accept them. After all, it had been a routine surgery for a minor condition. The patient was otherwise in perfect health. Maybe I *was* at fault, and deserved to be fined.

"What happened was much worse. The surgeon released the most incriminating report he could possibly write. He filled it with accusing words, speculations about my skills, things that definitely didn't belong there. But who can stop an author determined to write a tragedy? And that wasn't even the worst thing. Then he called the press. And told them I'd tried to bribe him.

"There were no riots that week, no activists going on hunger strikes; so, every news agency descended on his hospital. The bastard told them that I'd offered him money to keep his mouth shut. But he couldn't be bought, not he, with his conscience bathed in milk. Not even if I gave him a Mercedes. He must have emphasized that word, *Mercedes*, to every reporter, for it was used in every article. I imagine he wanted to make sure I read it.

"His accusation shattered my life. The telephone company released records of the calls I'd dialed—proof that I'd made all those frantic attempts to contact him. The resident who'd assisted in the surgery was a timid young man, and when the police questioned him, he just repeated everything his superior had said. My name was blackened in every newspaper in the city. Headline news, daily updates, rumors—my photo next to murderers and rapists.

"After two weeks of this, I was summoned by the head of the department. 'I sympathize with your position,' he said. 'Patients sometimes die from our mistakes, and we as doctors have to accept that possibility. But the public doesn't see it that way. They expect us to be perfect. And above everything else, they expect us to be honest. Exemplary citizens. All that bullshit.'

"By that point, he didn't care if the operative report was true. Nor if the claim of bribery was true. He was answerable to the trustees of the hospital, and they to the public. Someone had to be sacrificed, and it wouldn't be him. As I signed my letter of resignation, he asked why I hadn't come to him earlier. He knew people in the press, he said. He could've paid them to hold their tongues.

"The compensation the court made me pay wiped my savings away. It wasn't just for medical negligence—the accusation of bribery made the penalty ten times higher. I'm still astonished that my lawyer managed to save me from a prison sentence. No hospital would dream of hiring me now. Corruption, the secret friend of everyone from the top to the bottom of the chain, was a land mine when the world was looking. I had no money to open my own clinic. No bank would give me a loan, and no one would have referred any patients to me anyway. So I left the city, at my age, and came to work in this government clinic. The villagers respect me because they don't know my past. The government knows everything, of course, but it's better to fill a clinic like this with a disgraced doctor than with cobwebs.

"So there it is. It's a long story, but after everything you've been through, you don't deserve any more lies. I just want you—I need you—to understand that I'm not a saint. And I'm certainly not God. If you mistake me for either, you'll be very disappointed, I promise you."

Only as the surgeon neared the end of his tale did he truly realize he was delivering it to a patient, and to one so young. But the chasm between them—the living and the dead—had already made all earthly hierarchies seem pointless.

For a long time, the teacher remained quiet. Once or twice, he made as if to say something. When he finally did speak, it seemed to take him some effort to control his voice.

"Doctor Saheb, how does it matter if we think of you as god or man? When we were dying on the roadside, no one came to our help. No man, no god. For us, you are more than either. We're thankful for whatever you can do for us, and we won't have any complaint, no matter how this should end. I can only apologize again for everything, for all the trouble we're causing you."

The man's chest had finally been emptied of blood. A shrunken lung was crushed deep inside it. Behind it, the heart hid like a timid animal that had retreated into the depths of its cave. There was no flowing blood to inflate it, but it still appeared to have a beat, or, more precisely, a throb. It shivered under the surgeon's fingers, as though in fear or yearning for the moment when it would once again be entrusted with life.

The light was miserable, and even with the ribs propped apart with an improvised retractor, the lamps lit only a sliver of the interior brightly enough. Most of the cavity remained dark. There was a small battery flashlight on the windowsill, but it wasn't sterile. The surgeon wondered if it was worth spraying it with alcohol and holding it in one hand while he examined the interior of the chest with the other, but he decided against it. He would never be able to get it acceptably clean. So he just started feeling with his fingers, inch by inch, along the surface of every structure that could possibly have been the source of the bleed.

"Tell me, why do you want to come back? Some day or another, all of us have to die and end up in the afterlife, don't we? So why endure this anxiety, the uncertainty of this night?"

The teacher's eyes were fixed on the far wall. He was following, it seemed, an ant meandering up the tiles. So the fumigation hadn't accomplished anything after all, had it? But the surgeon felt no anger toward the black dot. The hapless little thing—even it had the right to live, on this night when the dead themselves were being smuggled across the border. It crawled across the cracked tile and vanished into the grime at its edge.

"We were murdered. My son deserves a full life."

"Yes, yes, you've said that before, but that isn't everything, is it? You're hiding something."

The teacher's ribs now moved for the first time in quite a while. The motion didn't disturb the surgeon, so he let the man breathe.

"When I first told you about the afterlife, Saheb, I was careful with my words. For the sake of my son. I would like to think he's still a child—that I have some control over what he should and shouldn't know. Or believe."

"Yes, but he's not here now. You can speak openly."

"But, Saheb, it's not supposed to be this way, the living aren't supposed to learn about the afterlife. Please understand, I don't want to hide anything from you, but there are some things you might be better off not knowing."

"And why do you think you have the right to decide what to keep from me?"

The teacher appeared wounded by the question. He straightened the arm that was folded under his head, and let it stick out from beneath the drapes, over the edge of the operating table.

"The afterlife is a barren place. There's no valley or mountain to catch your eye. Every direction looks like every other. You could walk up and down it forever, and so many have—the dead who don't even know why they're wandering anymore. Who would want to live in a place like that, Saheb? It's like being exiled to a desert. Worse. All we can do there is wander, hope that relief will come if we walk just a little bit more, find some magical resting place. Our legs don't get tired, we don't need food or sleep. But the soul, it gets tired. It wants to *feel* something, even pain."

"But that doesn't answer my question. You, all three of you, could live here till you're old and bent, and after everything's done, you'll still end up there. So how is this, all the suffering you'll have to face at dawn, how is any of this worth it?"

"It will be worth it, Saheb, I'm telling you. The suffering will be temporary, it will go away, and then we'll be able to feel things again, all the little things that we can only feel on earth. I want to drink water again, Saheb—ice-cold water. Sometimes I imagine it's collecting on my tongue, that I can roll it against my teeth, feel it in the bones of my head, smell it—water has a smell, I never realized that before my death—and then feel it in my throat when I swallow, that feeling right here in my chest, spreading outward, rib after rib, down to my stomach . . . I know I must sound half-mad when I talk like this, but it's these things that really separate life from death. Yes, I'll have to return someday, but now that I know what it's like, the time I spend on earth will be different. I know the value of every breath. I will live a life in which I teach others to appreciate it, help them lead better lives themselves. Maybe even become a farmer, grow my own food so that I know what it's like to sow life into the soil. All of these things . . . maybe they'll help me tolerate the afterlife better when I return."

The surgeon grimaced. It was too naïve, all of this. Not what he'd expected at all, certainly not from someone whose knowledge of life was supposed to surpass his own.

"Fine, but why not just wait until it's your turn to be reborn? Through a woman's womb? Why this plan to return in the middle of the night?"

The rapture that had entered the teacher's voice at the talk of water now drained out of it just as quickly. "I don't believe it, Saheb. I don't think anyone is ever reborn. Everyone talks about it in the afterlife. In fact, that's all they talk about. But I . . . I don't believe it."

"But didn't you say that your angel told you about it? Or were you lying to me?"

"Not lying, Saheb. Please understand, I just said what I did for my son's sake. All useless, I'm sure. My boy has seen so much—all it takes is a moment in the afterlife, and children remain children no more. But what else can a father do?"

"Get to the point."

"The angel isn't an angel. He's an official of the afterlife."

The surgeon stopped dead in his work. "An official?"

"Yes. One of the many who run the afterlife."

"I don't understand. Officials? The afterlife is run by *officials?*"

"Yes. It's all based on the promise of rebirth. Everyone needs hope, Saheb—the dead as much as the living. So they pray to the officials, who are said to be the gatekeepers."

"What—what are you saying?"

"That's how it starts, Saheb—appeals and rejections, rejections and appeals. The officials have different conditions for rebirth. Some say our lives are important, others our deaths. Some go through our sins, other talk about our penance. Every thought, every word we've ever said—things we did as children, before we even knew right from wrong—we are forced to justify it all until we have no dignity left. But nothing ever satisfies the officials. They say they need to think about it, they need to check with their superiors. They tell us they'll return when they've reached a decision, and we never see them again."

A crow, perhaps the insomniac from earlier in the night, cawed outside the window, and the night wind drew a soft rattle from the shutters.

"So you're saying the afterlife is like a bureaucracy? A government bureaucracy?"

"Much worse. No government on earth could create a bureaucracy like this. It's endless. There are probably more officials in the afterlife than there are dead people. The reason the three of us are here, the reason I'm telling you all this, Saheb, is that one official was different, and we were lucky enough to find him. Our story moved him, I don't know why. We had nothing to offer him, but still he decided to break his laws for us. Please, Saheb, don't tell my son these things. He's just a child. He deserves to grow up with some hope about life, maybe even about death."

The surgeon just stood, forearm-deep in the teacher's ribs. Because he had to do something, he tried to return to his work, but his hands kept falling still. The insane turn of the teacher's narration wouldn't let him focus, nor would the patina of sleep that, despite everything, kept building over his eyes. How much of the teacher's account had truly come from the man's lips, and how much had his own brain fabricated in its exhaustion? He was now passing his fingers in an unending circuit inside the man's chest, but he still wasn't sure that the large vessels hadn't been harmed. The walls had gained a darker tint, and it seemed that the door and windows of this shuttered room would never open again. The two of them— the dead and the living—would continue this conversation until the tiles blackened and crumbled.

"Is there a God?" the surgeon asked.

The teacher turned to the wall.

"Answer my question. You've been talking about all these officials, but not about gods."

The very act of speech seemed to age the teacher, making him softer and hoarser. "In the afterlife, we called out to God. We recited every prayer we had ever learnt. We searched so desperately that any God with a drop of kindness in Him would have come to us . . . at least shown us some sign. But He didn't. God is as hidden to the dead as He is to the living."

There was a coldness on the surgeon's face, on the back of his arms. But it wasn't from the teacher's words. The surgeon could now feel a hole under his fingers. In the vena cava, right where the vessel entered the heart. How could this be? Surely he'd checked the spot before. Had he himself poked a hole through it with his prodding? No, no, that wasn't possible. The vessel was in the path of the stabbing. The knife could very well have hit it. The hole didn't even appear to have a flap in front of it. There was nothing to stitch back into place. He pulled his hand out to take a look.

The teacher just kept speaking. "There are religions in the afterlife, Saheb. Just not the ones from earth. Even those who were faithful believers in life have to wonder how their priests and holy books could have been so wrong. But that has only led to new religions, made by stitching together shreds of the older ones. Some of the dead claim to be prophets and sages—men of God. They say they can hear His voice, that they want to spread His words to everyone who hopes to be reborn. I don't understand what they get out of this. There's no money or land or gold to gather there. Maybe it's just the sense of power."

No, it wasn't a hole. It was just another clot—a piece that had flattened and plastered itself against the vena cava so that it seemed to the surgeon's numb fingers like a portion of the wall itself. He had to stop obsessing over this. It would kill him if he kept looking for false alarms in the dark. The large vessels were fine.

But what could explain the chest full of blood? Not that little rent in the lung?

The small vessels running in the groove under the rib's edge were difficult to examine. The angle of light was completely wrong. The knife could very well have cut them, but he'd run his fingers over that area and hadn't felt anything suspicious. There was really no way to improve the positions of the lamps, so he asked the teacher to turn sideways, arch to the left, and inflate his rib cage as far as it would go so the groove under the rib could catch the light. As the man repositioned himself, the wound, framed by its green drapery, opened and closed like a carnivorous plant smacking its blood-flecked jaws after a feast. It took a few tries, but the man finally contorted himself into a pose that offered a reasonable view.

The artery and vein were so collapsed that it wasn't even clear which was which in the groove of the rib. And there was no spurting blood to act as a guide. The surgeon brushed his finger over the inner curve of the rib, but couldn't find a cut. Maybe it was best to assume that one of the vessels was the culprit, and close them off by tying blind knots on either side of the injury. He started to dissect what appeared to be the artery and vein away from what was probably the nerve.

"What did your angel, your official, say? Didn't you ask him about God?"

"I did, but he didn't answer. He didn't like to talk about these things."

"And didn't you ask him how all of this came into existence? The afterlife? The system of officials?"

"My official wouldn't say anything about that, either; but there was a wanderer I met, Saheb, a very strange man. He said he'd once been an official. He told me—"

"Once been an official? How do you know he wasn't lying?"

"I don't. I'm mentioning him only because he told me something that might answer your question. As an official, he'd been assigned to a province, he said. He kept an eye on things, recorded births and deaths. It was boring work, so he decided to play with his subjects. He took the form of a celestial messenger and appeared on earth—"

"In person?"

"Yes. He told me that he made his skin glow, just like a firefly. It was a simple trick for him, but it was enough to make any human who saw him drop to his knees. He appeared before a few men, told them that God was willing to offer them great powers if they could please Him with their devotion. The men all left their wives and children, went into caves, ate only seeds and roots, and spent their days in meditation. Some of them almost starved to death.

"So the official thought, why stop there? He started granting the powers he'd promised. To one man he gave the strength of ten elephants. To another he taught a spell to create fire from air. A third he gave the ability to cause agony with a glance. Awful things happened, and the official watched them, entertained.

"But he wasn't careful. After the men had taken revenge on their neighbors, they started intimidating people in other towns, threatened to kill them and their children if they didn't bow to them. That's when other officials began to notice these monsters with abilities that no human was supposed to have. The official tried to cover things up by killing his creations, but it was too late. He was discovered and exposed. His superiors judged him guilty, took away his authority and powers, and sentenced him to the worst punishment possible—permanent exile on the plain of the dead, as one of its wanderers.

"Whether this man was telling me the truth, or if he was just another one of us, a madman before he died or someone driven mad by the afterlife, I don't know. He said he had reflected on his actions, he'd changed, repented. Now he only wished to spread the truth. And so he told me that the officials themselves don't really know if God exists. They have a hierarchy, like a ladder, with steps that go on and on, the lower officials reporting to the higher ones and so forth. No one knows who's at the very top. No one even knows if the ladder ever ends."

The surgeon tied a knot under the teacher's rib and made two snips with his scissors. He then pulled out the segment of tissue, stretched it between his fingers, held it to the light. One of the cords, likely the artery, had a cut in its wall, right where the knife would be expected to have grazed it. It was tiny, but sufficient in the right situation to pump a man's chest full of blood. The surgeon kept turning it over, let the light glint off its neat rectangular shape until he was finally convinced that he'd repaired the fatal injury. Then he searched within himself for the slightest trace of relief. He could find none.

He used two rows of stitches to close the rent in the surface of the lung. A separate puncture, lower in the rib cage, would be needed for the drainage tube. He made a cut in the skin at the edge of a lower rib, and tunneled the puncture through to the inside, taking care not to injure the diaphragm. He threaded the chest tube from the outside of the chest to the space between the lung and the ribs, and once its tip was high enough in the thorax, he secured the outer portion to the skin with loops of sutures. After confirming that it was anchored in place, he drew the ribs back together and sutured the muscles between them. Then it was time to close the other layers of the chest wall—the muscles, the connective tissue, the skin. Once the drapes were lifted off, the incision with its closed lips made a macabre smile that stretched across the side of the chest. He dressed it with gauze and tape.

He now had the teacher sit up. Their eyes met, and the surgeon narrowed his and looked down at the man's neck in a pretence of clinical scrutiny. He'd forgotten where he'd left the glass jar, and he looked around until the teacher pointed to the stone shelf jutting from the wall. The surgeon adjusted the plastic tubes passing through the jar's lid so that the inner end of one of the tubes was submerged in the water, while the other ended an inch above the surface. To the outer end of the submerged tube he attached longer, flexible tubing, and into the other end of this tubing he twisted the end of the chest tube sticking out of the man's ribs. The tubes fit into each other neatly. After confirming that the seal around the rubber lid was tight, he asked the teacher to cough. Air gushed through the piping and bubbled to the water's surface.

"You'll have to carry this jar around with you. It's sturdy, but don't drop it. Take care not to tilt or spill it either—the end of that tube has to remain underwater, no matter what. Hold this glove to your mouth, and inflate it like a balloon repeatedly for the next hour. That'll generate enough pressure to inflate your lungs. There's a lot of air outside them, in the space where all that blood had collected. The air will bubble out as the lung expands to its original shape."

He'd kept his watch on his wrist during this surgery, and it told him now the time was a little after four in the morning. Less than two hours to sunrise. Somehow, in the hour and a half since they'd entered the operating room, the teacher hadn't brought up the one thing the surgeon had feared he would. Then, when asked to step down from the table, the man asked, "Will she live?" The only answer the surgeon could give was "I don't think she will." The teacher folded his face into his hands. Even through the walls of the room, the surgeon could feel the pressure of the heavy sky, and of everything beyond it.

TWELVE

THE PHARMACIST LEANED AGAINST the entrance of the clinic, waiting for the sound of a bicycle, waiting for the night to return her husband. The boy sat on the steps, examining a pile of boxes a few feet away. The boxes were rustling. He aimed a pebble at one, and a rat ran out from underneath it. With a small ball of cotton as its loot, it fled into its burrow and hid somewhere in the clinic walls.

The boy's mother was on the bench, her back pressed against the wall and her head set straight on her neck. She was still in the tattered green gown she'd worn for the surgery. A safety pin held the neckline together. The bandages were a thick white wrap above the gown.

She called out to him without turning, "Don't do that, my baby. Don't damage those boxes."

"No problem, really," the pharmacist said. "I was going to throw them out anyway. He can play with them if he wants."

The boy chose a box made of polystyrene.

The pharmacist knelt next to him. "Do you . . . did you go to school?"

"Yes." He began carving pieces of the box away with a thumbnail.

"And what standard were you studying in?"

The boy climbed down the steps and returned with some twigs from the mud. "Third standard."

"How nice. You're such a big boy. Did your father teach you in school?"

"No, he taught the ninth and tenth standards." He pressed the twigs into the squares he'd carved in the polystyrene.

She clapped her hands in delight. "You're making a house."

"It's not a house." He placed the box upside down on the floor. There were vertical twigs in the door and windows. "It's a jail."

She started, glanced at the boy's mother. With her neck held stiff, the woman had been looking at her son's creation from the corner of her eye. She looked morose, resigned.

"Is it for the men who did this to you?" the pharmacist asked.

The boy just adjusted the twigs.

"Bad people never end up happy," she said. "Sooner or later, they're punished. I believe that."

"It's not for them."

"For whom, then?"

"It's for us."

The boy had turned the box, placed it so that its door was facing the entrance of the clinic and its sides were parallel to the walls of the corridor. The pharmacist, despite herself, reached out to touch the boy, but then, remembering how he'd shrugged her off earlier, pulled her fingers back.

His mother held her hand out toward him. "Come."

The boy walked on his knees to her, leaned against her leg with his cheek pressed to the side of her thigh. She passed her fingers through his hair, tucked a few strands behind his ears. The pharmacist saw the woman's eyes go once again to the clock, the hands of which were moving so slowly that she wondered if the presence of the dead had somehow drained its batteries.

The door of the operating room creaked open, and the teacher stepped out. Physically he didn't look any different from when he'd entered, except for the glass jar in his hand and the tube sticking out from under his shirt. But his face appeared wooden. The boy ran to his father and pressed his face to his side. The man cupped his son's head, moved him away from the tube.

The boy touched the jar. "What's that?"

"I need to talk to you," the man said to his wife.

"The operation went well?" She pushed herself up with her hands while balancing her neck.

"Yes, everything's fine."

"Then what is it?"

"I'll tell you." He gestured to the back room.

The boy looked alarmed. "What are you going to talk about? I want to come too."

"We'll be back in a few minutes. Stay here."

"But why? What is it? Why can't I come with you?"

"Aai and I have to talk about something. A few things. We'll be back soon."

"You can stay with me," said the pharmacist. "I'll get you some glue and scissors. We can make a nice house out of this."

"It's not a *house*."

The boy stamped on the box, made a hole in it with his heel, flattened the walls. With a kick, he sent it flying out of the clinic.

His mother began to bend to his height, but then seemed to remember her tube. She held her son against her pregnant belly, scolded him in a voice that had nothing but love in it.

"What is this? Is this any way to behave in front of Saheb and this nice madam? She's just trying to help you. Why shout at her?"

The boy twisted his mother's gown in his fists. "Why don't you tell me what's happening? Why does Baba want to talk to you? The two of you are always hiding something."

"Why would we hide anything from you, my prince? There's nothing to hide. I'm sure it's just something ordinary, boring. Like when Baba used to read the newspaper and you just wanted to look at the pictures, remember? I'm sure Baba wants to talk to me about something like that, something that wouldn't be interesting to you."

The pharmacist forced a smile as she brought the smashed box back into the corridor. "We can still fix this. We can make whatever you want—a jail, a police station, anything. I have a lot of boxes. Come, sit with me while your parents talk."

The man and his wife left the boy with the pharmacist. She did all she could to get his attention, but he kept turning to the door they'd closed behind them.

Saheb was trying to sit on the bench, wincing as he did so. The pharmacist knew how bad his back could get, with the slipped disk or whatever he had. It took him some time to settle there and release the arm with which he was propping his weight up on the bench. Then he raised his finger and held the tip close to his face. A small red drop squeezed out of it. The wood of the bench had splinters, she'd been pricked enough times herself. But Saheb just kept looking at the growing drop with a strange expression. "I'll get some tape," she said, and he, as if startled, shook his head and rubbed the drop off between his thumb and fingers.

She found the scissors, glue, and some colored paper in the pharmacy, laid the pieces of the boy's jail out on the floor of the corridor, and glued the sides back together. Once that was done, she started cutting another cardboard box into long strips to make a fence. The boy showed no interest in any of this.

"They're discussing the possibility of another surgery."

It took a few moments for the boy to realize that Saheb was talking to him.

"Another surgery? When?"

"Now, before the sun rises."

"Why?"

The pharmacist stopped her scissors midway through the cardboard. Saheb was speaking to the boy as if to an adult. Actually with more patience than he'd ever shown any adult. The boy listened without interrupting. When Saheb was done, the boy had questions, some of which Saheb answered. She'd never heard him say "I don't know" so many times before.

Then the door of the back room opened, and the teacher and his wife returned to the corridor. The man nodded. "Doctor Saheb."

Saheb closed his eyes, stood up, stretched his back. "We'll be back soon," he said to the boy. "You'll stay with her, won't you?"

The pharmacist smiled and widened her eyes at the boy despite the ache in her chest. The boy did not argue, just stayed with his head lowered. His mother remained where she was, looking away, her eyes still dry, very dry.

The surgeon entered the operating room once again, this time with the teacher and his wife in tow. He felt crippled with fatigue. The woman held his hand as she climbed up on the operating table.

"Have you felt your baby move inside you since that evening?" he asked.

"No. I remember feeling it kick at the village fair, a few hours before we were attacked."

"So nothing in the afterlife? And how about tonight?"

"Nothing."

"Did your official say anything about this?" he asked the teacher.

"No. I—I have to admit it didn't strike me to ask. I assumed that when he gave her life, he would also give it to the baby inside her. Don't they have the same life, the same blood, until someone cuts the cord?"

"That would be too simple, wouldn't it?" The surgeon

placed his stethoscope against the woman's abdomen and listened at a few spots. "I don't hear a heartbeat," he said, and then, seeing their expressions change, added, "but I wasn't really expecting the fetus to have one. I did, however, expect it to move and kick, just as you can."

"What does this mean, Saheb?"

The surgeon lifted his glasses off his nose and tried to pinch with his thumb and middle finger the throbbing pain between his temples. "I don't know. I *can't* know. Whatever I've learned, all these decades of cutting people open and stitching them back together, nothing in them can help me answer your question. At this point, any guesses you can make will probably be more valid than mine."

The teacher looked ready to crumble. His wife clutched her womb with a desperate look, as though through that grasp she could awaken the creature that might just be slumbering endlessly within.

"You understand why I'm recommending this, don't you?"

They nodded.

"You understand that we don't know how things will go in the morning. If I have to do an emergency delivery then, it could be dangerous for both mother and child. It's better to do it now, in a controlled setting. You understand that, right?'

"Yes." They looked defeated, more dead now, so close to the morning, than they'd looked all night.

The surgeon replaced his glasses on the bridge of his nose. "Do you believe that the official who sent you here is wise?"

"Yes."

"And do you believe that he's benevolent?"

The teacher glanced at his wife, blinked at the floor a few times. "Yes."

"Then have faith in his wisdom and benevolence. Trust that he took every life, even the smallest one, into account when he arranged to send you here. Let's go ahead with the plan, but I should warn you, the child might not show any signs of life right now. It may be difficult for you to bear, but you'll have no choice but to wait until dawn."

The teacher helped undress his wife and laid her flat on the operating table, supporting her head so the tube in her throat wouldn't be disturbed. He sat on a stool while the surgeon examined her.

Long striae ran across her stretched skin, testifying to the months she had spent on earth carrying a creature that, one flesh with her while she lived, had perished with her final breath. It was the only member of the family to return from the afterlife without wounds to its own body. If granted life, it could well survive without any medications or surgeries. After all, its battles with death would be those of every ordinary infant that had ever left a womb.

The surgeon felt the woman's uterus. The head was in the expected position—pointed down toward the pelvis. In the left part of the uterus, he could feel small irregular lumps—the cluster of hands, feet, knees—and on the right, there was the neat, firm curve of the spine. Everything was in its proper place. He picked the razor and shaved away the upper part of the woman's pubic hair. He then prepared the skin and draped it, pressed a roll of cloth against either flank.

He tried to recall what little he could about cesarean

sections. The principles were simple enough, but he hadn't actually performed one in decades. He started with a neat horizontal incision, about six inches long, low on the abdomen, and cut through the skin, the connective tissue, the fat. He then cut through the fascia covering the vertical muscle in the midline, and pulled the two strips of muscle away to either side. Another few nicks with his scalpel, and he could peel the bladder and the fold of abdominal lining away from the lower segment of the uterus.

"Put on a pair of gloves. And take that fresh drape in your hands. Careful not to touch anything else, it's all sterile."

When the teacher was ready, the surgeon put his scalpel to the uterus. It sank into the spongy muscle without difficulty, leaving a clean, bloodless gash. He had now grown accustomed to the absence of flowing blood. What a mercy it was not to have to constantly swab and suction, not to have vessels to clamp at every turn.

The firm globe of the child's skull, covered with soft, wet hair, was under his fingertips. He stretched the edges of the incision in the uterus, just as in those old textbook illustrations. "It's time," he said, more to himself than to anyone else, and with his right hand he reached into the womb, grasped the globe, and pulled.

The head emerged in a gush of amniotic fluid, within which it had remained suspended even in this unearthly state. The woman on the table gave a cry, though it wasn't one of pain, her eyes told him that. He held the head in both hands and pulled with his fingers looped around the neck. Nothing budged. The baby appeared locked in that position. He pulled, first with a gentle tug and then harder, but his grip was weak, so very weak, and he was afraid of damaging the slender neck with the strain. But what if he wasn't able to get it out? What if it remained stuck there, and dawn jumped up behind him that very instant? Mother and child would both start screaming, one head above, another below—a two-headed howling monster washed with fountains of blood. His tired hands just kept slithering around, and he adjusted the grip of his fingers, crooked an elbow. "Come on," he said, "come on, don't be so stubborn." Just when he felt he couldn't summon any more strength, there was a sudden give, the shoulders slithered through the incision, and the rest of the fetus poured out in such a slippery rush that he almost stumbled back with it. The remainder of the fluid in which it had floated drenched the drapes, splashed on his gown, and the strong odor of the womb and its fluid filled the room. He clamped and cut the umbilical cord, from the ends of which, predictably, there dripped no blood.

The infant's skin had a bluish hue, but unlike its parents it had nothing to mark it as an unnatural visitor to this world. Its arms and legs tapered into slender fingers and toes, and its face was perfectly formed, carved by some skilled hand made masterful in its craft through countless iterations. But, as the surgeon had feared, the infant did not move. It lay in his hands, its limbs flaccid, its eyes and brow still, its mouth in an unmoving yawn, fluid pooled at the back of its throat that it made no attempt to cough out. On any other night, this could have meant only one thing, for the laws of the earth did not allow the dead to return to life. But this night was different, when death could perhaps be the precursor of life, the herald of breath and blood. Who could know for certain? Despite the resolve with which he had prepared himself for this moment, the surgeon's eyes welled up at the sight of this stillborn infant. Lacking any device with which to suction its throat, he held it upside down by its ankles and patted it until all that could drip out of its mouth had dripped out. After wiping it dry, he handed it over to its father.

The teacher received the limp body in the coarse green cloth draped over his cupped hands, and lowered it until it was level with his wife's head. "It's a girl," he said. Both of them seemed overcome, as though for them the very appearance of death were still as potent as death itself. Perhaps justifiably so, for now the surgeon knew that neither in the land of the living nor the dead were miracles ever guaranteed, and that, except in the rarest of cases, death did not display its colors without good reason. The dead held and kissed the blue infant and seemed to be praying, though whether to a wise and benevolent God or to His wise and benevolent official, there was no way to tell.

The surgeon himself couldn't recall the last time he'd prayed. It wasn't something one could summon up after a lifetime of disuse. So he just voiced under his breath a hope that the child be not dead but only unborn, and that at dawn its blood might flow again and its lungs draw in the morning air and it would let out its first cry. The teacher held his weightless infant in one hand, while with the other he caressed his wife's cheek, and who could say whether he ached more for one than for the other?

The surgeon turned his eyes from them and allowed them to pray and lament in peace. Returning to his surgical field, he stripped the bloodless placenta from the interior of the womb, and with careful sutures he restored everything he'd divided with his knife.

THIRTEEN

THE SURGEON RETURNED TO the corridor to find the pharmacist and her husband emptying five large bags and stacking their contents on a bench. The man had managed to bring everything—antibiotics, pain medications, sedatives, rolls of cotton and gauze, cases of gloves, syringes, needles, suturing thread, catheters, tubing for intravenous fluids, and more bags of saline than the surgeon had dared list.

"I brought the blood, too, Saheb." The pharmacist's husband opened the icebox, displayed six red packets glistening with frost.

The man's shirt was drenched. His hair, his face, were covered with dust. The pharmacist, with an embarrassed look, was trying to make him more presentable by wiping the sweat off his forehead with a handkerchief.

"I was afraid something had happened," the surgeon said. "I was beginning to wish I hadn't asked you to go."

"No, no, Saheb. Look, I'm back in one piece. No trouble

along the way. Oh, before I forget, here's the rest of your money."

He dug in his pocket and held out some notes. He was much shorter than the surgeon, barely taller than his own wife. In that moment, he looked like a schoolboy returning small change.

"Keep it."

The man looked at his palm. "I can't accept this. You're very kind to us. Too kind."

Too kind? The man had traveled to the city and back, on bicycle and by rail, at a time of night when the honest world slept and only people of ill repute roamed the streets. He had carried in his pocket a sum large enough to invite an ambush, and then lugged back these heavy supplies without a soul to help him. Now, bathed in sweat, he stood declining a reward. The surgeon felt words rise to his throat, but he couldn't force them out. Why was it so difficult for him to express true gratitude, to speak freely, perhaps even let his eyes water at this earnestness?

The money would have to suffice for now. With his left hand, he folded the man's fingers and pressed them back over the notes in his palm. His right hand he gently placed on the pharmacist's head. The young couple stood like newlyweds, heads bowed, solemn, as though before a priest sanctioning their union in a sacred place. The surgeon willed with every thread of his being that they be guarded from evil, that they be spared all torments, that they never have to know suffering. He granted them health, peace, prosperity. He knew he had no power over anything, but he still blessed them with all that was his to give, and all that wasn't.

"You must be tired. You should go home."

"No, Saheb. It's almost morning," said the pharmacist. "We can stay awake for a few more hours."

And indeed the night had almost passed. In the east there was a darkness that wasn't entirely dark. The first sparks of day were glowing against the night's edge. The birds had already awakened, and were twittering and cawing in the trees. Cowbells sounded in the village.

"I've made you some tea, Saheb. Extra strong."

He tried to smile, but the weight of what was yet to come was too great.

"Pour me a cup. I'll drink it soon."

The boy flung down his scissors and ran to his parents the moment they stepped out of the operating room. His mother was cradling a bundle in her arms. The boy peered into the small opening in the swaddling. She adjusted the drape and showed him the round face circled by green folds.

"This is your sister."

The boy studied the still face for a long time, then darted out his finger and tapped the little nose. "Why doesn't she move? Why doesn't she open her eyes?"

"She's sleeping."

"When will she wake up?"

"Soon. She'll wake up soon."

"What will we name her?"

The teacher and his wife looked at each other. The woman spoke a name. The boy whispered it to the baby. "Wake up," he said, "wake up," shaking it as though, now armed with a name, he might be able to cajole it to life. But the baby did not move. Its cheeks remained blue.

"Gentle, gentle." His mother folded a corner of the drape over the infant.

"I think it's time," said the surgeon.

In a somber and wordless procession, they followed him into the back room. He flicked on a light and saw that an extra mattress and sheet had been laid out on the floor. There was also a sturdy box padded with cloth to look like a crib. He hadn't had to ask the pharmacist for any of this; she'd done it all on her own. The teacher and his wife each sat on a bed while the son lay on the mattress on the floor. The surgeon could see the exquisite care they now took of the bandages and tubes sticking from their bodies. Maybe they too could feel how close it was, the moment when every stitch would be tested. The pharmacist and her husband waited in the doorway, and that left the surgeon at the center of the circle formed by them all.

"I'm doing something I've never done before. After all my years of preparing the living for their deaths, I now have the task of preparing the dead for life. Sunrise isn't far, and neither you nor I really know what will happen then. The angel promised you life and blood, and I don't have any reason to doubt him, but how much blood and how much life he will give you, I can't say. I only hope it'll be sufficient.

"For our part, we've done everything we could. But look at the cracks in the walls, look at the rusted bed frames. Look at where you are. You can't leave this village, so your fates are tied to this clinic. I'll do everything I can, but there's no other doctor to relieve me. And I'm not a young man. I will stay awake as long as my body allows, but at some point I'll have to stop and rest.

"I'm not saying any of this to worry you. I'm saying this so that the three of you—yes, even you, my boy—should fully understand, or at least take some time to think about, the obstacles in front of us. If dawn brings life, it will also bring everything that comes with it—pain and infection and suffering. Your wounds will try to bleed, and though I've stitched them up as well as I could, I can't promise you that every knot I've tied will hold.

"Place the baby in the crib, lie down flat on your backs, and don't try to get up. I can't afford to have you faint and fall and suffer new injuries. As soon as your blood starts flowing, I will insert cannulas into your veins, and we'll give you fluids and antibiotics. Thanks to this man—he traveled all night for you—we now have some medications to help control your pain, and sedatives to make you drowsy if needed. But beyond that I don't have much more to offer. I don't have the skills or supplies to make you unconscious. Some of you might find that you have trouble breathing. I have two oxygen tanks here, both half full, but no life-support machines to stabilize you if things get really bad. So I must ask you to endure what is beyond my ability to control. And finally, I know you're very aware of it, but I'm still going to remind you: I *don't* have any skills beyond those of a simple doctor. If your lives slip from my hands, they're gone. I won't be able to reach into the other world and pull you back.

"I've done everything I could. I just hope it will help you face what is to come."

He had closed his eyes while he spoke these last words, and when he finished, he found the teacher kneeling on the floor, shaking.

"Doctor Saheb, you have shown us more mercy than I ever hoped I would find. You, all of you, you are our saviors. As long as we live, and even beyond that, we will sing your praises to anyone who will listen. How can we repay your kindness, Saheb? I'll do whatever you want me to do, I'll work for you day and night, you won't need to pay me a single paisa. I'll help you care for your villagers. I hope they realize how blessed they are to have a saint like you among them. I know you don't like it when I say things like this, but that's what you are—a saint. More than a saint. And I can do nothing but fall at your feet."

The man dived to the ground, and the surgeon jumped back. "No, no, what is this? Don't do that." He waved the teacher back to his bed. To avoid any further ceremony, he turned without meeting the eyes of the dead.

The pharmacist and her husband were at the door to the room. "Keep a close watch," he said to them. "Call me if something happens."

The cup of tea that the girl had poured for him was still steaming on the table of the consultation room. He picked it up and stepped outside the clinic. The glow in the east had deepened, but the sun had yet to cut through the horizon. He groaned at the stabs in his knees as he sat on the steps at the entrance.

At the bottom of the hillock, the village was like a primitive engine cranking its pieces into motion. Even if, by some miracle, the dead were able to keep from screaming in pain once they came to life, the usual villagers would soon start hobbling up to the clinic. He could make the pharmacist and her husband swear to secrecy—he trusted they would hold their tongues—but how long could he keep the visitors hidden? The villagers would have questions, perfectly valid ones. Where did these people come from? Why these injuries? Someone might call the district police. There would be an inquiry.

No matter how many explanations he turned over in his head, he couldn't cook up a single one that even the stupidest of constables would find convincing. Here was how the newspapers would report this: Three corpses had been found in a village clinic. A young family. The autopsies revealed gruesome findings. All of them had tubes in their flesh, and the boy's organs had been cut out. The woman's neck had been shredded and then stitched together with row after row of sutures. Her uterus had been sliced open, her dead fetus removed and placed in a crib next to her. There was no evidence that any anesthesia was used. No trail of blood was found outside the clinic. No one had witnessed any struggle. The victims were clearly alive and intact when they reached this place. A crime of precise, horrific madness, planned and executed within the walls of this house of healing. A surgeon had become a butcher, brainwashed his superstitious assistants with tales of rebirth, and turned his clinic into a slaughterhouse.

He took short sips of his tea. It was remarkable, the detachment with which he was able to think about this mess. It was almost as though he were contemplating the misfortunes of some poor fool who'd managed to lose himself in a deranged labyrinth. *Deranged* was really the only word for this. It was impossibly deranged, like some device of torture, full of traps and locks and monstrosities . . . *dazzling*, now that he stopped to think about it. And it was exhausting, yes, dear god, all this thinking, it drained the life from every inch of his body, made his skin drape like a lead sheet over his bones.

He looked at his hands, so sore from the clamps and forceps and scalpels. There was life in them, precious little of it, but life nonetheless. The veil that separated the worlds of the living and the dead was now so thin that it might tear at the gentlest touch. Against this veil, he could feel his fingers pulse with a dull ache. And with blood—there was no separating the two, the blood and the ache, for, as he'd learned from the dead, one couldn't exist without the other. His hands, unused for so long, whose inertia had caused him so much misery, had just completed a task that no surgeon would ever face, no matter how profound his skills or resources. Everything might well be uncertain, but his accomplishment was true, and would persist even when there was no one to recall it.

Grandiose thoughts, perhaps, but he allowed himself to think them. After all, the brightness in the east was growing every minute, and the world was preparing itself for something that had never before come to pass and never again would. If ever in all of history a moment deserved philosophical meanderings, it was this one.

"Whatever will happen will happen."

With this thought he tried to rise, but the weight of the air pressed him back onto the stairs. The weight of his eyelids, too, heavier than the earth itself. He allowed himself to shut them, just for a second, just to blink himself alert, and he felt the teacup slip from his fingers.

Before him grew a tree. It was a raw bud first, then a quick sapling in damp soil. Then an eruption filled the world, gnarled and mottled bark churned out of the earth, and leaves, like fluttering moths, fled from the trunk, drawing branches and twigs in their wake until the full, familiar form of the banyan stood under a cloudy sky. He recognized it—his old, estranged friend.

A boy was effortlessly climbing the tree. From his shoulder swung a bag, empty except for a few pages of newsprint. The branches left dry scratches on his arms. His slippers flapped, caught in the leaves, and he kicked them off. Beetles, crickets, caterpillars oozed from the bark, crawled along the endless branches. The tree was trying to bewilder him. It had built a maze to conceal the nest. It was clever, but not *that* clever, and he would outwit it.

For days, there were eggs in that nest, and by now they had to have hatched. The impatient skills of a surgeon squirmed in the boy's hands. The chicks would soon be his. He would first render them inert in formaldehyde, then stretch them out on a dissection board, pin their wings and limbs with needles. And then he would bare their lungs, their livers, their hearts, with his scalpel. He would sketch diagrams in his books, unearth organs that had never before been described. The new organs would be named after him. He would be listed in textbooks. Students would memorize his name for their exams. But the tree was jealous. It wouldn't share its bounty. It tried to confuse him with its green curtains. Once or twice he went down blind alleys, slipped, and scrambled to regain his foothold. But he kept climbing.

And then suddenly there it was—the nest. He'd almost missed it in his hurry. The eggs had released their tenants into the world. The outsides of the shells were speckled with green, the insides white as ivory. The naked chicks thrashed. Twigs pricked their featherless sides, tried to warn them—they were no longer in their wombs; they should look around, beware. But they were still blind, their eyelids purple. The boy was out on the branch. It was flimsy but would support his weight. He extended his hand, cupping a piece of newspaper with which to scoop the chicks from the nest.

A crow flapped into view. It ignored him, brushed past his fingers, landed on the brim of the nest. At that sound, the nestlings balled themselves, opened their beaks, stretched their gullets. The boy pulled back his hand. The heavens opened, grub flowed from the mother's beak, and the nestlings fed. Their heads bobbed, their limbs scrabbled. And the boy allowed himself nothing more than the permission to perch on the branch and watch. Every nestling had something astonishing in it. Something that a single cut could destroy but not even a thousand stitches create.

But then the cloud that hung over the tree drifted away, dragging its shadow behind it. The lidless sun stared down. Walls of leaves keened in panic, darkened. Fire pruned them to meshes, revealed their hidden latticed veins. Spelled in them were the secret patterns of all life, glowing with a radiance he'd never known. The nest was just a ruse, a distraction the tree had used to draw his attention from the leaves themselves. He rushed to read them, to piece together this final mystery, but the sun burned everything away.

Only nest and branch remained, jutting out of a naked tree. He was trapped. There was no foothold below him. No earth to which he could ever descend. The nestlings in their charring nest weakened, dried, thinned to skeletons, and their mother flew to battle the tyrant. With her sharp beak, she pecked at the sun, cracked open its shell, swallowed a drop of its molten yolk. The morsel scalded her throat, and her eyes bulged. Her wings convulsed like a cloak in a storm, an awful wound opened in her neck—a wound that no suture could ever close, and she uttered a caw.

But the caw was not the caw of a crow. It was the cry of a human. A cry of pain or surprise, maybe even the first cry of a newborn child. The tree, the nest, the crow, the nestlings, all turned to dust, and there it was again, the village laid out before him at the foot of the hill. And above it, the yellow edge of that ancient, deathless orb, creeping over the earth's rim.

FOURTEEN

It was like being slammed against a wall, this awakening. How much time had he been under? It couldn't have been long—the sun was below the horizon one instant and above it the next—but still he'd been dragged to such depths that he felt like a diver struggling to reach the surface. He lurched, hit his shin against a bench, felt the pain crackle in his bone, but still pushed on, feeling his way against the wall.

The corridor felt longer than he'd ever known it. The sounds continued, what seemed to be wailing, or screaming, yes, that was what it was, that high-pitched sound. Then someone called out to him, the pharmacist, perhaps. Her husband was clutching the doorframe, and she was hiding behind him. He turned the corner to the back room, and the instant he reached the doorway, everything fell absolutely silent.

He closed his eyes, dropped his head, shook it from side to side to throw off the shades that kept folding over his vision. The teacher was standing by the side of his bed. There was dismay on the man's face, or something else, and his hand was held out in front of him, the wrist bent back and fingers fanned as if he were holding a blizzard at bay. The boy was on the mattress on the floor, propping himself up on a hand. When the surgeon looked at him, the boy started to lie down again, as though he'd suddenly remembered the instructions not to rise.

And then there was the woman. She was standing too. Her face was so different that the surgeon might not have recognized her were it not for the tube in her throat. It wasn't a grimace of pain, no, it was anger. Her lips were pulled back, her teeth pressed to each other. Was she the one who'd screamed? She was quiet now, though heaving with such emotion that he could hear her breath whistle through the tube.

But apart from this, none of the three looked any different. They weren't doubled over, weren't clutching their sides. They weren't fainting, falling. There were no rivers of blood. The baby in its crib was as limp as when he'd removed it from its womb.

The surgeon entered the room, and the teacher took a step back, raising his arm as though to shield himself. The surgeon grabbed the man's wrist. His own hand felt numb, as if someone had pumped it full of anesthetic, but that was just the residue of sleep still coursing through his veins.

"Stop moving," he said, and searched against the bones of the teacher's wrist. Once he'd found the spot, he held his fingers there.

There was no pulse.

He dropped the wrist, then pressed his fingers into the man's neck, poked under his jaw. Everything was still, lifeless.

With the other hand the surgeon felt his own neck, and instantly his strong, fast pulse tapped back against his fingertips.

"How? It's already dawn. Then why hasn't—"

"Ask him, Doctor Saheb, *ask* him," said the woman.

The pitch of her voice was so unlike the few meek sounds she'd made all night that he had to remind himself she was the same person.

Her husband cringed. "Maybe it will take a little more time, Saheb. It should happen any moment now, and—"

"Don't *lie*," said his wife, cutting him off in rage.

The boy jerked on the mattress at his mother's cry, drew his legs to his body, locked his arms around his knees.

"What . . . what's this? What's going on?" the surgeon asked.

The teacher kept avoiding his eyes. The woman stabbed a finger at her husband. "He just told me, Saheb. Right now, when I asked him why nothing was happening. Now, *now* he tells me, after everything—"

The man shrank under her. "Saheb, forgive me, I really didn't think this would happen, so I didn't mention it to you."

"Mention what?"

"The angel in the afterlife, he told me that things might not go exactly as planned. There could be a problem. He couldn't guarantee everything."

"Problem? What are you saying? Tell me exactly what he told you."

"The angel told us—"

"No," his wife said. "He told *you*. He didn't tell *me* anything. *You* alone."

"The angel told me that the state in which we would be sent back, this state between life and death, he told me . . . it wouldn't be easy to change us from this to living flesh. We have clots throughout our bodies—in every blood vessel, in the heart, in the brain. He would have to turn all of these to liquid and add new blood. Make it all flow. At the very same moment, he would have to bring every organ to life, all together, or we would immediately fall dead. He believed it could be done, but he'd never done it before. It was all very complicated. He tried to explain, but I didn't understand most of what he was saying. I just trusted him."

"But you didn't trust *me*." His wife was shrieking now. "You didn't tell me."

"If I'd told you, you would have refused. You wouldn't have come."

"How dare you. That's my right. I had the right to refuse. It's my life. These are my children too. You told me everything would work out without any trouble."

"That's not true. I never said that. I just . . . I didn't want you to say no just because you were afraid."

The surgeon put his hand out to shut them up. "Now tell me again, slowly this time. What exactly did the angel say? What did he say would happen if your blood didn't start flowing at dawn?"

"He said that this, our return to life, it could be delayed."

"How delayed?"

"He didn't say."

"But still, did he mean hours? Days?"

"I don't know, Saheb. I just . . . I don't know."

"So it could be months. You could just remain stuck here like this."

"No, I really . . . I can't believe that the angel would let that happen."

All the surgeon could do at this was shake his head. To have come all the way, *come back from the dead*, while leaving a question like this hanging. What could one even say about such folly?

"Did he at least tell you whether it would be the same for all of you? Or would this resurrection be more difficult for some than for others?"

Behind the teacher, the boy had been inching back along the floor. He was now cornered against the frame of his mother's bed.

The teacher pressed his eyes shut. "The angel mentioned that some of us might come to life later than the others, and there was no way for him to know which would happen when. I assumed he meant the difference would be a few minutes. I didn't give it that much thought then, didn't ask him."

An ear-splitting rasp jolted the surgeon. The woman had let herself sit down violently on the wire-frame bed, making the rusted legs scrape against the tiles. But no, nothing about her had changed. She just sat there with her palms pressed to the sides of her face, looking overwhelmed.

The surgeon's breath now drove through his nostrils in short, hot bursts. "All night, every time you opened your mouth, you spoke about the dawn. Nothing else. Not a word about this."

"I'm sorry, Doctor Saheb, I . . . really, I'm sorry."

"You didn't think I deserved to know any of this?"

"Saheb, I didn't want to complicate things. I hoped everything would go according to plan."

"You decided to give me just enough information to keep me working, so that I would do whatever you needed."

"No, Saheb, please don't say that. I trusted the angel. What else could I do?"

As abruptly as she'd dropped onto the bed, the woman now snapped to her feet and smoothed the gown that had bunched around her neck. Her face was stony. "I'm going," she said, a ghastly edge to her voice.

Her husband looked suffocated with fear. "Where?"

"Back." She reached into the crib, snatched up her infant. Its lifeless head rolled back, swaying against the side of her palm. She flung her other arm in her son's direction. "Come."

The boy cowered against the bed.

"Come," she said again, but the boy just stared back, frozen on the floor.

She took two steps in his direction. The baby flopped in her hand. The pharmacist stepped from behind the surgeon, her hands held as though ready to catch the child if it should fall.

The woman now stretched her neck into forbidden angles as she bent down to grab her son. The boy's hands were bunched into fists. He dug them close to his body, hid them between his legs, behind his back. After trying a few times to find and grasp his fingers, she forced her hand into his armpit, tried to pull him up.

"Where are you going?" the surgeon asked.

"To the village boundary."

The teacher now looked like a madman. "No. No, you can't do that."

"Why? That's better than this. Better than not knowing what will happen."

"But then, then, why did we even come here?"

"Because you tricked us." The woman's hair was smeared across her face. She tried to brush it away but couldn't, not with the infant in one arm and her son struggling in the other. "Since the moment we reached the afterlife, returning here was all you could think of. I was trying to console myself, console us: now we're here, let's accept what we have, it's not as bad as you kept saying it was, let's take what God has given us and trust Him. But you? All you could think of was coming back to life. And for what? So that some of us could live and some of us die again? At least there we were all together."

She dragged the boy to his feet.

"Baba, Baba." He clutched at the frame of the bed.

"Stop this. Stop right now," said the surgeon, but even his voice couldn't stay her. She tugged at her son until his fingers lost their grip on the metal rod. Her strength, her savagery, were astonishing. The surgeon tried to block her path.

"Please, just stop and think about this."

"Saheb, I know what it's like to have my neck cut. To die. When he first started talking about this, this new life, I was so afraid of what we would have to go through. But I agreed, because I thought it would just be one night of waiting, and at the end of it we would endure whatever was in our fate. But now what's left? Just this fear. It's morning. Soon it will be afternoon, then night. And what are we supposed to do, Saheb?

Wait for the pain? Lie down here until our bandages become wet with blood? No, I don't want to live like this. It won't be life. It will be worse than death. The afterlife might be bad, but not like this. I won't let my children suffer."

The teacher forced himself past his wife. "Please, just listen to me, I did what I thought was best. For us, for all of us."

"Come with us if you want. All of us can go back."

"You want to kill yourself? Kill our children?"

"Kill? How can I kill them? What's left in us to kill?"

The boy yanked his body back, snapped free of his mother's hold. She clawed at him, but her nails just scratched his skin as he fell back.

"Come, my baby, take my hand. Come with me."

The boy crawled away from her on all fours, quailed in the corner of the room, his body pressed against the wall. He shook his head in terror.

"Please, just think a little," the surgeon said to her. "Think about what you're doing."

The woman's face crumpled. With her fingers still splayed out, reaching across the room to her son, her eyes and lips twisted into a hideous, soundless wail.

The pharmacist tiptoed forward, slipped one hand under the infant's neglected head, the other under its buttocks, and the woman released it, slumped on the bed with her fingers like prison bars before her eyes, her nails digging into her scalp. The pharmacist's hands trembled as she replaced the corpse in its crib, and then, with a quiet motion, she slid the box along the floor and put some distance between mother and child.

It was a wonder the commotion hadn't yet brought every villager to the clinic. The surgeon looked around, but the corridor was empty except for the pharmacist's husband, who was standing outside the room with a look of bewilderment and fear. The portion of the hillock visible from the windows of the back room was fresh and serene in the morning.

The teacher returned to his bed and sat turned away from everyone, the weight of his body on an angled arm. He shielded his eyes with his free hand.

"Is there anything else?" the surgeon asked.

The man's hand remained where it was, concealing whatever shape guilt had given his features.

"Is there anything else you haven't told me?"

Through all this, the man had been protecting the jar connected to his chest. Air bubbled through it now with unseemly vigor.

"There's something more, isn't there? Put your hand on your son's head."

"Saheb, please try to understand, please don't—"

The surgeon's eyelids were turning unbearably heavy again. Despite all this chaos, they kept dragging him down to some foggy abyss. There was a sickly shade to everything: the walls, the sunlight, the dead. They darkened, grew murkier, every time he blinked. He couldn't deal with these abominations anymore. He just needed to fall on his own bed and lose consciousness.

"Swear on your son's head. Swear on the life you want him to have that there's nothing else I need to know."

The teacher now turned like a criminal at an inquest. His

face looked stretched across his cheekbones, his eyes seemed set deep under his eyebrows.

"Doctor Saheb, I should never have agreed, I should've said no when the angel told me."

"Told you what?"

"I know now, I should have refused his offer there and then—"

"Stop talking in circles and get to the bloody point."

The teacher's head sank into his shoulders. He raised his hands as if he were expecting his next words to be met with violence.

"The angel said that if something went really wrong, if there was a real risk that our secret might be exposed, he would have to pull us back to the afterlife. And with us, any living people who were involved in this."

A high-pitched ring rose in the surgeon's ears over a painful silence, as if his hearing had, at that moment, been deadened by fireworks. He strained to make sense of the teacher's words, but no matter how hard he tried, he couldn't force them into a coherent sentence.

"What—"

"Saheb, I didn't think about how—"

"Any living person? But that means—"

"You are good people. I had no right—"

"You gambled with our *lives*. Without even knowing who we were."

"No, Saheb, no, please, that's not how it happened. I was desperate. I was willing to do anything for my family. No one would ever have offered us anything like this again. I had to make a decision—it was then or never. I didn't think, I didn't consider how it would affect others, Saheb. I did an awful thing, but please don't blame my wife, my son. They didn't know any of this."

"You . . . you dared to talk to me about justice, about how unfair your deaths were—"

"I thought everything would go as planned, Saheb. I didn't expect any trouble. Even now, nothing bad has happened. We could come to life any minute, and then everything can just go on as it would."

The man's naïveté was horrifying. The surgeon felt a cold thrust in his marrow, a pressure in all his bones, the greatest in his skull. Behind him, the pharmacist gasped. He heard it, but couldn't bring himself to look back at her. He curled his fingers around the free edge of the door panel to steady himself, but it swung and slammed against the wall with a loud thud, and he stumbled back with it. The teacher's body was convulsing, with sobs, it might be said, but the dryness of his eyes, the tearless contortions, they were all too macabre to have any real meaning. It was as though the night had started all over again: the dead had just appeared with their mad predicament, and he was at the mercy of it all.

"Call your angel."

The man seemed not to hear him at first, and then his face flattened into a stare.

"He responds to your summons, right? Summon him now."

"But, Saheb, that was in the afterlife. He can't come here."

"You told me they could if they wanted to."

"Doctor Saheb, please understand. The angel can't . . . *won't* come to this village."

"Then what are we supposed to do? None of you know what's going to happen. Only the angel knows."

"But he won't—"

"You fucking fool, why are you wasting my time arguing? After everything you've done? Just summon him."

The teacher seemed to wither under the surgeon's fury. He slowly rose from the bed, joined his shaking hands together, pressed them to his lips.

Then he shut his eyes and started muttering, reciting some prayer in a tongue that the surgeon couldn't recognize. It went on and on. The man didn't stop for breath—of course he had no need for it, he could very well continue this till the sun was doused and the moon ground back to dust. The surgeon felt a sudden, racking chill at the thought of a celestial being actually appearing in his clinic, glowing like a firefly. What would he do then? Plead for his life and the lives of the others, beg for pity from this being that probably considered him no more worthy of life than a cockroach?

But nothing changed. Even the air stayed completely still. The surgeon looked around, and saw that the boy was still in the corner of the room. He was hugging his knees to his face, his head bent so that his terrified eyes peered through the mess of hair on his brow. His mother's face was turned away toward the far wall, whether from anger or shame or grief, there was no way to tell. Or maybe because she couldn't bear to see this, the figure of her humiliated husband in his useless prayer. A miserable rhythm had entered the man's recitation by now, the same incoherent string of syllables rising and sinking from the waves.

The surgeon turned. The pharmacist pulled back behind her husband. Their faces were pale, and there was reproach in their eyes, or at least that's what he saw. *You dragged us into this, Saheb*, he heard, but neither of them had spoken. There was no assurance he could give them now, so he just looked past them and walked into the corridor.

A few syringes, still in their plastic packaging, were strewn across the floor. They'd probably spilled from their boxes when he hit his shin against the bench. At that memory, the pain returned, and he bent, felt the spot with his finger. His trouser leg was wet there. The spilling of morning blood by the wrong character in this farce. The omen of death. The wait couldn't be long now. A few hours at the most. What would it be like to die at the whim of a bureaucrat? A brisk, banal leaving from a body that would then fall and fracture itself, at which point who cared—once you're dead, you're dead, no matter what anyone promises you. But the girl and her husband, for it to happen to them . . . No, it was too horrible even to consider. If there were to be deaths, he should die thrice, but not them, God, not them.

Tears formed under his eyelids, but he was tired, too tired, and they couldn't even wet his eyes, not even when he tried to massage them out with his palms. The muttering continued in the back room. It hadn't stopped even after he'd left their presence. It was idiotic, absurd beyond words, to expect an official of the afterlife to report to the insects of the earth. The entrance to the clinic was just a few feet away, so the surgeon stumbled to it. Who knew, perhaps the air there would be easier to pull into his lungs?

And that's when he saw. Some distance away, on the gravel path leading up to the clinic, the official. The one who had brought the polio vaccines the previous afternoon.

FIFTEEN

THE SURGEON FELT HIS innards churn with a sickening rush. He tried to convince himself that he was mistaken, but there was no doubt about it. It was the same official. As far as he could tell, the man was even in the same blue safari jacket he'd worn the previous day.

The official looked back at him, and the surgeon passed his gaze over the horizon as though he were just examining the morning landscape. Then he turned as calmly as he possibly could and walked to the back room.

The pharmacist and her husband were squatting outside the door, huddled against each other. The teacher was still standing in closed-eyed recitation. The woman, the boy, the newborn—all were just as he had left them.

The surgeon had to force the words from his throat. "All of you, listen very carefully. I won't repeat this. Lock yourself in and don't make a sound. And don't come out until I call you, no matter what happens."

The teacher stopped his prayer, returned to the surgeon a look that was initially blank but then curdled with shock. "How—" he began, but nothing else emerged from his lips. His hands remained where they were, the fingertips touching in front of his chest. He was taking too long to collect his senses, and his wife rose from her bed, swung shut the leaves of the door, slid home the bolt.

The pharmacist began to pull her husband into the pharmacy.

"Not there," said the surgeon, pointing out the open window in the front wall.

So the two stole to the other side of the corridor, past the autoclave machine, and into the operating room. The surgeon couldn't remember if he'd left the placenta lying on a tray there, but it was too late to worry about that now. The door closed behind the girl and her husband.

It would be better if he were seated when he faced the official, the surgeon decided. It would rid his legs of the obligation to be steady. On a whim he happened to glance at the autoclave, and saw the small red light glowing on its lid. At the very thought of its unpredictable shriek, he flipped off the wall switch and pulled out the plug.

A crunch sounded outside the clinic before he could reach the consultation room, and so he stayed in the corridor and turned to face the entrance. His fingers knotted behind his back, he straightened himself to his full height. Biting the back of his lower lip to still the quiver in his jaw, he tried to settle his forehead into some expression of bland and appropriate surprise. Before he could achieve any of this, the official appeared, framed in the doorway, the sky at his back.

"Good morning, Doctor Saheb. Hard at work, I can see."

He climbed up the few steps at the door.

"Quite a strange decision. Whoever it was that drew up the plans for this clinic, why did they put it high up on a hillock like this? The sicker your patients are, the less likely they are to make it to this place. A clinic only for the healthy, eh?"

The official didn't appear winded by the climb. That said, he wasn't carrying any boxes today. He cast a look around the corridor, at the supplies piled on the benches, the packets on the floor.

Now the surgeon had to say something, play host on this morning that was proving more grotesque than the night that preceded it. He unlocked his fingers from behind himself and gestured to the consultation room.

"Would you like some tea? I had made a kettle for myself."

The official showed no sign he'd noticed the tremor in the surgeon's voice. "Yes, why not?"

The surgeon led the way into the room, his back as stiffly held as when he'd received the official. The pharmacist had left the kettle on the side table as always. He poured a cup.

"You look tired, Saheb."

The surgeon hadn't glanced into a mirror since the previous morning, but he could imagine how darkly the night had shaded the folds around his eyes.

"I have to say," the official said, "this is quite a change from the welcome you gave me yesterday."

The surgeon placed the cup on the official's side of the table. The tea was lukewarm—no steam curling up from the surface. His own teacup, he now remembered, was somewhere on the gravel outside the clinic entrance. His chair gave its familiar creak under his weight, and his fingertips left moist oval smudges on the plate of glass on his desk. There were things flattened under it—yellowed receipts, scraps with faded scribbles, flowers with their anthers spread out.

"How did the drive go, Saheb?"

"The drive?"

"The vaccines. Did you end up using them all?"

"Yes, all."

"Good, that's good. It's to be admired, what you do here, and with so little."

"I try."

"There aren't too many surgeons working in broken-down clinics like this."

"Hmm."

"It must be difficult, working in this place."

"Difficult, yes."

"Especially with you having to spend from your pocket to stock the pharmacy."

"Yes."

"Unfortunate that you have to balance your needs against those of the clinic."

"I do what I can."

The official had settled in his chair, his soft, full hands folded on his belly. His nails were small and circular, with neat crescent edges. A second chin occasionally formed under his face when he spoke. He hadn't touched his tea.

"You've heard the story of the Brahmin and the Ganga, haven't you, Doctor Saheb?"

"Uh . . ."

"I'm sure you have. Maybe you've forgotten it. In any case, here it is. There once was a poor Brahmin who lived all alone. As the years went by, his spine bent from age, his hair turned white, and the time came when he knew he would die. Now he had only one wish: to bathe in the water of the Ganga before he closed his eyes for the last time.

"But our Brahmin had never left his little village. What did *he* know about the world? Someone told him that the Ganga was to the north. So this poor man sold all his belongings, settled his debts, and set off with a stick and a bundle of food.

"After half a day's walk, he reached a small stream. He put down his bundle, dipped his hands in the water, and started to pour it over his head.

"A farmer from his village happened to be walking to the market. He recognized the Brahmin and asked, 'Washing your clothes?'

"'No, I'm cleansing myself,' replied the Brahmin. 'This water from Gangotri, it will wash my sins away. Then I can die in peace.'

"'But this isn't the Ganga,' the farmer said. 'This is just a little stream. The Ganga is much farther away.'

"So the Brahmin, weak as he was, gathered up his things

and hobbled along. The hot ground burned his feet. For every hour he walked, he had to rest for two more.

"Two days went by, and he came to a river. He said his prayers, bowed to God, and entered the water. A shepherd on the riverbank asked, 'Why are you praying here, grandfather?'

"'My son, I'm washing my sins away,' said the Brahmin. 'I'm preparing myself for death.'

"'Washing sins? In *this* water? This is just a small river, grandfather. It feeds our fields, nothing more. If you're looking for the Ganga, you should keep walking.'

"The Brahmin had so little strength left, but what else could he do? He begged along the way for food to keep his soul tied to his body. He had to stop and rest his bones every few minutes now—under trees, under large rocks, any place he could find.

"A few days later, he reached another river—a wide and mighty one. He waded into it with tears flowing down his cheeks. So great was his joy that all the pain racking his body seemed to vanish. With all his faith and devotion, he said his final prayers, bathed in the water, and purified himself.

"A fisherman passing in his canoe cried out, 'Watch out, old man. You'll drown if you aren't careful.'

"The Brahmin smiled. 'We all have to die someday. Me much sooner than you. Drowning in the Ganga would be a blessing. It would take me straight to heaven.'

"The fisherman laughed so hard that his canoe almost tipped over. 'The *Ganga*? You toothless fool. Who told you this was the Ganga? This river is nothing, just a tributary. Go, cross the bridge and keep walking northward.'

"By now, the Brahmin had become so ill that he could hardly breathe. Every step he took made him feel lightheaded. His skin burned with fever, no food or water would go down his throat. He knew death wasn't far.

"A crowd of people joined the road. They were dressed well, all in a festive mood. 'Why are you so happy?' the Brahmin asked a boy in the group.

"'Because we're all going for a dip in the Ganga,' the boy said. 'It's very close now.'

"The old Brahmin was filled with despair, because he knew it was too late. He swung forward on his stick, as fast as he could go, and tried to keep up with the other travelers, but they passed him one by one. His legs became heavy as grindstones. The Ganga, the real one this time, blue and immense, stretched out at the horizon. But the fever had spread through his whole body, and there was a crushing pain in his chest. His stick slipped from his hand, and he fell on the mud, dead.

"His soul left his body and reached the other world. He stood in front of Chitragupta, who was there with his book of sins and virtues.

"The Brahmin cried, 'O great Lord, I couldn't cleanse myself. I'm full of sin. Send me to the underworld if you wish, for I was unable to bathe in the Ganga.'

"All Chitragupta said was, 'Ah, my son, but you're mistaken,' and he opened the door to welcome the Brahmin into heaven.

"That's the story, Doctor Saheb. Quite a touching one, wouldn't you agree? Now tell me, what would you say is the moral of this tale?"

On any ordinary day, the hectoring tone of this fable would have enraged the surgeon. Even now, he could barely believe he'd just allowed himself to sit there and be spoken to for so long in such a condescending tone. But when he tried to reply, he found he could only mumble.

"The moral? Even a stream can . . . can be as holy as the Ganga if . . . if you have faith. Is that what you want me to say?"

The official raised his forefinger with a lecturer's air. "That's what everyone thinks. You're not the only one to come up with this optimistic interpretation. But let me suggest something else. I've thought about this tale a lot, and I've realized that the true moral is actually quite different. It's that there is no Ganga."

"No Ganga?"

"Well, of course there's the river that starts at Gangotri, joins the Yamuna, empties into the ocean, all of that. But the Ganga that the Brahmin was looking for, the one that can wash away sins—it simply doesn't exist. There's nothing in its waters that gives it any magical powers. You know that, Saheb, as well as I do."

"So that's the moral? That there's no way to wash away your sins?"

"Not exactly. It's that everything about sin lies in how you choose to look at it. The Brahmin chose to believe he was washing his sins away, even though it was in a minor river. It was a compromise, but it was the best he could do, and, as it turned out, it was good enough for Chitragupta. That's what we're all limited to, you and I—compromises. There is no Ganga. You just pick a river and decide that its water is holy. And then it's better if you don't look back."

This new blend of delirium and fear the surgeon felt made even the terrors of the previous night seem mundane. Perhaps this was why the heads of the condemned were covered with sacks, so that they might be spared the horror of a final conversation with the executioner while the noose was being adjusted.

"Tell me, Saheb, what river have you chosen in life?"

"I just . . . I try my best to help. Help those who come to me."

"And what do you expect out of it? For yourself?"

"Nothing much anymore. Only that I be allowed to live my life. That the people who work for me not be harmed."

"That's it? A balance of lives? That's how you think about it?"

"I try not to, but there are times."

"And tell me, if you find yourself in a position where you have to harm someone to preserve your own life, what would you do?"

"Choose the just path. I hope I would have the courage."

"And what would the just path be?"

"It would depend on the circumstance."

"A different river each time?"

"If you insist on that word, then yes."

"And how would you choose between them?"

"As you said just a minute ago, you just pick one and decide that its water is holy."

The surgeon said this in as a grim a tone as possible, but somehow it still amused the official enough to make him slap his hand on his thigh. "Very clever, Doctor Saheb. My own words turned back against me. Very clever."

The suffocating coils of sleep, even at a time like this,

draped around the surgeon's muscles, folded over his brain. Whatever was to happen, no matter how terrible, he hoped it would happen soon. But the official showed no sign that he wanted to stop speaking.

"Tell me, Saheb, do you believe in God?"

"Me? No. I've . . . I've never been God-fearing."

"God-fearing . . . Hmm. People use the term all the time, but it's a strange one if you stop to think about it. Especially since God is supposed to be everywhere—in the earth, in the sky. But people don't spend their lives fearing the earth and sky."

"Maybe they should."

"But you see, when the earth or sky kills you, it does so indiscriminately, without making any plans. God, on the other hand, He has a mind, He thinks. That's what makes Him worthy of fear. Because no one knows what He's planning. So you play games with Him, try to understand His mind."

"Play a game with God? How do you do that?"

"Well, you can't. If you set up a chessboard on the street and challenge God, He won't come down to move His pieces. But a passerby might. That's how the game begins. And the passerby is already playing other games. He's quarreling with his brother over their father's will, extracting a loan from a bank, looking to fondle some woman's breasts without having to hang a mangalsutra between them. Each game is small, but they're all pieces of larger games, and the largest one, the one that contains them all, that's the game you play with God."

His life and the lives of everyone else in the clinic were in the hands of this unhinged official. And it wasn't just drowsiness he was feeling. It was a slippage into nonexistence—the world and everything in it scattering to pieces that no one, not even God, could ever put back together. The official kept talking about the stupidity of the pious: "holy threads around their bodies, eating certain foods on certain days, smearing ash on their foreheads," about how God despised worship: "The villagers who fawn over you, Doctor Saheb, do you feel anything for them but contempt?," about the mind of God: "He places puzzles in the world so that He can understand it better." The surgeon had been under anesthesia only once in his life, when his gall bladder was removed. What he was feeling now was no different from how he'd felt in the moments after propofol was injected into his vein. He selected a red spot on a scrap of paper on the desk, tried to keep its redness burning into his retina. The world couldn't dissolve, he declared, as long as he kept this redness from leaching out. A single mind, if it wanted, could hold all of existence to ransom with a single red spot.

". . . All you can do is play His games. That's why God keeps the universe going: to see what new moves he can learn from His creatures." The official adjusted himself in his chair. A smile spread under his mustache. "And death, that's the most ingenious of all His games. You've made your share of moves in that one, haven't you, Saheb?"

A bead of sweat cut a slow path down the side of the surgeon's face. When he saw the official's eyes follow it from brow to cheek, he wiped it away with a quick brush of his palm. On the official's face itself, there wasn't a trace of moisture. And his skin was smooth, incredibly smooth.

"You haven't had your tea. Please. It must be growing cold."

"I will, I will," said the official, without making any effort to reach for the cup. His mustache, his hair, were a deep, un-natural black.

"And what is this? Is this a game as well?"

"This, Saheb? You mean my visit?"

"Yes. Why are you here?"

"I have as much of a right to be here as you. Tell me, why did you decide to become a surgeon?"

"I . . . I don't even know anymore."

"Still, why?"

"It seemed, during my training, that holding a diseased organ in my hand and cutting it out, it was a straightforward way of doing things."

"That makes sense, yes. And tell me, what gives you greater satisfaction, cutting people open or stitching them back?"

"What?"

"Of all the creatures on earth, only humans can put things back together. But the ability to tear flesh apart—God gave it to every beast roaming in the jungle. So there must be something to it, some animal pleasure. Like eating and drinking. Or sex. It must fulfil some basic need."

"What a *horrible*—"

"I'm just asking. You have skills that I don't. So I can only learn these things through you. I like to ask questions, understand new things. Tell me, when you cut someone open, do you feel a thrill?"

"Stop, that's just, you can't—"

"To lower your hands into someone's body and know that you hold their lives in the snip of a scissor, it must give you such a sense of power."

"No, no—"

"What do you feel during surgery, then? Answer me."

"Fear, it's fear. Above everything else."

"Ah. Fear of what?"

"What do you want?"

"You can't just have fear. It has to be fear of something."

"What do you want from me?"

"Your surgical skills, are you satisfied with what they've brought you?"

The surgeon's lips, his tongue, scratched against each other now, rough as sandpaper. The official leaned forward.

"Whatever you're feeling, Saheb, it's quite understandable. It can't be an easy thing, accepting that someone you treated like a rat yesterday has more power over you today than you could have imagined."

The official now picked up the cup. The tea was clearly cold by now, but he still blew on its surface before taking a sip. "You see, after our little meeting yesterday, I went straight to the head office to take a look at your file. You were such an unusual character, I had to learn your story, find out how someone like you ended up here. There are rooms upon rooms there, you can imagine, cabinets to the ceiling. It took me all evening, but I found it just as I was ready to give up."

The surgeon's nerves, the strands of his hair, all stabbed like copper barbs. His eyes felt intensely clear.

"You know a lot about compromise, don't you, Saheb? People like you, you stand over others and lecture them about integrity, and then when it's time to save your own skin, you soil your hands in the same dung. Your file is quite thick, I'm sure you know. Newspaper clippings, court records, all those things.

"At one level, I don't blame you. Look, mistakes happen. If I were in your place, I would have tried to bribe that other surgeon as well. When a patient is dead, he's dead, it's bad enough. Why rake up trouble for the doctor on top of that? But you never know what the person on the other side will be like. Unlucky for you that your opponent ended up being a disciple of Gandhi."

The surgeon studied the flowers flattened under the glass, their dry, brown, dead petals.

"All these supplies in the corridor, Saheb, they weren't here yesterday when I checked. You'd hidden them somewhere. Just like you're hiding that dealer in the back room right now. Look, I'm an understanding man. I know they don't pay you enough. Selling supplies under the table, everyone does it— you're not the only one, I'm not judging you. But they don't pay me enough either. Not enough for me to keep my mouth shut when I see something like this."

A slow, heavy drip gathered in the surgeon's gullet, swelled painfully behind his breastbone. The official finished his tea, wiped off a few drops hanging from his mustache, and sat straight in his chair. His fleshy face beamed.

"It's all up to you. If you think I'm just bluffing, then fine, I'll make some calls, and my colleagues and I, we'll make a detailed search and inventory of the clinic, go through all past records, interview the villagers about suspicious activity, all the routine stuff. I'm a decent man. I can keep my mouth shut. But I can't promise you that the other officials won't let something slip to the villagers about your past."

The surgeon reached into his back pocket. "Here."

The official looked at the two notes the surgeon had held out. "I have a wife and children, Saheb. My daughters are yet to be married. Whatever we think of this world, we still have to live in it."

The surgeon blinked at the money, then stuffed the notes back into his wallet. As he rose from his chair, a sharp pain pulled at his spine, and he stayed that way for a few seconds, stuck in that awkward pose. Then he limped to the safe and turned the lock. There was just one bundle in it, and a few scattered notes. He pulled out the bundle.

There was no way for the surgeon to know if he'd overshot the usual amount for this sort of bribe. The official probably had enough practice with such dealings that he could keep his eyelids steady in a sandstorm. He took the bundle and started counting through it with the elegance of a bank teller.

"Promise me I won't see your face again," said the surgeon.

A softness entered the official's manner, ripened with his progress through the bundle. "I wish I could promise you that, Saheb, but I've been assigned to this clinic. Unless they replace me, it's my job to check in once in a while. From your point of view, it's good it's me and not someone else, because who knows what my replacement might be like? But let me promise you this: you won't see me for many months, let's say six. I won't stop by, I won't let any other official bother you, and what's more, I'll make sure all of your supplies are delivered without a hitch. Then you can do whatever you want with them, and put down in your account books whatever you like. I'll just rubber-stamp them."

Now done with his counting, the official folded the notes into a pocket in the lining of his trouser waist. He joined his palms to each other and made an exaggerated bow. And then he left. Feeling his eyelashes dampen, the surgeon turned to the wall.

"I almost forgot, Saheb."

The official was in the doorway again, pointing at the polio vaccine ledger that lay shut at the edge of the desk. The same ledger whose columns the surgeon had been filling with numbers and calculations before the dead first appeared. That was why the official had returned to the clinic this morning: to collect the ledger and file it away in the head office. The man stood there as though expecting the book to be handed to him, but after a few moments passed in silence, he stepped in, picked it up without bothering to check its pages, and stepped over the blister-packed syringes in the corridor on his way out.

SIXTEEN

THE HAZE OF MORNING seemed to give even the peeling paint a surreal air, making it appear as though the clinic were casting off its old skin in an attempt at rebirth. A particularly large flake hung from the ceiling of the consultation room like an icicle. The surgeon let his eyes rest on it between glances at the window. Watching the official's diminishing form was like staring into the sun—he could endure only a few moments of it before he had to turn his eyes away. There was a final insult in the man's indifferent gait, in the way he strode without looking back, without a shred of further curiosity about the clinic or its contents. At the base of the hillock, the road curved, and the official disappeared behind a crumbling wall.

"He's gone," the surgeon called out. A weariness of death and of everything on either side of it filled him.

The operating room was the first to open, and the pharmacist appeared at his door. "What did he want, Saheb?"

"Nothing. Some paperwork."

The way the pharmacist was staring at him, the expression

on her face, it made the surgeon wonder if he too had joined the ranks of the dead. Under the table, he placed the fingers of one hand on the wrist of the other. He still had a pulse.

Then the door to the back room opened. The teacher approached with a shuffling walk. He seemed to be in great pain, though not from his wounds. Nothing had changed there.

"Doctor Saheb, I don't know how to . . . I don't have any words, but please forgive me, please understand why—"

The teacher's jaw moved as he spoke, as did the flesh and skin of his face, all dead, of course, but imitating life with a terrible talent that the surgeon knew he would never understand as long as he lived. No amount of pondering would help, nor rummaging through ribs or guts. Perhaps that was why one died: so that one could finally fathom death.

"Close the door," the surgeon said.

The pharmacist and her husband remained in the corridor as the teacher pushed the door shut after him. The man sank to his knees, and the jar attached to the tube in his chest clattered to a halt beside him. He seemed to be searching the surgeon's eyes for compassion, but the surgeon wasn't sure he had any left.

"The official you told me about while I was operating on you—not the one who sent you here, the other one, the one who was punished because he gave all those unnatural powers to humans—were you telling the truth about him?"

"Yes, Saheb, all true. I told you exactly what he said to me."

"Now think very carefully, and answer me only after you've taken the time to do so. Is there any possibility that you lied to me about this other official? Is there any possibility that the official who sent you here and the official who was toying with humans, they were one and the same, and you just cooked up a new character to conceal that part of his past?"

"I swear, I promise you, they were different. Completely different."

It was a pity, thought the surgeon, that he would never be able to trust the teacher again, no matter how much sincerity the man put into his words.

"And the official who sent you here, is it possible that he's toying with you, and with me? That we're all puppets, and he's just entertaining himself?"

The man didn't blurt out an answer this time. This question was clearly not entirely foreign to his thoughts.

"When the official offered to help us, I have to admit that my first fear was that this was some kind of trap. But why would he play with us like this? What could he gain from it?"

"Does a puppeteer need a purpose?"

"With lives, Saheb? How cruel would he have to be?"

"Have you ever seen a cockfight? There was one in this village a few months ago. They attached knives to the roosters' feet."

"The official wouldn't do that to us, I'm telling you. He isn't that kind of person."

"He *isn't* a person."

The surgeon reached for the cup from which the earthly official had drunk. It was empty except for a sediment of tea powder at its bottom. One could read the future in it, or so he'd heard. He rolled the cup in his fingers, wondering whose future it was supposed to be—his or the official's.

"I don't know what's worse," he said. "A bureaucracy that forces you to bribe, or one in which bribery isn't even an option."

"Saheb, there's at least one official in the afterlife who's willing to break unjust rules. Someone who is kind. Maybe there are more."

"Yes, and look at what his kindness has brought you."

"It's helped us meet you, Saheb. Even if we die again this very moment, we would still be blessed by the hours we've spent in the presence of a great man."

The obsequious way the teacher kept twisting his fingers into coils aggravated the surgeon. He walked the teacup to the side table. If he were to smash it, it would just create shards for the pharmacist to sweep up. It was a sign of cowardice anyway, the venting of anger on inanimate things. The surgeon let the cup clatter onto the tray.

"When you speak this kind of nonsense," he spat, "it just makes me wonder if you have more lies to reveal, if you're fattening me with flattery before you betray me again."

The teacher recoiled at these words. His pathetic expression infuriated the surgeon further.

"Maybe I should just announce this in the village square? 'Gather around, O villagers, and listen to me. The dead are here to live, or rather, remain dead, among us. Let's welcome them into our community.'"

"I really, Saheb . . . I don't know if it's a good idea to even think about something like that. The official might be forced to kill everyone—"

"How the fuck does it matter? We're slaves in both worlds

either way. And your official wouldn't dare kill a whole village, would he? Maybe that's what I should do: announce this to the villagers right away, and then the officials, for once, won't have a choice—"

"Please, Saheb, please don't say that. The official is listening to everything, I'm sure—"

The surgeon was in a state beyond sleep now. It was a dense, saturating daze from which there could be no sleeping or awakening. He collapsed back into his chair.

"What the *hell* am I supposed to do with you people, then?"

The teacher looked shattered. "My wife was right. We should never have come."

"Yes, you shouldn't have. You should have stayed where you were."

"We'll go, Saheb. We don't want to make any more trouble for you."

The surgeon slammed his hands on the desk and planted his brow on the backs of his knuckles. He blew his breath out against the glass in frustration.

"Yes, keep coming up with more ridiculous ideas like that. Even if you make it to the village boundary without being seen, you'll still leave your bodies behind. With the surgeries you've had, no matter what happens, everything will be traced back to me. And *I'll* be the one who'll die in prison."

There was a long silence. And then the teacher spoke, his words so muted that the surgeon had to strain to hear them.

"We could . . . Saheb, if you know of any abandoned well, somewhere outside the village . . . Or I could help you dig a hole at night. Like a grave . . ."

The surgeon did not lift his face from the glass. And he did not reply. To his shock, his tongue did not lash out to reject the offer the moment it was spoken. Yes, he knew of a spot near the southern edge of the village, behind a decrepit temple that no one visited because the idol in it was said to be cursed. And yes, there was a secluded path to it from the clinic, down the side of the hillock farthest from the farms and huts.

He couldn't involve the pharmacist and her husband in this, of course. They'd done so much, and might be willing to do more, but he couldn't ask *this* of them. This would have to be his doing and his alone. After midnight, he would have to tiptoe with the dead to the thicket behind the temple. If they were careful, they could manage the journey without being seen. Yes, graves would have to be dug. Deep ones, capable of guarding their secrets. The teacher would have to do most of the digging—he was the younger, stronger man. He would have to ready the earth for the task of swallowing his family.

And then the surgeon would lead the dead to the village boundary. There they would drop. Return to their true forms. Become corpses like any other. Then they would have to be dragged. Pushed into graves. Soil would have to be shoveled over them.

The hypnotic horror of this contemplation was unfolding in the face of the surgeon's efforts to stop it. With the force of a hurricane, it was ripping through every vestige of sanity and decency in his brain. Ever since the dead had appeared in his clinic, he'd spent every minute in detailed planning. Every cut, every stitch, every surgical instrument—he had outlined and rationed them all. How was he supposed to switch off this faculty? Especially now, at the end of all things?

And indeed a logistical problem was already presenting itself: where exactly *was* the boundary of the village? There were stone markers at a few spots where one village ended and another began, but what was the precise location at which the dead would turn inanimate? Did the boundaries marked by the government correspond exactly to those respected by the afterlife? This question had to be answered before the graves could be dug. Otherwise, who knew what distance he'd have to drag their bodies?

It meant that one of the dead would have to walk ahead of the others. Like a canary meant to be snuffed. A mother couldn't be expected to endure the demise of her son. And a boy couldn't be asked to witness it of his parents. The man couldn't be the first to go, for he had to remain capable of digging. The best option was for mother and son to walk together. She would want to carry her infant. Step after step they would advance, the moon lighting their path. Ten paces behind them would follow the teacher. And the surgeon would trail them all, so that he wouldn't have to look upon the face of the father at the moment when his beloved ones crumpled to the ground.

The surgeon sat up with a jerk. The teacher, still kneeling on the floor before him, started at the movement. On the man's face was a gathering horror. The surgeon couldn't quite tell if the teacher had been serious when he'd offered his suggestion, but it was clear that he could see now that it was the only way forward. Perhaps he too understood what would be required of him.

And the surgeon saw in that instant the depths of his own degradation. How completely his soul had been eroded, how the years had torn the stuffing out of his humanity and left him hollow. He should never have become a surgeon. He should have remained a coroner. His place had always been with the dead who remained dead. Those who lay on slabs and did not speak. Who asked nothing of him and to whom he owed nothing.

A voice called from the corridor. "S—Saheb, Saheb."

It was the pharmacist. Neither the surgeon nor the teacher moved. There was a sound of knuckles rapping against wood, but neither of them responded. The rapping grew louder, more urgent. The surgeon finally stood, and the teacher shifted aside, his face averted, as the surgeon walked to the door. By the time he opened it, the pharmacist had already turned and was running to the back room. "Baba, baba," the boy called as well, and at that sound the teacher rose from his crouched position and followed them.

In the middle of the back room was the teacher's wife, seated with her legs folded under her. The tube in her neck was perfectly still. Her son was kneeling behind her, gripping the side of her arm and pressing his lips into the back of her shoulder. Their eyes were trained on the swaddling of green cloth in her lap. Then the bundle twitched, and the pharmacist fell to her haunches, joined her hands in front of her face, and started to rock back and forth.

There was a second twitch, and a third. Even though the surgeon could see each one, it took him some time to realize what was—what could be—happening. The woman raised the bundle to him unopened, as though he were a deity to whom she was surrendering an offering. He knelt and took it from her, placed it on the mattress between them, opened it.

The infant had her arms held up against the sides of her body, bent at the elbows, the fingers with their soft nails curling and straightening in slow grasps at the air. The plump wrists creased, and the feet with their splayed toes kicked away at the fold of the drape in which they were entangled. The eyelids opened, and under them swam large black irises. The lips exposed toothless gums—as smooth as those of an old woman, the surgeon thought, and then he realized that the comparison ought to be the other way around. It didn't matter, really—for whatever reason, life started and ended with the mouth polished of all its weapons. It was just the period in between that made everything so complicated. The baby was still blue—cool to the touch. The surgeon placed his palm on the newborn's chest and curled his fingers around the rib cage. The chest, delicate as it was, rose against his skin.

"Get my stethoscope."

Someone placed it in his outstretched hand, and he ordered them all to be quiet. Too many people were saying too many things, the boy loudest of them all. The surgeon bent over the baby and moved the bell over her chest. The hard plastic earpieces pressed a dull pain into the sides of his head, and a low, quick beat sounded in them now that all other sounds had been silenced. But that wasn't the infant, no, it was just the beat of his own blood pulsing in his skull. He listened, and when he was convinced he'd listened enough, he peeled the stethoscope from his ears.

"She isn't . . ." he began, his eyes brimming, but found he couldn't bring himself to add the word *alive* to the end of that sentence. If this baby, who was stretching her limbs on the green cloth, whose ribs rippled under her dusky skin as she breathed and moved . . . if such an infant wasn't alive merely for want of a heartbeat, then it was language and its prejudices that needed remedy. The infant's eyes were calm, almost solemn, with a slight wrinkle in the skin between them that gave her an expression of deep thought, as though she were indeed some ancient soul reborn, inspecting the world and its inhabitants for the last time before fully assuming the guise of a child.

"She isn't crying," the surgeon said, unable to draw his gaze away from the infant, "because she doesn't have any hunger or thirst or pain. Or fear. You've given birth to what might be the first creature on earth to ever know peace, because she needs nothing from this world."

He then raised his eyes, and moved to hand the infant back to her mother. But the woman and her son were no longer kneeling on the floor before him. He jerked his head to where the teacher had stood, and found no one there either. In his haste to stand, he almost tripped over the infant, and had to balance himself on both palms to keep from falling on her. Raising himself would require more strength than he could summon, and so he twisted and slumped back down, this time facing the door, with the side of his hip and thigh against the floor and his torso propped up on the mattress by a forearm. The baby remained nestled within the arc of his body. Apart from the two of them, only the pharmacist and her husband remained in the room. She was still rocking on her haunches, her awestruck eyes darting between the infant and the surgeon, her palms joined before her lips as she breathed loudly in rhythm with her rocking. Her husband, on the other hand, seemed barely to breathe. He sat with his back against the doorjamb and his hands balled before him, as if braced against some invisible foe who might try to strike him from the air.

SEVENTEEN

THE SURGEON CHECKED EVERY room of the clinic, and checked again. He tried a different sequence of rooms each time, as if it were possible for an entire family to play hide-and-seek with him in a place this small, and in broad daylight. The dead had vanished. All except the infant. The parts of the dead he'd extracted through the night—those were still in trays in the operating room. The things he'd attached to their bodies—the tubes and bottle and surgical dressing—had gone with them.

After his fourth circuit of the clinic, when it was clear that nothing more would be gained by his aimless wandering, the surgeon sat in the chair in his consultation room. This had to be the doing of the official from the afterlife. Perhaps he had realized that none of the three would survive their surgeries, and had pulled them back to spare them another death.

But why take them all back? The boy would have lived. His spleen was out. His wound wasn't bad. Why not give him a chance? Perhaps the official just couldn't make dead blood flow.

Dawn had come and gone, after all, and nothing had happened. Who knew what other warnings from the official the teacher had ignored in his haste to regain life? The official, if he had any intelligence at all, must have had a plan for exactly such a scenario. If he couldn't make their blood flow, he wouldn't just leave the dead stranded in the middle of a village, waiting for someone to stumble upon the truth. Or for a surgeon to devise a monstrous scheme to bury their corpses.

But why leave the bloodless infant behind?

And what if this weren't the doing of the teacher's official? What if other officials were involved? Perhaps the teacher's official, the benevolent one, had been working away in the afterlife, hammering the gears of his plan into motion, restoring movement to the infant as the first step of his grand resurrection, when others discovered his plot. Perhaps they immediately pulled back the three people he had sent, without realizing that portions of their bodies had been left behind.

The surgeon realized that the clicking sound he was hearing was the tips of his incisors striking each other as they slipped over the smooth edge of his thumbnail. He placed his hands before him on the table, and watched his fingers quiver against the glass. Was he even permitted to think about the afterlife and its officials? Perhaps the officials could read thoughts, and were spying on him this very moment. If he chanced upon the right explanation for all of this, would they consider him too much of a risk and snatch him up?

And in the midst of all this was the awful feeling of relief that the dead were gone. They were no longer his problem, he wasn't responsible for them anymore. At this thought, the surgeon pounded a fist on the table, making a pen on the edge rattle and fall off. What kind of person was he, to think like this? To have thought all those appalling things? What kind of selfish beast—

"Saheb?"

The pharmacist and her husband were standing in the doorway of his consultation room, at the precise spot where he had first seen the dead. They looked strange, but then so did everything else. The surgeon felt an urge to confirm their pulse.

"Don't ask me what's going on. Just . . . *don't* ask me," he said, rising from his chair and walking to the window. A glare of sunlight fell on his face, and he used the excuse to cover his eyes.

When the surgeon told the pharmacist and her husband to return to their home, the man looked relieved, but his wife pulled him aside. They argued in whispers outside the clinic for some time and then entered, having resolved their disagreement, one could say, though she did most of the talking while he stood by her side in glum silence. They couldn't leave Saheb here like this, she said. He was tired. Who knew what would happen next? It wasn't right that he should be alone. And if some calamity were to strike them, they wanted him to be around when it did. Besides, it was best if they didn't try to walk home in broad daylight. The neighbors would take one look at them and realize that something was wrong. And the baby, even if she wasn't a child like every other, needed a woman to look after her.

The pharmacist's husband looked subdued—too tired to argue any further. It was clear that he was struggling with his wife's resolve.

The surgeon asked for a few minutes to think. The pharmacist went to the back room to check on the baby, while her husband followed her and stood with a listless expression outside the door. Then they both returned and waited for him to speak, forcing him to come up with a plan.

"We'll make the clinic look like it's closed," the surgeon said. "Like when we go to the city for supplies. Hopefully the villagers will see the shutters and not disturb us. It'll allow us to get some rest. My head feels like it's packed with rocks, but after I've had some sleep, I'll decide how we should keep the baby hidden." He wanted to add "until she vanishes as well," but realized that would be unnecessarily cruel, especially in front of the pharmacist.

At the surgeon's instructions, the pharmacist's husband went from window to window, securing each one from the inside. A few of the latches were broken, and he had to tie their handles together with rope. Almost all the windows were made entirely of wood, and the ones in the operating room were of frosted glass, opaque from the outside.

The clots, the spleen, the placenta, all had to be disposed of before the heat and flies could start acting on them. The dead themselves had shown no evidence of decay while they were here, but who knew if their entrails would retain this immortality once separated from their bodies? The pharmacist ladled everything into plastic bags and, with the surgeon, carried them to the compost ditch. The sight of them puttering outside the clinic was familiar enough to the village for no one to give them a second thought. Nonetheless, as the surgeon emptied the bags into the hole, he could feel the muscles in his shoulders tense. It was deeply unpleasant, this feeling that he was disposing of evidence. He imagined everyone in the village stopping their work to look up at the hillock and memorize his every move. It reminded him also of the horrible thoughts he'd allowed himself to think. But there really was no other option. There were just two ways of doing this—fire or earth. It was no different from when the bodies of entire humans were bid farewell—either you sent up corkscrews of smoke to announce it to the heavens, or you chose the discreet path.

They packed enough soil over the ditch to prevent stray dogs from digging up its contents, and returned to the clinic. The pharmacist's husband closed the front door, placed a padlock on the outside, and climbed in through the small window where the pharmacist usually sat—the only window in the whole place without metal bars across it. He shut it from the inside, and the surgeon switched off the lights. Enough sunlight filtered through the cracks in the wood for them to see one another.

The pharmacist had peeled her blood-covered gloves off into the pit and, once back in the clinic, scrubbed her hands with soap until they were raw. Drying her hands on her dress, she walked to the back room. The baby was still on the mattress, as Saheb had left her. Her skin still blue and her face still calm, she was kicking her legs in the folds of the green drape tangled around them. The pharmacist brought her face close to the baby's and took a deep breath, but the infant gave off no smell. She tickled the baby's ribs and feet, but there was no response. The eyes were open, and the pharmacist moved her face back and forth in front of them. With the windows closed, the room was dark and, though the baby's eyes wandered, occasionally seeming to cross, it wasn't clear that she could truly see her. The pharmacist was struck by how seldom the baby blinked, and she realized that she'd never before seen a newborn this awake, one without a hint of drowsiness. She gathered the infant up in the drape, rested the head in the crook of her elbow, and held the scalp against her lips. After kissing it a few times, she placed the baby in the crib she had fashioned, and left the room.

At the far end of the pharmacy, she pulled out a sack of rice from beneath the stone platform. She pumped the stove to a high flame, set a pot of water on it, and added three cups of rice. While the water came to a boil, she picked around in a basket of vegetables for any still fresh enough to eat. Two potatoes, an onion, a few small tomatoes, a packet of legumes, an inch of ginger—it wasn't enough to make a single decent dish, so she just chopped them all up together. When the rice had softened, she took the pot off the flame and replaced it with a skillet. The tablespoon of oil she poured in took very little time to start rippling from the heat, and she added mustard and cumin and turmeric, let them crackle on the fire.

She thought of the boy, and the prison he had carved out of the polystyrene box. She would never see him again, she knew that now, and she felt a rush of sorrow. She hoped he was at peace, and cared for, wherever he was. She hoped he was with his parents.

She added the chopped vegetables to the skillet, and the hot oil sent up its fumes, making her cough. After draining the excess water from the rice, she swept it into the mix and covered it with a lid. A sound behind her made her turn. It was her husband, carrying the supplies from the corridor into the pharmacy and arranging them on shelves. She caught his eye, and he stopped. He looked morose, but she knew it wasn't the moroseness of someone forced to act against his will. It was the anxiety of someone afraid of false hope. Hope had been unkind to them in their young marriage. He placed a hand on her shoulder, and she rested her cheek against it. Then the skillet spluttered, and she returned to it, and her husband to his boxes.

The pharmacist hadn't mentioned it to Saheb—he didn't believe in this kind of thing—and even her own husband, normally a pious man, thought she was losing her mind, but she knew this was no ordinary baby. It was an incarnation of some goddess. Her husband and she were blessed to have been chosen for this task. It all made sense to her now—why it had happened to them, why the dead had come to this world. It was to deliver this child into their care. Difficult as things seemed now, wasn't Krishna himself born in a prison cell on a night filled with bad omens—storms and a flooded river, and everything else? And look what greatness He was destined to achieve. If she did everything in her power to protect this child, raised her, devoted her life to her, who could say what miracles the child would perform, what evils and injustices she would drive from this world?

The pharmacist ladled the rice out into two plates. She wasn't feeling very hungry herself. The cramp low in her belly nauseated her. It wasn't her time of the month yet, so perhaps this was just from the scars left after the tuberculosis in her ovaries had closed off her tubes. Saheb was sure that all those months of antibiotics had been enough to cure the infection itself, and he always insisted that the scars, though they would probably never go away, shouldn't cause her pain. But what could you do? You accepted what God decided for you without asking too many questions. After all, if He could make this world and everything in it, put in its place every star in the sky and pebble in the river, then He understood the path laid out for you, life after life, better than any human ever would.

She carried the plates out.

Though the pharmacist kept apologizing for the tastelessness of the food, the surgeon barely stopped to chew as he swallowed. The same was true of the pharmacist's husband, who ate cross-legged on the floor. After the plates were cleared, the surgeon remembered the packets from the blood bank, and he transferred them from the icebox to the refrigerator. Perhaps another farmer with a lacerated forearm would walk in one of these days, and he'd have a chance to use them.

He waited in the corridor while the pharmacist laid out the makeshift beds. She had spread out two thin ones in the pharmacy, and now seemed to be arranging the one in his consultation room to be as comfortable as possible. They hadn't had to discuss it, but it was obvious that none of them had any desire to sleep in the back room, on any of the beds or mattresses that the dead had occupied.

"We're like kites," said the surgeon.

"Kites, Saheb?" asked the pharmacist's husband.

"Yes. Kites with strings."

To relieve a crick in his neck, the surgeon turned his face upward until he felt a pleasant squeeze in the flesh at the back of his scalp. He found, to his bemusement, the pharmacist's husband mirroring the action, turning to the ceiling as if in search of kites.

"You have to wonder," said the surgeon, "what a kite would think if it had a brain. Maybe it would think of its position in the sky as the only steady point in the universe, and worry about constantly holding the rest of the world in place. That, too, on a single string. A single string, at the end of which is balanced the entire earth, as if on the tip of a pin. The earth has so many dangerous things on it, trees with branches like claws, constantly trying to poke holes through the kite's body, animals crawling all over, waiting to grab and tear it, and water, so much water everywhere—the kite has to make sure it never touches it, or it will be done for. The wind is strong, it makes the earth flap around the kite in every direction, but the kite holds on to its string, keeps the earth at a safe distance. There's sin and death and evil on the earth, the kite thinks, but the sky is pure, and as long as it controls its own little patch, things are good."

This seemed to perplex the pharmacist's husband. The surgeon waved a hand, dismissing the train of thought.

"Get some rest. Both of you. We'll talk again after we've slept."

The pharmacist brought the crib from the back room and positioned it beside her bedding in the pharmacy. The surgeon knelt at its side, examining the baby again to confirm that she was still in her placid, bloodless state. He caressed her cheek with the back of a finger.

"If only this were a normal child, we could pretend that she was abandoned at our doorstep. Now we'll have to just hide her. After it's dark, we can move her to my quarters, where no one will wander, and you can look after her there. Let's see how long we can keep this secret."

The surgeon dragged himself to the consultation room and closed the door. His eyes, of their own will, went to the side table, to the teacup that the official's lips had touched. He gave it a long, quiet look, and thought of the teacher and his wife and son, of the place to which they had likely returned. He remembered what the dead woman had said, that the afterlife wasn't as bad as her husband made it out. He hoped that those words, uttered though they were in a fit of rage, were true. Somehow the prospect of the afterlife seemed to cause the surgeon less distress than he felt it should. Perhaps if he were less drained, the ghastliness of it might have overwhelmed him. But now, in this little room, surrounded by the apparatus of this mortal world, one of which was a prepared bed, the afterlife seemed like a distant calamity, to be confronted at a later, mercifully unspecified, date.

He thought of his last conversation with the teacher, of how wretched the man had looked, kneeling on the floor. He recalled how harsh he'd been with him, how needlessly bitter and cruel their final moments together had been. What would *he* have done in the teacher's place? Refused the possibility of life? Far greater men had sinned for far less. One thing the surgeon knew: the remorse he now felt would remain with him as long as he lived. And perhaps beyond.

He thought also of the bundle of money, a good portion of his savings, that he'd handed over to the official. At that last thought, he pulled an old handkerchief from a drawer, spread it out on his desk, placed the cup in its center, and knotted the ends of the square to fold it into a bundle. He pinched the knots in his fingers, raised the bundle to the level of his eyes, and released it.

The smash was muffled, but apparently still loud enough to carry to the other rooms, for the pharmacist called out, "Saheb?"

"Don't worry," he said. "I dropped something in the dark. I'll take care of it."

An irresistible drowsiness overcame him. He lay down on the sheets without bothering to throw the handkerchief and its enclosed shards into the wastebasket. He had wondered if he would be able to sleep under the weight of everything that had passed, but as soon as his head touched the pillow, his eyes were sealed as though with a kohl of wax. His chest rose and fell. That wasn't a definite sign of life, of course. Only the few drops of sweat that pushed through his pores and trickled down his skin spoke of his persistence in this world.

The living slept as though death itself had scoured all thought from their minds. The clinic readied its bricks and mortar and settled into the silence of a tomb. In the corridor, a small green lizard, emboldened by the quiet, emerged from a crack in the ceiling and resumed its vigil beside the wall clock. Hours passed, marked by nothing more than the crawl of the clock's hands and the occasional dart of the lizard's flat tongue, until, in a box lined with cloth, by the side of a new mother deep in dreamless sleep, the slightest shade of pink crept into the cheeks of a newborn. Her fists balled, her face crinkled as she shut her eyelids tight, and her lips pulled back from her toothless gums while she drew in a breath, preparing to let out a cry.

ACKNOWLEDGMENTS

Many thanks to my editors: Peter Gelfan for helping this story find its direction, and Miranda Ottewell for helping it find its voice. Thank you to my agent Matthew Turner (Rogers, Coleridge & White) for his dedication and insight, and to Megha Majumdar and the stellar team at Catapult. My gratitude to Nate, Shruti, Shalaka, Christine, Chris, Adam, Dhruv, Tom, Thomas and Bruce for valuable conversations and comments, and to my parents for enveloping my childhood in books.

© Kimberly Kunda

VIKRAM PARALKAR was born and raised in Mumbai. Author of a previous book, *The Afflictions*, he is a physician-scientist at the University of Pennsylvania, where he treats patients with leukemia and researches the disease. He lives in Philadelphia.

Acknowledgments

These essays have been published in various magazines, some reprinted in more than one publication. Acknowledgment is given to the following publications. "The Language Wars" was published in Christian Education Journal, Vol. XII, No. 2, and is used here by permission. Other articles have appeared first in Evangelizing Today's Child, Family Resources, Home Education, Home School Digest, Homeschooling Today, The Moore Report, and The Teaching Home.

Table of Contents

PART I

Which articles in a collection should have the prestige of being up front? My daughter-in-law, Ellen, selected these. She said they are encouraging to parents who think publishers and textbooks have the answers, while they themselves know nothing. Chapter 3, on publishing, drew some flap of criticism when it first appeared, as I expected. But the publications which objected most loudly have continued some of the very practices described in the article, so I still stand by the opinions and observations given in this. The article does not say the practices are wrong; it just describes what happens. We can be better informed consumers to know these facts about the publishing business.

Curriculum 101

Do you sometimes feel you need a short course in curriculum in order to find your way among the flood of books and clamor of voices you meet at conventions or in magazines? If so, read on. This is it.

Sometimes the word *curriculum* is used to refer to books—to curriculum materials that you find in catalogs or conventions. Another meaning—the dictionary meaning—is more theoretical. It refers to the content or skills to be taught. It concerns the foundational questions of how and why content gets chosen to be put into the books.

These basic curriculum questions can be divided into three general areas:

1) Philosophy, values, and foundations underlying curriculum—the Why.
2) Psychology of learning and teaching—the How.
3) Organizing and presenting the content of curriculum—the What.

Why?

To keep this course short, we will pass lightly over this first category because Christian homeschoolers and Christian publishers of curriculum materials largely agree on the basic values underlying education. Small differences, as found among denominations, do not affect the big philosophic questions such as "What is man?" and "What is knowledge?"

Answers we give to the big questions are the starting platform for all other curriculum decisions. For example, Christians believe that knowledge is found in God and in His creation. Knowledge is "there" for us to search out, discover, and try to understand. By some other philosophies, people believe that knowledge is constructed in our minds, thus truth changes or evolves along with mankind.

Doctrinal differences among Christians, of course, affect the content of their teaching, but that is the "what" level of curriculum decision making. At the foundational level, all Christians believe that truth is found in the Bible, and their curricula, then, look to the Bible and its Author for truth.

How?

How do children learn? How should we teach them? What methods work best? These are psychology questions related to children's psyches. Probably most educational writing revolves around these topics.

More questions: Should children have formal or informal learning environments? Should learning be competitive? Should we hold out carrots and sticks, such as report cards? Should we start early or late? What can children learn at each age?

Methods. All the myriad activities we call methods are part of the psychology of education—learning by workbook, projects, field trips, questioning, discussion, lecture, reading, writing, simulation, practicing, TV, video, movies, computer, audio cassettes, games, team learning, cooperative learning, contests, memorizing, and so on.

Practically all research which compares two or more methods has been carried on in classrooms, so it says nothing to homeschoolers about what is best for them to use.

Implicit in some methods is a preference for one or another level or style of thinking. One factor in choosing a method is whether it will enable the child to *do* something with his knowledge, rather than just to know facts and information.

The materials you choose have some effect on the methods you use, but they need not determine methods entirely. For instance, instead of having your children read a textbook and answer its questions, you could have them use the book as a reference to help in a project. You can use more writing, discussion or questioning than the book includes. Or you can use less.

Organizing pupils. Ways to organize pupils for learning is also a matter of psychology. Do children learn best in herds of 30 age-mates? Or in mixed age groupings—family style? (In the 60s this was tried in many elementary schools.) Or do they learn best when tutored individually? When research favors this last arrangement, as it usually does, it has to be brushed aside by school officials because tutoring is financially unattainable in the schools, except for occasional instances.

Some texts and workbooks now being sold in home study courses were originally classroom books. They were aimed at an average level in each grade. They include amounts of review and reteaching that are appropriate for a classroom, where the teacher hopes that with one more repetition maybe some of the stragglers will at last catch on. Some publishers use these books at a lower grade level than they were written for and label them "advanced" or "accelerated."

You don't need to try to teach everything in every grade. As a tutor, you have many advantages over classroom teachers. Do not lose that advantage by trying too hard to imitate the classroom, but feel free to adapt your curriculum as much as you like.

What?

We have stated that the philosophy underlying Christian curricula differs hardly at all. We have noted that their educational psychology may differ, but you can adapt or change that in many ways. Now, we move on to the questions of curriculum content—the "what" of curriculum.

Examples: Does the history teach a view of American origins and the constitution that you approve of? Is the geography up-to-date, or does it teach that the major industry in Japan is raising silkworms?

In practice, it is often difficult to separate content questions from psychology questions; the *what* and the *how* become so intertwined that we have to handle both kinds of questions at once.

For example: Does your arithmetic book mainly drill on basic calculation skills, or does it also stress meaning, principles and logic? You may feel that it moves too rapidly to adding of large numbers and that it relies mostly on drill and rote memory rather than the understanding you would like to see. Thus you are considering both *what* it teaches and *how* it teaches adding.

In phonics, is a big chunk presented before starting to read? Or are phonics and beginning reading integrated together (as I prefer)? Does the science major on information, or does it also provide experience in the process of thinking like scientists? Is the curriculum gimmicky, attempting to develop excitement from overly clever teaching aids instead of from the subject itself?

You may have opinions on some of those questions, and the people selling you materials have their opinions too. If we turn to research, we usually raise more questions than we answer. One reason that research answers are so fuzzy is that most research gives too little attention to the human factors of the teacher and pupil and the deeply human interactions between them. Such factors are not easily tabulated, so they don't fit into what passes for scientific research in our day.

So trust your own opinions. What you believe in and what is workable for you, should be the main factors in choosing curriculum materials. I often wonder why researchers spend so much time trying to find by "scientific" means what most of us already know by common sense.

Homeschoolers who teach the cultural heritage of the Bible and their national heritage as well as they can, and who teach the basic skills for learning—the three R's—have already answered for themselves the most important questions of what to teach.

A best selling book called *The Closing of the American Mind* by Allan Bloom points out the weaknesses of glossing over the distinctive values and shared experiences that make a society cohesive. The attitude that all such values are equal is tantamount to saying that they don't matter. And that stops any further thinking about them.

After the important content mentioned in the previous paragraphs, you can add other studies about people and things (humanities and sciences), the arts, home or vocational skills, and physical skills in whatever mix your family likes. If your children learn how to learn, they can pursue any area of education.

Now, How Do I Choose Curriculum Materials?

We have looked theoretically at the why, how and what questions of curriculum, and if you're a newcomer to this you might feel overloaded. How are you ever going to examine all the books and materials your children might need and make decisions for even one year of schooling?

The obvious answer is that you can't examine everything, so just make the best choices you can in the time you have. You can always make changes—even in mid-year. If while using curriculum materials, you find a problem or find something especially good, share this information with your friends and support group and listen to such recommendations from them. Some parents begin by obtaining all curriculum from one source or publisher, and then, as they gain confidence, they begin to make changes subject by subject.

I do not agree with the advice sometimes given that you need to know your children's learning styles and analyze the materials to find what fits those styles, that you need to articulate your education philosophy, and other such overwhelming demands. Most of that which really matters has a way of working itself out as you go along.

Classroom teachers have committees to work at selecting books. And teachers sometimes try books for a while before deciding whether to continue using them or to look for something better. That's what a good deal of education research is all about, and this on-the-job research brings vitality to the teaching enterprise.

So if you feel you are researching and experimenting and don't know all the answers yet, you're a member of the club. Welcome! As parents like you think independently and let publishers know what they are looking for, the products will continue to improve. Publishers and users of curriculum together can strengthen the already strong homeschool movement, with happy results for everyone.

The Last Day of Curriculum 101

We will not have a test today, because a test might imply an ending, instead of an ongoing vital process. Instead of a test, please let me indulge in a little closing sermon.

Try not to be intimidated by other people's views and by the mountains of materials and competing voices you encounter at conventions. Just listen when you can, learn what you want to from all of these, and trust your own instincts about what is best for your family. I believe in you homeschooling parents. You are the best hope of our society. You are leading the way in the homeschooling movement, so don't wait around for someone to lead you.

Goodbye until next semester.
God bless you all!

Curriculum as Servant

In one of his books[1] John Holt told a delightful story of some first graders. He substituted for a week in a classroom where the teacher customarily put arithmetic problems on the board for the children to do if they came early. The problems were addition, with sums rarely over 10, and never over 20. One day Holt forgot to put the problems up.

Two or three children came in, worried awhile, and then asked if they could put some problems up. Holt said, "Sure, go ahead." They began with the usual kind but after a while grew bolder and began to write problems like 70 + 20 = ? It didn't seem legal to leave up a problem unless they could work it, so they argued until they managed to agree on the correct answer.

After a while they began adding numbers like 200 + 400 or even 230 + 500, or 340 + 420. Making their problems more complicated all the time, many of the children worked out for themselves most of the rules for doing addition. That week, working only a few minutes a day, they covered material that the school was prepared to spend years teaching them.

This story illustrates the freedom to explore that Holt's books are largely about. Some people instinctively like this way of teaching. Others worry that there is something wrong or dangerous in letting children "do their own thing." They also worry about achievement tests. Isn't it safer, they ask, to stick with curriculum?

Many Ways To Use Curriculum

This complex problem has more than two sides. It's not just a choice of following a curriculum or not. Here are six possible sides to the curriculum questions, and you may think of more.

1) Follow one complete subject-oriented curriculum with textbooks and/or workbooks in each separate subject.
2) Follow a "unit" curriculum wherein the traditional subjects (math often excepted) are integrated around topical studies. For instance: a unit on colonial times in America can combine geography, history, art, music, reading, spelling, and writing.
3) Mix and match curriculum materials to your own liking, instead of following one publisher's complete set.
4) Plan your own units or your own studies, using "real" books rather than textbooks.
5) Do any parts of any of the above.
6) Let children study whatever they become interested in.

If we wished to debate on the curriculum level, we could

probably find six people to give convincing arguments for each of the six arrangements above. And every listener could decide which he prefers to do. But this is an unsatisfactory way to make the choices.

Why is it unsatisfactory? Because it gives curriculum the uppermost position in the decisions. It puts curriculum in the position of master rather than servant.

Being Ready To Drop Curriculum

When curriculum is servant, you can easily drop it anytime something better is happening. My friend Karey Swan likes to do that. She phoned recently to say, "I just had to tell you what Heather is doing." She went on to tell how 11-year-old Heather had put state names on pieces of paper and spread them all over the house in proper positions. Then she drove from state to state in little cars. Two cars met in Colorado and Heather said, "I don't want to stay here. I'm going to drive on to New Jersey. Good-bye." Karey suggested that she bring all the states into the living room, but Heather said it was more fun to have Florida way off in a bedroom.

Karey had wanted to get "school" started for the day, but she changed her mind when she saw the strong learning that was already happening. The incident reminded me of a story I heard about Micki Colfax.[2] When her boys were engrossed in collecting butterflies, Micki decided it would be foolish to cut off that learning and impose something from the school books instead.

Discipline with Discernment

Common questions on this point are: But what about

the Bible instructions on discipline? What about foolishness in the heart of the child? Isn't it dangerous to just let the child have his way?

The verses that come to mind are all true, of course. It is important to discipline when the child's heart is rebellious and he thinks or acts foolishly. But in these instances the mothers did not discern foolishness. Being sensitive to what was going on in the children's minds, they were able to put real learning first and leave curriculum in its servant position.

These children had inner discipline, which is essential to learning. When inner discipline is working, there is no need to impose discipline from the outside.

Being Ready To Use Curriculum

That inner discipline and love of learning has grown so strong in some children that they range far beyond the boundaries of whatever curriculum they started out with. They hardly use it anymore.

But other children for various reasons do not fit that pattern. Sometimes their teachers spend a good part of their lives trying to make a subject interesting. They think up projects and activities so as to involve the children and hopefully to engage their minds fully upon the learning, and only once in a while their efforts result in the total engagement seen in the incidents above.

If you are wearing yourself out trying to work up exciting units or projects, then reconsider. It might be time for published curriculum again. Remember that if curriculum is a servant, not only can you drop it when that seems best, but also you can use it when that seems best.

If your family has been caught up in reading and

talking about books on ancient Egypt or some other topic and now the interest is waning, you need not dive immediately into another intense study. And if you need something to do during "school" hours, just use a textbook for a while. The next topic and mental challenge will present itself when the mind is ready.

What About Achievement Tests?

Parents often ask: What about achievement tests? Won't my children do better in tests if I stick with curriculum?

Most fears about achievement tests are groundless. I have met parents who believe in the writing method to good writing, but they reluctantly add more grammar than they otherwise would because they want their children to be ready for achievement tests. The good news for such parents is that achievement tests don't ask about grammar as such. They never ask "What is a predicate adjective?" or "Which of the following verbs is intransitive?" Grammar is considered a means to an end, and the testmakers try to test the end of good use of language rather than the means of grammar. About the closest they come to using grammatical terms is asking which are complete or incomplete or run-on sentences. (Much research shows that traditional grammar study does not achieve the end hoped for it, anyway.[3])

In content subjects such as history and science, many parents think that the tests will quiz their children on information in the textbook and not on information in library books. This is only partly true. Testmakers, of course, do try to include questions on the topics that are generally agreed as important for education in our society.

In science, for instance, they would include questions from broad topics such as plants and animals, electricity, the solar system, and so forth. But as for specific information being in the curriculum and the same specific information being asked on the test, that is the way semester tests work, but not achievement tests.

Achievement tests work on sampling theory. The test items represent a small sampling of the many thousands of items that could be asked in the topics. How the children score on the samples gives an idea of how they would score on all the items if it were possible to answer all the items. Put another way, those children who score highest on the sampling would likely score highest on the whole. This gives comparative scores, which is the way that achievements tests measure.

In my early years of classroom teaching, I had the same concerns about textbooks that homeschooling parents are having today. Only gradually did I move outward to the world of real books.

Then one year I gave almost complete freedom to a group of third graders to choose their own books. I imposed only the minimal structure that they had to read at least three books on a topic and then tell the class in some way what they learned. This freedom was so popular that we continued the system all year long. At the end of the year, their scores on primary achievement tests were too high to be an adequate measure, so I obtained some junior high tests. On these, most children in the group scored at junior high or high school levels. That was the upper third of the class. Scores were high not only in reading and language but in science and social studies, too.

That experience taught me that textbooks were not the route to high test scores. Further experience showed me that exclusive use of graded textbooks could actually hold back a child's advancement.

The case of Johnny will illustrate. Johnny was brought to my summer reading school one year. He had just finished first grade and was reading at second grade level. I said to the mother, "Johnny reads well. He doesn't need summer school." But she insisted on enrolling him because "His teacher said he was bright and she didn't have time to give him the extra attention he needs."

We enrolled him, got a pile of library books, and had a high school student read the same books as Johnny and talk with him about them. I inserted a couple of high-level questions like "What good can come out of pure research?" (as opposed to practical research). After one month of this "treatment," Johnny scored at fifth grade reading level.

The following year he was brought back to summer school and he scored fifth grade reading level. Evidently the year spent in second grade textbooks had done nothing for him. We gave him another month of the same treatment and he scored seventh grade level.

I wouldn't expect similar results with every child, of course. But what I would expect is that each child should come up to his own ability level when allowed to do wide reading in real books.

Achievement testing, like curriculum, should be viewed as a servant and not master over our children's learning.

Learning Styles

Another consideration in the decision of whether to use curriculum or not is the learning styles that children use. One way to categorize styles is into these three divisions:

1) Dependent
2) Collaborative
3) Independent

These categories are for labeling situations, not children. For instance, you may feel very dependent when you take organ lessons. You may want your teacher to be the authority, telling you what to practice next, how to practice it, etc. You may be collaborative in learning about home-schooling. Talking with other parents and sharing books and experiences with them are collaborative ways to learn. And you may be independent in learning to use your cookbook or in some other private learning project.

In a subject where a child feels dependent a "closed system" is needed. You could be that closed system if you want (like the organ teacher), but it saves time if you find just the right book (or tape or program, etc.) for the need.

In subjects where a child feels independent, an "open system" is what he needs. And in still other areas, a "mixed system" works best.

Complex Decisions

In the John Holt story given at the outset of this article, we should notice that the open learning of the first graders did not happen from a vacuum. The structure of working problems every morning had been built, and within that structure the exciting learning happened. Heather Swan did not invent her state project out of nothingness. She had been doing map work with her mother, and in an independent learning style she got better at it. And the Colfax boys' ranch environment, as well as the model of their parents' love of learning, set the stage for their phenomenal independent science learning.

The daily decisions that you must make are about as complex as the human mind itself. You will find your decisions more satisfying if you base them on your perceptions of the children's minds. Rise higher than the curriculum level. It's not "Should we or shouldn't we use curriculum?" Instead, it is "What does my child need at this time?" Curriculum is one of the means for meeting those needs. It is a servant.

---

1. *How Children Learn* by John Holt, Pitman Publishing, 1967.
2. See *Homeschooling for Excellence* by David and Micki Colfax, Warner Books, 1988.
3. See *You CAN Teach Your Child Successfully* by Ruth Beechick, Arrow Press, 1988.

Should We Buy an Encyclopedia?

Alongside the curriculum purchasing questions is the encyclopedia question. This is common among homeschoolers and is worth some time and thought. Here are a few comments I wrote in *You CAN Teach Your Child Successfully.*

Don't worry about trying to afford encyclopedias. They are not the route to a good education for your children. If you have that much money to spend on books, think what a library you would have if you used the money, instead, for family members to select books on subjects they are interested in, books they will read from cover to cover! Compare that use of book money with the shelves of encyclopedias that your children will use only occasionally, and in which they will read only a tiny fraction of the pages. Rewording encyclopedia articles is not an especially good way to learn to write, and it is a poor way to learn what research is.

If you really want encyclopedias, find out when the good used book sales happen in your area and buy an old set or a set with a volume missing, for less than one-tenth of the original price. That's about what it is worth to be able to look up a fact now and then. Old sets work fine for looking up most historical and literary information, but not so well for science.

With the pace of science these days, even textbooks can't keep up, much less encyclopedias. The same could be said for political geography and other topics with rapidly unfolding events. Keeping up with the latest—in any field—is not a viable argument for using encyclopedias.

Henry Beechhold comments on encyclopedias in his book, *The Creative Classroom: Teaching Without Textbooks.* Beechhold has much to say about *books* versus *non-books*. And encyclopedias generally come under his category of non-books. He has kind words about some European productions, including *The Encyclopedia Britannica.* This latter has a different philosophy than American encyclopedias, even though an American, Mortimer Adler, was head of the editorial committee. Adler was perhaps the greatest educator of our century, and he was the brains behind the "Great Books" programs.

Here are some of Beechhold's comments about encyclopedias.

In my list of encyclopedias, I pointedly overlooked the big American productions for the simple reason that I think of them as another species of non-book. I am appalled at the money schools waste on those flashy sets. Somehow, librarians (or whoever manages the job in lieu of a librarian) at every school level from elementary on up have got the idea that encyclopedia sets are desirable acquisitions. I know of many an elementary school that is virtually barren of books but which feels satisfied that several hundred (hard-to-come-by) dollars are well spent on a new encyclopedia.

Beechhold further comments that "the typical encyclopedia article is both oversimplified and overly general. . . . Not that an encyclopedia might not make entertaining casual reading (if one enjoys stuffing his head with odds and ends). Unfortunately, the volumes are far too stiff and heavy to make pleasant companions of this sort."

I had a grandfather who enjoyed reading the dictionary. Every time he looked up a word, he was lost for an hour or more reading about the next word and the next, straight through the pages. I have met a few children who read encyclopedias that way.

Families who like encyclopedias for such browsing or any other particular use, and who can afford them, should just buy whatever looks good to them. They don't need advice from any "expert." The expert advice implies that the sets are not really for enjoyment, but for medicine, instead.

I do not believe that encyclopedias are good educational medicine. They are not basic tools. They are not even particularly useful.

My life has consisted of teaching and editing (educational materials) and writing. Few other pursuits might make more use of encyclopedias than these three, yet I can practically count in my head the number of times I used them. I never gave children the dull assignment of looking up something in an encyclopedia and writing a report on it. Beechhold says that is teaching children how to plagiarize. In a publishing house, we sometimes received such plagiarized manuscripts from adult writers, and I had to realize that we start teaching children at about fifth grade to do that.

As an editor, I often had to check names or dates or other little facts, and for that the Columbia or International desk encyclopedias work as well as full sets. Once when I needed to check on obscure nineteenth century personages, I found that a decades old set still had a lot of those people who had been dropped from newer sets. I had bought the old set for $12 at a garage sale. In my writing, I find encyclopedias completely useless.

So from under my three hats, I find no reason to recommend that each homeschool family buy an encyclopedia set. Those who do buy should have their personal reasons for doing so—something more interesting than as medicine for their children's education.

References

Henry F. Beechhold, *The Creative Classroom: Teaching without Textbooks,* (New York: Charles Scribner, 1971).
Ruth Beechick, *You CAN Teach Your Child Successfully* (Pollock Pines CA: Arrow Press, 1988, 1993).

Insider Secrets of Publishers

I wish to share with consumers some of the insights I have gained through working in various capacities within the publishing world. My purpose is to help homeschooling families—and any book buyers. If some bit of information here helps some readers make better use of their book dollars, then it is worth the criticism that will probably come my way as a result of this article.

Advertising and Book Reviews

Magazines and other periodicals, in order to operate profitably, usually depend to a large extent on income from advertisers. The best that can be said for this arrangement is that readers pay less for subscriptions and that they may actually find help from the ads. The worst that could happen is that editorial content is controlled by advertisers. The true case for most publications is somewhere on a continuum between these two extremes.

Take book reviews, for instance. Any magazine that runs book reviews finds itself inundated with review copies of new books from publishers seeking this sort of free publicity. The fate of these books depends on staff and time and space allotted to reviews. In many cases the editor selects books she feels will interest her readers, and she sends those out to her reviewers, who often hold those jobs simply for the reward of receiving free books. The magazine publisher may place constraints on the editor, saying, "Don't review books from Publisher X because he never advertises with us." Or the advertising manager says, "Here's a book I'd like you to review. I told this client I was pretty sure you would do it."

This latter kind of deal can become a formalized arrangement. The client buys an ad and with it comes review space. And if he likes, he can write the review himself instead of leaving it to magazine staff.

Advertising and Articles

The same sorts of pressures, subtle or otherwise, bear on the choice of articles. Say that you're an overworked, harried editor. That's the only kind there is. Your next issue must go to press or to layout today. You've already included the articles you really like and really want, but you must select one more from your "maybe" pile. The top one is from a long-time, regular advertiser. Will that give it the boost it needs to be chosen over the others? And if the magazine is in tight financial straits and must encourage advertisers to stay with it? Most magazines have small staffs and the editor knows what's going on in all departments. She may even *be* the publisher or the ad manager. So the mixture of editorial and financial concerns is not unusual.

This, too, can become almost a formal arrangement, as with book reviews. I say "almost" because most people would not want to admit that they do this. But I've seen it happen—from several sides. Even from the client side. Once an ad salesman called, for about the third time in his campaign to persuade me to advertise in his magazine. In the course of the conversation I said something like, "It would help if I write an article so your readers would know who I am." His response was something like, "Yes. I can't promise anything, but the chances are better if you're running an ad." An under-the-table arrangement.

The magazine folded shortly after, and I believe it was because they were more talented in advertising than in the subject matter of their particular magazine.

Advertising as Teaching

About three decades ago was a period of rapid growth of Sunday schools and, consequently, of published materials to serve them. I had the experience of working in the midst of that movement during its exciting years. In many ways it paralleled what is happening now in the homeschool movement. There was what businessmen call a "growing market." When there's a growing market almost anyone can make money, with or without good products, with or without efficient business practices.

During those boom years no one was interested in saving money. As curriculum editor, I could plan a low-cost, reusable, or multi-use curriculum. But publishers weren't interested. They wanted more color, more consumable pieces, more products. Provide a course that worked for club or children's church and also for VBS? Unthinkable If competitors had the full, expensive set of VBS materials which had proliferated over the years, nothing less would do.

A basic principle in publishing is that if you print more of an item, the cost per item is lower. The multi-use idea and other techniques could bring costs down for consumers and also give them more flexibility through having more choices. But neither businessmen nor churches were swayed by that logic during boom years.

Why not the churches? Because much of the teacher training was sponsored by publishers. It was part of their advertising campaigns. Seminars, books, films and ads served to teach people that they needed curriculum materials just like what the publishers were producing.

Of course some salesmen in that work had high motives and skills and knowledge, and they no doubt accomplished a lot of good. But the system of mixing sales efforts with teaching has some built-in pitfalls.

For an example, take the "legend" that people remember a given large percentage of what they see. I read that repeatedly in ads and Christian education writings. My background had made me aware of how people often misuse single research studies by generalizing the results beyond any sensible boundaries, and I decided to track down the origin of this particular idea. The trail led to 3M Company, and they would never send me the actual research data, but only their own advertising brochures, from which Christian education writers had obtained their information.

So what was the research? We could guess that perhaps they used salesmen's meetings. One group was shown graphs and the other group was told the numbers. Or something like that. Then somebody tested to see how much the groups remembered after the sessions, or after a week. Our problem is that we don't know the age of the students, the content of the learning, the timeframe for remembering, or anything that could help us make sense of the information for our own teaching. All we are told is that people remember a certain percentage of what they see, and even that figure varies now because of so much retelling in the manner of folktales. But percentages sound scientific.

What is the business of 3M Company? Visual aids, for one. Overhead projectors and related materials. The percentages no doubt help their sales. Curriculum publishers, borrowing them, have sold mountains of flannelgraph and other visual aids. And teachers everywhere believe they must have them.

I still notice that I remember very little of what I see, even billboards which I pass repeatedly.

Another slogan spread by advertising efforts is that children "learn by doing." Even anti-Deweyites used these words from the philosophy of Dewey and applied them, instead, to method. Or misapplied them. If the lesson is "Be ye kind one to another," you would think the real doing is in performing kind deeds. Teachers could encourage and even arrange some of that among the children in their classes. But with publishers, too often the "doing" is tied up with a worksheet. If children color somebody else doing a kind deed, that sells worksheets.

"Now we come to the important part of the lesson," a workshop leader says as she holds up the worksheet and begins to teach that children learn best by doing. Doing with the hands is stressed. Overlooked is the fact that a child's mind may be occupied with coloring inside the lines, rather than with the pleasure his kind deed may bring to another.

Now, in homeschooling, a similar history is unfolding. Numerous slogans, cliches and legends in this community have come from advertisers. And a good many of these do not hold up when thoughtfully examined or when traced back to their sources. These legends are promoted both in "official" ads and also in the unofficial ads of articles, workshops and books. And they are picked up by other writers who believe the ad sources.

Boom Days for Publishers

The still-growing market in homeschooling makes it possible for all kinds of publishers to operate. I have my private, unscientific way of categorizing these. My categories, as with anyone's, are not clearly separate; they overlap. Also, as with any categories, they oversimplify. Only a few factors are taken into account, whereas in real life numerous factors exist. But for what they may be worth, here are my three major categories.

First, are the businessmen. Maybe Christian businessmen. They saw a market, an opportunity, and moved to fill it. Some of these already had curriculums they were providing for Christian schools, or they themselves set up schools to use their curriculums. Early in the market, some of these saw homeschooling as a threat to their schools, but as the market grew they saw its potential.

Other businessmen had no curriculum, but seeing the new market, they moved quickly to get one. They could buy copyrights to existing sets of workbooks. Old editions were obtainable. They could remove objectionable items like smoking, and call these Christian books, but it may have escaped their notice for years if the books taught Japan as a silk culture instead of teaching its auto and high tech industries.

If a businessman didn't have a curriculum, or didn't buy one, he could get somebody to write one. Whether his writers produced good curriculum or poor, he may not have known; his talent was marketing. His asset was a mailing list. It was fairly easy for a writer with textbooks on his desk to write bits of information and questions about them to form workbooks. These books could be, and sometimes were, produced rapidly.

My second category is the broader education publishing world, not limited to Christians or to homeschoolers. These companies had their niches carved out and their market outlets already working. When homeschoolers knocked at their doors they reacted in various ways, depending mostly on size. Some, for the first time, sold to individuals instead of schools. Some now advertise in homeschool publications. Many don't. Almost everything is available through them, except of course the Christian slant.

My third category is the curriculum which grows out of the grassroots of homeschooling itself. Parents who plan something successful for their own families may write those courses or teaching aids and begin to sell them. Parents who cannot find what they want realize that others are likely in the same situation, so they produce curriculum items to fill these needs.

This is opposite from the businessman approach. These publishers first have products they believe in, then they often must learn from scratch how to get them to market, and many are succeeding.

The quality of some of these grassroots products is super-great, better than in the other categories. The homeschool movement is, I believe, the healthiest movement in education today. And its publishing now is a growing part of its good health.

That, in brief, is this one insider's look at educational publishing.

Ruth Beechick Begins Teaching

I read the advice given to first-time homeschoolers, and I sometimes want to scream, "No, no! Don't burden them with all that." Each year the advice grows. More fads and jargon are added. More psychology. More philosophy. More of curriculum and testing.

I am amazed that so many new homeschoolers enter the ranks each year. I salute you all.

If the story of my bumbling first year of teaching will encourage anyone, it is worth the telling. I was 19 years old and arrived in Valdez, Alaska, on the old steamship Alaska, just after World War II, armed with a temporary certificate and a few back copies of a teacher's magazine. I had not yet done my "practice teaching," as we called it. But I had lived in classrooms all my life, I argued to myself, so I knew what happened in them.

I was hired to teach third grade and to teach music in all the other grades, including high school. No one asked me to submit a plan for the year. If they had, I suppose I would have handled it like an academic assignment. I could have looked in textbooks to see what third graders are supposed to learn, but it would have had little connection with reality. How many of my third graders were good readers? Were there enough high schoolers for a choir? Could we do anything instrumental? None of this I knew as the boat docked and some townspeople welcomed me.

The next day we teachers had a meeting—six of us, as I recall, including the principal/teacher. We were all new and only slightly aware of the town's tensions over the first year of combining Natives and whites in the same school. The Natives were going to bring their report cards and that's how we would know what grades to enroll them in.

I arranged furniture in my room and spent much time that day making plans for the first day of school. I scarcely thought of what the children might learn. My main goals were just to manage the day as smoothly as possible, and to get acquainted with the children.

Only eighteen third graders turned up. The principal's wife walked through my room, which was the route to the supply room, not really for supplies, I suspected, but observing. I was glad the class was controlled and quietly singing.

At lunch time all the children went home to eat; the town was small enough for that. The principal's wife came in to say she'd have to bring in the twelve second graders because there were too many children in the other primary room. Because of over-planning, I achieved my goal of managing a smooth day.

Now, if I had made a year's plan, or even a week's plan, I would have had to re-do it to include second grade. Anyway, my beginner's mind couldn't see very far ahead. The first week, I squeaked by a day at a time. Saturday I laid out a week of plans. I worked on school every night while my experienced teacher housemate pursued dates and other leisure activities.

The teacher at the Native school had believed that Natives were limited to third grade achievement, so all her children were assigned to a primary grade no matter what their age or accomplishments, and most of these were over-age for their grade, even if they were good readers. I began planning with some second graders to skip and skim through the arithmetic book so they could soon become third graders. Some of the third graders, too, I felt could cover fourth grade work during the year and then be assigned to fifth grade the following year. This would catch a lot of them up to where they should be according to age. One girl, in fact, made a triple jump from second grade that year to fifth the following year.

If some official had required me to plan out the full year, I might have been so intent on following my plan that I would have missed all that adjustment, which perhaps was the best thing that happened in my classroom that year.

I had some discipline problems, and struggles keeping things from becoming too boring for the children and me. The textbooks were a major problem and, neophyte that I was, I thought the trouble was with me. (Nowadays I would blame it on the books.) The health book had insufficient content. Several pages about a child learning to wash his hands before eating: How could we have a 20- or 30-minute lesson on that? The reading books contained short stories about Dick and Jane in trivial pursuits with their friends. How could I stretch out one of those into a 45-minute lesson?

I was always trying to fill time. I filled a lot of it with worksheets that I made late into the night hours. I returned checked worksheets for a while, but a secret pile of unchecked papers grew threateningly high. No child ever asked about one of those missing papers, and one late afternoon I remembered a professor saying, "You don't have to check everything the children do." Suppressing my guilt feelings, I put the whole pile into a waste basket, covered it the best I could with more normal basket contents, and walked home with a light, adventurous feeling of having turned over a new leaf in my teaching year.

We used the small town library (the school had none), and I learned some of my first lessons about how much children love to read if there is something interesting to read. We had triumphs like the all-school operetta at Christmas time. I had failures like not being able to teach a beautiful, gentle third-grade girl how to read. That haunts me yet, and is a reason I have since specialized in reading problems. I experienced fiascos like the time we made May baskets as described in a teacher magazine, then walked in the woods to find blossoms and flowers for the baskets, but could find nothing blooming in Valdez on May 1.

What helped me the most that year? Practical ideas of things to do, from the teaching magazines, from my housemate, and from the textbooks.

What did not help much? Psychology. In those days Skinner and behaviorism were the rage. Today it's brain-based learning. What will it be tomorrow? In those days we categorized learning styles as visual, auditory, and kinesthetic. Today there are other systems of categorizing. But any differences that matter have a way of showing up as we proceed with teaching and learning. I could hear that some children had more difficulty singing on tune. I could see that Victor's mind leapt to the answers in arithmetic and he hated to back up and write down his steps. The whole class knew that Emil liked to try fixing the record player when it broke down. Labeling children ahead of time and trying to choose special curriculum for them is something that beginners can forego—for now, and maybe forever.

What else did not help? Philosophy. It was years later in graduate school that I seriously met philosophy of education with its words like idealism, progressivism, essentialism, realism, existentialism. Today, researchers try to categorize homeschoolers according to these words, and writers admonish homeschoolers to decide which philosophy fits them. But I suggest that we Christians do not fit into any of the philosophers' categories. A more ordinary level of philosophy may be appropriate for us at some point in our careers. After I had taught a couple of years I could begin to write out some simple beliefs about teaching and learning. But if I had written this heading north on the SS Alaska it would have been only a schoolgirl essay. I can't see that it would have made any difference in my day-to-day teaching that memorable year in Valdez.

So, to all you beginners, I say you can safely ignore much of the overwhelming advice. Just dive in and stumble around and learn as you go. That way your teaching will be real, and not textbookish.

PART II

Most people I know who love history came by their love after they finished school and could read real books instead of textbooks. My own love of history, especially the most ancient periods, grows every decade. My all-time favorite article is Chapter 5 here. Some book reviews are included after Chapter 7 because I think these are books not ordinarily brought to the attention of parents and teachers. Books like these can change your view of ancient history.

Is Bible Knowledge for Everybody?

Does the Bible belong only in churches and religious schools, or does it belong also in the education of every child in Western society? To explore this question, we survey here several areas of the curriculum and show what children will miss if the Bible is excluded.

Cultural Literacy

A good argument is made that our low reading levels are not caused so much by lack of phonics or techniques, but by lack of knowledge of the shared culture. Thus the term *cultural literacy* has recently appeared in education writings. It refers not to the in-depth knowledge of an expert or serious student in a subject, but to the shallower level of knowledge that should be shared by everyone in a society in order for them to communicate well.

You might read on the sports page or the business page

the phrase "David and Goliath." Those writers take for granted that you know of the little underdog challenging the giant and thereby will understand the meaning. E. D. Hirsch, Jr. and his associates cataloged such items of specific information that are taken for granted in public discourse. They first set up selection criteria and then scanned numerous publications to collect items.

The resulting dictionary includes 26 pages of Bible information, which is almost 5% of the total. No other single book comes anywhere close to dominating as the Bible does. For instance, all other literature in English uses 30 pages of the dictionary, just a bit more than the Bible uses by itself. World literature, too, even with philosophy and religion added to the category, uses only 30 pages. A category of Mythology and Folklore from everywhere uses 19 pages.

These researchers note that "No one in the English-speaking world can be considered literate without a basic knowledge of the Bible."

Mythology in Literature and History

To literature professors, "mythology" is a technical word referring to foundational stories of how the world and mankind began and, in the case of the Bible, how the world will end. Whether the stories are true need not be answered for the professors' purposes. A civilization's mythology is important because it embodies its basic assumptions, and these affect all its literature. Students cannot understand literature without first understanding the foundational beliefs of the civilization.

In the West, those beliefs are derived from the Bible. This is not to say that all or even a majority of students and professors believe the Bible. But it is to say that Western civilization is built upon a biblical system of thought—such ideas as a linear view of time, cause and effect, or man as distinct from nature. A prominent literature professor, Northrop Frye, wrote:

> [T]he Bible forms the lowest stratum in the teaching of literature. It should be taught so early and so thoroughly that it sinks straight to the bottom of the mind, where everything that comes along later can settle on it. . . . it's the total shape and structure of the Bible which is the most important: the fact that it's a continuous narrative beginning with the creation and ending with the Last Judgment, and surveying the whole history of mankind . . . in between *(Frye[1], p. 110).*

Frye, as far as I can tell from his writings, does not claim to be a Christian—or Jew. He wrote from his literary viewpoint.

Historians ask a different set of questions about mythology; questions like Which story is the oldest, Which borrowed from the other, Who invented the ideas, or How did they arise.

How did the stories arise? One major hypothesis is that the ideas came from the minds of people as they observed their world. For instance, early agricultural societies saw death and renewal each year in plant life, thus stories all over the world of gods and goddesses reflect themes of death, underworld and resurrection. Great novelists, those stone age farmers, according to this hypothesis! But if it is wrong and the stories are not inventions of man, the obvious alternative is that they arose out of actual events or prophecies.

Which story is the oldest? Until recently, historians answered from our modern viewpoint. That is, they assumed that the oldest manuscript we knew was the oldest story, and others must have borrowed from it. For instance, the early Babylonians' Gilgamesh epic of a great flood predated Moses. Therefore Moses must have borrowed his ideas from the Babylonian mythology. That hypothesis worked until we dug up and decoded Sumerian mythology. Then the Babylonians and everybody must have borrowed from the Sumerians. Is this the end now, or will we dig up something still older?

Recently, some scholars have taken a new approach to studying the ancient stories, which any family can try as an educational project. To do this you need a minimum of three stories of an event, say the event of a worldwide flood. You need more than three to draw meaningful conclusions from your work, but three will do as a start. People have collected more than 270 versions of a flood story from around the world.

Place circles or dots on a sheet of paper and label them each to represent one of the stories you have collected. Then do the detective work of finding similarities in details among the stories. How many people were on the boat? Draw lines to connect any stories which have the same number. Where did the boat land? Draw lines to connect any stories that are similar in this detail. Continue analyzing each story until you have found all the similarities you can.

Do your lines tend to converge on one more than others? If so, that argues that the other stories borrowed from it rather than the reverse. Scholars who have done this on a large scale find a definite pattern of the biblical flood story being the root of all flood stories.

But Moses's Bible writings are not the oldest, so how could the Babylonians and others have borrowed from him? This research raises the distinct probability that the original story was older than any that we now have, and Moses and other ancient writers drew from existing records or oral traditions. The convergence of lines on the Bible's version of the story indicates that it is closest to the original. It has less corruption in its transmission than the others.

The Bible, as closest to the root source then, should not be neglected while the derivatives are studied. The Bible is neglected less in literature courses than in other areas of curriculum, but even there it is phasing out, as younger generations of teachers know less about it, and as schools in America have over-reacted to the Supreme Court decision about Bible reading and prayer.

The Bible story of creation is in Genesis 1 and 2. The story of the flood is in Genesis 6–9. Chapter 6, verses 1 to 4, has a hint of demigods and superhumans that fill the mythologies of other ancient peoples. Verse 4 says, "There were giants in the earth in those days; and also after that, when the sons of God came in unto the daughters of men, and they bare children to them, the same became mighty men which were of old, men of renown."

Can students be called educated who read the Greek, Roman and Norse stories of origins and early times but have these Bible stories banned from their education?

Ancient History

It is now common for historians to take the Bible as sober history. A century and a half of archeology has made it impossible for them to ignore the Bible. They now quote from it along with other ancient documents, but only back as far as Abraham and the Sumerian cities.

Before Abraham, are the times that historians refer to as "legendary" or prehistoric. We have no clear history from outside the Bible of those early times, so without that corroboration, historians don't take the early chapters of the Bible as clear history either. For one example, historians write that Menes is the legendary first Pharaoh of united Egypt. The Upper and Lower Kingdoms, with their supposed long history before him, are themselves legendary. That means that most of what is said about those kingdoms is conjecture, though in schoolbooks it may sound like well known fact.

The Bible doesn't have a long, fuzzy period before Abraham. History appears much shorter there. In Genesis 10 is the remarkable "Table of Nations," a unique ancient document. Listed in this chapter is Mizraim, which is an Old Testament name for Egypt. The man Mizraim (Menes, perhaps?) is the uncle of Nimrod, who founded Babylon, Nineveh and other Mesopotamian cities, and who gathered the cities together into the empire which led to the story of the Tower of Babel.

Thus in this account, if it is sober history, we read of the origins of Egypt and of Sumeria (later to become Babylonia and Assyria). It sounds there as though civilization grew up rather quickly. We get this picture even if we read between the lines to allow for migrations and settlements and wars and numerous births to enlarge the tribes.

Amazingly, the Sumerians' history also sounds as if civilization grew up suddenly. Our greatest historian of those times criticizes the Sumerians for that view. Noah Kramer wrote that the Sumerians had no concept of the slow development of civilizations. They thought their civilization came full-grown and full-blown upon the world. We moderns, according to Kramer, have the right concept, while the Sumerians were wrong about their own history.

Those histories from the Sumerians and the Hebrews

both tell a story of civilization rising rapidly after a great flood destroyed the world. The Hebrew history of that time is found in the Bible book of Genesis, chapters 10 and 11. Students who do not learn these Bible stories, or meet them only as mythology, have a more anemic education than their peers who consider the Bible more seriously as history.

Law

Schoolbooks used to refer to Hammurabi's laws as being the oldest code, also saying or implying that Moses was a Johnny-come-lately. Then, as with the histories, still earlier law writings from Sumeria were discovered and translated, so Hammurabi lost his place as the originator of law systems.

A scholarly view of these ancient laws comes from Professor Carl Ehrlich of Heidelberg, Germany, writing in the *Oxford Companion to the Bible*. Ehrlich says that the law writings from Babylonia and other ancient Mesopotamian civilizations were not "codes" of law in the Roman sense. Among thousands of legal documents from ancient Mesopotamia not one refers to Hammurabi's collection, nor to any other, for a precedent. Those kings compiled laws simply to enhance their stature as rulers in their lands. Thus these documents should be classified as literary, of historical interest, Ehrlich says, but not as the origins of legal systems.

The laws of the Hebrews differed from their neighbors' in fundamental ways. First, the authority for law was not the king, but God, in their conception. Moses and other leaders were mediators of the law; they were not above law. Second, human life was valued. The main concern of Babylonian law was to protect property belonging to the upper echelons of society. The main concern of Hebrew law was the sanctity of the individual, who was formed in the image of God.

It is this Hebrew law, rather than the Mesopotamian, which strongly influenced Roman law, both through its civil law after the empire became Christian and through church law, as the Roman Catholic church exercised influence during the disintegration of the empire. From these Roman roots, stem all systems of law in Western Europe and those which later branched out from Europe. Law that sprang up among people in their local communities came to be called "common law," and this, too, was based on the biblical beliefs of the people and of the judges, who often were under holy orders from the church. The non-western world was less influenced by the Bible.

Modern law has more immediate roots in law books from the 1500s to the 1700s. These writings often appealed to Roman law or to the Bible itself. They also began using the term "natural law," which was said by some of the writers to be given by God. As time went on, the original sources were acknowledged less, though the principles remain.

Professor Francis Lyall of the University of Aberdeen, Scotland, writes in *The Oxford Companion* that Bible principles are being secured more widely in our century through the United Nations' Universal Declaration of Human Rights and other covenants which followed that. These draw on biblical ideas, he says, but do not acknowledge this source.

Hebrew law is found mostly in the Bible books of Exodus, Leviticus and Deuteronomy. The Ten Commandments are in Exodus 20. Are students cheated in their education to have no acquaintance with these?

Politics

The idea of theocratic government has been powerful in Western history. The "divine right of kings" and of judges and others in authority has been defended by Romans 13:1, which states, "The powers that be are ordained of God." But through the centuries people have challenged this idea. They argued that kingship was not in early Bible history, and when the Israelites did get a king it was as a revolt against God.

Thus, although the Bible has not been shown to clearly support one system of government over another, it does contain ideas and principles which people have debated in relation to government. The Reformation idea of "the priesthood of believers" gave responsibility in religious life to individuals, rather than to priests of the church. This principle filtered into political thinking and grew into the modern democratic idea. By this route, democracy appeared in the West rather than in other parts of the world.

Ethics and Morals

Problems in our society have led to a call among educators to teach ethics and morals in the schools. That, in turn, has led to a lively debate about whose ethics, how we keep religion out of it and so forth. We all can agree on certain ethics, like honesty, and we should teach those, some argue. Yet, by law, we cannot hang a poster that says, "Thou shalt not bear false witness" or "Thou shalt not steal." If Hammurabi had written those words, they'd be okay. But they came through Moses and are in the Bible. So they're labeled religious.

Dr. Robert Coles, a prominent psychiatrist and social

scientist, proposes that we teach ethics and morals through literature. He has taught courses at Harvard designed to humanize some of the fields of study. These are "Literature and . . ." courses: literature and sociology, medicine, teaching, business and others. One course was called "Dickens and the Law." With this background, Coles has now written about using literature with younger students to teach ethics and morals.

Why literature? Professor Frye would answer that it's because literature reflects the foundational assumptions of our society, and that means it reflects the Bible. So by Frye's reasoning, the most direct ethical and moral teaching comes from the root source, the Bible. But Coles suggests secondary sources only, from obvious political necessity.

Learning from secondary sources, rather than the original, is weaker to start with, and in this case is likely to become more weak with passing time. If it is true, as some observe, that each generation of literature is moving further from its Western roots, then the Coles-type courses will move with them. In the future we may not agree on honesty or other principles that we could perhaps agree on today. We'd probably not even agree on whether that's decline or progress.

A truly educated person should not be ignorant of the shared ethics and morals that helped to build Western civilization. Through many centuries the Bible has had more influence in these areas than any other book. This phenomenon is unmatched anywhere, anytime in history. To quote Frye again: "This huge, sprawling, tactless book sit[s] there inscrutably in the middle of our cultural heritage like the 'great Boyg' . . . frustrating all our efforts to walk around it" (Frye[2], p. xviii).

The Arts

Bible themes appear extensively in art, music and literature. Much has been written on this. It is a common reason given for students' need to know the stories and themes of the Bible.

Biblical visual art aligns closely with Christian worship, as it decorated cathedrals and books. Biblical music and literature grew to have both their sacred and secular strains. From the 1600s and onwards, certain operas and orchestral works with biblical themes were written for performance in music halls rather than in church. We are richer for such works from Handel, Rossini, Gounod, Richard Strauss and other greats even down to our own century.

In literature, the influence of the Bible in Europe "has been so pervasive as to be almost incalculable" (Peter Heinegg in *Oxford Companion* p. 446). In America, writers used drama from frontier life, yet they infused biblical meaning. Puritan and Calvinist tradition influenced writers directly at first, and in the nineteenth century more indirectly, as people lived off their literary capital inherited from the previous century. This capital was so pervasive that "American writers almost unavoidably wrote in biblical language, whatever their subject" (David Jeffrey in *Oxford Companion* p. 457).

This unavoidability is seen perhaps especially vividly when the subject is anti-Bible. Walt Whitman recognized this in telling that he grounded himself in the Bible before writing *Leaves of Grass*. Then using Bible style in the poems, he praised self and man. Emily Dickinson, too, rejected the traditional views, but to fully understand her rejection, a reader needs extensive familiarity with the very words of the Bible. Melville's *Moby-Dick* can be seen as an anti-Calvinist message, of a failed imitation of Christ. Yet from the opening line—Call me Ishmael—Melville's knowledge of the Bible shows through.

When the Bible so permeates the arts, particularly literature, it is folly to try banning the Bible itself from the curriculum.

Science

Debates in our day seem to pit the Bible and religion against science. The Galileo conflicts in everyone's textbooks add to this popular conception of science as separate from religion.

So it may sound startling to hear that the Bible has played an indispensable role in Western science. But this is the view of Andre Goddu a professor of the history and philosophy of science who writes in *The Oxford Companion*. Also philosopher Alfred North Whitehead has said that Christianity is the "mother of science." And scientist J. Robert Oppenheimer and other great modern scientists, though not Christians themselves, concur with that view.

Copernicus believed that a creation by God would have rational design and thus would be knowable within human limits. These two ideas of design and knowability are critical in Western science. Johannes Kepler held these philosophical views, as well as agreeing with Copernicus that mathematical relations among the heavenly bodies favored a hypothesis of a heliocentric (sun-centered) system. Galileo was not satisfied with strictly mathematical relations but wanted also to demonstrate the Copernican theory. Complicated religious conflict ensued, which a Catholic Pope apologized for about 300 years later.

In the meantime, science grew into a profession and

proceeded with the method of empirical research. Francis Bacon is credited with establishing the method. Bacon was a Bible believer, as were many of the "fathers" after him: Robert Boyle, father of chemistry; Blaise Pascal, father of hydrostatics and analytic geometry; Nicholas Steno, father of stratigraphy; William Harvey, discoverer of blood circulation; John Woodward, founder of paleontology; Carolus Linnaeus, developer of today's system of biological taxonomy; Michael Faraday, electro-magnetics and field theory; Lord Kelvin and Clerk Maxwell, physics. This list could be vastly lengthened, as many of the great men of early modern science held the Copernicus view that nature is designed and knowable.

Because of the predominance of that view among scientists in those times, the evolutionary thinking of Darwin's grandfather and others made little headway among the general public. People preferred to believe what the scientists believed. But the times seemed ripe for a change when *The Origin of Species* appeared. Now that most scientists believe in evolution, most of the general public does too.

But observers and philosophers of the science scene point out that scientists *act* as though they believe in design and order and knowability of nature, rather than acting as though they believe in chance and other basics of evolution. In other words, the progress of science today can still be traced to its operating by the biblical principles laid down by the fathers from Copernicus through the eighteenth century.

Shall we tell that to today's students?

Summary

The Bible's "stories and characters are part of both the

repertoire of Western literature and the vocabulary of educated women and men. . . . Since its formation, the Bible has been a primary resource for Western culture." So state the editors of *The Oxford Companion* (pp. vi and viii). Hirsch writes that the Bible "is the most widely known book in the English-speaking world. . . . The linguistic and cultural importance of the Bible is a fact that no one denies" (p. 1).

The huge, tactless book sits sprawling through all curriculum areas. In education, it most certainly is for everybody.

---

1. Frye, Northrop, *The Educated Imagination,* Indiana University Press, 1974.
2. Frye, Northrop, *The Great Code,* Harcourt Brace Jovanovich, 1983.
3. Metzger, Bruce M. and Michael D. Coogan eds., *The Oxford Companion to the Bible,* Oxford University Press, 1993.
4. Hirsch, E. D. Jr., Joseph F. Kett and James Treffil, *The Dictionary of Cultural Literacy,* Houghton Mifflin Company, 1988.

The Neglected Period of History

If the world's history were divided into three equal segments, which segment do you know the most about? Which do your children spend the most time studying? Possibly your answer to both these questions is the most recent segment. That is the last 2000 years, the time from Jesus until now.

Certainly a lot has happened in those 2000 years. First there was the spread of Christianity throughout the Roman Empire and elsewhere, then the fall of the Roman Empire and a time of unsettled government in the West that we call the Middle Ages. Eastern peoples became Buddhist, Arabs became Islamic. Then followed the Renaissance, the Reformation of Christianity, world exploration, colonization and settlement of the Western hemisphere, the Industrial Revolution, wars and rumors of wars right down to the present day—an eventful 2000 years and a period we know rather well. You and your children in ten minutes could produce a long list of events and people that belong in this period.

The preceding 2000 years begins with Abraham and stretches to the time of Christ. If you know Old Testament history, you also could produce quite a long list of events from this time segment—at least events that happened in the Middle East. Abraham was promised a good land, his descendants migrated to Egypt and grew strong there. Under Moses and Joshua they returned and claimed their land. They lived under judges and then kings, and later were conquered and scattered by Babylonia and Assyria, which were in turn conquered by Persia. The Persian king Cyrus decreed that the Jews should return and they did, remaining through the Grecian period and into the Roman period. Rome was ruling when Jesus was born.

A still earlier segment of 2000 years stretches backward from Abraham all the way to Creation. A look at the timeline serves to remind us that many events could have happened then. The first period is just as long as the middle or the last. In a moment we will look at events of that period, but first let us consider the importance to us of each period of history.

Creation	Abraham	Christ	Now

For Americans and others in the western hemisphere it is important to know about the foundings of our nations. Especially in America, we need to know of the Christian roots that came across the ocean with the Puritans, Pilgrims and others and was built into our founding documents. By looking back across history we can see that our country's founders had long roots before them in the people who spread Christianity across Europe in the early centuries after Christ. And the historic roots of Christ's coming stretch back to Abraham, through whom God promised to bless the world, and even before Abraham to a more distant early time.

Some Americans came to our Pacific shores, during the settlement period, from China and other Far East areas, and they have their own ancient history to learn, but need also to understand the Christian founding of the government they now live under. Later waves of immigrants have similar multiple strands of history behind them. The earliest immigrants came to Western shores in the middle period of history as shown on our three-part timeline, or possibly even during the first period.

Why should children today learn about the past? One reason is to help them understand and deal with the present. For example, troubles in the Middle East today can be largely understood in terms of religious tensions that reach far back in history—to the beginning of the Arabs and Jews from the same father Abraham. Though some educators have wanted to minimize the study of religion and relegate it to the "superstitious" past, it is still much with us, playing its major role in history. Religious issues are involved not only in the Reformation, the Galileo episode and other past events and movements, but they are still here in struggles over atheistic communism, issues of public and home schooling, abortion and others which will be written into history if the world has enough years left to it.

History books which do include religion often have too short a view. They may try to help children understand an issue by understanding the differing views or backgrounds of the people involved. This, in fact, is a major trend in teaching—to go back far enough to show that differences exist and then try to develop a respect for all beliefs. Some educators would like to wrap up all religious beliefs into a warm blanket and say, "It's okay. Believe whatever you want. It's not really important." If they could succeed in putting religion into the fuzzy warm blanket, then, they think, it wouldn't raise its strong head and cause wars and other troubles for the world. We could live in peace.

The short view, then, may take into account only influences operating at the time of the event being studied. Or it may reach back to show some roots of the influences, such as the Arab and Jew example given above. But few history books go back far enough. They do not reach into the first period of history to find the common plight of Arabs and Jews and all of us. Where were we before the differences came to be? What caused the differences? Getting back to these origins is essential for understanding where we are now.

The first period is of supreme importance in the study of mankind's history, yet it is the most neglected. Major principles for interpreting history are found by knowing the beginnings of man, the beginnings of nations, the beginnings of religions. It's a weak history that neglects beginnings and tries to understand middles and endings without that foundation. It's also a weak history that postulates guesses and falsehoods for beginnings.

The greatest and most influential book ever written on beginnings is, of course, Genesis. Millions of people through all periods of history—even before Moses—have based their thinking upon the first beginning recorded there, that God created the heavens and the earth and everything in them. Those who don't take this view, if they are thinking people at all, hold the only other possible view, that matter always existed and somehow begat life and the gods. Ancient peoples included "real" gods in this scenario, but moderns prefer to say that mankind simply invented gods for their psychological needs. But in either case it is a difference of whether God was first or matter was first.

This difference in world view, accounts for numerous differences in outlook upon life today. One obvious example is the modern practice of killing babies. If we originated from matter, and we arrived on the scene by time and chance; if we have no souls or God who gave us life; then who can say it's wrong to kill babies for our convenience? This major principle of creation is paramount for understanding history and its issues.

Another major principle is the coming of sin into the world. This principle is not well understood even by many Christians. How common it is to hear someone lament that if God is good how can He let tragedy and evil happen in the world! But a close study of the beginnings of sin in the world shows also that evil exists in a spiritual realm outside this world. It shows the existence of Satan and his evil demons and their battle for control of the world. When people understand their place in this larger battle, they have a much clearer view of history. They know, for instance, that the religious issues cannot be swept away or wrapped in a blanket. These will be with us until the end of the age.

Pagan literature, that we call mythology, in some ways corroborates what Genesis says. Pagans believe that there were gods, evil ones, and that men and gods had some contact with one another. A careful look at Genesis shows that a lot of this original knowledge of the spirit world was wiped out in the Great Flood. What re-emerged afterward, was again judged, and confounded, at the catastrophic Babel event. Students of these events can see how all religions not based on worship of the Creator God are based, instead, on various garbled versions of Satan's original opposition to

God. All pagan religions can be seen as fanning out from their center at Babel.

Other major principles and sub-principles could be listed, but the point to make here is that these principles come from studying closely the first period of history. How many pages in your child's history book are devoted to this period? How clear is this period in comparison with later ones?

Many rewards await the student who looks closely at this period, using Genesis as a starting point. Small details and larger pieces of the historical puzzle begin to fall into place. Here's a small one—that has major ramifications. Genesis 2:10 says that "a river went out of Eden to water the garden; and from thence it was parted, and became into four heads" (KJV). Practically all translations carry that same meaning of a river parting and becoming four, but this apparently caused too much problem for the people preparing one recent version, and they arranged the words to say, "A river flowed through Eden and watered the garden. From that point the river was divided. It had four streams flowing into it." These writers made it conform to today's world where rain and snow bring water to the lands, the waters gather into small rivulets, which flow into streams, which in turn flow into larger rivers. In today's world four rivers can become one, but one does not become four.

But in the pre-flood world there was no rain. This information and the river information have led scientists to study what form of water cycle could have operated in those days. Their studies, combined with still other bits of the puzzle, bring us fascinating insights into the old world and the Great Flood which destroyed it. Our children should learn these events thoroughly and well so they can never be the ones Peter writes of, saying that they are willingly ignorant that "the world that then was, being overflowed with water, perished" (II Peter 3:6).

Here are some typical recent items that show even Christian leaders without a clear view of this early history:

Item: Radio preacher says that people laughed at Noah because his boat was 500 miles from water. (He was measuring from where the boat landed at Ararat, not from the unknown location where it was built.)

Item: Executive editor of a Christian publishing house returns from a trip to Bible lands and reports, "This is where they think the Garden of Eden was." (This puts Adam in the same land as Abraham or David, and ignores the destruction of the Flood.)

Item: A commercial timeline shows discovery of agriculture, Bronze Age, Iron Age, etc., as developmental periods, and the Flood and Babel disaster interpolated upon these as having no effect. (This mixes evolutionary history and Bible history in an illogical way.)

The past is important to us all, and the distant past is supremely important. That is where we study origins—the origin of the world and mankind, the origin of sin and religions, the origin of languages and nations, the origin of prophecy and our knowledge of God's plan for the world. Children who study these matters will have wisdom far beyond those whose schooling leaves them ignorant of the first period of the world's history.

Revise those Timelines!

Yes. You'll need to take scissors and paste to most of your timelines, charts, textbooks and practically all books of ancient history. If you have read that archeologists have it all figured out now, that what they dig up aligns neatly with Bible history, it's not true.

Speaking of the times before about 800 BC, there are more questions than answers about historical chronology. Biblical scholars try to decide which ruler was the pharaoh of the Exodus, which wall at the Jericho digs fell in Joshua's battle, and could a great man like Joseph be found in secular history.

Secular archeologists on their part, not usually caring whether the Bible fits, also have their problems. In civilizations of the Mediterranean area they have gaps of time which they cannot fill. What is needed for a good fit is either that traditional Bible chronology be stretched out or that secular chronology be shrunk.

Consider the Exodus problem, for instance. The Bible

gives a lot of detail. First, a pharoah whose daughter (Or perhaps sister, daughter of the previous pharaoh?) rescued Moses seemed to reign for about 80 years of Moses's life. Then he died and a new pharaoh reigned only briefly before being drowned in the Red Sea. The plagues that year ruined the Egyptians' crops, decimated their livestock, and killed the firstborn sons of all families. The departure of the Israelites deprived Egypt of its slave labor, and much of its wealth besides. Then the ruling pharaoh and his whole army were drowned. Further, the book of Judges never mentions Egypt among the nations which oppressed Israel in the land, although Egypt is known to have extended her empire that far in her stronger days.

What an event that was! Yet historians still wonder and guess which pharaohs were involved and when in Egyptian history it happened. Many secular historians don't believe it happened at all because they don't find evidence of such a devasted Egypt. Could it be that they don't find evidence because they are looking in the wrong timeframe, in the wrong centuries?

Actually there is a time where this event fits wonderfully well, and homeschoolers will recognize it because so many of you love to study ancient Egypt. It comes at the end of the Old Kingdom. The next-to-last pharaoh of this prosperous kingdom was Phiops II (or Pepi II) and he reigned for more than 90 years. He was followed by Merenre Antyemsaf II, who reigned for 1 year. Then the Old Kingdom collapsed for reasons that still mystify historians. That was followed by the chaos of an intermediate period leading into the Middle Kingdom which, though it lasted hundreds of years, never again achieved the splendor of the Old Kingdom.

The main problem with this scenario is that if you lay a

traditional Bible timeline alongside a Cambridge or other secular timeline there is no such match. The Exodus and the collapse of the Old Kingdom are simply are not close enough.

Such mismatches are so numerous that scholars are questioning the timelines themselves. Below are reports on two efforts to cut and paste the timelines. The first is from secular historians who propose shortening ancient history in the Mediterranean area by several hundred years.

Shrinking the Timeline

To get a picture of archeological problems, imagine yourself working on a jigsaw puzzle. Someone has already placed the left and right edges, and you are filling in the sky and ground pieces. After a time you struggle with too large a gap all across the puzzle. You can't make the ground meet the sky. The trees can't be stretched that far. Close study almost convinces you that some of your ground pieces actually fit into sky pieces. But you can't fit them because of the gap. If the framing on the edge wasn't there, you would be convinced. You would just slide the sky down and complete the puzzle.

That's exactly what archeologists have been struggling with. The framework on the edge was a chronology of Egypt developed by William Flinders Petrie early in this century. He based his work on ancient dynasty lists by Manetho, a Greek-Egyptian priest from the second century BC, and on something called "Sothic cycles," which are periods related to the rising of the star Sirius (ancient Sothis) with the sun.

Many events in the Middle East area could be connected with artifacts or pharaohs of Egypt and they were dated thereby according to Petrie's dates. These were assumed to be firm dates. W. F. Albright and a few others objected to the obstinacy with which scholars hung on to the dynasties as Manetho listed them. Isaac Newton had earlier criticized the Egyptians for their vanity in making their "monarchy some thousands of years older than the world." The Sothic theory, too, came under criticism. But mainstream archeology proceeded with Petrie's system.

That's how the gaps came to be—dark ages in civilizations great and small. In Greek history, for instance, your young homeschool historians probably know something about Homer's story of destroying Troy. Historians used to think that was just a legend of the Greeks, and not true. According to them, Homer, if he existed, lived 400 years before the Grecian city-states of real history. But then a century ago, archeologists dug up Troy, several Troys in fact, one on top of the other. Their new problem, then, was where to fit the 400 years. The diggings showed no such gap, but they put it in anyway. They could explain it: the survivors moved elsewhere and made the same kind of pottery for 400 years and then came back and rebuilt Troy, so naturally there would be the same pottery in the next level 400 years later.

Peter James, in a book called *Centuries of Darkness*,[1] takes on this problem among others. He redates the sack of Troy to where the diggings say it should be, thus cutting 400 silent years out of the Greek timeline. He tackles numerous such absurdities in the Mediterranean area, closing the gaps and solving many problems. For instance, regarding the Palestine area he concluded:

> By redating the beginning of the Iron Age in Palestine from the early 12th century BC to the late 10th, a completely new interpretation of the archaeology of Israel can be offered: one which is in perfect

harmony with the biblical record. The search for the riches of Solomon's reign can be brought to an end—they have already been found, but simply not recognized, in the material remains of the Late Bronze Age.

James points out some problems with Egyptian chronology—the edge pieces of this puzzle—but he does not solve them in his book. That is left for other historians. A few decades ago Immanuel Velikovsky, a controversial figure, wrote a series of books in which he explained the Egyptian problem and he, too, proposed shortening its chronology by several hundred years.

Centuries of Darkness uses much technical language of archeologists, so most homeschoolers may just want to know that such a book exists and know its message as described above. But hopefully a few serious history students will pursue it in more detail. Will some of them eventually solve Egyptian chronology problems and bring order to the history of Old Testament times?

Stretching the Timeline

While some historians work at cutting out the gaps and shortening ancient secular history as we know it, others work at stretching the Biblical timeline to make a better match. One effort of this kind is by Dr. Gerald Aardsma, a Christian scholar conversant with radioisotope dating and other physical sciences. He is the scholar who suggests the Exodus at the end of Egypt's Old Kingdom, as described above.

How does he stretch the Old Testament back far enough to make Moses fit with Old Kingdom times in Egypt as that is traditionally dated? By pasting a new section of timeline between Judges and I Samuel. The time there is fuzzy to Biblical chronologists, anyway. And Aardsma has a theory about it that he argues in great detail in a monograph on this subject.[2] Dr. Aardsma has worked for over ten years on Biblical chronology problems and is now devoting full time to this work.[3]

Where Do We Go from Here?

We obviously are at an exciting juncture in the study of ancient history. Are we about to overturn a long-entrenched system? Here's how Velikovsky described the circular thinking that set up this system.

> The specialists in astronomical chronology made their calculations and announced their expert results. The specialists in pottery took the results of the specialists in Sothic [astronomical] computation as a firm base on which to build. Specialists in the history of art, the history of religion, philology, and history in general followed. Difficulties were swept away and the findings of the specialists corroborate one another, and so they have scientific proof that their systems are constructed with precision and are well fortified on all sides. The readers of cuneiform borrow dates from the readers of hieroglyphics; the Bible exegetes from the archaeologists; the historians from all of them. Thus there came into existence an elaborate, entrenched system that bears very little resemblance to the real past.[4]

What will the textbooks of tomorrow look like? Will the timeline shrinkers win out or will the stretchers win. I personally hope the shrinkers win, on most points at least. But either way the end will be, as Peter James said, "in perfect harmony with the biblical record."

Further, I hope that many homeschoolers participate in the process. You are in a unique position to do this, because you are not so bound as classroom students to the traditional textbooks that sound as if they have all the answers. Your older students can read books like those mentioned in this article that question the entrenched views. And some can go on to specialize in history and related fields, and contribute to rewriting history for the next generation.

---

1. Published 1994 by Rutgers University Press.
2. Described in detail in *A New Approach to the Chronology of Old Testament History from Abraham to Samuel,* available from Institute for Creation Research, PO Box 2667, El Cajon CA 92021; $17.95 including shipping.
3. He publishes a bimonthly newsletter, "The Biblical Chronologist," to give ongoing reports and information. It is available from Aardsma Research & Publishing, 412 N. Mulberry, Loda IL 60948; $18 per year ($19 US dollars in Canada).
4. *Peoples of the Sea,* Doubleday, pp. 243, 244.

How, then, Shall I Teach Ancient History?

1. Children of all ages can learn more about Old Testament history, becoming familiar with people and places and events.

2. Children meeting ancient dates in their books should master the idea of counting backward for BC dates. This requires time and attention; it's not easy to see that 400 BC is later than 479 BC. Note also the modern terms BCE and CE, which stand for "Before the Common Era" and "Common Era." This is a way of avoiding the name of Christ at the center of our dating system.

3. Children studying ancient history should be told that dates before about 800 BC are uncertain, regardless of what a particular book says. They should know that scholars are debating the problems and some dates may eventually be changed by as much as several hundred years.

4. Try to find two books which present differing views on a topic in history. Children who read a lot may stumble across this themselves. Take advantage of this situation to compare the two views and analyze, if possible, why the writers differ. This is an especially valuable lesson, as children learn that history isn't just black or white and all known at this time. Not only are ancient dates a case in point, but motives of historical personages, whether particular actions turned out for the better, and practically all other history topics are open for historians to dig up additional information and to reconsider.

ere was translated: Ships from Phoenicia, cargo
as this a sign telling merchants where they may
ps that will pick up their wares?

from Tarshish left a drawing and inscription on
e, Rhode Island. Over 500 inscribed grave markers
d in the Susquehanna valley. In Iowa were found
s written in ancient Egyptian, Lybian and Cartha-
nguages. Stone tables can be seen at Bartlett, New
ire, and North Salem and Westport, Massachusetts. If
near the Colorado-Oklahoma border you may find
ions in caves and on cliffs along the Arkansas and
on Rivers and their tributaries.

ould ancient history be buried in your back yard? You
discover it if you learn from this book more about ruins
ancient scripts. Unfortunately, the index in this book
ides no help in locating references to your state. You will
e to read the book and form your own index as you go
ng.

5. Children who show special interest in the ancient dating problems (or other history problems, for that matter) should be encouraged to pursue this as far as resources and time allow. This study will integrate math and astronomy and other sciences, as well as ancient languages and other subjects you never thought to put into the curriculum, so you don't need to worry if something else in your curriculum gets slighted for this.

Two More Books To Change Your Views of History

The Pyramids: An Enigma Solved by Dr. Joseph Davidovits and Margie Morris. New York, Hippocrene Books, 1988.

The most often asked question about pyramids has been, "How did they lift those stones of such size to such heights?" and it now appears we have asked the wrong question for centuries. These authors point out that even if you propose a lifting technique the ancients might have used, you haven't solved the main problem.

One common answer is that slaves pulled stones up dirt ramps. But nowhere is there any evidence of the ramps. And unanswered are the related questions of where that many stones were quarried; how men cut, polished and fit them so perfectly; and where all the rubble was left. Moreover, arithmetic concerning the number of slaves required to build the Great Pyramid during the 20-year reign of Khufu (Cheops) yields a result of 750,000 men cooperating on the plain of Giza!

If I give Davidovits's answer to the puzzles, it should not spoil the ending of the story for those who want to read it, because much of the fascination of this book is reading about the evidences—in chemistry, in geology of the areas, in ancient writings, hieroglyphics as well as Latin and Greek. Anyone with even a mild interest in pyramids will be drawn to at least one of these chapters. The solution, according to Davidovits, is that the stones in most pyramids were poured, being cast in place.

This thesis, with the reasoning and evidence given, is strongly convincing, and history textbooks over the next decade or two may be changing their information. But that will be too late for today's children.

The book is adult or teen level reading, and the authors seem to take for granted that their readers know such things as the Old, Middle and New Kingdoms of Egypt and that they are well acquainted with its geography. So you may wish to be ready with a map, a historical chronology and other references, and keep in mind that there is not full agreement on dates, particularly of the more ancient periods of Egypt.

America B.C.: Ancient Settlers in the New World by Barry Fell. New York: Pocket Books, 1976.

Did the ships of Tarshish carry on regular commerce with the New World? Are ancient Egyptian words found in some American Indian languages? Were Celtic peoples settled in New England before the time of Christ?

The answer to all these questions is Yes.

The Atlantic Ocean seemed to be crossed regularly by Phoenicians, Celts, and other Mediterranean peoples from at

least the early Bronze Age (th[...] the Roman Empire. The Pacific [...]

Celts in America worshipe[...] goddess found in all pagan religic[...] were built here, with inscriptions to[...] townspeople thought these structure[...] own ancestors; so, many were destr[...] for fences or bridges and dams. You[...] inscriptions thousands of years old.

Why did we take so long to recogniz[...] these inscriptions? That is the major st[...] fascinating account of deciphering an ancie[...] Ogam. Fell's view of this script is controv[...] historians do not believe it is a script at a[...] studies this, you can form your own opinion.

A couple of chapters give considerable deta[...] monuments, which you may not want your childre[...] book is rather difficult reading, anyway, so you cou[...] your family and pass on to the children some of[...] which probably is not in their textbooks.

The author, Fell, takes an evolutionary view of[...] Thus he presents the fertility rituals and sun wors[...] harmless superstitions which grew among agricultural p[...] Any connection with Babel and the false beliefs of p[...] peoples everywhere escapes non-Christian historians.

If you live near North Salem, New Hampshire, you m[...] visit Mystery Hill, where several temple remains and inscrip[...] tions have been preserved and are available for public viewing. These date about 800 to 600 BC. More temple remains and other relics are scattered around Vermont and other New England locations. At the island of Manana, near Moneghan Island off the coast of Maine, is a flat horizontal surface of rock where Phoenicians may have unloaded cargoes, as an

inscription th[...]
platform. W[...]
meet the sh[...]
A shi[...]
Mount Ho[...]
were fou[...]
inscriptio[...]
ginian la[...]
Hampsh[...]
you liv[...]
inscrip[...]
Cima[...]
migh[...]
and[...]
pro[...]
hav[...]
alc[...]

PART III

Reading became a specialty of mine during my teaching years, and in these chapters I share some of what I learned, with an effort not to duplicate what appears in other of my books. I think the message on phonics is especially needed among homeschoolers, to bring common sense into what could be called the phonics wars. I include reviews of some books (and a drug) as Chapter 11, because this is information not readily available elsewhere.

Once More on Phonics

Bob was leaning against the doorjamb of my office telling me about the young boy he was tutoring. The 10-year-old knew phonics backwards and forwards, yet he could not read.

I was supposed to help Bob solve the reading case, but it was overshadowed in my mind by the teacher case standing before me. Bob had written a book lambasting the public schools for not teaching phonics. It was what I call a "second-hand" book, one where the author reads some books on a subject and then writes his book on the subject—not enough time allowed for digesting the thoughts, not enough life experience to temper the thoughts, just book to book, for the second-hand quality that I detect all too readily in my field of education. Bob's book preached the message that Christians should send their children to Christian schools where phonics is taught and therefore wonderful results follow.

Now Bob was up against his first real, live, squirming

reading problem. Life experience was beginning to temper his thoughts.

That little scene happened in the midst of the rapid growth of Christian schools. Now, a generation later, we are in the midst of the rapid growth of homeschools, and the phonics zealots are back in greater force than ever.

One factor, naturally, is money. Suppliers of phonics kits and materials never had it so good. Now instead of selling one set per classroom they can sell one set per home. So everybody and his brother is writing a new phonics program. Reviewers follow. Ads bombard from all sides. True believers contribute their articles and books, and the combined result is an atmosphere filled with phonics, phonics, phonics.

New homeschoolers might be excused in this setting if they feel intimidated. You veterans should remind them that they know phonics. They've been using it for years. Where's the hidden secret that they must search for and pay high prices for? There is none. Most parents could teach reading without any phonics program if they wanted to.

And most could teach it in lots less time if they weren't so bombarded and pressured by the phonics zealots. When I was a child I taught my toddler sister to read in about three months. When I was a teacher I found that I could teach phonics in about three weeks if the time was right. Homeschooling parents teaching it for the first time need not aim for the three-week schedule. But, to be conservative, how about four times that, or three months?

I would like to quit writing on phonics and move on to other topics. But since the phonics hype won't go away, I take one more stab here at trying to defuse some of the myths I see in the atmosphere.

The Myth of Wrong Ways

Some ads and ad-articles use their space to tell what is wrong with other systems and how their own system is right. I suppose this is normal in advertising, but it does contribute to homeschoolers' fears of doing something wrong.

I suggest that you think of your child's mind as reaching out to understand, rather than as you pouring in the phonics. With this picture, you can't pour the wrong formula or pour in the wrong order or pour at the wrong time. It won't go in. If the child is reaching, he will understand what he can understand of your offerings. The rest will spill over.

This explains why any phonics system, or no system, will work for most children. It is human minds that learn. The curriculum materials are a minor part of the process.

The Myth of Right Ways

The converse of wrong ways is, of course, the right way that each advertiser wants you to believe he has. One expensive phonics system announced a new, revised edition. It was said to be more phonetic! That makes me wonder what they were marketing before. Unphonetic phonics?

While I refrain from saying that one curriculum is right, I have some general preferences which I will pass on to you. Most important, is that I prefer the systems which do not teach all the phonics up front. If a system teaches a few sounds and then provides practice reading material using those sounds, I consider it much more efficient. This is my main technique for shortening the learning time. Those who do teach all the phonics up front naturally criticize this approach. Mainly, they point to the type of reading material which must be used in the early stages: Nan can fan; Dan ran the van. My rejoinder is that children don't criticize this reading matter. They are caught up in the excitement of figuring out patterns in the language and are as mentally absorbed as a linguist researcher making his new discovery about the language.

Teaching up front all the phonics and related rules works okay for some children bright enough and mature enough and with memories good enough. Knowing rules and deciding which rule to apply and figuring out how to apply it are sophisticated mental operations, quite a lot to ask of 5- or 6-year-olds. I'm sure that many children who seem to accomplish this are actually using their own shortcuts and patterns that they see, just as the "Nan can fan" children do. And yet they have to labor over the rule memorizing, too.

When I look at a phonics system and see consonants or vowels presented in alphabetical order, I take this as a clue that the author has little or no experience teaching children to read. This is a neat adult arrangement. It takes no account of which sounds are easier to learn, which are used more often, and so forth. Now, I am not a stickler for the curriculum being arranged in a "right" order, because of the spill effect mentioned earlier, but if I suspect lack of experience in the author, then other, larger problems may appear in the program. With so many to choose from, I don't need to choose this.

My final general guideline for choosing materials is that expensive ones are unnecessary. Phonics is simple knowledge that we all have, so unless a family has money to burn, they can purchase inexpensive materials or none at all. I know parents who have returned expensive sets for a refund, saying they make phonics more complicated than it needs to be. One argument for those kits is all the bells and whistles, more specifically the tapes and tunes and color. But these can become drawbacks rather than helps. There's an artificiality in memorizing facts by tunes and rhymes. This works for a while, but if phonics is learned that way, then grammar rules learned that way, then state capitals, and so on, the fun doesn't last and a type of memory overload sets in. I prefer to use memory for better music and Bible passages and poetry and such, not for trivia. It's less artificial to learn phonics by understanding and seeing its patterns than by memory gimmicks.

The Myths of Phonics and Learning Problems

As Bob discovered and as reading teachers have long known, phonics is not a cure for most reading problems. Only one problem does it cure: the lack of phonics knowledge. By citing specific examples of children who were taught phonics and at last learned to read, the myth perpetuates that phonics is a cure-all.

A concomitant myth is that lack of phonics is a *cause* of reading problems. That is, if children are taught sight reading, or phonics is brought in slowly instead of up front, the children actually develop dyslexia. One detailed report circulating around argues that learning sight words is like learning Chinese symbols, and that supposedly programs children so they can't learn to read words from left to right. This makes them dyslexic. Well, I ask, why are not the Chinese all dyslexic? And why can they learn to read English at all ages, even after long programing with "whole" words?

The area of learning problems is rife with its own problems. Children are over-labeled and mis-labeled, the labels themselves are controversial, Federal money tends to distort reality, and so on. But underneath it all are numerous children with problems that a dose of phonics cannot cure, or that a lack thereof did not cause.

Probably about ten percent of children have modern problems of allergies, sensitivity to food additives, environmental poisons, fetal alcohol or drugs, problems which hardly existed thirty years ago. Another ten percent have other physical or neurological problems, which may be little understood, but which nevertheless are real to the teachers and parents who work with these children and the doctors who treat them, not to mention to the children themselves.

I believe it is a disservice to the homeschool movement for phonics zealots to make their broad claims and easy promises. This is pressing guilt upon about twenty percent of the parents, those who are dealing with real reading problems. And it is causing many others to begin phonics instruction too early so that they spend, in total, far too much time on it. If you wait for the right time you may get through the phonics part in a few months. If you start too early you may spend years at it.

I urge experienced homeschoolers to pass on their encouragement and common sense to each year's newcomers. And pass on the used phonics materials along with the outgrown clothes.

How To Shorten the Time You Spend on Phonics

- Wait until your child is ready. If he has too much difficulty learning the phonics you are trying to teach, he probably is not ready yet, so don't waste time on it. Use the time instead for learning from real-life work, play and conversation. Later, when he is ready, he will learn more rapidly and will have a larger vocabulary and knowledge base to bring to his reading.
- Don't rely overmuch on rote memory of isolated sounds and phonics rules. Learn a few sounds and put them to use as quickly as possible in real reading. Then learn more sounds and put those into practice, and so on. This efficiency principle works with phonics and practically all other learning also.
- Remember that once a child is started and realizes that phonics makes some sense—it's not all just memory—he usually works out some of the rules and sounds for himself. Don't worry about leaving gaps if you fail to teach every rule and sound in your curriculum. If there's something the child doesn't know, it will show up in his oral reading and you can teach it then.

Beyond Phonics

On the way to good reading and high literacy much more happens than acquiring phonics skills. Both before and after the "phonics stage" are other essential stages in the progression toward high level reading.

Research has shown that children must have information and thinking skills in order to become good readers. They might learn phonics in primary grades and be able to sound out words, but if they come to fourth grade without a general knowledge and interest in the content of books, they fail to progress in reading. Those who do not read lose even the skills they once learned, and they end up in our illiteracy statistics. Every stage is essential.

Prereading Stage

Through all the preschool years, beginning even in babyhood, loving parents are the experts. They read stories to their children. They let children choose a story and participate in it. Their children say some of the repeated or rhyming words, ask questions, guess what will happen next, comment. Parents and children together interact with stories. They enjoy them, and favorites are read over and over. Later, children may pretend to read these favorites to themselves or to a teddy. Such follow-up activities are voluntary and not obligatory.

Classroom teachers wish they could do as well. One book admonishes them: "Because so many children who have a background rich in such experiences are able to read before they begin school, teachers should consider attempting to replicate this successful home-learning environment within the constraints of their own classrooms."

Besides book experiences, young children in a loving environment have rich oral language experiences. Older people talk to them. Every day they learn new words, new ideas, new ways to say things. If you want this in academic terms, you could say the children's vocabulary expands, their grammatical usages and sentence structures become more complex, their thinking skills grow, and their knowledge increases.

What can you do during this stage to help build toward reading? Besides the natural activities mentioned above, you could sometimes connect real-life with books. For instance, after observing clouds, you could find a book about clouds. Read part of it and look at its pictures.

Use writing, also, during this stage. Your children could draw clouds and you could write for them the captions they want on each drawing. Hang the pictures for display or form several into a book. The children learn that books are written, as well as read.

When your toddlers first begin to scribble, encourage them just as you encourage their first attempts to "read" books. These scribbles are valuable learning. They are steps toward understanding that thoughts can be saved on paper. The idea of writing should grow alongside the idea of reading. Let children see you write notes and shopping lists and other items. They might help you think of what to say.

Overall goals during this prereading stage are for children to learn what reading and writing are for and to learn that they are useful and enjoyable enterprises.

Fluency Stage

After children learn basic phonics, they need a relaxed time to build fluency. You won't find much written about this fluency stage. It is much neglected, especially as compared to the over-hyped phonics. Even most curriculums neglect this as they, instead, push children forward through ever more difficult reading material.

But children need unpressured time for consolidating their learnings of the phonics stage. They need to read, read, read, and write, write, write. In order to read enough books and stories, they must be allowed to read easy ones.

At this fluency stage parents often observe, "My son can read big words, but he stumbles over little words like *when.*" This is entirely normal. Big words in children's books might be *helicopter* or *dinosaur,* and the little words are *when, was,* and *the.* Many little words are connectors, articles, prepositions and such. These evoke no image. *Helicopter* is memorable; *the* is not. Moreover, *the* does not abide by the child's phonics rules, and this is true of a great many of the little words.

Now, these little words happen to be the high frequency words in our language. They are used repeatedly in easy books as well as in advanced books. If your child reads easy books, he may read 10 or 20 or more pages, but if he reads difficult textbook material, he may read only 2 or 3 pages. So in the easy reading, he gets much more practice reading *was, could, people, many,* and other common words that are not concretely memorable or that are not readily sounded out by phonics.

This explains part of the rationale for allowing time for building fluency. When children are constantly pushed through lessons at their "grade level" or their "reading level," they read only a few pages a day, but when they have real books to choose from, they devour quantities of easy books and they taste some hard books as well. From the difficult books, children learn from pictures and from reading parts that give information they want. From the quantity of easy books they become fluent with the common words, and they also practice phonics until these skills become automatic habits. From all books they are exposed to ideas, information and words. Their vocabulary grows by leaps and bounds. They learn a great deal about what is in books, so they naturally learn more about how to write.

An extra bonus of easy reading is that it boosts children's spelling ability. Children who read a lot get used to seeing words correctly spelled, so misspelled words begin to look wrong to them. This skill of recognizing possible misspellings is the way we adults get our letters or important documents polished up. Even a computer spell-checker will not tell us that we spelled *peak* for *pique.* And phonics does not solve such a case. Memorizing lists of words provides only limited help, because children remember for the long term only those words they see and use repeatedly. But wide reading of easy materials is a powerful help to better spelling. During this fluency stage, the invented spelling of the phonics stage gradually fades away.

On a computer homeschooling echo, a graduated home-schooler touted the great "cirriculum" that he had used. He bragged about how many spelling words he had memorized per week, how difficult the words were, and so forth. It was a great "cirriculum" in his view, and he highly recommended it to all comers. He seemed unaware that he could learn spelling by reading other people's postings, and after several weeks of conversation about curriculum and "cirriculum" someone finally said, "Look up the spelling of curriculum."

This ability to sense when a word might be wrong is arguably the most valuable spelling skill a person can possess, and children grow in this ability by wide reading (and writing). So, add spelling to the list of advantages from easy reading.

How much time for the fluency stage? Two years. One full year at the least. For instance, if children learn basic phonics in first grade they can spend second and third grades reading widely in easy books. Then at fourth grade they will be ready for the kind of studying that is typical of the following stage—information. The timing varies widely with different children, of course. Homeschoolers know that, but they often feel pressured by society to push children when instinct tells them to relax.

Even with good readers, there is no need to push on with what textbooks call reading skills. When children read real books, they get practice in the skills. Reading is learned by reading.

Overall goals during this stage are that children will practice enough to become truly fluent in reading and that their writing and spelling abilities will grow alongside their reading ability.

Higher Stages

At about fourth grade—on average—children reach the information stage of reading. By this stage they have learned basic skills and have had additional time to master the skills and become fluent readers. Now instead of learning how to read, they use reading to learn. They read for information and recreation.

They gained information and pleasure during previous stages, of course, but now these become the main characteristic of reading, and thus it is named the information stage. This is when children can read more books than most will ever again have time for in their lives. They should explore a wide variety of topics and literature. Some will discover during these years the field they will pursue for a career. All should build a knowledge base upon which their higher education and thinking skills can be built.

This stage lasts through the middle grades and, I believe, through the junior high years as well. Some educators who are on the brain-fad bandwagon propose leading students into deeper thinking during junior high because that is a time of growth spurt in the brain. But efforts to do this have not worked as hoped. At times of physical growth spurts we do not push forward with skills teaching, but allow children time to adjust to their growth. It seems wise to do the same with brain growth and allow time for consolidation and continued improvement of the information stage skills of reading.

In high school, teens can think more deeply about issues in literature, history, politics and so forth. And college aged young people can bring a more mature outlook yet to complex issues and questions of life, and they can read advanced material in specialized subjects. So two more stages can be called the high school stage and the college stage.

Now, after these stages, are people educated or are they equipped so that they can become educated as adults? Mortimer Adler, one of our greatest educators in this century, wrote that after college (or its equivalent non-classroom learning), people possess the skills for learning and they can embark upon a lifetime of becoming educated. Now that they are mature, he wrote, true education becomes possible in a way that cannot happen with immature young people.

If you like Adler's view, you might see that you are the one becoming more educated while you try to give your children the skills of learning. A number of teaching mothers have written about this, having discovered it on their own.

All the stages overlap, of course. Each stage is named for the major kind of learning that happens in it, but some characteristics of the preceding stage and of the following stage appear also. If you know the route, as a tour guide you can help your children benefit from their current position, rather than anxiously pushing into the next stage.

Hope for Dyslexics

Either you have a child with reading problems or one of your friends has. That's because about ten percent of all children have this problem to some degree or other. And the good news is that at least ninety percent of those can be helped or thoroughly cured by simple home remedies.

We'll get to cures in this article, but first, what is dyslexia? From the meaning of its Greek parts it simply means trouble with words. Thus it is a name for symptoms, rather than a name for any underlying cause. The World Federation of Neurology defines it as a disorder "manifested by difficulty in learning to read despite conventional instruction, adequate intelligence, and sociocultural opportunity." This wordy definition says the same as the Greek *dyslexia*.

We now try to be sophisticated and call sub-groups of the syndrome by such names as attention deficit disorder or perceptuo-motor impairment. But these, too, name only symptoms and show our ignorance of underlying causes.

Though theories abound, it is still disputed whether or not there is a biological cause. But neurologists and others who work with these children agree that there is a real disorder of some kind or kinds.

Each case of dyslexia is different from others. Impairments and symptoms are not the same from person to person, and the degree can vary from hardly noticeable to quite severe. Yet the cases have enough in common that simple home treatments can cure or significantly help the vast majority.

Can this be true? Doesn't dyslexia call for professionals and complicated diagnosis and expensive treatment? Natural questions. Almost everybody asks them. My experience says, Yes, it is true that parents can solve probably ninety percent of dyslexia problems. And No, it isn't complicated.

Why isn't this information emblazoned in headlines in education publications? Why aren't parents and teachers given the help they need? No doubt, several factors in our society have played a part in this silence. We will come back to this question later, after looking further into the phenomenon called dyslexia.

I Learn about Dyslexia

In the early sixties, I met Ken in a graduate class on teaching reading and asked if I could help at the reading clinic where he worked. He seemed happy about the offer and the next Saturday I walked into the homelike atmosphere and informality of a small class, seven children of differing ages. I could observe and help a little with some of the activities. But when Ken had the children crawling on the floor, I didn't know what to think. Could I help with this? I had read about Carl Delacato and the clinic in Pennsylvania where people were doing this sort of thing. Patterning, they called it. Cross pattern therapy and exercises. Educators looked with contempt upon the whole idea. Articles for the general public, too, were highly critical.

I managed to keep my thoughts to myself and returned each Saturday. After classes Ken and I sometimes reviewed the children's records, discussing their progress, which usually was remarkable. Sometimes Shirley joined our discussions. She was the one who had gone to a Delacato training session and explained the theories to us. I timidly began to assign eye exercises and cross pattern exercises to children I worked with. The results showed in a few short weeks and I became fully sold on the method. By summer I felt ready to take on classes of my own at the clinic.

This led to a career of teaching reading—several years at Shirley's clinic and a few more years with one of my own. Practically all the children who came to us had neurological problems. I decided it was because the schools did everything else. They could teach missed phonics. They could encourage and motivate psychologically defeated children, and so on. But they didn't believe in the "mythology" of curing neurological problems with the method of exercises.

School teachers had their own methods in those days, methods which still persist and which have some usefulness, but which I came to view as cumbersome compared with what we used in the clinics. The idea in the cumbersome methods is that if children do not learn well through their eyes and ears, then we should use their sense of touch. Children should trace shapes and letters with their fingers, feel letters made of sandpaper, and so forth. Gradually, by this more difficult route, they could learn what most children learn easily.

The idea in our clinics was to cure the neurological problems, not just cope with them. Maybe it's too much to claim actual cure in a medical sense, but to us reading teachers cure did not seem too strong a word at all.

I remember Jake, for instance. Jake's mother brought him into my clinic in Anchorage, and as we talked she told me how they had lived in Nome during Jake's early years. The floor there was so cold that she never let him crawl on it. He spent most of his crawling days in a high chair instead. So we set him to crawling at the clinic and at home, and in just one month's time he advanced from first grade reading level to third grade, which matched his age. Was that a cure?

And I remember Sarah. She couldn't copy my drawing of a diamond. She knew there were "corners" to be made, so she struggled to make them, with results as shown in the illustration. Sarah was a bright fourth grader who tested at low second grade reading level. Sarah's mother looked at the drawing and said, "Oh she can draw diamonds!" She and Sarah went home that day determined to bring me proof that Sarah certainly could draw a diamond. But the next day the mother said, "You're right. There is something strange about the way she sees them." They were motivated to work on the cross pattern exercises and eye exercises, and within a few weeks Sarah could read at fourth grade level. Was that a cure?

I will never forget Sammy. He had just finished sixth grade and his family sent him from another state to enroll in our summer reading classes. A young teenager who tested at beginning second grade reading level, Sammy appeared to be a potential delinquent, as often is the fate of those who do not learn to read. Sammy mumbled answers to questions and could not look me in the eye. He shuffled on his feet and

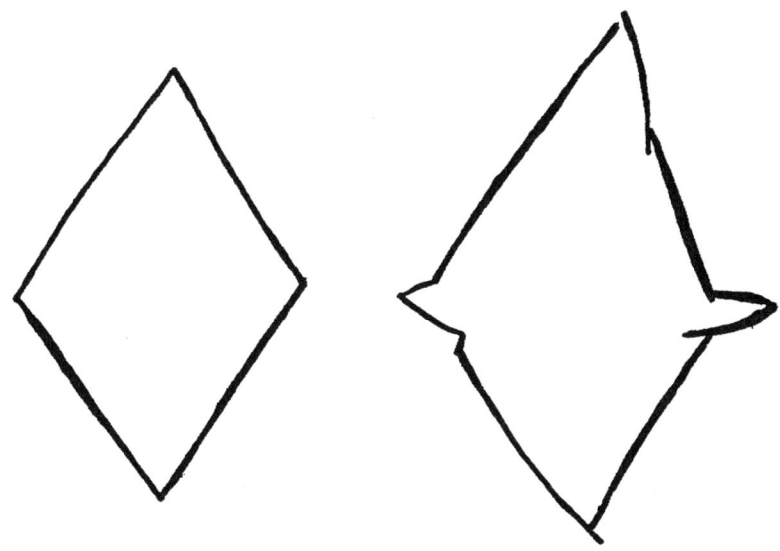

Diamond drawn by the teacher.   Copy drawn by fourth grader.

never smiled. But he did cooperate in the testing. The second day, I explained to him what some of the tests were about. We had found that his left eye and left foot were dominant but he wrote and threw balls with his right hand. I further explained, the best I could, the theory that this kind of crossed dominance could mix up messages in the brain. That could be the reason he had had such a hard time with reading.

I sensed a little softening of his exterior shell. Students are always relieved to hear this kind of information. They are not dumb, they begin to realize; it's not their fault they can't read. Coupled with a plan for conquering the problem, hope enters their lives and self-confidence begins to return. With a boy Sammy's age, confidence building is slower than with a boy Jake's age. Did Sammy remember if he might have been left handed? Yes, he did remember. He was living with his grandmother and she made him color and draw with his right hand. Every time she caught him with a pencil in his left hand she made him switch to the right.

The boy's parents were in another state, and I proceeded tremblingly. Would Sammy want to try acting left handed for a while? He could experiment and if he didn't like the results he could give it up. He was eager to try, so we thought up a few ideas. He would play ping pong with his 7-year-old cousin and offer to play left-handed to even things up. In class he wouldn't have to do any writing unless he wanted to. He would work on larger motions first.

The results exceeded my hopes. Sammy very quickly became a competent left-hander. Meanwhile he rapidly learned phonics and reading skills that had eluded him before, and after only four weeks he tested at a late sixth grade level. Scoring the test, I exclaimed, "Look what you have done!" I tried to show him what a remarkable job he did, bringing his score up from second grade to sixth grade. "Oh," he said, "I thought I did something wrong." Yes, I should have been more careful with my exclamation.

Sammy worried that sixth grade level was not good enough for the next year in seventh grade. I tried to explain that seventh grade level meant the middle of the class. Lots of kids in that grade score sixth or lower. But if he would read every day for the rest of the summer he would be seventh grade level by the time school started. Sammy smiled some during that conversation. And he looked me in the eye a couple of times.

The Theories

What accounts for such miracles? One theory, in a

nutshell, says that messages from the right side of the body go to the left side of the brain and vice versa, and if this normal pattern is disturbed in any way the result is some confusion in the brain. For instance, if a child is writing with his right hand but reading the words with his left eye leading, one message goes to the left brain and one goes to the right, and the brain has a bit of trouble coordinating them. Exercises which restore normal dominance of one side of the body, then, solve the problem.

Very young children have not yet developed a dominance; they are non-dominant. But by about age 5 they show a definite dominance for either right or left side, according to their genetic inheritance. Some few inherit a mixed dominance or ambidexterity, but the vast majority can be called right or left sided.

Sometimes this normal development is disturbed by an event such as a high fever or oxygen deprivation during a difficult birth. This may cause what has been called a minimal brain dysfunction. Sarah's mother surmised that Sarah's problem may have begun this way, from her difficult birth. Jake's case of not crawling as an infant and Sammy's case of forced hand change are examples of disturbed development. According to Delacato's theory, creeping and crawling and other normal activities are necessary to normal brain development.

Since these theories involve the brain, our society tends to think that diagnosis and treatment are mysterious and complicated and beyond the reach of most of us. But the truth is that no one understands the brain very well. Brain specialists say that the more they learn about the brain the more they realize there is to learn. Neurologists, who know the most, are the most cautious about drawing conclusions concerning the complex human function of learning. It is not neurologists who start fads about right brain learning, whole brain learning and such.

Scientists writing about the brain practically always have a chapter on the evolutionary history of how the brain came to be as it is. If this reasoning actually helped them to arrive at their views about the brain, I would lose confidence in their views. But as far as I can see, their evolutionary beliefs have nothing to do with their beliefs about the brain's functioning and abilities. They ascribe incredible abilities to the brain. The brain seems over-designed, a feature that could not come about by evolution—through survival of useful features. So I ignore the evolution portions of these books and prefer to believe that the brain was designed by the Creator God.

Because of overdesign, if one part of the brain fails to function normally, other parts can be trained to take over. This is likely what happens in cases like Sarah's. Also, if the brain misses some aspect of its development, it can still catch up at a later age. This may be what happened in Jake's case.

As an ordinary teacher, I had no knowledge of what was actually happening in the brains of individual children I worked with. I doubt that neurologists would either. The term "minimal brain dysfunction" was coined to theorize about abnormalities so small that they cannot be seen or measured by any means now available to us.

So there need be no mystery about treating these children. If your son can't crawl in a cross pattern (right hand and left knee move simultaneously, then left hand and right knee), you can have him practice crawling in cross pattern. If your daughter can't walk and on each step point to the front foot with the opposite hand, she can practice this exercise until it becomes easy for her. Skipping, walking a rail and all sorts of coordination activities are helpful.

Families who suspect they have a dyslexia problem can obtain one of the books now available for parents and read more about the theories and suggested treatments, and try some of them. Even if these don't help reading in a particular case, the time won't be wasted because the exercises are good coordination or physical activities, anyway. I am convinced that about ninety percent of dyslexic cases will find good success with home treatment. Some few, particularly of the eye problems, will require help from a professional. Each metropolitan area now has a few ophthalmologists or optometrists who treat the type of eye problems we are concerned with here.

Also, some few cases cannot be cured. From my experience, I came to believe that the problems with developmental causes were most easily cured, and that the inherited ones may not be changed. I later found this view corroborated by Dr. Hilde Mosse in *The Complete Handbook of Children's Reading Disorders*. Some children with inherited differences have exceptional talents in music or in athletics and other physical pursuits. Reading may not be their favorite hobby, but they can learn it by putting forth more effort than others. They probably should be allowed to start later, to use more kinesthetic methods and to progress at a slower pace.

Secret Information?

If so many children (and adults) can be helped so easily, why isn't this common knowledge? Why is it one of the best-kept secrets in education?

I think several factors contribute to this. At first,

there was the natural skepticism that people have toward something unfamiliar and not mainstream. Later, when the word *dyslexia* was spoken by everybody, there was some protection of turf, and our society falls easily into the pattern of letting specialists have their turf. The attitude is that reading specialists or medical people know what to do, but parents can't be expected to know. Their function is to pay fees and follow directions.

Money plays too large a role in still other ways. We see a parallel in medicine. If some country reports that a food or herb is useful in the treatment of an ailment, what company in the US will put a lot of money into research and publicity? Only if they can get the substance reclassified as a drug will it be worth such investment. Likewise in education. If a company can produce expensive materials or high cost seminars, then they can go to the public with a lot of publicity. But a single book? That you will have to search out for yourself.

The low cost books usually suggest that families seek professional help if the home remedies fail to work. Some suggest consulting a doctor before trying any home remedy. This latter suggestion may get the publisher off the hook in a lawsuit, but I can't see that it should worry a parent who wants to try some simple exercises that can't possibly damage either a normal child or a dyslexic child. If there is any problem in home remedies, it lies not in trying them for a few weeks or a few months, it lies only in continuing unduly long when they are not working, and thus delaying to seek professional help. No guarantee comes with the professional help either, of course. But at least everyone has done his legal duty by suggesting it.

Cures?

Just as we can't be sure about what kind of "disease" we have, so we can't be sure about "cures." The proverbial physician may say, "Take two aspirin and call me in the morning." Similarly, the reading specialist may say, "Take these exercises and try the reading lessons again next year." The waiting itself does the trick for many children. A recent study by the Yale School of Medicine found that two-thirds of the children who were identified as dyslexic in first grade were not so labeled in second grade.

Families armed with a little information and their knowledge of their own child can make good decisions about delaying or slowing reading instruction and about experimenting with the various exercises and treatments suggested in books. A large proportion of them, with patience, will find success from their home efforts. The remaining few may wish to pursue further help from professionals.

There is hope for dyslexics.

Reviews

A New Start for the Child with Reading Problems by Carl Delacato.

This fulfills the promise of its subtitle, which is *A Manual for Parents*. The first half tells clearly how to evaluate a child according to Dr. Delacato's theory. Can the child crawl in a cross pattern? Can he do cross pattern walking—pointing to each front toe with the opposite hand? What about his eyes? Do they follow an object smoothly when he holds it at arm's length and moves it in a full circle, up and down, sideways, and in other patterns? Or do the eyes exhibit a jerky start-and-stop motion?

The second half of the book explains how to provide therapy, which consists of the same exercises used for diagnosing. This lets out the secret that you don't need a specialist to diagnose first and tell you what therapy to use. Diagnose and treat with the same exercises.

Some school districts now are using this system, and parents may obtain the book from The Chestnut Hill

Reading Clinic, Plymouth Plaza Suite 107, Plymouth Meeting PA 19462. Some homeschool suppliers also carry this.

Help for the Hyperactive Child by William G. Crook.

This book addresses a different set of problems than the neurological ones mentioned in the preceding chapter, but a growing number of children now struggle with these problems.

Dr. Crook wrote for parents of children with hyperactivity and/or attention deficit disorders, also problems of fatigue, depression, respiratory allergies, digestive disorders and bed wetting, and history of prolonged antibiotic drugs. He points out that we did not have many of these problems in the 1950s, but began to see them in epidemic proportions in the late 1960s and early 1970s. This timing coincides with increased use of food additives and highly processed foods. Chemical contaminants may also be a cause.

Seventy-five percent of children with these problems can be helped by diet, and the book is packed with nutritional information and directions for an "elimination diet" to help families do their own detective work in locating the culprit or culprits causing their problems. The format is easy to read and easy to use.

In addition to special diet, these children need discipline and consistent management of rules and limits, Dr. Crook believes.

Available from most bookstores or from Professional Books, Inc., 681 Skyline Drive, Jackson TN 38301.

Better than Ritalin?

This is a review of the drug phenytoin (PHT), which can help in a variety of learning problems but which has been effectively hid from the public and their doctors since its discovery early in this century. The brand name by which PHT is known in the United States is Dilantin.

Why don't we all know this as well as we know Ritalin? Especially when it does not stimulate or sedate like Ritalin, and has no dangerous side effects and is non-habit-forming? A quick answer is that Ritalin is still protected by a patent, so the drug company spends money getting its message to doctors.

But there is far more to the story, and it has been told by Jack Dreyfus of Wall Street fame. (You've heard of Dreyfus mutual funds?) Dreyfus suffered from depression so severely that he had to let his partners run the business while he sought a cure. Psychotherapy did not help. Through a series of mental connections, Dreyfus got the idea that his problem might be electrical. His doctor mentioned that epileptics have a problem with body electricity, so Dreyfus asked for their medicine—Dilantin.

Telling it later, Dreyfus realized what a crucial moment that was. The doctor could have said No, and the rest of this story would not have unfolded. But the doctor said, "You can try it if you like. I don't think it will do you any good, but it won't do you any harm."

Dilantin did help. Immediately. Later it helped friends and acquaintances of Dreyfus's. Dilantin neither sedates nor stimulates. It is better described as a "normalizer" of bioelectrical functions. Nerve cells and brain cells transmit information by means of electrical impulses. Excessive electrical discharge causes problems up to the severity of seizures. A medical "bible" describes the effects of PHT this way:

> Coincident with the decrease in seizures there occurs improvement in intellectual performance. Salu-

tary effects of the drug PHT on personality, memory, mood, cooperativeness, emotional stability, amenability to discipline, etc., are also observed, sometimes independently of seizure control. (Goodman & Gilman's *Pharmacological Basis of Therapeutics*.)

Dreyfus found that most doctors knew PHT only as an anti-convulsant, and most had never read the other information in their drug reference book. Back when PHT was listed by the FDA, people believed in using a drug for one just symptom, so only the convulsion use is put into the package insert, and that is what doctors read. But once drugs are approved for marketing, doctors can legally use them for other than the conditions listed in the insert. In the case of PHT, numerous doctors use it for heart patients with arrhythmia. The head of the Heart and Lung Institute assumed that it was listed for such use and told Dreyfus he was surprised to find it was not.

Dreyfus ran into brick walls in many efforts to spread the message about PHT's uses to the medical profession and to obtain more indication-of-use listings for it from the FDA. Even the drug manufacturer, Parke-Davis, was no help with what had become a crusade with Dreyfus.

Dreyfus felt it was a sin to know something this good and not tell everybody. He wrote that he was a most unlikely person to become rich on Wall Street, and he felt that his wealth had been "given" to him for such a purpose as trying to breach the brick walls. So with his own money he set up a foundation in New York, now known simply as The Health Foundation. He eventually left Wall Street and devoted full time to this work. The foundation conducted research and collected research that had already been done—about 2000 studies to start with, over 10,000 now.

There followed a ten-year odyssey of trying to achieve a tiny helpful move in government bureaucracy. Even with encouragement from presidents and other high officials, Dreyfus's efforts with the government came to naught. The foundation published a synopsis of selected studies and published Jack Dreyfus's story to show what he calls, with monumental understatement, a "flaw in our system of bringing prescription medicines to the public." Now the foundation has announced that it is no longer in the communications work. But their files are available to physicians who are interested, and copies of everything are offered to the government.

PHT has now been used for over fifty years by thousands of physicians in 38 countries and has a good record of safety. Side effects are said to be "rarely serious." The only side effect I found mentioned in the reports was a mild dizziness. A standard drug reference book lists about the same possible effects that they list for Ritalin, but apparently these rarely happen.

Physicians now prescribe PHT for at least 100 medical uses. A few of these mentioned in the research studies are: hyperactivity, excitability and temper tantrums, distractibility, fears, neurological deficits, short attention span, irritability, impulsiveness, poor concentration, emotional and behavior disorders, and retardation (particularly when caused by slight brain damage).

Dreyfus describes his condition of an overactive brain. Others call it a turned-on brain or over-thinking. He devised a test of asking a person to list on paper the thoughts he or she could not turn off. An over-thinking person might name 9 or 10 or more thoughts. An hour after taking 100 mg. of PHT the test is repeated and the list may be only 3 or 4 items long. He calls this the one-hour test.

Neither the government nor the medical establishment at this time is going to suggest that some of our children with various learning disability labels might respond to PHT treatment. The ball is in our court. If we think a child's problems are related to bioelectrical functioning, we can ask our doctors about trying it. They might at least say, "You can try it if you like. It won't do you any harm."

The Language Wars

All the King's teachers and all the King's men
Want the King's English together again.

Who broke the language? And what is involved in the current movement to teach whole language again?

The Long Roots of Language Debates

The first cracks may have appeared in the time of the Greeks. Ancient grammar, at first, was a wholistic study of Greek classics, but scholars intruded into the process, analyzing literature by its techniques and language by its elements. Their abstract study of language parts we now call grammar.

Dionysius Thrax, in the first century B.C., compiled all grammar research which had preceded him, and his book became a code of grammar used in teaching. Other Greek writers ridiculed this as the degeneration of education into barren formalism.

The Romans incorporated Greek grammar without adapting it enough to truly fit their Latin language. And English teachers, in their turn, did the same with Latin grammar. Through all those centuries, the original grammar lived alongside the narrow formal grammar. Study classic texts as wholes? Or study the techniques of literature and the elements of language? Educators have long grappled with this tension between wholeness and formalism. A sixth grade class recently expressed their view of formalism as what only the teacher can comprehend.

> Grammar is when nouns are nouns
> and verbs are verbs
> until the time comes
> that nouns become verbs
> and verbs become nouns,
> and only the teacher can say
> when the time is coming.

In our century, the debate about wholeness erupts particularly around the topics of phonics and grammar (with its narrow modern meaning). A popular view is that we now know the parts of reading and writing, so let's get busy and teach them. If children don't read well, let's hammer in the phonics. If they don't write well, let's pound in more grammar. On the other side, wholistic educators see grammar and phonics as a little like vitamins—to be included in a healthy diet, but not sufficient by themselves to add up to a whole diet.

The Politicizing of Language

Two circumstances help to make the debate today both vigorous and visible. The first is its politicization. In 1955

Rudolph Flesch's book *Why Johnny Can't Read* became a runaway best-seller.[1] This brought the public into the debate. Every man on the street had an opinion on how to teach reading. Special interest groups pressured their school boards or legislatures. Reading scores were pounced on by the press, and the public has never since let go of this issue. Phonics advocates are accused of being part of an organized far right, and whole language advocates are accused of being part of a socialist conspiracy to dumb down American education.

Educators who would like to achieve some kind of balance or to change the question to, "What is the best way to teach reading?" find themselves, one by one, embroiled in the public's question of, "Are you for phonics or against it?" After *Why Johnny Can't Read,* the Carnegie Foundation funded the research of Jeanne S. Chall of Harvard University. Her sweeping research was reported in *Learning To Read: The Great Debate,*[2] and she is added to the "for" side. In preparation for a 1992 assessment of reading by The National Assessment of Educational Progress (NAEP), a Maryland state reading official, Barbara Kapinus, headed the planning group whose job was to reach consensus on what is important to test. She found herself attacked from both sides every step of the way. "I haven't had reason to be attacked, or take major stands until this project," she said. "I considered myself eclectic. [The debate is] fiercer than I ever thought."[3]

Its fierceness leads some observers to point out that more is involved than meets the ear. The war operates more like a power struggle than a debate over what is good for children. Perhaps it really is a question of who will control the schools. Whose ideology will be taught? And further, whose textbooks will be purchased?

Christian Educators and Language

Christian schools show considerable unanimity in this debate. They are firmly on the phonics side and just as firmly reject whole language, according to Dr. Ollie Gibbs, Director of Academic Affairs of the Association of Christian Schools International. He adds that publishers are happy to supply what the schools want. [Written in 1991.]

Among homeschoolers, the publishers expend many advertising dollars to convince parents that they need those same phonics and grammar materials. But also among homeschoolers, is a movement toward using "real" books rather than basal reading textbooks. One influence in this direction is Susan Schaeffer Macauley's *For the Children's Sake,* which urges Christians to use what she calls "living books" in the education of their children.[4] This is in the tradition of one of America's greatest educators, Mortimer Adler, who spent a lifetime helping people read "great books" which contain the great ideas that men have written about through the ages. The real-book movement promotes reading, thinking, discussing and writing about books of value instead of doing workbook exercises on "skills."

The Scientizing of Language

A second circumstance that fuels the debate on language teaching is our modern propensity to scientize education. Linguists have dissected the language much more thoroughly than Thrax and the Greeks, so we now have a lot of material to teach as phonics or as grammar. Much of this has happened in the last 150 years. In McGuffey's time beginning reading was still seen as a process of learning letters, then learning one-syllable words, then longer words.

A line in a McGuffey primer says, "Here are boys at the pump." These are all one-syllable words, but only the word *at* might fit into a modern linguistic primer which fine tunes the one-syllable stage. A linguistic primer says, "Wag can tag Dan."

Reading beyond the phonics stage has also been dissected, and we have numerous reading sub-skills laid out end to end in the textbooks and scope and sequence charts. One such program was elaborate in its trappings of giving pretests on each skill, then a lesson or two on the skill, then a posttest. Some districts in my state adopted it, at least partly because it provided a way to meet the legislature's demands for accountability. I visited a classroom on the day the children learned about one thought being imbedded within another in a sentence. The teacher told me the class never had time to read whole stories, let alone whole books, and he worked every night making reports about skill learning that had to be sent to state officials. That teacher and others quit at the end of the year, and not too long afterward the legislature let up on its demands that had led to such extreme dissecting of reading.

In grammar teaching, also, experiments have been tried and dropped. It has long been known through research that a good knowledge of grammar does not necessarily correlate with good writing ability.[5] Some surmised that this was because we taught Latin grammar instead of a grammar that really fit English language. So in the 1960s there were movements to teach two or three of the English grammars that linguists had developed. After about a decade those experiments "came to a screeching halt" in the words of one district curriculum coordinator. Now we are back to the traditional Latin-style grammar, but modified, with clear imprints of the English grammars upon it. These changes have made grammar learning somewhat easier, but they have not solved the larger problem of achieving better writing. To solve this problem is an aim of the modern whole language movement.

Whole Language in the Classroom

One commonly used plan for whole language is to call certain blocks of time the "writing workshop." Even kindergarten children know that when it is workshop time they should get out their writing folders. In the right side of the folders are unfinished papers, so each child can pull out one of those and get started. At each table there is a mixture of abilities. One child may be scribbling on his paper or watching what others are doing. A second child may practice writing his name or something else that he happens to know. A third child may actually be writing a "story" or illustrating one he wrote yesterday. Children can help each other, but that usually doesn't happen as much as the busy teacher would like. A teacher's aide or an adult visitor sitting at the table soon becomes the main helper, because kindergartners think every adult is the source of spelling and writing information. Whenever a paper is finished, it is slipped into the left side of the folder—at least by some of the children. When it is time for music, all the folders are closed and put away for the day.

At the beginning of writing workshop, the children gather around the teacher for whatever kick-off she has planned. Some children may sit in the "author's chair" and show-and-tell their drawings or stories. The teacher may read a picture book. A new breed of giant books has been developed for these occasions, so a group of children can together practice reading the book. If it's a snowy day the children will talk about the snow stories they're going to write. They may write one together, which the teacher prints onto a large chart and they all practice reading.

In one of these kindergartens, Yvonne, who is now a first grader, visits regularly. She reads to the children and watches the gerbils with them. Her father was going to let her take home one of the new babies as soon as it was old enough. But one Monday morning all the baby gerbils were dead. Yvonne cried a lot that day. On the next, she asked to join the kindergarten writing workshop. For two or three days she worked on a book about the gerbil she did not get. A few days later it was "published," with a cover and illustrations, and she sat in the author's chair and read her story to the class.

Writing workshops or its various equivalents are found in all the grades. Younger children learn to write the simple repetitious or accumulative tale that they have understood and enjoyed since they were preschoolers. Older children write more complex stories and non-fiction, real-life accounts as well. Teachers write, too, so their children can see that writing is a valued activity, just as reading is. Various kinds of journal writing are used. In some of these, to get things rolling well, the teacher responds for a time to each child each day, so that a child's journal contains a two-way conversation between him and his teacher.

Parents or sixth graders act as publishers, typing books with proper spelling in place of invented spelling, laminating, "manufacturing." Student authored books hang in the halls, sit on classroom shelves, and get catalogued into the school library. Some books have space on a back page for a signature and comment from each of its readers.

Another type of whole language program appears more loosely structured than the writing workshops, but the teachers say it takes even more planning and structure on their part. When you walk into one of these classrooms you will see children scattered all over, doing all kinds of activities. Some may be lying on cushions looking at books, others in a group listening to a story through headsets, others at a table writing or drawing, still others watching video or cleaning up an art mess or puttering with a science project or playing with the pets. The teacher may be having a conference with one child or be reading to a group in the library corner or checking on a child who is having trouble coping in this environment.

Many whole language programs emphasize what is called the "writing process," which can include: 1) experiencing, thinking, and getting ready to write about a topic; 2) drafting a tentative form; 3) revising, often with peer or teacher help; 4) editing the details of spelling, grammar and mechanics; 5) publishing, which can take various forms, but basically means to present the writing in some form to some audience; and 6) receiving response from others. (Process, too, is an old debate; Dewey wrote on it in 1917.)

In some kindergarten and primary classrooms, teachers use their tried and true phonics programs alongside the whole activities. In others, they say, "I'm completely whole language." In the higher grades, there are similar differences concerning the teaching of formal grammar.

Parents are often enthusiastic about whole language programs in their schools. Many of them volunteer to help with the work that such individualizing and book publishing requires in a classroom. And families moving into a state sometimes call education officials to ask where whole language programs are available, a phenomenon not seen for a long time.

Whole Language in the Homeschool

Bill and Mary Pride, with their large family, are famous and influential homeschoolers because of their writing. Here is Mary's account of some recent language teaching in their home.

We are now at the point where the Bible forms the core of our entire language arts program. Here's how it works:

1) Each school day begins with one of our "readers" reading a chapter of the Bible aloud to the others, who take notes. With appropriate guidance, this develops oral reading and dramatic skills. It also provides excellent opportunities for teaching outlining, thinking skills, and speedy handwriting. The children also have the chance to ask questions about the passage and are provided commentary on what it means. Our main emphasis here is on using and developing new skills to increase the children's understanding.

2) Each child then narrates what was read, the oldest first, proceeding to the youngest. Skills: oral presentation and memory.

3) Next comes dictation. Bill or I read a verse for the children to copy down in their notebooks. These are not disjointed verses, but portions of a larger passage they are memorizing. We want them to memorize a key verse or passage from each book of the Bible. Examples: Genesis 1 and 2, Exodus 3:7–8 and a list of the ten plagues, Leviticus 17:11, the Ten Commandments in Deuteronomy.

4) Finally, memory practice. The children repeat their memory passages.

The Bible is the world's greatest literature; by copying and reading it, our children absorb its rich sentence structure. It stretches their vocabularies, helps them practice spelling, and tunes them in to the kind of language God uses (e.g., honest words for *good* and *evil*). The Bible also teaches character development (God's Word applied to everyday life); philosophy and theology; history (ancient world history); cultural studies (they get to see that late twentieth-century America is not all there is, was or will be!); sex education (just say no); and logic (see Ecclesiastes, Proverbs and the book of Job for conspicuous examples of logical and illogical reasoning contrasted). We could also mention biblical instruction in practical storytelling, training in family living, practice in persuasion and debate (you may recognize this as witnessing skills), and piles of other benefits. . . . All this and eternal life too! What a wonderful book![6]

Underlying Theory

Behind all the varieties of whole language programs, lies a common theoretical belief. To state it in a nutshell, it is an attempt to help children learn written language in the same natural way they learned oral language. How do children learn to talk? One principle is that they are immersed in the language. All around them, family members talk to one another, ask for things and obtain results. The talk is purposeful and whole, not broken into tiny teaching bits.

A second principle is in the feedback we give children. We reward anything that's close to conventional or even recognizable in a distant way. We're happy with *dada* for a time and do not insist on *daddy,* much less on *father.* True, we may gently model by saying, "Yes, Daddy is home," not only modeling the pronunciation, but adding words to help express the child's meaning more fully. But we don't issue a red check mark the next time and say, "I told you it's *daddy.* When will you ever learn to say it right?"

This is related to the third principle, which is that we respect the child's own timetable and his own order of learning. We let the child direct his learning. We don't set aside speech periods of twenty minutes and drill on words or sentence elements in a preordained order of learning. Moreover, it would be impossible ever to lay out language in such a fashion, whole language teachers believe. Frank Smith, a leading American proponent of whole language, points out that usage and grammar conventions are so numerous and many of them so subtle as to preclude their being taught to children in any systematic order.[7] On my own shelf full of grammar books sits the two-volume set by George O. Curme, which totals to about 1000 pages of fine print, perhaps the most complete compendium of English grammar ever assembled. Yet there are times when that set and all the other books on the shelf do not hold the answer to a question I have decided to ask them. Though language scholars have reached far beyond the work of Dionysius Thrax, we still face the ancient question: Is this scholarship able to scientize language teaching for us, or is there a better, natural system which the younger generation has used ever since Cain, Abel and Seth?

Whole language teachers in their differing ways are acting upon these principles of: 1) immersion in language, 2) accepting and encouraging the child at his present level, and 3) respecting the child's natural rate and order of learning.

What Does Research Say?

Besides scientizing grammar and phonics, we also try to scientize teaching methods and curriculum. We look to research for definitive answers to age-old questions, but even research results dissolve into controversy.

Concerning phonics, for instance, proponents can always cite research to support their views. Recent decades have seen a lot of such research, two major citations being the Jeanne Chall book already mentioned and *Becoming a Nation of Readers,* a report by a federally sponsored commission on reading.[8] These are broad syntheses of researches. But those who think phonics is overemphasized counter by arguing that while phonics may give an edge to readers in the early years of schooling, this advantage disappears by about fourth grade.[9] What is needed, say these voices, is much experience with the language and literature and culture, much in the way of information and ideas and thinking skills, so children have in their heads something to bring to the printed page. Reading is more, they say, than sounding out the words on a printed page. This argument earns them a point.

The phonics team rebuts, saying, ". . . whole language does not have research evidence [and] they are deliberately turning their backs on the existing, solid research that exists for the opposite."[10] They score a point—temporarily. Though their opponents cite a variety of researches about how children learn, research on results in whole language classrooms is only now being accumulated. In typical American fashion, we have jumped into a fad first and we'll get the research later. Most research reports at this time are glowing success stories, individual in nature, not overviews or syntheses.[11] Australia, New Zealand and Canada are somewhat ahead of the United States in having results to report, since they started earlier on this kind of teaching. One major program in New Zealand is now formalized into a set of books—supposed to be real books, not textbooks—and it is now meeting with criticism that such formalization is not in the spirit of whole language philosophy.

Blowing at cross currents with the either/or debate, is a secondary debate that might be labeled "educators" versus "the public." Educators accuse phonics enthusiasts among the public of being roused by emotional books, such as Flesch's, and of twisting information from research studies. Instead of subjecting the research to debate and possible refutation, they bypass the scholars and go directly to legislators and to an uninformed public, presenting their information as propaganda, says Kenneth Goodman, a professor at the University of Arizona.[12] The public, in their turn, accuse educators of ignoring the Flesch-type messages that reach them.

After a century of educational research, we continue to debate most of the very points the research was designed to resolve. Research seems not to end the debates but only to fuel them.

A Perspective for Today

I once interviewed a lady who taught kindergarten in the 1920s, and she described the reading program she had created and used in her classes. Today this program would be called whole language, but no one had invented the term in those phonics days. The teacher's sister taught in the same school and she said, "Neva's children came into my first grade each year already reading."

In my childhood country school there was a first grade

teacher whose career spanned the years just before and after the introduction of sight reading via Dick and Jane and Spot (who were in giant books as well as primers). But Mrs. Naugle taught two generations of children to read by her alphabetic method. Her set of babies (Baby A says *a, ay,* and *ah,* etc.) never seemed to wear out.

So, each era has its holdouts and its innovators. Good teachers are independent souls and they do what works for them. But in spite of diversity, today's era may soon be called the whole language era—which is not the same as sight reading, and which can include phonics (although not with intensity enough to satisfy the strongest phonics advocates). Are we moving forward or are we back to where the early Greeks began?

We Christians view man as a far higher creature than others view him. Language (and the thinking behind it) is a God-like characteristic. Theologian Gordon Clark wrote that the mind, rationality, *is* the image of God.[13] Even speaking with scientific logic, it is an impossibility for the mind of man to search and understand the mind of man. Thus we Christians, more than others, ought to be humble about our knowledge of teaching and learning language. The answers are not all in. They likely never will be. And someone who thinks differently than us about these matters may very well have something valuable to share with us.

This is a time to keep open minds on language teaching.

1. Rudolph Flesch, *Why Johnny Can't Read and What You Can Do about It,* (New York: Harper, 1955).
2. Jeanne Chall, *Learning To Read: The Great Debate,* (New York: McGraw-Hill, 1967).

3. Robert Rothman, "Reading's Great Debate Escalates to Full-Scale War," *Education Week* (March 21, 1990), p. 11.
4. Susan Schaeffer Macauley, *For the Children's Sake,* (Westchester, Illinois: Crossway Books, 1984).
5. See, for instance, C. W. Hunnicutt and William J. Everson, *Research in the Three R's,* (New York: Harper, 1958).
6. Mary Pride, "The Resourceful Home Schooler," *The Teaching Home* (February/March 1989), p 33.
7. Frank Smith, *Writing and the Writer,* (New York: Holt, Rinehart and Winston, 1982).
8. *Becoming a Nation of Readers: The Report of the Commission on Reading,* prepared by Richard C. Anderson, Elfrieda H. Hiebert, Judith A. Scott, and Ian A. G. Wilkinson, with contributions from members of the commission (Champaign, Illinois: Commission on Reading, 1985).
9. For instance, a national bestseller by E. D. Hirsch, Jr., *Cultural Literacy* (Boston: Houghton Mifflin, 1987).
10. Jeanne Chall, quoted by Robert Rothman in "From a 'Great Debate' to a Full-Scale War: Dispute Over Teaching Reading Heats Up," *Education Week,* vol. IX, No. 26 (March 21, 1990), p. 10.
11. See, for instance, several schools and their programs reported in *Educational Leadership,* vol. 47, No. 6 (March 1990).
12. Rothman, *op. cit.,* p. 10.
13. Gordon H. Clark, *Language and Theology* (Phillipsburg, New Jersey: Presbyterian and Reformed Publishing Co., 1980), p. 138.

What Is Creative Writing?

Jane sat across the table from me and if there is such a thing as stars in the eyes, this was it. "I want to be a writer," she said.

Willing to be a good listener, I asked, "What do you want to write about?"

"I don't know. I just want to be a writer."

Jane was not a "reader," and till that time had never tried to write anything more than an occasional letter, but some recent contact with writers had evoked this starry-eyed dream. She thought she could sit down with a piece of paper, and some creative magic would take over and make her a writer. Awhile later, Jane later signed up for a creative writing class at the local community college.

What is a creative writing class supposed to teach? Or a book or course labeled "creative writing?" Are these simply titles devised by clever advertising writers, or do they differ from other writing courses? If there is such a thing as creative writing, then what is uncreative writing?

Not Just Fantasy

Fantasy is high on people's list of what is creative. Other fiction may trail a bit lower on the list. And poetry is there too. But history? Biography? Political commentary? Student essays about books they have read? Do these belong on the uncreative list?

Definitely not on the uncreative list is a story called "The Feeling of Power," which science fiction writer Isaac Asimov wrote back in the days when a single computer filled a gym-sized space. His story is set in the future time when computers designed computers, and men had lost track of the ancient history of humans directly designing computers. Everyone carried a hand-held calculator, and no one knew how to calculate in his head or on paper—except for one hobbyist. This low-grade technician discovered that the calculator always gave 63 as the answer for 7 times 9. He didn't know what the calculator might say in the future, but it so often said 63 that at least he might count on it practically always giving that answer, so he could just remember it in his head if he wanted to. Working backward this way from the computer, he figured out many laws of calculating. Programmer Shuman discovered this odd man and, with effort, convinced government officials that he could indeed perform wonders of calculating. Why, this would liberate men from machines, he told the officials. What a weapon it would make against an enemy with only computers in their missiles! What could it do for the long stalemated war?

It would take awhile, of course. They would have to launch a highly secret Project Numbers. But already Shuman knew that 7 times 9 was 63, and he knew how to work out other laws of calculating. It was amazing the feeling of power it gave him.

Do we call this creative writing because it is set in an imaginary future time? Because it contains hand-held calculators and other things which existed only in imagination when the author wrote? On one level, readers might enjoy the predictions, but Asimov said that he did not intend to predict. He was only writing satire. Reading on that level, we find much more to engage our minds—questions of man and the machines and environment he makes for himself, questions of the mind itself. On this level, we are closer to the reasons why this is creative and why it is one of Asimov's most frequently anthologized stories.

What Is Creative in Creative Writing?

If this deep or original thought is the most creative feature of a science fiction story, then are similar thoughts creative when written in essay form? I think so. Some people will read stories and some will read non-fiction, but in either case a creative writer can set them to thinking, can stretch their minds, can show them a new view of something.

So here is my quandary about creative writing classes. Is it their job to teach the craft of stories and essays—and poems? Or should they teach people to think creatively? Most of the courses I know are on the craft level. Thus I think they might better be called simply "writing classes." If the enrollees learn to write well, then they have a vehicle for being creative, for expressing the creativity that is within them.

This view of the matter can lift a burden from teachers of children. You don't have to plan "creative writing" lessons. Just set the stage for writing lessons, plain ones. If creativity comes along, nurture it, but don't worry if it doesn't seem to be here today.

A common attempt at eliciting creativity from children is an assignment related to study of Pilgrims and the Mayflower: "Pretend you just came over on the Mayflower and you're writing a letter home." Mothers say, "I tried that and he just looked at me blankly. What should I do?" These families may have read two or three books about the trip, perhaps drawn a picture or roleplayed events or visited the Mayflower replica—some of the standard lead-ins. Yet sometimes the child's mind is on another voyage. He isn't ready to write what his mother or the curriculum planner asks him to write.

In such a situation, if the studying has in fact been done rather thoroughly, it might help to notice an aspect of the topic that particularly intrigues the child and get him to talking about it. In the Mayflower lesson it might be something technical about sailing vessels or navigation instead of "the trip." If you find something that really animates him, that his mind seems full of, then try suggesting that he write about that. If this works, then you can see how future writing topics can come from your child's mind in this way and be related to any current interest of his. In fact, he can learn to find his own topics to write about, and this is a giant step forward from writing on assigned topics.

But if there isn't any interest that bubbles out in words, if the look is still blank, then what do you do? One possibility is to turn to another level of writing lesson, as listed on the ladder below. Forget about pushing for creativity. Just get the child to practice writing, so he'll be ready for the day when he does have something in his head that he wants to express.

Four Levels of Creativity

Any work of children involves some measure of creativity, if they are thinking at all or producing anything at all. The degree of creativity ranges from low to high, and in writing assignments a ladder of creativity might look like the following list, which begins at the bottom of the ladder and works up toward higher creativity.

1) Copying. The child copies sentences, proverbs, poems, paragraphs. In doing this writing and the subsequent proofing and correcting, the child gives close attention to numerous details of spelling, capitalization, punctuation and other aspects of writing—thus the learning power in even this simple exercise.

2) Dictation. The child writes short passages, as above, but from dictation. This writing may either follow a study of the passage, or precede it, depending on the passage and the ability of the child. He may also at times write from memory a poem or Bible passage or other literature. This requires all the close attention of the preceding level plus additional decision making, such as punctuating on the basis of meaning, or spelling by phonics.

3) Conversing. This involves input and output—a two-way dialog. Children learn to speak by listening, imitating, listening, responding, listening, inventing, and listening again, in a recurring cycle. In the same manner they must immerse themselves in written language, with input and output taking their turns.

For instance, after becoming familiar with a particular kind of literature, the child may write something in the same form. Primary children can listen to or read "patterned" stories—those which have various forms of predictable patterns or refrains—and respond with similar patterned stories of their own. (See child's story at the end of this chapter.) Older children can observe simple plot elements in stories and try to construct plotted stories. Children should gain experience in learning from and imitating all kinds of writing—including letters, descriptions, instructions, persuasive arguments, news reports. Poems too. Trying to match a particular rhyme and meter pattern is a good exercise, not only for learning various formats of English poems, but also for sharpening the ear for the sounds of language. Writers who spend considerable time playing around with poetry will afterward write more clear and graceful prose.

Children (and adults too) do not learn only from the form of writings that they study. More importantly, they learn ideas. They react to ideas by agreeing, arguing, wondering and the whole range of thinking. This thinking is what leads a student to gradually move from level 3 writings to the more creative writings of level 4.

4) Creating. This is not a jump above level 3, but only a step up. The child has an idea and wants to try writing it. Because of his practice on the lower levels, he also has a pretty good idea of the form he will use. But this time he may bend the form to suit his purposes, because this time he is driven not by the task of imitating but by the task of saying what he wants to say. As a person continues to work on this level of the ladder, he continues to push out from the boundaries of his previous work. And his work, if it is good and is understood by others, is viewed by others as being creative.

Using the Ladder Creatively

These four levels do not constitute a curriculum plan which should necessarily be followed in order. Young children can produce writings by working essentially on level 4. And some older children have great difficulty with this level. So the usefulness of the ladder is in the view it gives you as teacher. If your child balks at "being creative," you can back down the ladder to one of the lower levels and insure that the child continues to practice writing skills. Then when the child has something he wants to say, he will be able to say it well. Also, if your child's writing is not as skillful as you would like, you can provide practice at any of the lower levels.

The day will come when your child no longer needs to practice at levels 1 and 2. But he never will outgrow his need for the learning from other writers that happens in level 3.

Professional writers continue to require input. Most of them say they read far more than they write. Their reading and writing conversation often takes this form: read and think, read and think, read and think . . . then write.

So the blank look your child may give you in response to a writing assignment, could mean that he or she has not had enough input and thinking time on the topic. One college writing teacher watched a young man in her class who seemed to be dreaming and looking out the window most of the time. He never brought writings for class critiquing. But shortly thereafter he turned out a first novel which became a bestseller and has lasted for decades, becoming something of a modern classic. Was he in need of thinking and input time instead of writing time while he was in class?

My friend Jane learned from her teacher that she needed lots of ideas and research before she began writing. This surprised her. It sounded like ordinary hard work and not at all like the mysterious, creative secrets she was looking for. But the ordinary hard work is a necessary ingredient.

To examine this aspect, let's consider a type of assignment previously mentioned—that of imitating poems. One such assignment often used is to arrange seventeen syllables in the form of haiku. This seems to be popular since it looks like a route to instant creativity because it produces instant poetry. In fact, some people with such a student poem in hand want to send it off to be published. Isn't it poetry? Isn't it creative?

If you evaluate the poem by the creativity ladder, it is not creative simply because it is in the form of a poem. The ladder is not built of school reports on the bottom and poems at the top. Both reports and poems can appear on any level of the creativity ladder, and a child's first imitations of haiku or any poem form are simply early efforts in the long conversation that should come. A child interested in poetry needs to pursue the ordinary hard work of writing poems again and again (preferably in English forms for English language students), and spend even more time reading poets, studying what they say and how they say it. After much of this level 3 work, the child's poems may begin to reach level 4 quality. He can gradually push his own boundaries outward.

This same hard-work principle is demonstrated over and over again in the lives of people who achieve creatively. It applies in all fields—in art, music, science, every human endeavor. In writing, your teaching efforts may bring your children to a solid level 3 and not as much as you'd like to level 4. But watch them in other fields. Nurture creative effort wherever you find it.

Jane and her husband bought a new house, and she forgot writing while she became absorbed in arranging and decorating and planning for the house—probably never realizing how creative she was in this area. There was nothing mysterious about it. It was just work that she loved.

A Second Grader Writes a Story

After daily exposure to picture books with patterned stories, Alfredo, age 7, wrote this story which has a pattern—sort of.

Once upon a time there was a man.
He was going on a walk.
He found a old radio.
He took it home.
He thote he was rich.
But he wasint rich.

He was going on another walk.
He saw a broken computer.
He thote he was rich.
But he wasint rich.

He plugd up the computer.
But it didt work so he was not rich.
He plugd up the radio.
It did not work.
Now he knows hes not rich.

PART IV

If a language oriented person like me can become interested in math, then I think almost anyone can. I taught a seventh grade class the first year I seriously worked at getting students to visualize rather than just learn math procedures. The results amazed me. Their test scores on arithmetic understanding shot up higher than I had thought possible. Chapter 14 emphasizes this visualizing aspect for younger children. Chapters 15 and 17 illustrate a couple of the numerous applications and hobbies which connect with math knowledge.

How To Teach Arithmetic in Less Time

Do we have the horse following the cart in teaching arithmetic to young children? Yes, according to much research, we do. Many writings, including Jean Piaget's, support another approach to beginning arithmetic than that commonly found in textbooks and workbooks for kindergarten and primary grade levels.

It's not very difficult to learn how to put the horse first. If you make the effort, you will save your child from a common malady known as "Arithmetic Anxiety," and you will help him toward better thinking skills.

What is the horse? And what is the cart? They are concrete thinking and abstract (symbolic) thinking. If you ask a friend which one comes first, you can be almost sure she will answer "concrete thinking." It's only common sense. We don't need education books or the research of a Piaget to tell us that. (Concrete refers to the kind of things that can be seen and touched. Ship is concrete; navigation is not.)

But, strangely, most arithmetic textbooks and workbooks use symbols from the very beginning. Why? Several reasons might be cited, but one important reason is simply the nature of books themselves. If a child has to read a problem and write an answer, then you must teach him the symbols we use for doing this. The symbols are the digits, plus and minus signs, equal sign, and such.

Young children need real objects to think about. We don't teach five- and six-year-olds about "democracy" or "the American way." No, we give them stories about Pilgrims worshiping the way they choose, about heroes Washington and Lincoln, and so forth. After sufficient build-up of concrete information—over several years of schooling—children gradually come to the place where they can discuss and debate political abstract ideas such as democracy, freedom, and states' rights.

Three marbles, three jacks, three children—are all concrete. But the digit 3 is a symbol, and the "threeness" it stands for is an abstract idea. In some problems three is more abstract than in others. Consider five marbles in the ring, and you shoot two marbles out. How many marbles remain in the ring? This three is quite concrete. Many children will be able to "image" the marbles in their heads or count on their fingers and figure out the remainder. It is actually three marbles in the ring. It is concrete and image-able.

But Dale jumped over the rope five times and Susan two times. How many more times did Dale jump it than Susan? For children thinking concretely, this is not the same kind of problem at all. They cannot image Susan's two jumps and take them away from Dale's five jumps. It didn't happen that way. Thinking about differences is more abstract than thinking about remainders. And jumps are not as touchable or image-able as marbles.

If you look at primary arithmetic books around your house, you are likely to find that they do talk about marbles and apples and children. Problems are about concrete, image-able things that interest children. That's because all educators agree that we should start with the concrete.

But the great mistake in our age of books is that we move from concrete to symbolic on almost every page. A workbook page may begin with pictures of apples which the child is to count or color or draw rings around. Then it may end with something like:

$$3 + 2 = \underline{\quad}$$

This moves from concrete to abstract in every lesson or every unit.

But the growth of children's thinking is not that way. Growth moves from concrete to abstract over the years, not each day. This is an important principle for arithmetic teachers to know. Violating it—using abstractions too soon—is the greatest single cause, almost the only cause, of Arithmetic Anxiety and of later difficulties with advanced arithmetic.

This is an ironic situation to be in. Books, which are supposed to help teachers and pupils, turn out to be part of the problem. We can't entirely blame authors and publishers of these books. They usually are well aware of the concrete thinking of young children. But the public has demanded books, so they do their best to provide work on a concrete level. They get as close to real life as they can. If they can't have real apples for children to count, they do the next best thing and have pictures of apples for children to count. If they can't ask the child what three apples and two apples are, they write $3 + 2 = $ ___.

The other side of the irony is that parents and teachers think that books are where learning is found. Homeschools have real life all around them, and too often they ignore it and use books instead.

So books—and schools—try to imitate real life. Meanwhile teaching parents try to imitate schools and their book learning. What a circular reasoning we have fallen into!

As mentioned earlier, it is not difficult to break out of this pattern. You can quite easily put the horse before the cart if you are convinced that this is the proper way. If you already have books and you feel security in following them, experiment with oral arithmetic. Use the book as a guide, but you read it instead of having the child read it. Ask questions orally. Obtain real marbles, M&M's, and other objects and let the child manipulate them to work out problems. After a few hours spent this way you are likely to find that the child can do problems one or two grade levels beyond what he does with written work.

Why can you expect such remarkable results? It is because you allow the child to use his strong mode of thinking. He uses real objects instead of digits, plus signs, equal signs, and so forth.

You won't experiment very long before you find your pupil sometimes giving you an answer without manipulating the objects. He works a problem in his head faster than he could on the table. When that happens, he is imaging the objects in his head. If you understand imaging, you will be an excellent arithmetic teacher.

Imaging is another word for concrete thinking. It describes perhaps more clearly what goes on in a child's head at this stage of his development. When a child starts doing arithmetic in his head, we adults tend to assume that his thought processes are like ours. We think he is ready for the symbols of arithmetic. But, no, he is still using objects. He is mentally visualizing objects.

By the mental-image mode of thinking, the child can do more and more arithmetic. But sometimes you will stump him with a difficult problem. What then? Let him use M&M's, popsickle sticks, an abacus, or other real objects to work it out. The real objects develop his imagery, and the imagery develops his arithmetic understanding.

This is quite different from saying, "Now you're supposed to write this number directly under the larger number, borrow one and write it here, put your answer in this column . . ." It's very different. It builds genuine understanding and thinking skills. It leads to success and enjoyment of arithmetic. It lays the foundation for later abstract thinking in advanced arithmetic and higher math.

Oral and mental arithmetic are not new inventions. They probably have been around since ancient times. And a recent reprinting (by Mott Media) of Ray's Arithmetics, which were used a century ago in our schools, allows us to see how arithmetic was taught in that era. In the beginner book is a picture of a teacher and children informally gathered around a table with fruit on it, and teachers are instructed to use real fruit in their classes for counting and other number work. The next book is called *Intellectual Arithmetic,* and it is planned for mostly oral and mental work rather than written work.

It is a rather recent phenomenom for us to think that the magic of learning is contained in workbooks. But, of course, learning happens in the head. And with young children, real life and real objects can cause more arithmetic to happen in the head than books can.

After you begin experimenting with oral and mental arithmetic using a book, you're likely to find yourself expanding beyond the book. You will challenge your child with arithmetic in all kinds of daily activities. (The accompanying list gives ideas that many parents use.)

It's another article to consider when and how to gradually introduce the writing of arithmetic problems. But you can experiment with that, too. Do it considerably later than the textbooks say and you will save months of plodding time. Your child will quickly learn to write what he long has understood.

Arithmetic in Real Life

School books try to teach about real life, but you can bypass the books and teach from real life directly. This list of simple ideas to use with young children may help you form the habit of looking for arithmetic all around you.

Make milk drinks, fruit drinks, sandwich fillings, and other snacks. Measure, count, and follow recipes.

Use the television program list. Find the time of favorite programs. Plan which programs to watch within the total allowed time for a day or for a week.

Help in the yard, garage, or workshop. Measure, count, plant rows, learn wrench sizes.

Help with grocery shopping. Count or weigh produce.

Calculate or read figures on the cheapest brand or package size. Keep a running total on a calculator.

Read speed limit signs, mileage signs, street numbers, odometer; calculate miles traveled; count blocks from the store to the library; read road maps. Make up problems.

Learn to use phone numbers—local, long distance, toll-free, and emergency numbers.

Read some household bills. Talk about how to save money.

Read advertisements and cents-off coupons. Discuss what savings may or may not be realized by using them.

Read the calendar, the thermometer, the speedometer, the scales.

Make up problems about news stories. If the team had made one more touchdown, what would the score be? Were there fewer traffic deaths this year or last year?

Play games—all kinds of games. Plan strategy, count moves, keep score, compete and think.

Numbers in the Bible

How did our number system originate? Why do we use a base of ten? And why on earth do we measure some things with sixty and its divisors and multiples?

Base Ten

By far the most popular theory about base ten is the evolutionary theory that it arose because humans have ten fingers, and this is repeated in many arithmetic and history texts. A typical statement reads: "Very probably when the fingers of one hand came to be used in counting, the fingers of the other hand were soon used. It is only natural that the base 10 would come into use." Another book omits "probably." It announces, "The only reason for basing our system of counting upon 10 is the fact that each of us has 10 fingers."

This is pure guessing, of course. And as scholars learn more about ancient times, this seems less and less likely to have been the case. Since the mid-nineteenth century, archeologists and others have continually pushed back for us the boundaries of history. As we learned more about older civilizations we learned gradually that the Greeks did not originate so many ideas as they had been given credit for. Some ideas came, perhaps, from the Assyrians and Babylonians. Now we're realizing that the Babylonians didn't originate so many ideas as they had been given credit for. Some ideas came, perhaps, from the Sumerians before them. We could continue this kind of thinking until we get back to Noah or Adam—or to God.

Historians are not that far yet, but are at early Babylon and Sumer—the Biblical Shinar. In the Bible view of history, this is not long after the Great Flood or the Babel judgment. People of those days had both a decimal (10) and a sexagesimal (60) notation system, place value, algebra that could solve quadratic and linear equations with several unknowns, cubic and biquadratic equations, and the geometry of areas and volumes. They could add, subtract, multiply, divide, raise to powers and extract roots.

Evolutionary thinkers say this all must have "developed," so they keep looking for earlier times in which man was developing from the finger counting stage to the early Babylon stage. It is still a mystery to historians how and where all this happened.

One possible answer is that such "development" never happened, but that man was created with intelligence and knowledge directly from God. Even evolutionary historians who puzzle over the base ten idea have concluded that this came not from nature, but from the mind of man instead. We, then, who believe that man is made in the image of God, may well ask whether base ten—and other mathematical ideas—originated with God.

Theologians since early times have, in fact, pondered this question. *Ten* is often cited as signifying the perfection, or completion, of Divine order. It implies that nothing is missing; the whole cycle is complete. Thus the Ten Commandments contain all that is needed and no more than is needed; the tithe represents the whole that God's people owed to Him, and this "whole" portion symbolizes God's claim on the larger whole; the ten plagues are God's complete judgment on Egypt; the ten generations to Noah are the complete pre-flood age; the ten "I am's" in the Book of John are a complete description of Christ's provision for us; the ten words in Psalm 119 are a complete description of God's Word; and so on through numerous other examples that could be given from the Bible.

Daniel heard an angel ask "the wonderful numberer" how long a certain time would be. (Wonderful numberer is the Hebrew word "Palmoni" in Daniel 8:3). God tells the number of the stars (Psalm 147:4). And God weighs the waters by measure (Job 28:25).

Did our number system originate with the Wonderful Numberer or did it come from early man counting on his fingers?

Base Sixty

The early Babylonians used sixty as a base, at least at times, for their calculations. Moving over one place meant a sixty-fold increase rather than a tenfold increase. Though we don't use a base sixty, we retain remnants of that system. Our geometry of circles is built on 360 degrees (6 X 60), and our solar calendar is based on this system. One degree is one day (approximately); 30 degrees are one month; and twelve of those equal a year. The hours, minutes and seconds are further divisions of sixty or its divisors. Our use of dozens also is related to base sixty rather than base ten.

What is the origin of this system of sixty? One text, speaking of Sumer and Babylon, says, "Most strange of all is the fact that their system of counting was based on 60!" Another says, "It is probable that 60 came into use because it has so many integral divisors (2, 3, 4, 5, 6, 10, 12, 15, 20, and 30) which made working with fractional parts easier." Still another says that "The circle was originally divided into 360 equal parts for astronomical instruments, because that was the supposed number of days in the year. This division of the circle into 360 degrees led to the sexagesimal scale used by the Babylonians."

Even a theologian is puzzled by this number: "No one can tell us why the great circle of the heavens (the Zodiac) should be divided into 360 parts, instead of any other number, for apart from this it appears to be perfectly arbitrary."

It would not be arbitrary if there actually was a time in the world's history when the year was 360 days. It may be significant that not only the Babylonians, but the early Egyptians and other ancient peoples also used these figures for the great circle of the heavens. It was only later, based on astronomical observations, that various adjustments were made, such as adding five extra days between years, to keep the calendar on track with the actual solar year. If at one time 360 days was indeed the length of the year, it would be perfectly natural for the ancients to divide the sky into that many parts and to calculate other calendar divisions on that basis.

Writers on the Bible have often pointed out to us that a prophetical and Biblical year is 360 days, and we may well ask, Is this concept based on fiction or on historical reality?

The Genesis record of the Great Flood contains hints that the catastrophe of that year may have changed the earth's rotation enough to lengthen the year from an original 360 days to about 365 days.[1] The long day of Joshua and the backed-up sundial in Hezekiah's time are other Biblical hints of cosmic catastrophes. Other ancient writers, including Plato and Aristotle, also recognized such an event (or events) in the history of the world.

A base sixty is referred to in the parable of the sower, where some seed brought forth thirty, some sixty, and some a hundredfold. Here we have both base sixty and base ten number systems used in the same story. The number sixty is also used repeatedly in reference to the number of animals to sacrifice.

As for the number twelve in the Bible, various theologians have considered it to signify government, or rule. They point out the twelve tribes of Israel, whose names are on the twelve gates of the holy city, and the twelve apostles, whose names are on the twelve foundations. The walls of the city measure 144 (12^2) cubits and its length and breadth each measure twelve thousand furlongs. This last number combines both twelves and tens (12×10^3). The hundred and forty-four thousand also is a combination—$12^2 \times 10^3$. The city will have no need of the sun and moon, but until that time these rule over day and night. The moon marking its twelve monthly cycles, perhaps? And the sun passing through its twelve divisions of the sky, marking seasons and days?

The origin of the 360 degrees seems not arbitrary at all. The base sixty system may have perfectly sensible foundations. When a child learns that a right angle is 90 degrees (one-fourth of 360), he is not learning just a bit of modern geometry. He is learning knowledge that may be as old as mankind. Perhaps Adam himself talked to God about such numbers when they talked about the heavens and their signs and seasons and their rule over the earth.

A Long History

Ancient Jewish historians and theologians wrote about Bible numbers. Early Christians did the same. Even before the canon of Scripture was complete, Christians tried to decide by numbers whether or not to include certain books in the canon. Augustine, Jerome and others down through the centuries have pursued the topic.

Christian students today can enrich a sometimes dull subject by adding a bit of number history to their study and by learning some of the uses the Bible makes of numbers.[2]

---

1. Explained in chapter 11 of *Adam and His Kin* by Ruth Beechick (Arrow Press, 1990).
2. See *Number in Scripture* by E. W. Bullinger (reprinted by Kregel, no date given). This was written in a former century and contains science information that today's readers may find out of date, but contains much valuable study material.

Math Content

Do Math Texts Repeat Too Much?

A study of repetition in three major textbook series startled a lot of teachers recently. The figures below show the percentage of pages on which any new material is introduced. That is, if any part of a page included new material, the page was counted. Kindergarten earns 100% simply because no book precedes it. But, of course, the children may already know some or all of this material either from real life or from books at home. Here are the percentages as the researcher found them.[1]

Grade	Percentage
K	100
1	75
2	40
3	60
4	45
5	50

6	38
7	35
8	30
9	90

At grade 2 and at grades 6 to 8 there is a shockingly low percentage of new material. Grades 4 and 5 are not much better. One simple move that homeschoolers could make is to examine their books and decide what they might safely skip. The children themselves are often good at this and can take responsibility for pointing out what they need to study and what they already know. The time saved can be used for more advanced math or for whatever goals the family has.

What Do Math Teachers Recommend?

The National Council of Teachers of Mathematics and other groups, after years of work, published their recommendations on goals for math. Quite surprisingly there was little controversy around these. Instead of the usual emotional debate, teachers of other subjects said, "If the math teachers can agree like this, so can we."

What do the math teachers recommend? Number 1 on the list, as might be expected, is problem solving. Number 2 is "the ability to think mathematically."

Number 7 is estimation. Many people find they use estimation more often than calculation in daily life. And people who work with math a lot, find estimation highly useful in the midst of their calculations.

Another topic the math educators recommend is probability and statistics. This is not for researchers only, but for every citizen who wants to be educated and able to think for himself. It is useful to homeschoolers, for instance, to understand the difference between percentile ranks and percentages. And it is useful for all of us to recognize when advertisers misuse research figures to get us to buy their products.

Another topic, perhaps less widely understood, is understanding and using mathematical structures. Math, as with all academic disciplines, is invented and organized by people in highly literate societies, and understanding the structures leads to great learning power. An elementary example of structure is the law of commutation. Understanding that 5 + 2 is the same as 2 + 5 helps students figure out problems with large numbers. Three + 18 is simple when children can turn it to 18 + 3. This knowledge carries over into algebra and other situations throughout the study of math. Rote learning of addition facts without understanding is useful only within limited boundaries, but understanding the underlying structure empowers a student to continually expand the boundaries. Knowing patterns allows a student to solve whole classes of problems. Structure is explained more fully in a couple of books by Jerome S. Bruner—*The Process of Education,* and *Toward a Theory of Instruction.*

Function is another topic the math teachers would like to see treated well in our curriculum. For an example, the weight we gain is a function of the difference between the calories we eat and the calories we burn. Weight gain is x, the dependent variable. It depends on y, which in this case is $C_{eaten} - C_{burned}$ (C for calories). This relationship can be shown on a graph or in a formula. Is ozone depletion really a function of the chlorofluorocarbons we humans release? Is national prosperity a function of the tax rate or the interest rate or the consumer confidence index or any particular combination of factors?

Mathematical thinking enters into most areas of modern life. And to be educated, thinking citizens requires a far higher level of understanding today than it did 50 years ago. We may want to set our goals higher than the ability to balance a checkbook or to fill out an IRS form. That is what math educators would like to see.

The list of skills below is a composite from several organizations and individuals involved in textbook production, state adoption standards and other aspects of mathematics education. Some items in the list are for secondary level and do not apply to elementary grades.

1. Problem solving
2. Communication skills related to mathematics
3. Integration of topics within mathematics
4. Relating mathematics to other subjects and to the learner's real world (closely associated with number 1)
5. Understanding and using functions, relations, and patterns
6. Probability and statistics
7. Approximation and estimation
8. Using number sense and number systems effectively
9. Computational ability—both written and mental computation—with rational and some irrational numbers
10. Two- and three-dimensional geometry, including both synthetic and algebraic arguments in geometry
11. Understanding and using mathematical structures
12. Measurement

13. Algebra
14. Trigonometry
15. Discrete mathematics
16. Intuitive foundations of calculus
17. Using technology (calculators, computers, etc.) to help solve mathematical problems[2]

---

1. Flanders, J. R. (1987) "How Much of the Content in Mathematics Textbooks Is New?" *Arithmetic Teacher* 35:1–3.
2. From Stephen S. Willoughby, *Mathematics Education for a Changing World,* Association for Supervision and Curriculum Development, 1990.

Math and Music

The ancient Greeks included music as one of the mathematical studies. Here is an experiment which shows how math and music are related.

A Music-Math Experiment

1. Make a simple musical instrument. For materials all you need are a rubber band and a small box. You could use a cottage cheese container or an oatmeal box cut down to a height that fits your rubber band. Leave the top of the box open. Stretch the rubber band across the open top and down around the box.

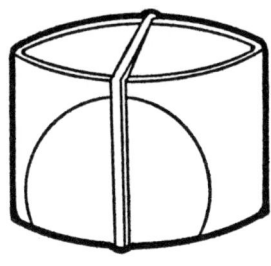

2. Try out your instrument. Pluck the rubber band to see what kind of musical sound it gives. If it is very low or very high, you can make it more pleasing by stretching it more or less. You can change either the size of the box or the size of the rubber band to do this.

3. Learn some musical ratios. A ratio of 2:1 (two to one) is easy. Try pinching the rubber band in the middle with one thumb and finger, and then pluck one of the halves. The sound should be one octave higher than when you plucked the full band. If it's not exactly an octave, move your thumb and finger until it sounds right—to you or to someone whose ear can tell an octave. That will be the exact center.

An octave is from *do* to *do,* in *do, re, me, fa, sol, la, ti, do.* The string for the low *do* is twice as long as for the high *do.* Or we could say the reverse, that the high string is half as long as the low. You can think of these as ratios or as fractions; it's all the same thing. That octave ratio of 2:1 or 1:2 is the most important in music.

The second most important ratio is 3:2. This gets you from *do* to *sol*. If you sing the first two twinkle's in "Twinkle, Twinkle, Little Star," you are jumping from *do* to *sol*. To play this, think of the rubber band as having 3 parts. Use all 3 parts, or the full stretch of rubber band, for *do*. Then use 2 parts (two-thirds) for *sol*. It might help to make an ink mark on the rubber band one-third of the way across. Then pinch on the mark and pluck the longest section of the rubber band. With those two notes now, you should be able to play "Twinkle, twinkle." Try it several times until it sounds right.

Now maybe you can play the phrase, "Twinkle, twinkle, little star." Let your ear tell you how far to move your thumb for the word "little."

Another important ratio is 4:3. If you pluck three-fourths of the string you get *fa*, which is the word *how* in "How I wonder what you are." See if you can play that note.

If you like music best, you could go ahead now and try to play the whole song, or play another song of your choice. Also, you could try playing on a string of a violin or guitar to see if they work like the ratios you just learned about.

If you like math best, you could read more now about the ratios of music.

Harmonic Proportions

Did you notice in the rubber band experiment that the ratios were in order? They were 2:1, 3:2, and 4:3. Other musical ratios continue with 5:4, 6:5 and so on. It probably didn't happen that somebody decided by arithmetic to make those rules. It was more likely the other way around. That is, people sang and made instruments to sound pleasing to the ear, and then somebody discovered that music followed these mathematical patterns.

Historians usually give credit to the Greeks for discovering these proportions in music. The Greeks knew how the ratios worked on the length of strings. Later, Galileo and a Frenchman named Marin Mersenne figured out the ratios according to the vibrations of the strings.

The vibration ratios were the same as the length ratios. On your experimental instrument, for instance, the half string you pluck for high *do* vibrates twice as fast as the whole string you pluck for low *do*.

Here's another look at the three most important ratios in harmony.

2:1	an octave
3:2	a fifth
4:3	a fourth

Why is one called "a fifth"? Because the space, or interval, between its two tones is five notes. Remember how you played "Twinkle, twinkle" and they were five notes apart? If the ratio between these two notes is just right, they sound good when played together. But if the ratio is wrong, the vibrations fight against each other and cause us to hear an unpleasant beat in the vibrations. We might say it sounds out of tune. Or it sounds unharmonious.

An interesting thing happens with the fourth. If we move from low *do* up a fourth, we come to *fa*. But if we move from high *do* down to *fa*, we find that it is an interval of a fifth. The musical ratios are related to each other in many ways that lead to beautiful harmony.

If you want to learn more about them, try looking in the library under the topic "physics and music." What you find is likely to have a lot of advanced and technical information.

Do Stars Sing?

The Greeks' four math studies were arithmetic, geometry, astronomy and music. We've shown here a bit of the reasoning for linking music with arithmetic. Could we link it also with astronomy? The Bible does. The Lord asked Job where he was when the morning stars sang together. David wrote a song that went, "Praise him, all ye stars of light." Are the stars singing God's praises?

If you study deeply into the physics of music you will find that the numbers don't work out quite as neatly as it might seem from this lesson. Instrument makers have to adjust the ratios a tiny bit if they want their instruments to produce more than one scale. Do you think that the vibrations might work out exactly right some day when the curse is removed and God makes the new earth? Do you suppose we will then hear the stars sing?

A Primer on Achievement Testing

Where Do Norms Come From?

Essential to understanding tests and their scores is the basic concept of the "normal" curve. Graphing practically any attribute in any population of large enough size will result in a curve close to the example shown in the diagram. The vertical axis on the left shows the number of people, and the horizontal axis along the bottom shows the attribute being measured.

If the attribute is height, then heights are tabulated along the bottom of the graph and children are counted up the left side. We can place dots to show how many children are 4' tall, how many are 4'1", 4'2" and so on.

In a normal group, we find that the dots at the far left and the far right are lower than the dots in the middle. People's heights, or any other attributes, tend to cluster around the middle, or average. So those dots closest to the

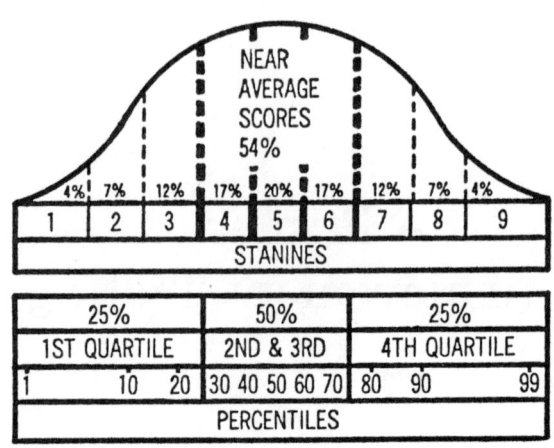

center of the distribution are higher. The farther outward you go, either left or right, the smaller the population and, thus, the lower the dots.

When the dots are connected with a line, the line resembles the shape of a bell. For this reason it is often called a "bell curve." For this bell curve, the group must be normal. For example, when measuring heights, a normal group could be 100 teenagers or 137 toddlers, but not 98 teenagers and 2 toddlers. Two toddlers in a group of teenagers would skew the bell, making its left edge extend outward much farther than the right. That would not be a normal curve.

Population Groups

When people standardize an achievement test, they use such a large population that the curve can't help but form a nice bell. And the "norms" we read so much about come from these bells, or at least from the figures which would make up such a bell. To obtain national norms, the test companies select students (the norming group) who proportionately represent all socio-economic levels, and all areas of our society. Their scores are graphed as described above to obtain national norms.

Homeschoolers are a select population. Compared with unmotivated drug users, non-English-speaking immigrants, families who have no magazines or books in their homes, and others who would help to pull averages down, home-schoolers are highly select. They *should* score higher than the general population. Some homeschool families, of course, adopt foreign children and begin from scratch teaching them English; some homeschooled children have learning problems or handicaps of various kinds; some are less motivated than others, and so forth. As individuals they have wide variations. But as a group they differ from the general population in ways that affect academic achievement, and it should be no surprise that research reports show them, as a group, to exceed national averages.

Percentile Ranks

Different kinds of scores can be placed along the bottom axis of the bell curve. One widely used score is called the percentile rank. Misunderstandings arise from confusing percentiles with percentages. Percentile rank refers to a position or standing among a population, not the student's percentage of correct answers.

For instance, if a student's score fell at the middle of this lower axis, we would say he was at the 50th percentile; 50 percent of the population scored lower than he did. A student at the 25th percentile is not one-quarter of the way along the lower axis; he is closer to the center than to the left edge. This is because most scores cluster around the middle, or average.

The highest percentile rank assigned is 99. You cannot say of the highest score that 100 percent of the scores are lower. Thus there is no percentile rank of 100.

It gives us a better picture of percentile ranks to notice on the graph where the middle half of the scores lie. Between the 25th percentile and the 75th percentile lie half of all the scores. But notice that those scores take up nowhere near one-half the length of the horizontal axis. This middle half clusters closely around the center. This area is sometimes called the second and third "quartiles," and test scores falling in this area can be thought of as average or close to average. The first quartile consists of the lower scores to the left of these, and the fourth quartile consists of the higher scores at the right.

When you first meet percentile ranks, it takes practice to think of them differently than you think of the more familiar percentages. Sometimes even in published articles this term is misused. In our height example earlier, a student at the 55th percentile would not be 5 percentage points taller than a student at the 50th percentile. And he is not 10 percent taller. The statements that people ordinarily make about percentages don't work when the figures are percentiles instead.

Standard Scores

Several kinds of scores have been developed that divide the horizontal axis representing raw scores, or the number of test items answered correctly, into *uniform* units of measure. Stanines are one common kind. This name was coined from STAndard NINE. The line is marked into nine equal lengths called stanines. The middle three—4, 5, and 6—are considered average, and 54 percent of all scores fall within this range. Only 4 percent of scores fall into stanine 1 and another 4 percent into stanine 9.

In terms of raw scores, there would be as much difference between stanine 5 and 6, which are near the middle, as between 8 and 9, which are near the high end. By contrast, the distance between the percentile ranks of 50 and 60 is less than the distance between the percentile ranks of 90 and 99.

Stanines have a number of advantages for statisticians and researchers who wish to compare various kinds of measures. An advantage for students and their parents is that nine divisions are about as precise as anyone ought to be in interpreting something like an achievement test. To make fine distinctions, as between the 66th and 68th percentiles, is not appropriate.

Grade Level Scores

Grade level scores are another widely used—and misused—kind of score. A grade level score indicates the grade in which a student's performance on a specific test would be average. Thus if he scores at grade 3 on a test, this means he performed on the test as the average third grader performed on that test. For convenience, a school year is divided into 10 months, and decimals are used: 3.4 means grade 3, month 4.

These scores work fairly well in the middle of a test range, but not near the high or low end of a range. In other words, if your child takes a test for third graders and scores at grade 2, 3, or 4, you can interpret that according to our usual idea of what is meant by grade 2, 3, or 4. But if he scores at grade 6 or 7, you must be careful. He may have scored as well as the average sixth or seventh grader would on the third grade test, but that doesn't mean he would get an average score on the sixth or seventh grade test. The third grade test doesn't really show what an average seventh grader can do. Thus, at the extreme high and low ends of a test, grade levels become an artificial unit of measure and cannot be interpreted in our commonsense way of thinking about grades.

If you know that your child is quite advanced or considerably behind the average for his grade or age, you should request a test that is closer to the level you estimate him to be on if you want more meaningful scores. All major tests have various levels, so you can match the level to your child.

Standardization

All the "brand name" tests are standardized according to the technical meaning of the word. If brand X is rumored to be "harder," you might expect that your child would score at grade 5 instead of the grade 6 he scored on brand Y. Such a situation would make standardization meaningless.

If someone opens a test booklet and says, "Look, these questions are harder," and if they do actually seem harder to you, then remember that the standardization process evens everything out. If questions are easier, more children get them right, and your child would have to get more right to keep up with them. Conversely, if they are harder, he has to get fewer right to keep up with children of his age or grade.

Actually, for statistical reasons, a test item works best if about one-half of the children taking the test can get it right. An easy item that practically everyone passes is a waste of space and time. It doesn't help to distinguish those who know the subject from those who don't. It would have been thrown out or revised early in the process of making the test. Likewise, a test item that hardly anyone passes is also useless.

Content of Achievement Tests

The brands vary somewhat in the sub-scores they give you. One test may give language subscores in mechanics, spelling, and expression. Another may give scores in capitalization, punctuation, spelling, and usage. If you prefer one set of categories over another, you could choose which test you want to use on this basis.

Most achievement tests, in addition to the main categories, make quite detailed lists of content and skills and report the results just as if they were meant to be diagnostic tests. This probably has been forced onto the test companies by public demand and marketing considerations. But there may be only three items on a particular skill, and on the basis of those, a child is scored as average, below average, or above average on that skill. If you spend any time at all helping your child with his studies, you already have a more insightful assessment than such a test score gives.

The actual content—the subject matter and skills—which the tests cover in elementary grades is quite standardized. The selection procedures, involving input and consensus from curriculum specialists and teachers, tend toward uniformity. Content is checked against widely used textbooks, and the textbooks, having had the same standardizing pressures, don't change things either. So the major brand tests are not much different from one another in content.

Misuse of Test Results

Most college courses on testing teach that no important decision concerning a child's education should be made on the basis of one test. A recent survey confirmed that many schools practically ignore the results of achievement tests. These schools go right on trying to achieve their own goals while the test scores languish in the files. Teachers, like parents, already know more about their students' learning than the test scores tell them.

Turning these scores into standards that children should meet is a misuse of the result and indicates a gross misunderstanding of measurement statistics. On the bell curve, we can see the layout of scores which were developed from the population of children used for standardizing the test, this population being representative of the total population in the country.

Now, to say that every child should be brought up to the 50th percentile, or any particular figure, is absurd. Such an event is impossible unless the norming group was very badly chosen. When the statistics are accurate, always half the children will score below the 50th percentile. Ten percent will score below the 10th percentile, and so on. Yet we have the absurdity today of laws and regulations requiring homeschoolers to bring every child above a given percentile rank or lose the right to homeschool. This amounts to saying that the lowest children on the curve cannot homeschool, and often those are the children who need homeschooling the most.

Media attention, public pressure, and public money bring other misuses. Every state and many districts are under intense pressure to be above average. In a recent year every state except one claimed to be above average. So we have lost any sensible meaning for *average*.

Districts have various techniques for pushing their scores above average. One is to classify more children as learning disabled and then test only the "regular" classes. Another is to test the children every six weeks and work and drill between tests to raise the scores. The whole year, then, becomes a training course for taking achievement tests. More sinister reports include practices not so widespread as those. One is to enroll everybody long enough to get them counted and collect the public money for them, then let the uninterested drop out. Or suggest to their parents that the children should be homeschooled. These, then, hunt for a homeschooling family who will take in their chidren.

The Place of Tests Today

Today there are legitimate concerns about achievement tests. Misuses such as those mentioned above have led to a loss of credibility of test scores. Professionals concede that they are less trustworthy than 20 or 30 years ago.

Yet the tests are not altogether useless. One of their best uses is for group assessment, and in the homeschooling movement they have played a large part in convincing the world that this type of education works. To assess any one child, they can give general information, but are limited in the kind and amount of specific details they provide. They are not meant as diagnostic tests.

The real test is life. As homeschoolers, your goal will be realized only as your children show the beneficial effects of home education in their lives.

PART V

I have written about memorizing for longer than any topic in this book. My first article appeared in "Moody Monthly" in the 1950s and told the story of my own toddlers memorizing Scripture. From almost a dozen articles, I have selected the "Tom Sawyer" one for inclusion here. It first appeared in "Evangelizing Today's Child" and was reprinted in several publications which I have now lost track of. The follow-up on my toddlers is that Allen eventually memorized about half the New Testament books, the book of Proverbs and other long passages. He was memorizing the Gospel of John in Greek when his first child was born and the memorizing suddenly slowed down. Andy memorized quite a lot also, and to this day he organizes annual memory programs for churches he attends. The other chapters here, on creativity and thinking, also show a lifelong interest I have had in how the mind works.

It's Time to Bury Tom Sawyer's Memory Method

Sunday morning for Tom Sawyer was a trying time because he had to get his verses in mind before leaving for Sunday school. On a particular Sunday morning he chose five verses from the Sermon on the Mount because he "could find no verses that were shorter." Good-hearted cousin Mary tried to help and began hearing him recite.

"Blessed are the —a—a—".

"Poor—"

"Yes—poor; blessed are the poor—a—a—"

"In spirit—"

"In spirit; blessed are the poor in spirit, for they—they—"

"*Theirs*—"

"For *theirs*. Blessed are the poor in spirit, for *theirs* is the kingdom of heaven. Blessed are they that mourn, for they—they—"

"Sh—"

"For they—a—"

"S, H, A—"

"For they S, H—oh, I don't know what it is!"

"*Shall!* "

"Oh, *shall!* for they shall—for they shall—a—a—shall mourn—a—a—blessed are they that shall—they that shall—they that—a—they that shall mourn, for they shall—a—shall *what* ? Why don't you tell me, Mary? What do you want to be so mean for?"

Mark Twain was writing of the time around 1840 and we find this familiar yet today. Tom was using what we today would call his short-term memory ability; he hoped to remember only long enough to say the verse and earn his points.

People can hold in their short-term memory somewhere from five to nine items, or an average of seven. If there is interference from other items jockeying for one of the seven places, the person is likely to forget some of the original items. For instance, if you have just read a seven-digit phone number and then someone talks to you, you may have to look at the number again before you dial it. You can group items into "chunks," and that increases your capacity to seven of the chunks. Tom's chunks, with the exception of two phrases, were only one word long.

If you wish to move items from your surface, short-term memory to long-term storage, you must process them in some way. Each person has his unique way of going about that, but the important point is that it must be processed in the mind. Simply hearing or seeing is not enough except for certain rare individuals.

Sunday morning cramming does not accomplish this processing. Long term memory requires time to "set" in the brain, time for physiological processes to complete themselves. It also requires review, overlearning, and multiple associations of contexts.

Multiple associations are actually more important than multiple repetitions. Tom did associate "the kingdom of heaven" with the poor in spirit, and that helped him over the largest chunk that he managed. But his other associations were simply remembering which word followed which.

A system of memory which best incorporates these and other known factors about memory is called the "whole" system. The whole system has been shown in research to have three distinct advantages over the part system: 1) it is more efficient, 2) it results in greater understanding of the meaning, and 3) the passage is remembered longer.

Briefly stated, the steps in memorizing by wholes are these:

1) become familiar with the whole unit
2) practice the whole unit many times with concentration
3) put extra work on difficult parts, if necessary
4) overlearn.

Using this basic sequence, you can devise an infinite number of teaching-learning plans. You can teach passages as long as the Twenty-Third Psalm or even longer to a very young child who is just learning to talk. To do this, begin by saying a short phrase and the child repeats it after you. Then you say the next phrase and the child repeats it. Continue in this way through the whole psalm. Repeat the procedure daily, and gradually increase the length of the phrases. Later, just start the phrases and let the child finish them himself when he can. At this point your help diminishes with each repetition of the psalm and the child says more of it on his own and eventually he says the entire psalm with no help at all.

A child who has learned the psalm in this way will see it as one piece. He will recite straight through it as most children recite through the alphabet, without stopping at the end of a verse and wondering which verse comes next, or without stopping as Tom Sawyer did at the end of a word and wondering which word comes next.

The verse-by-verse system, or the part system appears at first to give quicker results, but it takes more time in the long run. And the final result is not as meaningful or as long lasting as memory by the whole system. Also, using the whole system, the child is more likely to achieve a smooth recitation that proceeds straight through the passage without the problems of connections and proper order of parts that so often accompany memory by the part system.

With older children, you can use a variety of methods to familiarize them with the memory passage and to practice—steps 1 and 2 of the memory process. They can read the passage, answer questions about it, discuss difficult parts, have relays to put phrases in order or play various other games with it. When they learn the passage, continue the games and drills for a time so that overlearning can happen.

Then, ideally, they should review the passage. Space reviews closer together at the first and then space them farther and farther apart. It takes only a little ingenuity to adapt activities or to think of original activities to enliven the drills and practices and reviews. But if you have never tried the whole memory system, it takes a pretty big dose of perseverance to stay with it long enough to see it work.

Teens and adults can follow the same basic sequence but they are not as likely to need games and variety of methods to help motivate them. One high school student devised for himself a simple plan of reading a chapter five times each morning and evening. By the second morning he began trying to anticipate, or to think ahead of his eyes as they glided down the chapter. By the second evening he found he knew the chapter pretty well, but he completed his five repetitions anyway, referring to his Bible only when necessary. His review system began with reviewing daily the first two weeks, then reviewing weekly for a time and eventually tapering off still more. This student went on to learn a number of complete books of the Bible by his system and one review each year is enough to keep them in his memory.

As early as 1900, researchers compared the whole and the part methods of memorizing literary passages. With both adults and children, the whole method resulted every time in faster learning. The early studies have been corroborated many times by other researchers.

Later researches began uncovering other advantages for the whole system in addition to efficiency. These included the facts that when associations were made they remained; everything was always in the same place; the interrelationships of parts and the organization of the whole became clearer. Thus there was a deeper understanding of the poem or prose passage, and what was memorized lasted longer.

How long is a whole? The unit should be as large as the learner or learners can handle meaningfully. This varies with age. And it also varies with exposure to and familiarity with the type of material. As a person becomes more familiar with the style of writing, the kind of language, the concepts, and other characteristics of the writing, memorizing becomes easier. The first chapter one learns from Paul's letters will take longer than the second. Children not used to the vocabulary and sentence construction of Bible verses will take longer to memorize a verse than will children who have had much exposure to it. There is conflicting research on whether modern translations are easier to memorize than the KJV style of sentence construction.

Perhaps one reason the whole memory system is not more widely used is that progress is not highly visible in the early stages. The memorizing appears to have a slow start. Most teachers on the first day would rather hear the children recite "The Lord is my shepherd; I shall not want." This tangible evidence of learning may be more satisfying to the teacher. And she reasons that she can tack on verse two at the next session and continue working on parts in this way until the whole psalm is learned.

With this method, it is better not to leave memorizing entirely up to the children until after they have had considerable training and experience in the method. It works better if you take time and build the memorizing into your lessons. Help the children through the steps of the memory sequence by a variety of procedures. These are usually motivating in themselves and children are not disturbed if they leave class the first day and cannot quote the first verse of a passage they are starting to learn. It is usually only the teacher who is disturbed by this. Those who persevere in the method in spite of the seeming slow start are often greatly surprised by the results. After children have had considerable training and experience in the method, they may take charge of their own memorizing.

What to do about the hard parts of a passage? After working for a time on steps 1 and 2 of the memory sequence the easy parts will already be learned and some hard parts will remain unlearned. For this reason step 3 has been inserted into the recommended sequence. Putting extra effort on the hard parts is actually a departure from the whole method, and an emphasis on the part method for a time. But this further increases efficiency.

In actual use, the steps overlap each other. That is, work should continue on the whole while hard parts are attacked one at a time. This work on parts is step 3 in the sequence to indicate that it should not start too soon. The learning must be well along before it even becomes clear which parts are going to be the hard ones.

The four-step procedure explained here is built upon the best knowledge of memory that is available at the present time. It is a general outline and allows for much flexibility in specific methods. In your own memorizing and in teaching children, you can work within this framework while tailoring the specifics as you like.

Sample Lessons for Teaching Psalm 23

1. Look at and talk about various sheep and shepherd pictures. As you talk, use the words *still waters, valley, rod, staff, shepherd, oil,* and others which may appear in the pictures. Read together through the entire psalm. Or if the children are too young to read, read it to them.

2. Read or recite the psalm phrase by phrase and have the children repeat carefully after you. Correct any mispronunciations. Insist on accuracy, as this pays off in later lessons. Review a couple of the pictures by having the children tell what

they know about them. Teach the meaning of one or two phrases such as "preparest a table" or "cup runneth over."

3. Read through the psalm together. Or recite phrase by phrase. Repeat again while the children stand on one foot, then while they sit cross-legged. Let them think of other positions and repeat some more. Talk about sheeps' enemies. Do the children have enemies or other things to be afraid of? What does the shepherd do about it?

4. Explain that *restoreth* means *make new again.* Illustrate with a story of a sick sheep that is now well again because the shepherd took such good care of it. Read or recite several times through the entire psalm. Can the children find a part that will be good to think about when they are afraid. Have each child tell why he chose his part.

5. Read or recite the psalm together. See who remembers what *restoreth* means. Teach one or two other difficult words. Have the children close their eyes and see if they can finish each phrase of the psalm after you start it.

6. By reading or listening, have the children find four words that name themselves. (I, my, me, mine.) Write these in a list. Read or recite the psalm together and say those four words louder. Have identical copies of the psalm cut into several pieces—with straight, horizontal cuts. Teams or individuals can race and see who can first assemble a set in order. Scramble the pieces and try this again. If there is only one child he can see if he does it faster the second time. If the children are old enough to write, they could prepare these pieces in a couple of days of writing lessons before doing lesson 6.

7. Find all the words that refer to God. (Lord, shepherd, He, his, thou, thy.) Read or recite through the psalm emphasizing all those words. If this is difficult, try marking the words with color and reading it again. See who remembers the meaning of *restoreth* and any other words you taught in lesson

5. Do the puzzle races again, as in lesson 6.

8. Read or say the psalm together. Pass out pieces for one puzzle (lesson 6), or make a new set with the number of pieces you want for this activity. In a small group each child could have more than one piece. Let the child who thinks he has the first piece place it on a bulletin board or floor. The child who thinks he has the next one places his below it, and so on. All children watch and raise their hands if they see a mistake. Everyone must agree on correcting the mistake before proceeding with the remaining pieces.

9. Have the children find Psalm 23 in their Bibles. Each should select the verse that is hardest to say and work with a partner to learn it better. If a child does not read, you or the child can select a hard part and work orally on it. After sufficient study time, repeat the entire psalm together.

10. See if the children remember the hard parts they studied in lesson 9. Review those and study them again if necessary. Or select a different hard verse to work on. Then repeat the entire psalm together. Begin planning for an audience to recite the psalm to.

11. Use the puzzle pieces from lessons 6 or 8. Scramble them and have the children put them in order. Have races. Remove one piece. Can they put the others in order and leave a blank in the correct position? Let the children think up tests for the group. Recite the psalm together. Are you almost ready for the audience?

12. Pretend there is an audience and practice reciting for them. Speak together. Use good expression. Try it several times.

13. If you are not yet ready for the real audience, repeat any of the lessons and continue as long as needed. After the performance, review once a week for two months, then once a month for a while. Work on other passages.

Who, Me? Creative?

Creativity—what is it? Is it for everyone?

Nine-year-old John was an orphan living with an older brother who resented his presence. John wanted to play musical instruments but was denied use of his brother's music. So, late at night by moonlight, he secretly copied the full library of music. His brother, upon discovering it, burned the music.

George, at the earlier age of seven, also desired to play, but had a father who disliked music and insisted that George would grow up to be a lawyer. George and his mother sneaked a small keyboard instrument into the attic and wrapped its strings in cloth to muffle the tones. There George secretly practiced through several childhood years.

These cases, you may have recognized, are Johann Sebastian Bach and George Frideric Handel. And they can encourage parents today who worry that they may make a wrong move and stifle their children's creativity.

Creativity is not fragile. And it is not rare. It is in all of us because we are created in the image of God.

What is the image of God? Theologians point out many aspects of God that may be included in our heritage. But which of these aspects do you notice first upon reading the opening chapters of the Bible? Scientists, literature professors, and others can say a lot of complex things about these passages. They can so confuse an ordinary reader that Genesis becomes an obscure ancient document instead of a plain message from God.

But if you imagine yourself to be twelve years old again and read the chapters in that frame of mind, it is very clear to you that God is the Creator. An obvious trait we must inherit as His image bearers is creativity. What are you doing with yours?

In our day there is a tendency to link creativity mostly with the arts and with certain science endeavors, especially researchers building new knowledge. In Bach's and Handel's hometowns, music did not have the prestige it does in our times. These two men were born within one month of each other in Germany. In their time and place, musicians were humble, hard-working craftsmen, just as the local cobblers and tailors. They often were government employees, playing church organs, directing choirs, composing music for the services, giving lessons. Sometimes they composed funeral anthems or operas by request of royalty.

Bach's family for generations before and after him were musicians. Johann Sebastian never strayed far from his birthplace. He held positions as *Kapellmeister* for several Dukes, and he ended his career as cantor for a church and school. He was poorly paid in these positions, and lived in cold, unsanitary conditions, which may be why six of his first eight children died. His first wife died young, also.

Pupils were undisciplined. Musicians in his choirs and orchestras were incompetent. Church officials tried to defraud him. The rector who was his boss treated him with contempt, and often humiliated him. He had a pauper's funeral and was buried in an unmarked grave. That was the life of a musician in those days.

But throughout his life Bach composed as a worship to God. It was the main purpose for which he lived. He used existing forms of music, but carried them to more majestic heights. He experimented with polyphony, the interweaving of multiple melodies, so exhausting the possibilities of this style that his successors could develop it no further. His peers did not understand the greatness of his music. It was considered stuffy and old-fashioned at his death, and a pile of the cantatas sold for forty dollars. His sons did not preserve his music and much of it was lost. Obscure music teachers had musty copies. One such man was the teacher of Felix Mendelssohn. Thus Mendelssohn learned of its value, and when he grew up he was able to reintroduce Bach's music to the world.

Handel's father was like many fathers in wanting his son to follow a professional life. As a lawyer, George could help people, perhaps save someone from the gallows. If he were great enough he might even argue a case before the Emperor. And above all, he would make good money.

But Handel loved music. Unlike Bach, he left Germany for Italy and London in search of audiences. He enjoyed times of popularity and endured times of despair, facing debtor's prison and fierce attacks by jealous competitors. But always, he composed, composed, composed. Much of his life he wrote operas for entertainment. He was not as deeply religious as Bach. But in his later years he turned to biblical oratorios. Handel is such a master of the oratorio that those who follow him can only be imitators. He poured all his talent, experience, and energy into "The Messiah," and felt that God himself visited him during its composition.

"Messiah" was not particularly popular during Handel's lifetime. Church leaders, including John Newton, opposed it on grounds that sacred music should not be presented in concert halls, but only in churches. Others objected to the fact that the words were prose instead of poetry. And still others just plain didn't appreciate the music. Handel presented it annually, the proceeds going to charity. There was no indication in his time that the oratorio would live to inspire millions.

Are these two creative giants in heaven today reaping rewards that eluded them on earth? And along with them, the cobblers, tailors, parents, lawyers and others of that era who lived creatively, worshiping God with their talents?

Some parents have recognized the bent of their children, or perhaps helped to bend them, from a young age. The father of Wolfgang Amadeus Mozart, though a musician himself, recognized a greater talent in his son and devoted himself to teaching him, beginning at age four. Mozart was surrounded by music from birth, and even in the womb he heard music, as modern science has shown is possible.

Mozart had a brilliant career while he was a child. But later he was never able to get satisfactory employment. Through all the troubles of his short life he, too, composed, composed, composed. He wrote graceful, lively, inventive music. When he was thirty-five years old, a stranger appeared at his door and asked him to compose a requiem. The person who wanted it and who would pay the fee was to remain a secret. Mozart completed "The Magic Flute," and then began feverish work on the requiem. He became obsessed with the idea that he was writing his own funeral song. He was dying, as he said, ". . . before I could enjoy my talent." The deeply moving, other-worldy beauty of "Requiem" was not heard at his pauper's funeral. Music there was directed by a man who because of jealousy had long been an enemy of Mozart.

Today we can only guess at the spiritual tranquility and strength these men must have possessed to achieve such creative feats in the circumstances of their lives. Creativity is not fragile. Parents help or parents hinder, but creativity remains. God put it there.

God invented music, we know, since stars sang before man was created. And God invented the beauty and complexity of nature, from which artists and scientists obtain inspiration for their creative efforts. God started, and man carries on within the patterns and channels set out by God in the beginning.

Artistic and scientific endeavors are commonly seen today as "creative." But this is not all God started in those early days of the world. Often overlooked, is the fact that God invented work. He himself worked during creation week. He told Adam to dress the garden and keep it. He told the first couple to subdue the earth and have dominion over it. He told them to be fruitful and fill the earth. Sin brought thorns and other problems, but the commands are still the same. Subdue the earth. Bear children. Have dominion.

Within those mandates, fit our many and various fields of work. For instance, while multiplying and filling the earth, people must study and work in the human fields—sociology, education, government, child development, economics, and so on. To subdue the earth we must study it through various avenues of science. And to have dominion, we apply our knowledge to pursuits such as farming and manufacturing.

Why, then, do we often think of artists as being the most creative? Perhaps because most of us feel we understand the arts less than other human work. And the mysterious we easily view as creative.

Actually, if you look for Bible verses on human creativity, you find none. In the strict, biblical sense of creating something out of nothing, God is the only one who can create. In the looser, human sense, we use the word to apply to someone who makes new forms out of what God has already put here. The poet presents a new image for an old, profound thought. The painter presents a new view of a landscape. The musician arranges melody, harmony, rhythm, and form in new ways.

But what about the cobbler in Bach's hometown? In this life we will never know how creative he was. Did he figure out a way to fit a shoe to a child's deformed foot? Did he improve on the materials and cut of his shoes? How did he handle the issue of extravagant, high-fashion styles the world wanted versus the conservative styles espoused by the church in his day? Was he as devout in his work as Bach was? Did he arrange financing or charity to enable a poor family to obtain shoes? How did he use his opportunities to creatively serve God?

God created the world. We, made in His image, should creatively carry on the work of the world—as shoemakers, mothers, secretaries, executives, or musicians.

If your habit is to view your work as dull, if you suffer from put-downs by your boss or others, if you think your circumstances are too harried or restrictive for creativity, try a creative new look this week at your possibilities. Remember Bach, poorly paid, unappreciated, writing a chorale not for publication and royalties, but for worshiping God on Sunday. Remember Handel, in debt from failed operas, trying to write a better opera in order to pay the debts, and asking whether God might want him to write music in another form—maybe an oratorio. Remember Mozart, in pain, racing to finish "Requiem" before he ran out of time.

Here is none of the glamor we tend to associate with the creative life, only situations most of us can identify with. Debt, tragedy, uncertainty about the future, being misunderstood. These are the situations in which people work. This is where creativity counts.

What kind of community could we make if we all work as eagerly as Mozart, as devoutly as Bach, as persistently as Handel? What will happen when we create from the depths of our spirits? What inner wells will we find when we live out the creative nature God has put within?

We can put our hearts into our work in whatever the present circumstances, and then watch how we grow into greater and more exciting creativity. If no one encourages, it doesn't matter because heart work is happy work with God for an audience.

Christians Can Be Better Thinkers

The Beginning of Wisdom

Solomon wrote a great deal about wisdom. God gave him more wisdom than anyone else ever had or will have. His gift from God and his selection as a writer of Scripture qualify him more than any person in history, aside from Jesus, to advise us about wisdom—and about knowledge. Solomon told us that knowledge begins the same place as wisdom, with the fear of the Lord.

A Fatal Flaw?

Knowledge and wisdom, of course, are what we hope our children attain through our teaching and through their thinking. A mountain of education journals and books tells about developmental stages of thinking, higher level thinking, critical thinking, styles of thinking, and on and on.

Through it all runs a humanist trail that can become a fatal flaw for Christian educators.

You don't read far into this mountain of print before you come across the word *indoctrination*. It is always a dirty word, and its supposed opposite is rational thinking or the educative process, or a similar term that is hard to object to. I have spent many years studying these topics, and to this day I can't quite figure out what indoctrinate means. It often seems to mean a way that we Christians have of tricking children into believing what they wouldn't believe if we weren't so sneaky about it. If we wouldn't teach spiritual matters early in life, if we would teach children how to think, then at a proper age they could make rational decisions about what to believe.

Right here is where the fatal flaw pokes its deceptive head into Christian education systems. The word *rational* isn't so bad, is it? Doesn't it mean reasonable, civilized, and things like that? In ordinary conversation, yes. But in philosophy, rationalism means that reason is the source of knowledge. Knowledge does not come by revelation or from God or any other source, but solely through human intellect. That is humanism. It sounds suspiciously like what the serpent offered Eve. "You will know, like God," he said. "You will be wise." If he were a modern educator he might say, "You shouldn't be expected to assent to God's restrictions until you have developed cognitive skills and have the capacity to think critically and make rational decisions."

The Trap

Are these thinking skills, then, only for humanists and not for Christians? No, not at all. Christians can have superior thinking skills—superior because they are built upon the Solomon principle—the fear of the Lord.

A well known exercise the schools have used for thinking about values is the "fallout shelter." In the shelter are a doctor, a clergyman, a farmer, a child, and a variety of other people. But there is a shortage of food. Who must be put out and who should remain to rebuild society after they can safely leave the shelter? The idea is to promote thinking about values in society. A group of students roleplays the parts or discusses the hypothetical situation, and their assignment is to agree on who goes. Christian thinking is outside this format. It blows the whole lesson plan if students decide to pray and ask God to show them how to make the food last longer, or to bring a strong wind so they can leave sooner. A student might suggest that a Christian in the shelter could give his testimony and tell how to be saved; then he could volunteer to go because he is ready to meet God. But if he did, the teacher probably would point out that they don't know the religious beliefs of the people, but that on the basis of what they do know they should decide who goes.

Lawrence Kohlberg has given the Heinz story to use for testing or for developing moral thinking. Heinz's wife will die if she doesn't have a particular medicine which Heinz cannot afford to buy. He can obtain it neither on credit nor in any other way except by stealing. Should he steal the drug or let his wife die? A student who says "Heinz should not steal; it's against the law" scores on the law-order stage. A student who says it's all right to it would save his wife's life, scores higher. He s higher value in this case. It's a thinking values like this. We might notice that, ag restricted. A child who says, "Heinz s

God to heal his wife," would stymie the tester. There is no way to score that answer. Or a student on a high level of thinking may say, "Well, if Heinz is a Christian and there's no way for him to get the drug, that may mean it would harm his wife instead of helping her. He should believe Romans 8:28 and trust God." Again, not a scorable answer. Answers must come from the choices offered.

Scriptural teaching of right and wrong fits only so far as unsaved humans can agree with the right and wrong. The idea of eternal values has no place in the system.

This humanist system invades even Christian education. A couple of decades ago in England, Ronald Goldman did some research on children's thinking about Bible stories that excited a lot of people on this side of the ocean. In a question about Moses and the burning bush, children were asked how it happened that Moses saw the bush burning but it was not consumed. Some older children said that perhaps Moses was over-tired and he hallucinated. Other children dreamed up science fantasy kinds of ideas, and they all scored high for their thinking. A few children said, "God did it." They scored low. They were supposed not to be thinking, but were repeating beliefs they had been indoctrinated with. Similar scoring was done on the Red Sea story and others. If children tried to explain away a miracle, they were scored as better thinkers than others.

How was this scoring system developed? By asking clergymen to rate possible answers. So, the humanist scoring scale came from the intellect of liberal clergymen, the majority of whom apparently did not believe in miracles. The underlying assumption was that the miracle could not have happened as the story says. On the basis of this false human thinking, many Christian educators thought the human research was telling them not to teach Bible stories to young children because they could not understand them. Only when children were older could they come up with the kinds of inventions that scored high in Goldman's research.

Such slippery reasoning happens not only in moral thinking, but in scientific thinking too. The general assumption in much of the scientific world today is that there could not have been a creator. So scientists pass over the most obvious answer to all they observe and try to find another answer. If they begin with false assumptions, they naturally will take some wrong paths and slow the progress of science.

A More Excellent Way

The foregoing examples show how thinking cannot be separated from its content. A dose of "How To Think" need not be added on top of your other subjects for two reasons. One reason is that it doesn't work well that way; thinking is better taught throughout all subjects. The second reason, and the one we have been examining in this article, is that the content of thinking affects the quality of thinking.

The Bible is the basis for all knowledge and wisdom that counts in this world. In the field of literature, even a non-Christian professor has written that the Bible should be taught so early and so well that it settles to the bottom of the mind and everything else can settle on top of it. We all know that the greatest of painting, music, architecture, and other arts were inspired by the Bible. Hospitals, schools and all humanitarian efforts grew because of people living by biblical principles. Our most treasured principles of law and society come from the Bible. Many significant advances in science came from great Bible-believing scientists.

Profitable knowledge is not facts, facts, and more facts.

To say that we live in an "information age" does not mean there is more knowledge in our day. The travel agency which has the most information about low fares is likely to get your travel dollars, so information may lead to money, but it does not add up to an education. Information is replaced day by day with new information. Knowledge builds up slowly. It comes by thinking about worthwhile matters. And who has better matters to think about than Christians?

In short, Christians can be better thinkers because their content is truer. The road to thinking begins with fear of the Lord. This proper heart attitude makes knowledge possible and knowledge makes thinking possible. With more knowledge comes ever higher levels of thinking.

Solomon knew that many centuries ago.

The High Road to Learning

King David asked "What is man?" In education we ask "What is mind?" and it is almost the same question. Mind in its classic sense, as people have used it for centuries, is the same as soul, or man himself. Whoever holds this high view of mind travels the high road to learning. Behaviorists and others with a lower view hold theories of learning that do not work as well as ours.

Behaviorists and Mind

Here we are using the word *mind* in its ancient, classical sense, thus it is necessary to point out that others in our times use it with a shallower meaning. During the earlier decades of the twentieth century, behaviorist psychology was a dominant view and nobody who wanted to sound knowledgeable and scientific would use the word *mind*. It was associated with religious views or with "superstitious" views that man had a consciousness—the ability to think, feel, desire, will, perceive, remember. Though they did not use *mind* as a noun, behaviorists, inconsistently, continued to use an adjective form of the word, as in "mental arithmetic."

Behaviorists banned mind from their vocabulary because of their basic view of man, which is stated succinctly in this chapter opening sentence from a psychology textbook: *Man is a vastly complicated mechanism, a mechanism that functions by responding to stimuli in order to adjust to the environment.* A key word here is *is.* Of course man is complicated and has in his body many complicated organs—we might even say mechanisms—but the behaviorist is not saying that man *has* certain complexities. He says that's what man *is.* For Christians, not used to thinking in such terms, it takes quite an effort to understand this behaviorist view.

If you ever studied from a behaviorist psychology textbook, you may remember how the opening chapters were all on sense perception—anatomy of the eye and ear, studies of optical illusions, and such. You may have wondered, as I did, when you would come to psychology. I leafed back to the later chapters and found topics like mental tests, which were closer to my idea of psychology. It took years before I realized why I was so bewildered in those classes, before I saw how fundamental sense perception was to those professors, how basic to their view of man.

Most psychologists today see inadequacies in the behaviorist system. Its "scientific" answers to the problems of education have failed us. It always seemed to concentrate on the trivial, simpler types of learning. So a new school called "cognitive psychology" has arisen.

Cognitivists and Mind

Cognitive psychologists reintroduced the word mind because they needed it in order to talk about the higher kinds of thinking and learning that they study. But as they use the word, it does not have its ancient meaning. They have not reintroduced anything akin to soul or spirit of man. Instead, they hope that neurologists will uncover a "neurological linkage mechanism that produces conceptualizations from related associations." That's textbook language again. Concepts are the higher kind of learning the cognitivists study, and associations are the lower level learning the behaviorists studied. (Remember Pavlov's dog that associated food with the sound of the bell and salivated at the sound).

Cognitive psychologists, then, retain the view that man is a mechanism. They just hope to discover a more complex mechanism than behaviorists had in mind (or in their response mechanism!). And when we read the word *mind* in their writings, we must be careful not to interpret it according to our infinitely richer spiritual meaning.

What Is Mind?

Now we return to the original question, "What is mind?" Using our minds to understand mind will never totally succeed. It's not at all like comprehending a machine. That is, we might grasp fairly well how a simple machine like a food grinder operates and less well how a complex mechanism like a computer chip operates, but if we studied these long enough our minds could wrap around them. Mind is superior to and exterior to a machine. Thus mind can understand machine.

But trying to understand ourselves from inside ourselves is a different story. We sit just about where all former generations sat—still debating how to draw a neat little diagram of how man is put together and how he learns.

The Christian is better off not to be swayed by what Paul referred to as science falsely so called. The Christian has an infinitely higher view of man. You know intuitively that the child you teach is a living soul just like you, made in the image of God. The image, according to some theologians, is none other than what we refer to as *mind* or *heart*. It is the *person,* who can think and choose and desire and learn. The image, when regenerated by God's Spirit, is alive unto God and gains wisdom by a spiritual route that educational psychology knows nothing of. Even the unregenerate image has more powerful learning capabilities than we will ever find, no matter how many new discoveries we make about the brain or glands or muscles or nerves.

Scholars have long been baffled by aspects of man that they cannot explain by physiology or chemistry. Freud popularized the idea of the "unconscious," and that has been a convenient place for theorists to hide motivations and whatever else they couldn't put into the muscles and nerves. The words *intuitive* and *innate* are also used in this way—as dumping grounds for all the unexplainable. Certain linguists, for instance, unable to prove that children learn language by behaviorist means, have suggested that children are born with an innate mental structure by which they can learn to understand language. They are getting awfully close to saying that children are made in the image of God.

Traveling the Low Road

For practically a century now, behaviorist thinking has led us down a low road. Much of educational research was about such sensory matters as whether people learn better by seeing or by hearing. And long after secular educators had dropped that particular question, realizing that factors such as motivation far outweighed the sense factor, Christian education books continued to teach that seeing is better than hearing. And they quoted percentage figures to add an aura of science to the claim. Once I tracked someone's figures and the trail led to a study done by a visual aid company. Of course. I should have suspected that. The education writers never questioned whether the learning tested in a sales meeting was anything like a third grader learning a Bible story or a three-year-old learning new vocabulary every day. They did not wonder whether other variables could have affected the outcome. The percentages were just quoted from book to book, applied generally to all ages and any learning situation, and most writers did not even know where they came from. But they sounded scientific, and Christians seemed to like that.

I was a young teenager when B. F. Skinner's teaching machine was the talk of the nation. By today's standards, it was a crude affair. It presented a bit of information to a student and asked him a question about it. Then it gave immediate feedback—a reward or otherwise for his response. Excitement ran high. Teaching was now a science. Everybody could learn everything, and there would be no need for teachers anymore. My classmates delayed an algebra lesson one day by inveigling the teacher into in a "Brave New World" discussion about what life would be like in a few years—with no teachers. Wise Mr. Crum let them all have their say, and at last someone asked what he thought. "We will always need teachers," he said. "Machines can do some things for us, but they will never eliminate the need for human teachers."

The first teaching machine gave way to programmed workbooks—more affordable than machines. Then came computerized versions of stimulus-response teaching. Companies contracted with school districts to teach all their children to read, and newspapers showed us pictures with rows of children in front of computers earning M&M's. What started with much fanfare ended with the districts quietly taking back their children. Now, decades later, in a second wave of computerized reading instruction, IBM is selling school districts an expensive beginning reading program—hardware and software. Today's programs include a lot more variety than the earlier stimulus-response versions, but they demonstrate our society's obsession with technology.

A research idea I have never seen carried out is to study whether this or any other "scientific" program can outdo the alternative of a loving mother and her child together on a couch or at the kitchen table with a few good books and some simple teaching materials. In my thinking, it doesn't matter much what teaching materials the mother chooses. That is a minor factor. The minds and hearts of mother and child are the major factors.

Education research has majored on the minors because hearts and minds aren't amenable to research and also because most researchers don't believe in hearts and minds anyway. The usual research is like studying a book by examining its paper and ink, and perhaps getting sophisticated enough to learn how the presses managed to get everything together in just that way. We could write a book about the book we study and never once touch on its "soul."

That's the way with much writing that comes out of education research. We may read about the wiring of the brain and other sophisticated (to our times) topics and never get close to mind or heart. Even secular educators can weary of the constant stream of such writings flowing through the journals. One of them sounded a little exasperated when he wrote recently, "Of course there are different styles of learning. Some children are motivated and some are not."

Traveling the High Road

The high view of man puts thought (or mind or the image of God) first. Thought can act upon sensation. That is, it can organize and make meaning out of what the body sees, hears, feels, etc. The low view reverses that. Sensation comes first—that is, the sight or sound or feel. Somehow, in the body, sensation is supposed to get turned into thought (not the high view of thought, only the mechanical view). But not philosophers nor psychologists nor theologians, who all have wrestled with this problem, can show that it happens. Logic fails them; experimental science fails them.

In a nutshell, the great gap between a biblical view of learning and all behaviorist and humanist views is this: Does learning happen from the inside out or from the outside in?

In my lifetime I have seen church education leave the high road bit-by-bit and veer toward the low. The glitter of "science" was usually the reason. Church educators added the latest twists from psychology to the Scripture. Later, some reversed that order, starting with psychology and adding a little Scripture. A few voices of protest were raised in the land, and at least one seminary dropped its counseling major in a move back to the high road.

Christian home educators are in a healthy, vigorous stage of their movement. Most are on the high road. But as they become more initiated into the beliefs of modern education, they are in danger of losing their strength, as happened with church education. Bombarded from all sides with information and ads, parents, wanting the best for their children, begin to wonder about their own wisdom. The answer is to stay deeply rooted in the Bible.

Take, for instance, the current fad of the brain, with curriculums and methods claiming to be "brain-based" or similar terms. You wouldn't necessarily have to know that educators have run ahead of neurologists on this, coming to conclusions mostly unwarranted at the present state of neurological knowledge of the brain. You wouldn't have to judge that most of what's happening today will turn out to be passing fads. All you would need is your biblical view of man that would immediately question such a physiological view of thinking and learning.

The word *brain* is never used in the Bible. Most references to thinking seem to attribute it to *heart*. When you tell that to people, they are quick to say, "Oh, but ancient people thought that heart was the center of emotions and thinking. We know better today." I answer that I believe the ancients were at least as intelligent as we are. And anyway God authored the Bible. Or someone might say, "Heart is just a metaphor when used like that in the Bible." I answer that it's a strange metaphor to be used so often with never a hint of its real meaning.

How often? When I wrote *A Biblical Psychology of Learning,* I said it was over 800 times. Now with a computerized Bible, I see it is almost 1000 times—989, to be exact, including the Hebrew *leb* with its denominative verb form *labab,* and the Greek *kardia,* and including their plural and compound forms. Heart is definitely an important word in the Bible, and a great many of its references have to do with thinking.

I am not saying that learning happens in a muscle, even such a central one as the heart. John Dewey once wrote that knowledge resides in the muscles. By that he meant that the body's responses to stimuli, the habits that it forms, and the behaviors it emits *are* the learning. There is no mind or heart to choose or to direct the body responses. Our meaning here is a far cry from that.

The Bible definition of heart encompasses most aspects of life and physical, or fleshly, life is only a minor one of them. Five other aspects are: spiritual life (belief and unbelief), moral life (knowing right and wrong), emotional life (joy and sorrow), motivation (willing or purposing), and thought life (perceiving, knowing, understanding, considering, pondering, meditating). It begins to appear that heart is almost the same as the person, or the same as mind when we use the word in its ancient sense. It appears to refer to the immaterial aspect of man, the man who lives on eternally, not to muscles and nerves and brain that will go to the grave.

Nowhere in the Bible do we read that thinking is a function of the brain but in numerous verses we read that it is from the heart. I listed some of them in *Biblical Psychology.* Kenneth H. Clark researched this thoroughly at Temple Baptist Seminary. He found that over 25% of the Bible uses of *heart* refer to thought life, while only 1.6% refer to physical life. The others are spread among the categories of moral, emotional, spiritual, and motivational life (listed in descending order), and an 11% category called "combination," in which two or more meanings are inferred. At least a little study of these heart verses will give perspective for viewing the claims of brain-based teaching methods or other fads that come along.

Road to the Future

What a great outlook we could have for the future if homeschooling parents stay on the high road themselves and help to lead others to it! A few years ago the Department of Education wanted to find out why over half the high school valedictorians were Vietnamese, and why the Vietnamese generally were among the top students. Their research led them to conclude that it was due to strong family values, particularly a value for education. These Vietnamese were exposed to the same methods and materials, in all their variety, as other groups, so none of those factors could account for the results, but family values could.

The same is now happening with homeschoolers. They are showing the world a better way. So far, much of the "showing" has been by means of test scores, which are limited in what they show. But as more homeschool students reach their adult years of service in the world, the impact will spread.

As to impact upon the world, it has occurred to me that we have another strong force besides the students. What about you parents? When your children are grown and you perhaps are looking for a second career, many of you could look to teaching. Schools are experimenting with what they call "alternative routes to teaching." A few states now offer teaching positions to people switching from other careers. They can begin teaching almost right away, and work on completing education courses as they go along. While the unions complained, one state insisted that it has raised the quality level of applicants. I hope that states like this will receive some resumes which include homeschool teaching as the first career.

Many of you also could begin taking courses now and work toward fulfilling local qualifications. You could study alongside your children and share your learning with them. One homeschooling mother of two teenagers had her children included in the cast of a Greek drama her class was performing, and in other of her activities. This way they learned English, history, speech and other skills together. And as a bonus, the mother earned some credits.

Schools are trying everything these days. Just wait till they try a new wave of teachers who have never lost their high view of learning!

PART VI

Middle class families are doing better with their preschoolers and kindergartners than government or educators or day care centers or anyone else. I hoped that the articles used as Chapters 23 and 24 would help to keep families on the right track. These articles have been reprinted in multiple publications. Closing the book with "Homeschool Boomers" was the suggestion of my daughter-in-law, Ellen, mother of four, who also chose the opening chapters. She wants me to remind readers that other Christian young people besides homeschoolers are included in this great hope for our future.

What's Happening in Early Childhood Education: The Big Picture

In the past few decades there has been a massive amount of research in early childhood education—and much controversy along with it. One major controversy can be called the "academic" versus the "developmental" approaches to learning. On the academic side, people point to research showing that direct instruction in academics in kindergarten helps children do better in primary grades. But on the other side, developmentalists counter with research that shows the boost does not last into later years and that it comes at too great a cost in stress and attitude toward learning. Moreover, the research does not apply to middle class children.

One year I had opportunity to check out for myself the value of the kindergarten boost. I taught a first grade in which some of the children had had kindergarten and others had not. So as not to know which were which, I did not look at the records. And you might say that I undermined the research by teaching reading by a rapid system that I liked and which was not the usual method in the district. By this system the children learned the sounds of letters and began immediately to sound out words. They did not need the names of the letters nor did they need to know their alphabetical order—matters which the kindergarten children had been drilled on.

Within a few weeks most of the children were reading, some choosing books at well above first grade level. At conference time, a mother was apologetic that her daughter had not gone to kindergarten. I said, "I haven't noticed any problem. Julie is doing very well." On the other hand, a couple of the children who were struggling and not ready yet to read were ones who had gone to kindergarten. In checking further, I found that no correlation could be made between the kindergarten head start and the ability to read in that first grade class.

You can argue that if I had used a more traditional reading approach or gave instructions in which I called letters by their names, or in other ways followed directly the path the kindergarten children had begun, I could easily have discerned those who had a "head start." But that is precisely the point I wish to make about research and its claims. A research study may yield persuasive numbers, but the numbers have limited application in other situations. People who have different goals or philosophies or methods or populations of children can always bring good arguments for a contrary view. They can usually cite research, too, for a contrary view. A good rule to follow is: never base your beliefs or decisions upon the findings of one research study.

Parents tutoring their own children should be particularly cautious about making decisions based upon research findings. Your child is not "average." No child is. Research may sometimes guide schools or nations in educational decisions but it is not that useful when you are facing one child whom you know well.

In recent decades there have been researches connected with "Sesame Street," with Head Start and Follow Through programs, with the High/Scope Foundation and with numerous lesser known programs. Specialists study such high quality researches and examine them together, finding where they agree, asking what might explain their differences and so on. Such a research of researches is sometimes called "meta-research."

Out of this, emerges a big picture which practically everyone agrees on. Three major principles in the big picture are:

1) Involving parents is important to the success of any program.
2) A low child/adult ratio is needed.
3) It helps to have a comprehensive program—with health, nutrition, medical and social services added.

Another major principle that is seldom explained in plain language is that adding the three factors above produces academic improvement in populations we have come to call "disadvantaged"—families in poverty, non-English or limited English speaking, dysfunctional and so forth. THERE IS NO CLEAR MESSAGE FROM THESE RESEARCHES THAT FAMILIES LIKE YOURS CAN BENEFIT AT ALL FROM EARLIER ACADEMIC EDUCATION. So why do they want your children in compulsory kindergarten and preschool education? Here's one reason why.

. . . right now most of the children in public preschools are disadvantaged. Learning from and along with their more fortunate peers would enhance children's preparation for success in school and later life. To better our programs, we must broaden the student constituency to include all the children of poverty *and* the children of mainstream America.[1] [Emphasis in the original.]

They want your children, and they also want you.

If we open school programs to all 4-year-olds, then we would also have the interest, commitment, and the potential financial and political resources of a larger and more powerful group of parents.[1]

This scheme sounds like a recipe for disaster. First, it would take the "more fortunate" children away for several hours each day from the parents who have made them fortunate, thus diluting their fortunate status. Next, the strong family influences are filtered through these little preschoolers and supposed to spill onto the less fortunate. The strong helping the weak is admirable in adults, but tiny children should not be exploited in this manner. If the strong families themselves were to give time and thought to these social problems, they no doubt could creatively come up with far better ways to help the weak than that of using their young children in this way.

Meeting Needs

Writings on early childhood development are full of noble sounding words about meeting the needs of young children. This "needs" message is so pervasive that even strong and fortunate families begin to believe that their children are missing out on something. Maybe they should enroll in a program, they think. Or at least they should bring a program into their home.

But what needs are these early childhood specialists are talking about? Typical, is a recent list in an education publication which gives demographic information: half of all infants have working mothers, 59% of 3- and 4-year-olds have working mothers, there is a growing number of single-parent households, and so forth. So all these children "need" child care and educational programs.

This pattern of thinking has pervaded American early childhood education for most of this century. In the thirties, there were depression "needs" and a few programs developed. During and after World War II, more mothers joined the work force and the number of early childhood programs rapidly increased to meet this need.

But children of homeschooling families generally do not have need for child care social services. And their children do not need public help with nutrition and the other aspects identified as important to the programs.

In short, all the hype from government and education sources about young children needing early schooling do not apply to middle class Americans and, in particular, do not apply to the kinds of families interested in homeschooling. Thus even if a state allows for families to homeschool while they lower the compulsory schooling age a year or two, they still are intruding into family life in an unnecessary way. These laws allow government to require that some kind of schooling and reporting of it goes on in the home. And there is no research base to show that this helps middle class children.

An irony in all this is that the best of schooling

programs are trying to give children a homelike atmosphere. More than one specialist has written that if they could just take each child on their lap and read to him or her regularly and could talk with children one-on-one and give them time to play and explore, both alone and with a *few* others, then they could achieve the good results that homes achieve. They agree that the parent is the child's first and best teacher. They envy the interaction that happens with such a low child/adult ratio. And numerous classroom activities are artificial ways to learn what is learned more naturally in everyday life in the home and family setting. Families, when they are not feeling pressured to be academic, are the ideal setting for young children to develop emotional stability, language and communication skills, knowledge about things and events around them, and a quality called "disposition to learn." These are the important developmental tasks of this age.

Most experts on early childhood support the developmental approach as being superior in many ways to the academic. Lilian Katz is one of these. She is director of the ERIC clearinghouse for research on elementary and early childhood education. She points out in a recent report that disposition to learn is a most important quality that children seem to be born with and which must be preserved during the early years. For this, children need time and opportunity to "lose themselves" in self-directed learning. Studies show that early pressure to perform "academic tasks introduced through direct instruction (e.g, practice in phonics or workbook exercises) appears quite harmless, or even beneficial, in the short term." But longitudinal studies suggest that teachers must be careful lest the disposition to learn is lost in this process. Though academic programs may claim to be individualized, Katz points out that what is individualized is the day on which a child completes a task rather than the task itself. And she believes that "after a year or two of such schooling, the effect on the disposition to learn is likely to be deadening."

General positive feedback is often part of the academic programs. This includes vague comments like "very good" or a smiling face sticker or gold star. This goes along with current belief that we must help children think well of themselves. But research on these rewards, according to Katz, "strongly suggest that children may suffer academic burn-out after two or three years of experience with general positive extrinsic rewards." Children lose interest in the tasks for which they are thus rewarded. This sounds odd at first hearing, but children seem to reason that it must be wrong to like doing x, if they are given a reward for doing it.[2]

Specific rewarding comments are better than general. These include information about the competence of the child's performance—he remembered more cards than yesterday, his writing looks like the model in specific ways, etc.

David Elkind, leading researcher on child development and professor at Tufts University, also warns that the usual academic programs do not reflect what we now know about young children's thinking.[3] This new knowledge that he refers to is the view of most researchers and experts today, that is really not new to Bible believers. It is the view that within children's minds is more complexity than we have heretofore acknowledged in our education theories. They do not call it soul or heart, but they are moving in that direction from the nineteenth century industrial model of education—a model in which everything depends on the teacher inputting the right information in the right order and being careful not to skip anything. The newer model, instead of postulating that the child's mind is passive and depends on us pouring information in, says that the child's mind actively constructs meaning. This change in view implies a change in methods.

But the education bureaucracy, the textbook industry and all related systems are so solidly entrenched in its current view (the academic) that it resists change in the direction that research would point it. A recent survey of principals, for instance, shows that they believe in the developmental approach, but their schools actually practice the academic approach.

In another survey, school principals ranked ten possible priorities for their kindergarten programs. With a couple of ties as shown, their rankings appeared in this order:

1. Language development
1. Social development
3. Emotional development
3. Self-discipline
5. Physical coordination
6. Motor development
7. Health and safety habits
8. Work habits
9. Academic achievement
10. Artistic expression

Looking at that list, particularly the first eight priorities, one finds nothing that a child can't do better in a fortunate home than in a schooling institution. And fortunate homes have no problem with the last two either.

In summary, the big picture in early childhood education today shows research and the experts' views differing from general practice in the schools, and controversy still common in the field. Yet school and government officials are forging ahead to require more schooling for younger children. "We can't wait until all the answers are in," says one leader.

Even as I write this, another state has passed a bill in its Senate and is sending it to the House. A report in "Education Week" quotes several experts involved in this state's debate.[4] Existing programs may be inappropriate for some 5-year-olds, says one. Probably 60% of programs do not meet criteria for good developmental programs, and the schools may not be equipped to offer the small classes that experts recommend, say others. And this strange anti-excellence argument: Mandating attendance at 5 may be the only way to address the inequities that now exist when middle-class parents delay their children's school entry, giving their children the advantage of being older when they go to school. (!) Read that again: If some parents do what's best for their children, we'd better pull them down to the level of other families.

The legislature cannot wait until more of the answers are in and more schools are ready. But they are willing to delay implementation for a year because of money. Why the bulldozer approach? A major reason is one of the goals set by the governors' summit on education—that by the year 2000 all children will enter school ready to learn. So state after state will join this race.

Parents who do not want their children sucked into these great experiments while educators reach for answers or try to catch the schools up with research, will have to be particularly vigilant and wise. One thing we all know is that the home works best. Early childhood experts, researchers, educators, and probably even legislators agree on this. Legislators may need reminding that you are helping them reach their goal of better educated children.

Let us not lose the best approach with young children while experimenting with other approaches.

---

1. Association for Supervision and Curriculum Development, *A Resource Guide to Public School Early Childhood Programs* (Alexandria VA, 1988) p. 29.
2. Ibid., p. 40–41.
3. Ibid., p. 53–62.
4. Deborah L. Cohen, "Bill in Maryland Puts Spotlight on Readiness Debate" in *Education Week,* 3-27-91:1.

What's Crucial about the Crucial Preschool Years?

In our time we often hear how important the early years of a child's life are. Parents and teachers are made to feel a heavy responsibility for the way they handle these tender years. So we teach numbers and letters and phonics earlier and earlier.

Does research really say that earlier is better in these academic matters? To answer this and related questions, we will discuss the present state of research knowledge in three areas of the child's development—the intellectual, the emotional, and the moral and spiritual.

Intellectual Development

The intellectual area is where the most pushing happens. Even in Christian education, where we presumably are more interested in spiritual growth, we constantly hear about the intellectual. Repeatedly in our conventions and literature we hear that according to science half a child's learning happens by age four, and we are admonished to redouble our efforts to teach before age four.

But this argument is flawed from the beginning, and it has not proved to work out in practice. The origin of this is some statistical work which Benjamin Bloom performed on results from IQ tests at all ages. Some complex reasoning was involved, because children's tests are different from adult tests, but insofar as we accept the validity of Bloom's work, we can say that one-half of a child's mental development takes place by age four.

Now that is quite different from saying that one-half of learning happens by age four. Bloom's message was that a child's *mental capacity* is half-formed, or his *mental ability* is half-developed at age four.

It is no wonder that when we tried to pour learning into a half-formed brain the results were disappointing. And when we tried to develop the brain faster the results were equally disappointing. The whole approach was wrong. It simply is not true that there is something magic about the first four years that most of us have been missing.

It is true that some children are deprived intellectually in these years. They live in families where no one talks with them so they lack opportunity to develop language. Or they are physically restricted to a crib or a single room, so they lack opportunity to explore and manipulate objects and interact with reality, and thus their thinking ability does not grow normally. Such deprived children are often used in the researches by which people claim to raise children's IQs.

Much of the frantic search for something better than normal is triggered by the hope that we can raise the level of the next generation of mankind—that we can guide our own evolution and raise it to a new height. This philosophy leaves out God.

The frantic search has not so far been successful. Research on early childhood programs is at best controversial. Researchers and writers often seem to be arguing from their own philosophical views or from the view that will get more government money for their projects. The scientific evidence that we can improve mental development in the early years has not yet come forth—except in the cases of deprived children.

Though we cannot increase the *amount* of intellectual development or speed up its rate of growth, we can understand more about the *process* of intellectual development. We know, for instance, that young children are egocentric; they think from themselves outward. In the physical world, they cannot visualize what something looks like from the other side; they think it looks the same as from their side. If you move an object out of sight of an infant, he thinks it is gone.

This egocentricity applies to the human world also. Children's years of roleplaying—playing House, playing Church, and so on—are the years of exploring other roles so that eventually they become able to understand two views or two sides at once.

This kind of information from child development studies can help us aim our teaching at the appropriate levels for children. But nothing in the research shows that we should push or speed up the development.

Emotional Growth

The area of emotional growth is much like the intellectual, in that deprivation in the early years causes problems. Infants who are not cuddled and loved, toddlers who do not receive a normal amount of affection, grow up with personality problems.

Emotional health is intertwined with other parts of the person, so that problems in this area affect other areas, including the intellectual. In our society there probably is more lack in loving little children than there is in providing intellectual stimulation for them. But among Christian families it should not be so. The biblical view that children are a heritage of the Lord, that parents are responsible to God for them, is perhaps all we need to know.

Psychology cannot tell us more than God already has about loving our children. Are Christians looking to science to solve the problems of bringing up children? We should, instead, be the ones who have answers and are showing the world a better way.

Moral and Spiritual Development

In the moral and spiritual realm it is definitely true that Christians have what the world is looking for. But the educational world wants to find answers that are not religious.

In moral development, the research of Lawrence Kohlberg has attracted attention. The technique called values clarification has risen to popularity and has spilled over into Christian education. But nothing that the world is doing is superior to what the church was already doing.

In spiritual development, James Fowler of Harvard researched the development of faith and has concluded that if the faith stage of the early years is missed, it is an irretrievable loss. Fowler's definition of faith is not an evangelical Christian one, but the research may be of interest anyway.

Fowler's finding is roughly comparable to findings in the intellectual and emotional realms—that deprivation in the early years has permanent, or at least long-lasting effects. In the spiritual realm, a great many children in our society are deprived. Comparatively few are emotionally deprived, and fewer yet are intellectually deprived. And the spiritual is the basis for the others, so this is the area where we can do the most for children's development.

This is shown by the late psychiatrist Bruno Bettelheim. Bettelheim expounded a view that is remarkable from our Christian standpoint but which has gone without the widespread notice it deserves. Bettelheim showed how fear and discipline in early life are essential not only to later moral development, but also to learning itself—to intellectual development. Bettelheim wrote of a time when the fear of God and of hell, and the hope of heaven were instilled into young children, and how these fears formed the basis of children's later moral and intellectual development. He showed from a psychiatric viewpoint how the early fears are necessary to all learning. This is what Solomon taught centuries ago.

Bettelheim added that we cannot use the fears of an older generation. Fear of God and of hell are not appropriate to today's society, so we must substitute some up-to-date fears for these old ones. He suggested fear of losing parental love, and later the fear of losing self-respect. Even this diluted advice is not widely accepted in our day; we are told repeatedly to let our children know that we approve no matter what their behavior. Society is not admonished to reject moral delinquency, but to accept such ways of life as valid alternatives to the historically accepted way in our Western Christianized society.

Thus the world is failing to teach moral and spiritual

values. And we Christians have the answers the world needs.

Who Is Doing It Best?

Christian parents and teachers who love children with Christ's love are doing better than they think. Recent education writings may tend to make them feel that science has moved ahead and left them behind with ineffective approaches from their dusty Bible. But the world's education emphasizes the intellectual and a superficial emotional development, and it gives little thought to the spiritual. Even when they see it, as Bettelheim did, educators do not advocate beginning at the spiritual. Thus they miss the foundation of all development.

Christian parents and teachers know the proper order of things. They know that the fear of God is the beginning of wisdom. Children under their care are not deprived of this essential ingredient in their learning. Neither are they deprived of love. With these two basics in their lives there is not much to worry about in the intellectual realm. The intellect will grow in a healthy, normal manner unhampered by a lack of the basics.

We can at times learn from science and secular educators, but let us not follow them so avidly that we give up our own great strengths. There *are* some things important about the early years, and we Christians know them, and we provide them better than anyone else.

When the Homeschool Boomers Come of Age

Pioneers of the current homeschool movement have already come of age. They have made it into trades or business or service careers. They have shown college and university officials that homeschoolers are good prospects for their schools. They have set up homes in which they now homeschool their own children. In many ways these pioneers have paved the roads for the boom generation of homeschoolers which follows them.

When the boom generation emerges from their homeschooling years, what effects will they have on society? I, for one, look forward to watching what they will do, and I want to add some suggestions to those I see already being discussed.

It is safe to predict that many in the boom generation of homeschoolers will be entrepreneurs, setting up businesses in their communities, others will be responsible workers in existing businesses. Many will take the route of apprenticeship to their chosen fields. All these will strengthen the fabric of society. Christians among them will be salt and light wherever they are.

Others will go to college in spite of the good arguments being given against it these days. For them, I hope they are able to meet the evolutionism, humanism and modern or sloppy theology they may find even in Christian colleges. Many of these, I am sure, will become missionaries or go into ministries at home. Others will pursue careers in numerous science and technical fields, and some few in the humanities.

All of the above will set up strong homes of their own and most will probably homeschool another generation.

This is the picture I have from talking with home-schoolers and reading their publications. It brightens the future for us all.

Take Back the Public Schools

Now, on to my two suggestions. The first is to consider teaching as a career—even teaching in the public schools. Especially teaching in the public schools.

Christian teachers add a strong element of Christianity to a school. The atmosphere of their classrooms and their world view are part of the "hidden curriculum" which influences children perhaps more than textbooks do. A recent edition of "The Christian Family Advocate" (Winnipeg) mentions "a strongly religious town south of Winnipeg where most people consider the public school as a Christian school because of the number of Christian teachers on staff." In former times this could have been said of many of our schools, but today in most areas we have only a few faithful Christians holding out in the schools and they desperately need reinforcements.

We need to take back the public schools. I think this is a more achievable goal than that of getting society to abandon them.

The strategy of taking back is being used successfully on the streets of some large cities today. Areas that were controlled by muggers and drug dealers, where the residents were afraid to be on the streets, are experimenting with ways to regain control of their own streets. Simply being there, walking on the streets, patrolling them in organized or unorganized fashion has been highly successful. If local businessmen are talking on a street corner, the drug transactions that would have happened there move somewhere else. In one neighborhood the men make it a point to be out walking on the day that elderly people pick up their Social Security checks from the mail boxes. Would-be purse snatchers have to find other pastures.

With this strategy of taking back, citizens need no changes in law. They need no courts. They just need to be there.

Opportunities for Teachers

There is opportunity for Christians to enter the public schools in record numbers during the next decade or two. In the United States, the nation is facing an imminent shortage of teachers. Not enough good students are currently being attracted to teaching careers. Former periods of shortages have been times when weaker students went through the courses, obtained teaching jobs, and then through the tenure system managed to hold on to the jobs long after the shortage was over. School districts saw their teaching quality deteriorate during such a time. Not much is said publicly about this, but school insiders comment that as soon as certain teachers retire they can have a good staff again.

So the government is considering measures to attract good students to teaching. In one proposal, scholarships may be offered in exchange for commitments to teach for a specified time in particular locations, such as inner cities, or to teach in the subjects of science or math where shortages are most severe. I know that many independent homeschoolers are averse to taking government money because of strings attached, but one of our Colorado congressmen says, "The government attaches strings to everything you do anyway, so what does it matter?"

With or without government money for their own education, Christian students can look upon teaching as a missionary opportunity of enormous proportions. The mission field is all around us. It's about to bury us. Millions of illegal Mexican immigrants sneak across our southern border each year. Eighteen million Central American refugees are already in the southwestern states. Hispanics in some areas are the majority, and this will increase. Add to those the Asians in the Pacific states, Cubans in Florida, and other smaller groups, and we have a task that exceeds that of any previous wave of immigration.

Homeschooling will not be the answer for these people who want their children to learn English and become successful in the land where they have taken refuge. During previous immigrations, public schools played a major role in integrating the children into our American, largely Christian, society. Can we do it again?

Homeschoolers who belong to these currently minority groups can be especially valuable in the task ahead. Others with a missionary heart can begin learning the languages and cultures and preparing themselves for a missionary career in which the taxpayers will pay their salaries. Black homeschoolers, Puerto Ricans and others can be more valuable than whites in the mission field of our inner cities. But whites will be needed too, because of the enormity of the task.

Parenthetically, I will add that the large immigrant population presents opportunities in other careers besides teaching. All these people need goods and services—and jobs. They need churches. They need new magazines and papers designed for them. Among homeschool boomers, with all their varied skills, are surely some who will find a useful future serving these people.

Improving Teaching

Everyone concerned about education is talking today about improving the quality of teaching. The press is full of it. This time around, leaders are cautious enough to realize that fads will not suffice; neither will simple infusions of money (although there will be lots of fighting over both). They realize that genuine improvement will come slowly. But imagine the swift changes that can happen when the schools are hit with a generation of teachers who did not grow up in classrooms, homeschoolers who love learning, who experienced the power of individual tutoring and self-learning, who with their parents spent their growing years trying this and that system of learning, who, in short, have an education in education before they ever reach the teacher training institutions, who have stronger character and more logical thinking because they missed out on peer pressures, and who, in addition, are Christian and have a biblical view of children as creatures of God—what will these young teachers do in classrooms when they arrive there on the teacher side of the desk?

I hope we will have a chance to find out.

The Humanities Revolution

My second suggestion is in a broad area we might call "scholarship"—particularly in the humanities. During the last hundred plus years most eyes were turned onto advances in knowledge of the physical sciences and technology, and history textbooks tell us of the Industrial and Technology Revolutions.

But I want to turn eyes toward another revolution of great significance that was happening at that same time in the fields of archeology and linguistics. Scholars here pushed back the line between history and prehistory by over 2000 years—perhaps almost to the Tower of Babel and the Great Flood! Moving that line was no simple task. Historic times are defined to be the times for which we have actual written records. That is, Abraham becomes a historic figure not when a later figure like Moses writes about him, but when his name turns up on documents written in his own time.

Though this revolution in history has been quiet, and though it proceeded with much painstaking work, it is immensely exciting to people who love these fields of study. The first step in the revolution was deciphering numerous ancient languages that had been lost to mankind for millennia. In the Near East were the Sumerian language, and Aramaic, and several Semitic languages. Before this revolution, historians did not even know of a pre-Babylonian civilization called Sumerian. So finding these people and decoding their language and their cuneiform writing was an advance of major proportions. Pioneers in the 1800s accomplished this breakthrough.

Next, came the job of translating thousands of ancient monuments and tablets that were dug up in various Near East sites. Presently, work on several comprehensive dictionaries is proceeding but there is a dearth of scholars in the field. Tens of thousands of clay tablets are awaiting translation. Some say 25,000 per year are being added to them. The University of Pennsylvania, which has underwritten many excavations in the Near East and has a large collection of tablets and other materials for study, has available a postdoctoral fellowship (a paid research position), and no applicants for it for the past three years. [Written in 1991.]

For a long time to come, scholars can work on translating these tablets and making whatever studies of them they are inclined to according to their interests. Christians can work on connecting this secular history with biblical history. What more might we learn of the peoples who lived in the centuries just after the Great Flood?

Evolutionists, who dominate in history as well as in the sciences, are constantly amazed at the high level of art and language and other aspects of Sumerian life, and they are puzzled when they find that earlier art is superior to later art. Their "developmental" view of early man precludes their considering an opposite, "degenerating," view that is implied in the Bible's early history. One scholar of Sumerian life, in fact, attributes this non-development view to the Sumerians themselves. The Sumerian thinker, he says, "saw historical events coming as ready-made and full-grown, full-blown on the world scene, and not as the slow product of man's interaction with his environment. . . . [their civilization] had always been more or less the same from the very beginning of days. That Sumer had . . . only gradually come to be what it was after many generations of struggle and toil, marked by human will and determination, man-laid plans and experiment and diverse fortunate discoveries and inventions—such thoughts probably never occurred to the most learned of the Sumerian sages."

Future historians may be able to show that the Sumerian sages were right, that there was no long period of development preceding their civilization. Were the Sumerians, perhaps, only rebuilding with knowledge that had survived the Flood and the Babel catastrophes?

For scholars with a biblical view, there is much exciting work yet to be done. There is need for a biblical interpretation of the new knowledge turned up in this revolution of rolling back history. Anyone interested in mankind, languages, literature, art, religion, or history could find a niche here—also anyone who can update textbooks or write other materials on a popular level concerning the history and literature of the Sumerians and other ancients.

Sciences, Too

Creationist scholarship is proceeding at a rapid pace in the sciences, but here, too, there is need for reinforcements. Science educator Dr. Richard Bliss pointed out that in all the world there was only one Ph.D. in paleontology (study of fossils) who is a creationist. This man recently earned his degree under one of the leading evolutionists, and that in itself is a breakthrough. Other pioneers have paved other roads, and they need more scholars to travel the roads with them. Dr. Bliss said the need is greatest in physics and astronomy.

Creation scientists have come so far in their work that

many fields give evidences that the earth is young—only thousands of years old as indicated by a literal reading of the Bible, instead of billions of years as the evolutionists would like. The major remaining block to young earth thinking is astronomy. People look at the stars and think of "light years," and that requires eons of time. This mind-set is so entrenched in our society that creationists are extra cautious in greeting what may be a breakthrough in our knowledge of light. They are taking an "it's too good to be true" attitude toward a recent proposal that is just what young-earth advocates want. More research is needed, and of course this requires more scientists.

A side-effect of having Christians become scholars in either the humanities or the sciences is that we may begin to take back the institutions of higher learning, too, because some of these Christians will end up with teaching positions in them.

Start Early or Start Late

A friend of mine was already deeply into astronomy at age 10 when I first knew him, and he now teaches astronomy at a university and does research for NASA. This will happen to some of the Mozarts among our children. Parents will know early in life what to help them learn. If this happens in your house, you have no curriculum bureaucracy to battle except yourself. You can do what Mozart's father did and bend the education to fit the child.

Other children need more years to explore more topics until they find one that can be a lifelong interest. For these children, too, you may do some curriculum bending. How many Sumerian scholars will we have if we depend on the two sentences or two paragraphs on Sumer that may be found in the history text? How many lovers of ancient languages will we have if we depend on the couple of pages devoted to ancient writing systems and the Rosetta Stone?

To do what no others or few others are doing in life might mean traveling an education road that few others are on. That diversity and possibility for diversity are major strengths of the homeschooling movement.

I hope that many in the boom generation of home-schoolers will become public school teachers and that some will follow the less-traveled scholarship roads suggested here. Whatever this generation ends up doing, they are certain to make an impact on society worthy of the efforts their parents are investing in them.

The world may not be waiting breathlessly now, but they are going to notice as more boomers come of age.

Index

About
the
Author

Dr. Ruth Beechick lives in the Rocky Mountains of Colorado, which she says is "second best to Alaska" for its beauty. She has degrees in music, in elementary education (with English major), and a doctorate in curriculum and instruction. She spent about half her career teaching. This was a varied experience spanning all the grades, including college, and ranging from a one-room school on an Alaskan island to a large school in a wealthy suburb. The latter half of her career was spent in publishing educational materials. As editor, she produced scores of Bible courses for church use, as well as homeschooling materials. Now from her mountain home, she works to help the homeschool movement, which she says is "the healthiest movement in education today." The achievement she is most proud of is raising two wonderful sons, who are her two best friends.

This book brings together writings which have been published over a period of twenty-five years in homeschooling and other magazines.

More Homeschooling Books by this Author

You CAN Teach Your Child Successfully: Grades 4–8

A basic guidebook telling what to teach and how to teach each subject in each grade. This classic book of almost 400 pages will replace a tall stack of teacher's manuals and workbooks and textbooks. $14.70.

The Three R's: Grades K-3

This is the classic to read if your children are preschool or primary ages. Packet includes three manuals—on reading, writing, and arithmetic—and a two-sided poster with phonics on one side and a 100-chart on the other. This packet will replace a tall stack of teacher's manuals and other curriculum items. $12.70.

Adam and His Kin: The Lost History of Their Lives and Times

A narrative of the little-known period of time from Creation to Abraham. Your children (and you) can learn history of the early world from this "real book" better than they can from textbooks. $9.00.

Order from:
Education Services
8825 Blue Mountain Drive
Golden CO 80403